HAYDN CORPER is passionate ab
wrote his first novel when he was fi
ing ever since: novels, scripts, and
and for his website. He's been an
a public affairs and marketing consultant, a business advisor, a politician, and a guest house owner; but always a writer.

Haydn is an active a member of the Historical Novel Society and of the Society of Authors. He loves conversation, good company and laughs a lot.

www.haydncorper.com

THE SCENT OF LILACS

HAYDN CORPER

SilverWood

Published in 2016 by SilverWood Books

SilverWood Books Ltd
14 Small Street, Bristol, BS1 1DE, United Kingdom
www.silverwoodbooks.co.uk

Copyright © Haydn Corper 2016

The right of Haydn Corper to be identified as the author of this work
has been asserted in accordance with the Copyright, Designs
and Patents Act 1988 Sections 77 and 78.

All rights reserved. No part of this publication may be reproduced,
stored in a retrieval system, or transmitted in any form or by any means,
electronic, mechanical, photocopying, recording or otherwise,
without prior permission of the copyright holder.

This is a work of fiction. Names, characters, places and incidents either
are products of the author's imagination or are used fictitiously.
Any resemblance to actual events or locales or persons,
living or dead, is entirely coincidental.

ISBN 978-1-78132-517-9 (paperback)
ISBN 978-1-78132-518-6 (ebook)

British Library Cataloguing in Publication Data
A CIP catalogue record for this book is available from
the British Library

Page design and typesetting by SilverWood Books
Printed on responsibly sourced paper

I have a rendezvous with Death
At some disputed barricade,
When Spring comes back with rustling shade
And apple blossoms fill the air.
I have a rendezvous with Death
When Spring brings back blue days and fair.

It may be he shall take my hand
And lead me unto his dark land
And close my eyes and quench my breath.
It may be I shall pass him still.
I have a rendezvous with Death
On some scarred slope of battered hill,
When Spring comes round again this year
And the first meadow-flowers appear.

God knows 'twere better to be deep
Pillowed in silk and scented down,
Where love throbs out in blissful sleep,
Pulse nigh to pulse, and breath to breath,
Where hushed awakenings are dear...
But I've a rendezvous with Death
At midnight in some flaming town,
When Spring trips north again this year,
And I to my pledged word am true,
I shall not fail that rendezvous.

Alan Seeger
Died 4 July 1916, Belloy-en-Santerre, the Somme

ONE

The sound rattled the window panes and rumbled around the room. Tanya blinked and sat bolt upright. Her mouth was dry with fear. She swung her legs out of bed onto the cold linoleum floor as light flickered through the thin black curtains. A word leapt into her mind: *bombs*. Fear clenched her gut. Not now, she begged. Please, not yet.

She fumbled for the matches and the candle she kept on her bedside table. Another rumble rattled the panes of glass louder; the bombs were creeping closer. The candle sputtered. Shielding the delicate flame with one hand she stumbled to the telephone, picked up the receiver and listened. There was nothing but the usual dial tone. Anger replaced her fear; she'd invested a lot in the box attached to the telephone, the box which was supposed to warn of danger, but it was silent.

Then another silence struck her: there were no sirens. And where was the sound of guns firing to protect the city?

She shivered; the room was cold. She knew that she should get to the cellar to join her neighbours, who undoubtedly were making their way down as they had most nights for the previous six months, but she hesitated. Something was very wrong. It didn't *feel* as the other times had when the bombers came.

Then, as she wondered, white light flickered around the edges of the blackout curtain, casting eerie shadows across the walls. This is it, she thought, feeling strangely calm. She had always imagined it would be like this: the sudden light, the shock, then darkness forever. She felt detached and waited for it.

Rain pattered, uncertain for a moment before the sound rose suddenly to a drumming roar on the roof. Tanya stepped back, felt the edge of the bed behind her knees and sat down abruptly. Rain. She drew in a ragged breath. Have I come to this? she wondered. Frightened by thunder and lightning like a child? She squeezed the cover of the bed in both hands, twisted the fabric, let the breath out in a long, low sigh. Have they reduced me to this?

She opened the small drawer in the bedside table and pulled out a bottle. Slowly she sipped from it, savouring the juniper flavour as the liqueur washed across her tongue and down her throat. She didn't take much. It was the last of her Doornkaat schnapps, all which remained of a case she'd bought on the first day of the war. Since then she'd eked it out, hoping she had enough to last until the war ended, but the war had dragged on for longer than anyone had imagined, and although peace must be close, she was no longer certain which would end first: the fighting or the Doornkaat. She peered at the near-empty bottle with its grubby white label, smiled ruefully and replaced it in the drawer. Then she lay back as another flash strobed the room and another deep rumble rattled the window panes. She drew the blankets over her head and let the alcohol calm her. Momentarily she felt as she'd done as a child, snuggling under the bedcover, warm, *safe*, but Tanya knew that there was no safety. She could not hide from what was coming. Once more, she shivered.

After the night's storm, the day had dawned misty, but now late afternoon sunlight slanted through the bare trees of the woodland. Walter stopped pedalling, rested one foot on the ground, relished the warmth on his face, the soft breeze and the scent of early-blossoming lilac. He came here many Sundays, detouring on his way home from the former Boy Scouts' hut where he and the others in his Hitler Youth section spent many hours of training and indoctrination. It was a refuge from the dreary little apartment where he lived; from the dreary battered streets; from the dreary exhausted people. These stands of trees set amongst open heath were where he'd spent many happy days in better times; a place which the war had not changed much; a place of comforting familiarity. Few others came here, except during the summer when the ground was dry enough for strolling families and picnicking lovers.

Berlin had many such woodlands, but most had been denuded of their trees to provide firewood as supplies of coal dwindled and were diverted more and more to feed the factories. Even the Tiergarten, the huge wooded park at the heart of the city, had been stripped bare, but this little enclave had survived, for it was used for training by the Hitler Youth, SA storm troopers and the home guard: the Volkssturm. Walter, who liked to think of it as *his* place, found them annoying, but it was worth putting up with their occasional noisy presence to see the trees preserved. He looked about him and smiled: he had the place to himself today. Carefully he leaned his bicycle against a linden tree. He was expected back at the apartment for dinner, but there was still some time. His mother loved the scent of lilacs; he would take some to her.

"Well, Comrade Lieutenant, what do you think?"

Junior Lieutenant Leonid Andreivich Barakovski looked at the mass of unkempt men in the brewery yard and turned to Guards Sergeant Pavel Agranenko.

"I'm not sure," and truly, he wasn't. Not at all sure. The men's undernourished bodies were clad in patched brown uniforms; they wore broken boots or filthy rags on their feet, and Leonid's boyhood memories stirred. They looked like the victims of the famines he'd seen years before and never forgotten: the long shuffling column of men, women and children which had passed the outskirts of his village. Afterwards no one ever mentioned them; no one asked questions, and nor had Leonid. Even at an early age he'd understood that there were some things it was best not to talk about.

"I know what *he* thinks." Agranenko sounded irritated, jerking his blond head towards the short, plump officer haranguing the men.

Leonid knew that Agranenko respected Major Polyanski, the Deputy Battalion Commander for Political Affairs, but didn't like or trust him, and Agranenko's opinion mattered, at least to Leonid. It was months since Leonid had left the Kamyshlov Military Infantry Academy, and although he'd fought in several skirmishes alongside them, Number Two Platoon still put Agranenko first. Leonid was the platoon officer, but he was not *the boss*. Of course, Agranenko made sure that Leonid received the polite deference due his rank and position, but it was Agranenko whom the platoon followed.

Leonid watched Polyanski. His party slogans were doing little except elicit sullen looks and nervous shuffling. There was resentment, anger even, and Leonid wondered if Polyanski had noticed.

"Sergeant?" Leonid heard the questioning note in his own voice, knew he should be more assertive. His stepfather had hoped going to war would toughen him, but it hadn't.

Agranenko turned to face him. "Comrade Lieutenant?" He glanced at Leonid and then at Polyanski. "Yes." He clearly thought what Leonid did but would not say, 'do something before someone else says or does something they shouldn't'. The men were on edge; they could both see that, but Polyanski seemingly did not.

Suddenly Agranenko walked forward to stand next to Polyanski, who seemed oblivious to his presence, but, as the men's gazes turned to him, Polyanski paused and turned his head too. He raised his eyebrows, then turned back to face the men.

"You have a chance to redeem yourselves," he droned on, "a chance to show yourselves worthy of Glorious Comrade Stalin, of the Motherland, of the Revolution. Line up. Show yourselves the soldiers you once were." Someone in the rear ranks laughed, a sarcastic, mocking sound. Polyanski hesitated, glared along the ranks, then squared his shoulders and resumed his peroration. "Show yourselves…"

"Comrade Political Officer." Agranenko's voice was soft; Leonid was sure the men couldn't hear what he was saying, but Polyanski obviously did for he blinked like a round-faced owl and fell silent.

"Comrade Political Officer," Agranenko repeated, "with your permission?"

Polyanski again turned to face Agranenko, who saluted. Leonid smiled. Agranenko had a way of making any request for permission sound like a mere formality, as if he was simply being polite in asking, but he never crossed the line; he was never obviously insolent.

Polyanski's mouth set hard. He glanced at the mass of men who seemed to radiate an air of suppressed violence and cleared his throat nervously.

"Very well." He nodded acquiescence and came to stand by Leonid.

Agranenko swept his gaze slowly along the ranks. Dull eyes stared back at him from pale, emaciated faces and most wouldn't meet his gaze. Some, more bold, he faced down. Gradually the mood lightened, the sense of anger faded and the men shifted nervously.

"Well, boys," Agranenko now sounded unusually jovial, "you know the saying 'Sniff out, suck up, survive.'" A few of the men chuckled; Polyanski raised his eyebrows again but stayed silent.

Agranenko nodded. "Well, you survived all right. Well done. Here's another saying: 'Soup and porridge, that's our fare.' Time to eat." He jerked his thumb over his right shoulder to where the battalion's field kitchen lay hidden behind the long grey brewery wall. The brown mass of men rippled at the word 'eat'. "Line up over there, three ranks. You remember? Sort yourselves out and then we'll feed you. Like soldiers." Agranenko smiled grimly, and one man even smiled back, briefly. "And then a wash, fresh clothes, rest." A barely audible sigh seemed to rise from the men. Agranenko glanced at Polyanski who nodded his agreement. Then, slowly, the men shuffled to line up along the wall, falling into place with the rediscovered habit of soldiers whose well-drilled instinct is to form neat rows at even intervals.

"Food first," Agranenko said as he turned to face Polyanski, who nodded again. Agranenko saluted and joined the men. Watching him walk along the line chatting to them, Leonid wondered how he did it: men seemed to listen to him easily, and would follow him where they'd not follow another, including Leonid.

He wondered whether he should join them, but the sour look on the Polyanski's face made him think better of it.

Tanya was picking her way carefully down the stairs onto the first floor landing, laden with blankets, a pillow, torch and thermos flask when Walter came up in a rush. She stepped back to avoid him, banging the back of her legs against the two buckets kept on each landing in case of incendiaries: one of sand, the other water.

He halted abruptly, looking embarrassed.

"Why the hurry, young man?" she asked.

Walter dropped his gaze. "Sorry, Miss Klarkova."

Tanya looked at him with amusement. He and his mother Ida shared a small apartment on the first floor with Ida's brother-in-law, Mathias. Tanya knew it was an arrangement of necessity since Walter and Ida had been bombed out of their house in Brunswick by the British, but it was an awkward one. Walter's father Fabian had not got on with his brother. Mathias had been a passionate Social Democrat, an ardent trade union organiser on the national railways where he worked; Fabian, an army veteran of the first war, was angry at Germany's defeat and had welcomed the Nazis. He'd joined the Party when Hitler came to power in 1933, and Mathias and Fabian had stopped speaking to each other. Then they had stopped seeing each other. But Fabian had disappeared in Stalingrad, and when Ida and Walter were made homeless, Mathias opened his home to them. He was that sort of man, but it wasn't an easy arrangement.

Tanya liked Walter in many ways. Perhaps he reminded her of the son she could have had, but never did. She'd made a conscious choice to remain unmarried and she seldom regretted it. To Tanya, marriage seemed like the cakes her Berlin neighbours were famous for: sweet and momentarily fulfilling, but insubstantial. She wanted more of life than to be a dutiful housewife; she preferred something more sustaining like the traditional Russian pancakes, the blinis she loved so much.

She looked at Walter, standing awkward and embarrassed on the stairs, bony knees showing below the long dark shorts of his Hitler Youth uniform, body painfully thin beneath a pale brown shirt and dark necktie. A brown cap accentuated the lightness of his straw-coloured hair. Only his vivid blue eyes and the bright red and white of his armband provided any colour. Has he ever tasted a blini? she wondered. Deliciously thick, lathered in sour cream, spread with caviar, dotted with smoked salmon. His only experience of Russia, she was sure, would be the endless horror stories pumped out by propaganda minister Goebbels. She thought of Chekhov's words: 'The blinis were deep golden, airy and plump; just like the shoulder of a merchant's daughter.' That made her smile; Walter was anything but plump. There and then she resolved she must do something about that, although where she was to find the ingredients for blinis, God only knew.

"Well, Walter, did you have a good meeting?" she asked. He nodded mutely and then pushed past her, keeping his eyes downcast as he opened the door to Mathias' apartment. It was seldom locked.

He always avoids looking at me, Tanya noted sadly, watching him disappear inside. "Good evening," she called, but the door banged shut behind him with no reply. After a moment she carried on down the stairs with a sigh.

Walter thought of the encounter as he walked down the short hall into the apartment. He'd been embarrassed, as he always was when he met her. Just a Slav he thought, and then felt a stab of guilt. In truth she'd only ever been nice to him. He pictured her smile, wide-mouthed below penetrating but kindly pale-blue eyes. She seemed such a cultured lady, on good terms with Uncle Mathias and with his mother, but nevertheless she was one of those routinely described as subhuman, bestial, murderers. It confused him: he couldn't reconcile his experience of her with what he was taught. She even looked like an Aryan. Of course, he didn't believe everything he was told, even though it was dinned into him that he must trust the Führer, he must trust the Party. To be a good German was to be loyal to people and Fatherland, to believe all they told him and obey, but he didn't: he couldn't.

He wished that he was like those around him who cast aside all doubts and followed. Life would be so much easier. He'd tried to conform as his father would have wished, but often he just could not. Then he tried simply ignoring the awkward questions in his mind, burying himself in his own interests and looking inwards, ignoring the outside world and the nagging doubts it provoked. People like Mathias, however, challenged him with their questions and objections, and people like Miss Klarkova challenged him simply by being around. He very much preferred to be left alone; life was less uncomfortable that way.

His mother's voice interrupted his thoughts. "Is that you, Walter?"

"Yes."

"Where have you been, boy?" Mathias sounded annoyed; but then, he often did.

Walter sighed and went to get his dinner.

Tanya walked down the steps into the cellar and nodded a cold greeting to the block warden. Mrs Boldt used to sit in the small alcove by the entrance to the apartment block. From there she could watch all comings and goings. Now she sat in an old chintz armchair at the bottom of the cellar steps and did the same.

Mrs Boldt didn't acknowledge Tanya as she came down the steps but carried on knitting, something she always seemed to be doing. With her stolid, lined face, her greying dark hair tucked up inside her knitted wool turban, Mrs Boldt reminded Tanya of a *tricoteuse*: one of the women who sat by the guillotine during the French Revolution and knitted as victims of the political terror were executed. The first time Tanya had sheltered in the cellar from British bombers years before, the moment she'd seen Mrs Boldt take up her knitting she had thought of the description of the guillotine-women in Charles Dickens' *A Tale of Two Cities*. Dickens was one of her favourite authors. He was popular in Russia; everyone, it seemed, had read him when Tanya was a girl.

The guillotine-women were often informers and denouncers for the regime, and block wardens, ostensibly appointed to act on behalf of a building's or street's residents, did just that: they watched and noted. They were also responsible to the Party for morale and morals, and for organising communal activities, for developing fellowship. Mrs Boldt had kept a noticeboard by the block front door festooned with official bulletins. And it had a list of the rising and setting times and phases of the moon: British bombers liked to come on clear moonlit lights. That board was now nailed up on the wall by the cellar steps, although no new bulletins had appeared on it for weeks.

Tanya made her way carefully across the cellar. It was lit only by a few Hindenburg lamps: paper cups of candle wax with a string wick which were easy to make and lasted quite a long time, but cast little light. Tanya went to the alcove she shared with Mrs Körtig. The old woman was not there, probably still upstairs, but she'd be down in a minute no doubt. She knew that Mr Körtig would not: he was away on a visit to his daughter in Fürstenwalde. The alcove was set into the outside wall, a bricked-up coal chute. There Tanya had placed her wicker chair and a few personal supplies and had hung an old blanket as a curtain to provide some privacy. It was her home when the bombs were falling.

The Körtigs' old stove stood in one corner of the cellar, elegant in blue and white tiles, its long iron chimney poking up through another bricked-up chute. The Körtigs had kept it when central heating had been installed in the apartment block, and Tanya was grateful that they had: it kept the cellar warm and provided the means to prepare hot drinks and food.

The cellar was well equipped in other ways. A lavatory had been rigged up behind another blanket screen: a lidded bucket of lime and sand, simple but effective. Mrs Boldt had grudgingly provided a table, but only after Mathias and Mr Körtig had insisted.

Mrs Boldt had at first reacted with her usual petulance, asking if they thought that she had nothing better to do than move furniture around, but after a lengthy verbal tussle and the support of the other residents, she'd finally caved in. The table was taken from its place by the front door, where once the post had been left, and now stood in the middle of the cellar. Stored under it was a selection of tinned and packaged foods, bread wrapped in cloths and bottled drinks brought by the residents to be shared out.

As Tanya made herself as comfortable as she could for the night, Mrs Körtig clattered carefully down the steps carrying her basket of embroidery. Tanya smiled a welcome and wondered if the old lady might have any buckwheat flour for making blinis.

Cheslav Barakovski left the barn and took the piece of cardboard offered to him by Pankov, the battalion political officer who was standing by the door. It was in the shape of a large key. Printed on one side in bright red letters were the words 'To Berlin', and on the other 'Red Army Soldier, the hour of revenge has come!' Pankov nodded to him, then handed another key to the next man to come out.

The company had just been watching *At Six O'clock in the Evening After the End of the War*. It was a good film about a gallant artillery lieutenant meeting his true love in Moscow during the victory celebrations. The story was premature, the victory had yet to be achieved, but no one now doubted that it was close, and the film had struck the right note. Ostensibly a musical comedy, it managed to convey a serious message of triumph and continuity without being pompous. Cheslav had wept at one point, for the young hero reminded him of his older brother, Leonid.

Others too had wept. Many sang the words which had been handed out on crudely cyclostyled sheets of paper as they'd filed into their seats. Especially popular was the 'Song of the Artillerists'. Pankov liked to encourage participation, but he'd been more successful than he'd intended. The song was repeated again and again until the film had to be stopped and quiet restored. After the screening, Pankov strode to the front of the hall and read from a *Pravda* article. It spoke of a previous occasion when Berlin had been taken by an avenging army from Russia. The keys of the city had been taken to St Petersburg, now Leningrad, for permanent keeping in the Kazan Cathedral. Pankov spoke of their duty to emulate that victory, indeed to surpass it, for now they fought not as subjects of a Tsar and nationalism, but as citizens on behalf of the Workers' State for socialism and world freedom. A crusade to make the world a better place. They fought, Pankov reminded them, even on behalf of German workers who waited for the end of Hitler and the Nazis.

Cheslav found that sentiment a little strange. On the one hand they were being told to exact revenge on the fascist beast in its lair; on the other, they were coming fraternally to liberate oppressed fellow workers. Cheslav didn't think that any of his comrades felt very fraternal; he felt little himself after what he'd seen on the long advance westwards through the devastation that was Russia and Poland. Pankov's audience had listened quietly. Some had applauded, but most just waited to be let out. It had taken nearly four years to drive the Germans and their allies back. Now the Soviet Army stood at the outskirts of Berlin and they wanted to finish things. They needed no pep talks from the Party.

Cheslav stood back and watched the company pass. They were of many nationalities, all ages: nervous teenagers from the towns and peasants old enough to be their grandfathers; soft-featured boys and hard-faced women who might be their mothers; Russians and Balts; Ukrainians and Crimeans; Kazakhs and Georgians. The Soviet Union on the march, he thought, and smiled wryly to himself. It was the sort of phrase the Party liked to come up with, and for which Leonid would have teased Cheslav had he been foolish enough to express it aloud.

He looked again at the key. Perhaps they're right, though, he thought. Perhaps this is a crusade. He hoped that it would make the world a better place; that the deprivations of the war and the years before it would be replaced by something worthy of the struggle and sacrifice. He watched the groups of soldiers standing talking quietly amongst themselves. Some smoked; some sipped from canteens or small vodka bottles; others just stood quietly. He wondered what thoughts were passing through their minds. Wives? Husbands? Lovers? Children? Cheslav listened to the low murmur of voices and his heart was filled with a longing that all of them, each and every man and woman now before him, would live to see the end of conflict, but he knew that it wouldn't be so. The assault on Berlin was due to take place in a few hours, and many wouldn't be there when finally they took the city in a bloody sacrifice of revenge and expiation. He hoped that he would be one of those to see it through to the end.

Leonid stiffened his back as the colour party marched along the front of the company drawn up in ranks behind him. As it passed, he saluted the scarlet banner, rich with embroidered images of Lenin, star and hammer and sickle, bright against the walls of the brewery yard. He watched it go, carried a little awkwardly out through the narrow gate to where another company waited to renew their soldiers' oath: a solemn rite; a blessing from the atheist Soviet State to those shortly to be sent into battle. Leonid was a little awestruck, which no doubt was what had been intended.

"Company, stand at ease!" The voice of Captain Chuya snapped him out of his reverie and he turned his attention to the red-faced portly company commander facing them. Next to him stood Polyanski, who, during the reaffirmation ceremony, had spoken expansively of revolutionary ideals; aspirations of freedom; victory over Hitlerite Germany. He'd read out the order of the day, full of worthy sentiments and stiff phrases.

Now Chuya spoke. Characteristically his words were simple and few. "We've come a long way. We've done a lot, seen a lot. There's a lot to avenge. Berlin is just over there." He pointed over Leonid's head. "Just do your duty. Kill the Fritzes. End it. Company, attention! Dismissed!"

Leonid stepped forward in line with the officers of the other platoons, saluted Chuya and turned smartly to the right. Agranenko approached him.

"Fine words, Comrade Lieutenant." His face was impassive as ever and Leonid was unsure whether the comment was approving or ironic. Agranenko had a fine line in irony. He followed Agranenko across the yard and down into the cellar which the platoon had called home for the previous two days. It was crowded and musty, smelling of part-washed bodies, cabbage soup and buckwheat porridge. Soup for breakfast, porridge for lunch, soup for dinner, every day, week in, week out, supplemented by supplies acquired from German houses: pickled vegetables, dried meats, smoked cheeses. Hidden by frugal German housewives during the hard years of the war and discovered by ever-hungry soldiers, they were a welcome addition. There's no scavenger as efficient as a Red Army scavenger, Leonid thought when first he'd witnessed his men systematically rooting out anything edible, and much that wasn't.

He looked across the crowded cellar and remembered the first German place they'd come to: a Prussian farmhouse. It had reminded him of *Hansel and Gretel*: thatched roof, neat little windows with closed wooden shutters and a chimney that was still smoking as the platoon approached. Clean and tidy; even the yard was clean. Fat cattle and fat pigs and fat chickens; the vegetables stored in the wooden barns were fat, too. Inside the small house was a paradise of abundance. At first everyone had wandered about silently, touching, awestruck. Then the mood changed and the platoon turned violent. Cupboards were wrenched open, drawers emptied onto the floor, curtains were torn down and upholstery ripped up. Ivanova, the platoon's quiet, home-loving, tidy medical orderly, tossed ornaments and crockery onto the slab floor, repeating as she threw each one down, "Look at this, look at this."

Leonid had moved to stop them, but Agranenko touched his arm and shook his head and they'd kept out of it.

After that farmhouse, the platoon's anger gave way to a sense of entitlement. There was plenty to go around, and after a time they'd become selective, picking only the best. There was, of course, an official edict: a rule for German property, as there was for everything else. The Party decreed that anything captured in battle or abandoned by the enemy was the property of the Red Army and of the State, but the interpretation of 'captured' and 'abandoned' was liberal. Although looting was officially forbidden under the heading of antisocial activity, officers were allowed to send home 15kg per month and soldiers 5kg, but few stuck to the limit. Leonid saw a bewildering array of items wrapped up and sent to the field post office for despatch home. Corporal Babich, the platoon's Chechen radio operator, had sent home an electric gramophone, although his home had no power supply. Babich had a fascination for all things technical.

At first, Leonid held back from the bounty, but one day he found a book lying undamaged by the burned-out ruins of an elegant house. *Little Dorrit* lay amongst other books on the grass of a trampled lawn. He'd wrapped it tightly in official brown paper and marked it 'approved literature': Marx had praised Dickens and the writer was much-quoted at school. It would be safe to send even if it was in German. Cheslav would love it. For himself, Leonid kept a companion volume, *A Tale of Two Cities*.

He smiled and crossed the cellar to the small room set aside for himself and Agranenko. There he sat on the two sacks of barley which constituted his bed and took out his officers' leather satchel. He laid it across his knee, extracted the letter he'd been writing to his mother and stepfather and looked at his last entry.

At this moment, we are sitting in our quarters, readying ourselves for the great day. The men are in good heart and we hope to have the business done soon. He sucked at the end of the pen his stepfather had given him as a leaving gift. Since departing for the academy, he had written something every week; and he wrote something for Cheslav nearly every day.

He chose his words carefully, not wanting to say anything the censor might cut out. *I am well enough and hope that you are too. We are fed more than enough. I hope that the sausage and tins of sardines I sent you have reached you safely.*

Little enough, he thought, looking at his words, but food was more appreciated back home than anything else. He added: *I haven't heard from Cheslav for two weeks, but that's nothing to worry about. Everything is so busy here and the post has to catch up with us when it can.* He smiled sadly. It had been much more than two weeks since he'd heard anything from his mother and stepfather. He didn't know yet if they'd received his letters and parcels. *So, my dearest Mamma and Papa B, I must go now and get some rest. Tomorrow will be very demanding. All my love as ever.*

Tomorrow, he thought. Despite his cheerful words, he knew rest was something he'd not get that night.

Walter found the table already laid for dinner. Mathias sat at it, his craggy face set in a deep frown. Being late for a meal was never a good idea. Mathias didn't like Walter being in the Hitler Youth, but it was the law. He disliked even more that Walter was away every Sunday and Wednesday evening for training and indoctrination in the section hut. The fact that Walter himself disliked going didn't make Mathias any more sympathetic, and matters were not helped when Walter chose to follow his best friend and fellow Hitler Youth Friedrich Jürgs to a new unit. Friedrich's parents had been bombed out the previous autumn and moved to a distant part of Berlin. Friedrich's father pulled strings to get Walter transferred, which had pleased the boys, but not Mathias. It was never advisable for Walter to return late.

He rushed to change out of uniform and wash his hands. When he got back, his mother was placing the pot on the table. It was something the Party approved of: the Sunday one pot meal, part of their ideology of folk community, sharing, being homely. Mathias invariably made sarcastic remarks about the latest news when they ate from it. This night was no different, but his annoyance with Walter imbued his comments with even more barbed anti-Nazi remarks, despite Ida's attempts to change the subject. Walter tried not to hear Mathias; lack of belief in ultimate victory was a criminal offence. Hitler Youth members were encouraged to report any disloyal talk they heard and Walter dreaded being put on the spot by his section leader, Vogel, who knew Mathias' reputation as a closet Red. Vogel invariably made a point of asking Walter what his uncle had been saying, and Walter was a bad liar: his face always gave too much away.

After dinner, the table was cleared to make room for Walter's books and he began his homework. Mathias sat by the iron stove as he always did, listening to the *People's Receiver*. Provided to every household cheaply, ostensibly it was intended to make radio available to everyone, but Mathias regarded it as yet another Nazi trick.

"So that we can all listen to *that man*," he'd commented after Mrs Boldt had delivered it. When Mathias first used the euphemism Walter had been surprised: evasion was not one of Mathias' characteristics. 'That man': it was a common expression in Berlin now. Hitler was no longer 'our beloved Führer'. It was as if people wanted to disassociate themselves from Hitler as the success and victories of the early years of Nazi power turned to failure and to fear; as if the German nation could somehow disassociate itself from guilt. Despite his overt cynicism, however, Mathias spent much time by the radio. Mostly he listened to music concerts and talks given by eminent speakers, except when the speaker was a representative of 'that man'. Then Mathias would leave the room.

Walter glanced at Mathias sitting in his shabby cane lounger, reading one of his old railway magazines and listening to a performance of Bruckner's Eighth Symphony, and frowned down at his homework. Mathias really had been difficult over dinner, but he'd try to forget what he'd said before the next Youth meeting. The trouble was, Walter couldn't get the words out of his head. Mathias had been critical of the conduct of the war as usual, but then he'd told an anti-Nazi joke that had been funny:

> After a bad air raid, Hitler and Göring are standing on top of the Chancellery inspecting the damage to Berlin.
> "I want to do something to cheer the poor city up," Hitler says.
> "Have you considered jumping?" asks Göring.

Despite trying not to, Walter giggled, but the words were treason. Walter picked up his ruler. Tonight was geometry, which he hated. Still, it had to be done, and with a sigh he set to, but he'd hardly started to get his head around the problem when the sirens began a long, dismal wail. Almost immediately came the bark of anti-aircraft guns and the dull *crump, crump* of distant bombs. Everyone looked at the radio in surprise: Bruckner was still playing. There was supposed to be a warning on the radio. The system had worked well for years, but lately there were more and more failures.

"Not again!" Mathias snorted. He sighed, placed his magazine on the floor by his feet and cocked his head slightly. He was counting, his lips moving silently.

"Eight," he announced and the sound of bombs stopped. The guns continued to fire. "Could be just a nuisance raid."

Walter relaxed slightly: eight was a magic number. The British often sent over solitary aircraft at irregular intervals to keep people awake by random bombing, and these aircraft usually carried no more than eight bombs. If you'd not been hit by the eighth explosion, you should be safe.

The radio was still playing and the sound of flak trailed off. With a dissatisfied grunt, Mathias reached for his magazine once more, but suddenly there were more explosions, closer and all in a rush, too many to count. The sirens wailed once more. Abruptly, Bruckner was replaced by hissing static and a slow, regular beep.

"Damn it," Mathias said, "I was just settling in." He stood up, retrieved his magazine and placed it on his chair. "I suppose we'd best go down."

There were more explosions now, not too close but getting closer.

Ida disappeared into the bedroom to fetch the overnight bag and Walter began gathering up his schoolwork.

"Bring that with you," Mathias ordered, and Walter sighed.

TWO

Tanya turned on the small torch she kept on the stout box beside her chair, careful to keep the beam away Mrs Körtig who was sleeping on her antique divan opposite. Its elegant carved wooden frame and red plush contrasted oddly with the bare brick and iron piping of the wall. Faded elegance was how Tanya had come to think of the Körtigs; that and kindness. When Tanya first arrived in the apartment block fifteen years before they'd been quick to cross the landing and knock on her door with welcoming offers of help. Since then they'd been good neighbours, but never really close ones. They had a knack of knowing when to be helpful, born of many years serving in a great country house before the previous war. That house no longer existed; it had been destroyed during the Russian offensive through East Prussia in 1914. Then the Körtigs had followed their employers to Berlin. They'd stayed in the city when the employers left for South America, leaving them with a small pension which had helped the Körtigs greatly during the hard years that followed, supplementing Eugen Körtig's income as a handyman at the Hertie Department Store and the occasional sale of Mrs Körtig's embroidery work. They weren't rich, but it was enough.

Tanya smiled at Mrs Körtig and reached forward to brush away dust that had fallen on the old woman's shoulder, but then she paused and snatched her hand back and looked up. Dust? It drifted down from the wooden boards, motes in the narrow beam of the torch. Tanya stood up. She was tall enough to reach the low ceiling and she placed her free hand between the thick joists. The rough planking was cold and damp and it vibrated. She stood on the box, switched off the torch and gently tugged back the blackout curtain which covered the small window high up in the wall. Leaning her head forward, she pressed her ear against the cold glass. She felt a continuous vibration, rising and falling irregularly.

"Has it started, then? Are *they* coming?" Mrs Körtig's sleep-hoarse voice drifted up through the darkness.

Tanya replaced the curtain and switched he torch back on. "I don't know." She stepped down, noticing the emphasis Mrs Körtig had given the word they: the enemy; the Reds; the Bolshevik Beasts. Tanya's former countrymen.

"What time is it?" Mrs Körtig gently touched Tanya's arm. She glanced at her wrist and held it out to show her: three o'clock. It would be dawn soon. Tanya wondered what the sun would bring with it. The two women looked at each other and Mrs Körtig touched Tanya's arm once more.

Then a dim light flicked around the edges of the blanket across the alcove before it was drawn back by Mrs Boldt.

"What is it?" Her face was ghoulish in the light of a Hindenburg lamp she held carefully on one hand, palm upturned.

"'The Twilight of the Gods.'" A voice, soft but deep, carried confidently from behind her. "'The End of Days.'" A match flared as another Hindenburg lamp was lit to reveal the speaker: a nondescript looking fellow, brown eyes in a pale face beneath brown hair – brown like his worn suit. He came every night to hold hands with Klara Winckelmann, the mouse-like woman who lived opposite the Schleys. Tanya had wondered who he was ever since he'd appeared three weeks before, for he'd only given them his name, Axel Götz, no more. Probably he was one of the myriad Nazi bureaucrats ordered to remain at their posts. He had an air of authority, but was not bumptious with it.

Mrs Körtig had suggested to Tanya that Klara kept a refugee camp. It was typical Berliner slang. Nazi officials had been allowed to send their families out of the city to safety and, separated from wife and children, many found refuge in the arms of other women. Perhaps, Tanya and Mrs Körtig had speculated, Klara was Axel's secretary; they knew she did something administrative in a government building. Or perhaps she was merely an acquaintance. She might even be a total stranger whom he'd bumped into by chance; relationships were more casual now. But neither Tanya nor Mrs Körtig knew for sure; Klara kept herself to herself, and really it was none of their business.

"What do you mean by that?" Mrs Boldt turned her head and stared. Her tone was the sort that schoolteachers reserved for pupils whom they suspected of impertinence but couldn't quite be sure.

"I meant," Axel detached his hand from Klara's and stood, "that the Russians will soon be here."

Mrs Boldt bristled. "Nonsense. The Führer has said…"

Axel cut her off. "The Führer is, of course, quite correct." He smiled deeply. Klara too stood, smiled and whispered something into his ear. He glanced at his watch and made a slight bow to Mrs Boldt. "Duty calls," he said and moved towards the cellar steps.

Tanya heard a chuckle. It came from the shadowed corner where Mathias, Walter and Ida had spent the night on fold-up camp beds.

Mrs Boldt looked annoyed and glanced at Mathias. "The Führer has said that the tide will turn. This must be it. They're our guns, I'm sure."

Axel stopped at the bottom of the steps and pulled out a torch. He flicked it on before turning with a rueful smile. "Well then, we have nothing to fear, do we?" He trained the beam of the torch on the steps and strode purposely upwards. At the top he turned again – "Heil Hitler!" – and with that he was gone, banging the door behind him.

Ida murmured, "Perhaps they are."

No one answered her, and above Tanya's the ceiling buzzed quietly and more dust trickled down. She thought not.

*

Agranenko gently shook Leonid's shoulder and held out a steaming mug of tea. Leonid blinked sleep from his eyes, sat up and took it. The luminous face of the German watch on Agranenko's wrist showed 02:00 hours. They all had German watches these days; every Soviet soldier seemed to possess at least one; some had several. Once, Leonid had watched a member of the platoon barter his German tinned food in order to add to an already impressive selection of watches lining both his arms. Leonid wondered what the attraction was. Was it the exquisite workmanship? Was it rarity, for watches had been hard to come by back home? He didn't know. It was another thing he didn't understand about the men he was supposed to lead; another gulf between them. Of all the platoon, aside from himself, only Agranenko restricted himself to one watch, a particularly fine model taken from a German colonel. The man had been pompously outraged that a mere sergeant had taken a fancy to it, but nevertheless he'd handed it over. Wisely, Leonid thought at the time. Unlike many NCOS Agranenko rarely used force to get his way, but he'd taken a definite liking for *that* watch and it would have been unwise to cross him.

"Time," Agranenko said softly, and Leonid knew that it was. The watch, like all German watches it seemed to him, was never wrong.

Leonid nodded and stood up, stretching his back to ease the ache. Despite the months spent sleeping on makeshift beds, or sometimes none at all, he was still not used to the discomfort. Always he woke with a back that chided him like an old man's. The thought made him smile slightly. 'Old Man' was the nickname with which his younger brother Cheslav had labelled him from the first day he'd attended the Stalingrad Technical School and had returned very solemn and self-important. The nickname had stuck for a few years, but no one called him that now. How Leonid wished that they would; he wished to be called 'boss' or 'The Old Man' by the platoon.

Agranenko moved amongst the men while Leonid sipped his tea. The cellar was full of activity. Weapons were being checked, food and clothing packed away in oft-practised routines. The platoon could do it in their sleep. There was little talking, but one man hummed a few bars of a jaunty tune. Leonid recognised it: 'The Road to the Front'. Agranenko whistled under his breath as he picked his way between sprawled bodies and stepped over carelessly piled equipment, stopping to check the tightness of one very young conscript's belt. The boy had arrived the previous afternoon just after the parade and Leonid still couldn't remember his name.

Agranenko stopped whistling and jerked so hard on the young conscript's belt that the boy almost fell against him. "Tighter," Agranenko admonished, "and higher. Don't wear it around your arse. It's not there to support your balls."

"If they've dropped yet," someone called out and there was laughter.

Agranenko continued his inspection, murmuring words of encouragement. He was met with lopsided grins or solemn nods. It was a ritual observed between those whose bonds had been forged by ordeals which Leonid had not shared; bonds tested time and again by terror, deprivation, suffering and loss, but strengthened by humour, shared pleasures and hope. The platoon had been formed by war: disparate threads woven into a tough fabric. Between themselves, they spoke an intimate language which could only be understood fully by those who had been through it together: the language of comradeship.

Agranenko finished his inspection and came to sit next to Leonid. He reached under his soft field cap, his pilotka, and scratched the close-cropped blond stubble on his scalp.

"Not long now."

Leonid nodded; he felt queasy. They would be moving to their jumping-off positions shortly and he'd really rather not be reminded of it.

"It'll soon be all over." A rueful smile touched Agranenko's lips. He murmured quietly, as if to himself, "'Nearly six months now we've been fighting. Six months of battle's roar an whine. Cruel are the sufferings of our nation, your sufferings, Dariya and mine.'"

Leonid sipped his tea. "Pushkin?"

Agranenko looked at him for a moment. "Now why is it that everyone seems to think of Pushkin when they hear poetry? Olga Berggolts, Comrade Lieutenant. Conversation with a neighbour. She wrote it in Leningrad. During the siege."

Leonid looked down for a moment. He knew that Agranenko had been through that siege, one notable for its horrors even amongst the pitiless experiences of the Nazi invasion. "I see."

"Do you?" Agranenko's face was expressionless, but his eyes were troubled. "She read out her poems over the radio. For us."

Leonid was wondering what to say next when the door to the cellar flew open and Chuya lumbered down the steps. Leonid sprang to his feet and went to meet him, trailed after a pause by Agranenko. Leonid saluted smartly, but Chuya's acknowledgement was a perfunctory wave.

"Five minutes to go, Comrades." He said it to Leonid, but his eyes were on Agranenko. "Are the men ready?"

"Yes, Comrade Captain."

Chuya turned to face Agranenko who bobbed his head in confirmation. It was that which seemed to content Chuya and now he turned away. He was halfway up the steps when he paused as if remembering something and turned around. "Carry on," he said, sketching another salute, and then he left, banging the door behind him.

Agranenko spoke wryly. "'But no, my friends, I do not wish to leave; I'd rather live, to ponder and to grieve.'"

"Berggolts?"

"No, Pushkin."

For a moment they smiled at each other, and then Agranenko nodded, his face once more impassive. "Time," he said.

Slowly they made their way out of the cellar, followed by the platoon which formed up on the road by the brewery. All around was bustle and sound; the area around the brewery was full of motor vehicles and horse-drawn carts alongside a mass of soldiers, sitting mostly as they waited for their turn to move forward. More men and equipment passed in an endless column down the road towards the ridge which faced them from the west where the Germans waited: the Seelow Heights.

Leonid's platoon was part of a reserve battalion intended to follow up the initial attack once positions below the Heights had been secured, so for now, they too waited. They took their turn on the road and then turned off it with the rest of the company into a trench running down the middle of a soggy field. The bottom of the trench was lined with duckboards, but even so water seeped up and around their ankles. To keep their feet dry they sat exposed along the parapets; wet feet were a soldier's particular bane and to be avoided even at some risk.

Leonid sat with Agranenko in the centre of the platoon and stared into the blackness ahead, waiting, but not for long. It was only a bare ten minutes after they'd arrived that Agranenko stiffened.

"Now," he said when three red flares leapt high into the sky behind, one after the other. For a moment all seemed motionless except for the arching red lights. In the darkness Leonid felt as if he were suspended in a void. Then the dark was dispelled by myriad flashes behind him. He turned to look, but the intensity of light forced him to close his eyes. He winced as a thunderous roar of guns broke over him like a monstrous symphony of drums, then the howling of rockets. 'Stalin's Organs' the men called them after the unearthly moaning they made as they shrieked overhead on tails of fire.

The air trembled like a living thing, humming with liquid movement, sound that was felt as well as heard. Leonid's head ached. The ground vibrated, and here and there, clods of earth detached from the trench wall and fell into the grey water, the sound of the splashes lost in the general cacophony.

In front of Leonid lay the Oderbruch, a narrow flat plain studded with small villages, prosperous farms and manor houses all enmeshed in a network of drainage ditches and canalised streams. He remembered the briefing maps at Battalion Headquarters. By the intense light of the guns and rocket launchers he now saw an eerie landscape of grey and deep blue shadows, the flickering making it look like an old film shown on defective reels. Beyond it, and still invisible in the dark, were the Heights: a sharply rising but low ridge. It was the only substantial natural feature between them and Berlin, but the Oderbruch was itself a formidable obstacle. Although as flat as a pancake, each crossing place, each crossroads, each village and building had been turned into a strongpoint. The ground, Leonid had been told at the battalion briefing the previous day, was flooded; the defenders had opened sluices, blocked drains and diverted river waters further north. Now the narrow watercourses were ribbons up to twenty metres wide, perhaps three or four metres deep in the centre. The land was saturated: a quagmire difficult for those on foot, and completely impassable to vehicles except along exposed embanked roadways. These were barely wide enough to allow two cars to pass each other, let alone cater for the thousands of wheeled vehicles and hundreds of tanks which the Soviet commander, Marshal Georgii Zhukov, would hurl at the enemy.

Leonid saw a forest spring up on the plain, tall, thin, dark fingers reaching to the sky like poplars, but it was not a forest; they were not trees. He was looking at the impact of thousands of artillery rounds and it was a bad sign. Normally the rounds exploded outwards, spreading blast, fragments of steel and death around the point of impact, but the ground was so soft that the shells were being sucked deep into the mud before erupting directly upwards where the explosions would have little effect. Still, Leonid felt uplifted as he watched. It was a massive set piece barrage, the sort at which the Red Army excelled. Nothing, no one, Leonid felt sure, could stand before it, wet ground or not. 'Red God of Battles' the soldiers named their artillery, and it was a mighty god. If this were not enough, he heard the sound of aircraft passing overhead to drop many bombs. He was awestruck.

He'd witnessed bombardments before, but nothing like this. The advance across eastern Germany had been an affair of movement and very little fighting. They'd trudged across a freezing landscape, occasionally hitching a ride on tanks or in lorries, pausing only to let following supporting units catch up. There'd been little chance, or even need, for pre-planned assaults with artillery. It was only when an unusually stubborn group of German defenders refused to give up a position that field guns, howitzers and mortars were brought into play, and even then only in small numbers and briefly.

This was different. It seemed to Leonid that this whirlwind, this maelstrom of sound and light, was not born of mere man; and mere man, he felt, surely could not stand before it.

He glanced to either side of him. The platoon was peering forward, each figure lit up momentarily by the rippling lights and then vanishing into darkness before being lit once more. It was as if he sat in the darkened People's Theatre in Stalingrad where his stepfather used to take him and Cheslav on Sundays to watch newsreels proclaim the great successes of Soviet society. Now he felt that same curious mixture of intimacy and detachment he'd felt in the theatre, but also he felt as he'd done before taking school exams or asking a girl out on a date: he was anxious.

He began to notice that the explosions were receding, drifting away towards the unseen Heights, and he glanced at his watch. It was just two hours to dawn.

Suddenly more rockets leapt into the sky, these straight up in a long multi-coloured line running north to south behind him. He craned his head to watch them as they climbed and flickered out. Then a single bright searchlight beam shot upwards, and moments later a harsh white light burst over the Oderbruch as dozens of searchlights joined the first, but their beams were pointed directly across the plain towards the German positions. Staring into the light, Leonid was overwhelmed and turned his head away, blinking tears from his painful eyes.

Next to him, Agranenko muttered, "Holy Mother."

Leonid blinked, slid into the trench with a splash, and heard the sound of others all around him doing the same. He pressed the balls of his hands into his eye sockets, and before too long his eyesight began to return in black flecked dimness. Agranenko stood beside him, blinking rapidly. Out on the plain came the sound of artillery and machine gun fire; it didn't sound friendly.

Agranenko fumbled in the top pocket of his tunic and extracted a pack of cigarettes. He held it out and Leonid took one of the ready-rolled tubes, normally only issued to officers. Soldiers and sergeants made do with rough makhorka tobacco rolled up in whatever paper they could find. He wondered where Agranenko had got them and then dismissed the thought. Agranenko always seemed able to obtain such things; the entitlement of rank was not something he seemed to pay much attention to. The two of them stood listening and smoking; overhead the sky held a glare like daylight. The bright lights and the aroma of the cigarettes mingling with the reek of the trench and chemical explosives made Leonid feel slightly nauseous after a while. He got onto the firing step and raised his head over the parapet to draw in fresher air. There wasn't much, but it was better than that below.

Agranenko joined him and together they peered out across the plain, which was now alive with tiny figures, thin spikes like pencils, moving forward. From the nearer ones, Leonid saw dancing black shadows cast forward by the glare behind, grotesquely outsized and distorted. They were infantry, he realised. Amongst them flickered lines of red tracer: enemy machine gun fire and shell bursts. Yes, pencils, he thought, looking at the moving figures. A typical army nickname for soldiers, pencils were cheap and expendable.

Agranenko cast away the stub of his cigarette and lit another. "They should turn those off."

Leonid nodded. The searchlights, meant to blind the defenders and illuminate the way for the attackers, seemed to have no effect other than to silhouette targets for the Germans. They watched for a while, then, as if in response to Agranenko's demand, the searchlights began to go off in ones and twos, and then in great groups until the plain was dark once more.

Leonid noticed that the air was clearing of dust. Behind them, in the east, the sky grew brighter: nothing to do with searchlights. He drew in a deep breath and let out a sigh. The darkness was pleasing after the harsh light, and no doubt those out in the open appreciated it even more than he did, but his relief was premature. Star shells began to burst over the heads of the soldiers on the plain, showing them as targets once more, and the machine guns fired and the shells fell. Still it was better than the intense light of a few minutes before.

Leonid glanced behind him. It was still very dark, with no hint of dawn.

"Just as well," observed Agranenko. "Better for them to be crossing the open in the darkness. They're sitting ducks out there."

Leonid was about to agree when suddenly the harsh white light burst over them again: the searchlights were back on.

"Oh shit," said Agranenko quietly.

The platoon stood in the trampled garden of a house watching the junior lieutenant. "There are three types of *panzerfaust*: the thirty, the sixty and the one hundred." He pointed in turn to three identical brown tubes laid out on a trestle table by his side. Each was about a metre long and terminated in a cone slightly smaller than a man's head, flaring outwards and ending in a rounded cap. "That means they have a range of about thirty, sixty or one hundred metres."

"You don't say," muttered Kolchok, who was standing next to Cheslav with an air of complete boredom.

The lieutenant began fiddling with the cone and detached it. "The warhead comes off like *so*, then you insert the detonation charge like *so*, and then the firing percussion cap." He replaced the warhead and pushed up the lever. "And lock this up. Before you fire it, you have to take out this safety plug *here*." He demonstrated. The weapon was, he went on to inform them, now armed.

He turned and st rolled across the field next to the garden. The boundary of the field was a grass bank, its surface pockmarked by small brown craters that looked like rabbit holes. The lieutenant faced it, holding the *panzerfaust* as if couching a lance. He was still speaking, but his voice was drowned out by the sound of vehicles passing in an endless stream along the road the other side of the house and flanking the field. Added to that was the noise of the artillery, which had been firing continuously since well before dawn. It didn't matter; they could see clearly what he was talking about. He stopped speaking, turned, and, with a *whumpf*, a jet of flame surged out of the back end of the *panzerfaust* followed by a whirling cloud of grey-white smoke. There was a smaller flash near the front of the tube and the conical top flew off and leapt down the field like a darting bird. Moments later there was a sharp *bang* and a small volcano of earth and pulverised grass erupted from the bank where the warhead had struck. The platoon applauded. Grinning, the lieutenant bowed to them like a kid who's just let off a firework on New Year's Eve, then walked back.

How young he looks, Cheslav thought. He seemed even younger than Leonid, another baby-faced junior lieutenant.

"Your turn, Comrades."

Kolchok caught Cheslav's eye and smiled slightly, his thin, almost emaciated, peasant face crinkling like old leather. "He's not old enough to be wiping his own arse," he muttered. Kolchok held out a cigarette as they watched the first of the pairs the platoon had been separated into walk forward. "Smoke, boy?" Cheslav shook his head and Kolchok grinned.

Cheslav had chosen to pair with him for he trusted the old man's common sense. Kolchok had years of experience handling weapons, gained in the previous war against Germany and then in the civil war at home that followed it, and he had an old peasant's matter-of-fact approach to things.

"Bad for your health, eh? Quite right. Smoke less, drink less, fuck less, live longer. Or at least it'll seem that way, boy, eh?" Kolchok laughed sardonically. He called everyone younger than himself 'boy' or 'girl', except officers, of course. With officers he was formally polite to their faces. Behind their backs he was not always complimentary, but he gossiped less about them than he did about his comrades. It was traditional for soldiers to moan about things; their officers, their food, the weather. A laxer atmosphere prevailed at the Front than at home. When Cheslav had arrived fresh from the training camp, he'd been shocked to find that the *frontoviki*, veterans who had seen active fighting, had less respect for and less fear of the Party than those back home. At the Front, being a Party member did not guarantee deference, nor were the pronouncements of the Party received uncritically. Cheslav found that many frontoviki hoped their greater freedom would outlast the war's end. Cheslav doubted it; he was sure that the Party would restore its grip, so he followed Kolchok's lead and was careful who heard his criticisms.

"What do you think?" Kolchok gestured towards the ruined bank. "Seems easy enough."

Easy was not how Cheslav felt about it.

"Can't be that difficult," Kolchok went on, "if Golden Boy there can manage it." He stabbed his smoking cigarette again, this time towards the lieutenant. Cheslav grimaced. 'Golden Boy' was soldier slang for a homosexual, and homosexuality was illegal in the Soviet Union. Worse, it was despised, but Cheslav knew that Kolchok didn't mean it literally. It was also a term often applied to officers fresh out of training academies, seen as impractical dandies, full of theory, dapper, perhaps a bit soft and unmanly. Inconsistently, the rank and file also admired their neatness as a sign of higher culture; of those with a greater sophistication and learning.

Seeing Cheslav's disapproving look, Kolchok murmured, "Don't mind me, boy." He jerked his head towards the lieutenant. "He'll do all right."

Cheslav nodded, and then sighed as Platoon Sergeant Lopakin beckoned to those from his place by the table. "Our turn."

"Barakovski," acknowledged Lopakin as they approached. The lieutenant held up a *panzerfaust*. Cheslav hesitated for a moment and then took it. As he stared down at the surprisingly heavy weapon, he saw pieces of shredded cardboard on the ground.

"Proceed," said Lopakin.

Cheslav started to sweat. He wasn't practical and he struggled to remember what the lieutenant had said.

"Well, Barakovski? Weren't you paying attention? What happened to that fancy brain of yours?" Lopakin looked irritated. He resented Cheslav's education; Cheslav wasn't an officer, and Lopakin, rumour said, had spent most of his teenage years in a reformatory and could hardly read or write.

The lieutenant pointedly consulted his watch. Cheslav looked closely and saw small cartoons printed on the side of the tube and instructions in German.

"Come on, Corporal. The rest of us want to eat!" Lopakin barked. It was nearly midday and the company cooks would be stewing up lunch.

Cheslav ignored him and concentrated on working out what the instructions were telling him. He wished that the lieutenant would guide him through it, but the officer just stood and watched him intently. Kolchok was no help either. Fumbling at first, but with increasing confidence Cheslav managed to reproduce the lieutenant's actions, then he turned away from the others so that they wouldn't be caught in the ferocious back blast, tucked the *panzerfaust* under his arm and fired. For a moment nothing seemed to happen, and then he was wreathed in smoke that stank like an extinguished candle. When it cleared, he could see no sign of having hit the bank. His ears rang.

The lieutenant, however, seemed pleased. "Good. Next time, a Tiger."

Cheslav hoped not. The Tiger was the most feared of German tanks. He wondered what use a little rocket would be against a steel behemoth with a huge gun.

The lieutenant took the empty launch tube from Cheslav and tossed it onto a nearby pile. "Where did you learn German?"

Cheslav froze for a moment and then mumbled, "Uh, I don't understand, Comrade Lieutenant." He sounded unconvincing, even to himself. Lopakin and Kolchok looked at him with interest.

"You were reading the instructions." The lieutenant was smiling.

"Not really, Comrade Lieutenant." Cheslav paused. "I picked up a few phrases along the way, that's all."

"Really? Are you sure?" The lieutenant seemed disappointed. "Battalion Headquarters has been asked to find German speakers to act as translators. We're short. It'd be a good post, back at Regiment."

For a moment Cheslav was tempted. It would get him away from the worst of the fighting, and the 'rear area rats' had an easier life – better food, drier accommodation, more sleep, cleaner clothes – but he shook his head. It would be unwise to draw attention to his German skills. At Regiment he was more likely to run into those who would take an acute interest in them and who might ask awkward questions.

"It was the pictures, Comrade Lieutenant. I didn't really understand much of the words. I guessed."

"Guessed?" barked Lopakin. "You should have been paying attention."

The lieutenant came to his rescue. "No matter. You did well. Dismissed."

Cheslav saluted and he and Kolchok made their way across the trampled grass to those waiting by the house, smoking and talking. Cheslav glanced back to see Lopakin speaking animatedly to the lieutenant, who shrugged.

"Next pair," Lopakin bellowed.

Half an hour later they were sitting on the other side of the road, watching the traffic pass. Kolchok offered Cheslav his water bottle. Cheslav sniffed inquisitively and smelled alcohol. Brandy? They were all getting good at guessing German liquors: they'd commandeered a lot of it.

"Courtesy of a Fritz cellar. Don't drink it all."

Cheslav shook his head and swallowed. It was good, smooth, mellow, not like vodka, nor like the powerful birch-sap wine they'd brewed at home.

"He didn't believe you." Kolchok took the bottle back, sipped and made a face. "Comrade Rocket didn't believe you when you said you didn't speak German."

Cheslav looked away, not wanting this conversation, and pretended a keen interest in the passing vehicles. Many had slogans painted on their sides: 'On to Berlin'; 'For the Motherland'; 'Hitler Kaput'. Red flags fluttered on some, and the soldiers going forward to fight waved their weapons and shouted.

Kolchok looked at him and then snorted. "All right, boy, you keep your secrets." He offered the canteen once more and Cheslav took it. "Though if it were me I'd have taken the offer. Regiment. Now there's a thought. Nice billets and maybe a campaign wife or two."

Cheslav couldn't help but smile at that: 'campaign wife' was slang for women soldiers who, rumour had it, provided senior officers with more than administrative services. It might even be true, although most soldiers' tales were greatly exaggerated. Nevertheless, he found the idea pleasant and swallowed more brandy.

Maybe I should have taken the offer, he thought, but that he'd made the right decision, both for himself and for Leonid. Some things it was best not to draw attention to.

"Don't drink it all, Comrade," Kolchok admonished and held out his hand.

Mrs Boldt was trying everyone's patience more than usual.

"I tell you," she said, waving a piece of paper under Tanya's nose, "it's a relief force. Look, look. See here." She stabbed at the tabloid-sized newssheet with her stubby fingers so that the thin, cheap paper crinkled and bent. Her red cheeks, thick lips and blue eyes reminded Tanya of her favourite childhood doll with its painted china head. The resemblance ended there, however, for Tanya had been fond of her doll.

"Nonsense." It was Klara who spoke – she who rarely said anything at all, let alone a contradiction.

Mrs Boldt turned and glared at the younger woman. "Don't tell me it's nonsense," she snapped. "Herr Dr Goebbels himself has assured us, has *assured* us, that...that..." she stumbled over her words, scanned the page for a few seconds and read "...the Bolsheviks will meet the ancient fate of Asia, which means they shall and must bleed to death before the capital of the German Reich. There! The minister himself says it. Look! Look!" and she stabbed her finger at another section.

Tanya sighed. She didn't need to read it. After twelve years of Nazi rule she was more than familiar with their bombast. The newssheet was *The Armoured Bear,* printed to replace the usual Berlin newspapers when paper became scarce and production erratic as the war wore on. The bear was Berlin's ancient heraldic symbol; the newssheet banner showed one holding a rocket launcher in each paw.

"You read it," she said.

Mrs Boldt scowled. "You think you're so clever, madam, you wait and see. The Führer himself has told us that at this moment, *at this moment*, our army is on its way to save Berlin. You'll all see."

"Oh well, if *he* says so, that's all right." Klara's words were quiet, but everyone heard them. Mrs Körtig snorted.

"Do *you* doubt it also?" Mrs Boldt turned her attention to the old woman. "Call yourself a German? Why, you should be ashamed. You should *all* be ashamed."

Mrs Körtig cut her off. She didn't raise her voice, but it was steely. "Madam, do *not* speak to me like that." She stood suddenly and locked stares with the block warden. "My husband, madam, fought for Germany. *Your* husband, I recall, did not."

There was a frosty silence. Mrs Boldt seemed at a loss as to what to say. Tanya had never met her husband, but she knew that he'd been some sort of minor clerk in the admiralty, a post he'd held all through the last war, safe from any fighting. He'd died before Tanya had moved into the apartment. Cancer, Mrs Boldt had claimed. Drink, Mathias had said, driven to it by his wife.

Mrs Körtig and Mrs Boldt glared at each other for a moment longer, and Tanya thought that the block warden looked like a bull preparing to charge. Then she turned away and walked to her chair. With pursed lips, she sat and picked up her knitting. Mrs Körtig looked at her for a moment longer, then went to her sofa and picked up her embroidery. Both women bent to their tasks, studiously ignoring each other. A strained silence fell across the cellar, disturbed only by the distant, faint rumble of artillery, which had been going on for some hours now.

Cheslav was disappointed. After the *panzerfaust* training they'd had lunch, porridge of course, and then moved into a small orchard near the farmhouse. There was nothing to do so he cleaned his rifle and slept, woke and watched the passing traffic, then slept again. It was not as Cheslav had expected it. He'd imagined they'd march forward into battle immediately the offensive commenced to drive back the fascists, just like in the film reels. Instead they waited. A few of the platoon had started games of cards, but he could dredge up no enthusiasm for them. Twice he'd pulled out a book Leonid had given him when he'd left for the academy, but he was too restless to read, and too restless to write to Leonid. He had the book out now, lying on his lap. It had been a favourite of Leonid's when he was younger: *How the Steel Was Tempered*. On the face of it, an odd book for Leonid to like. The characters were Bolshevik archetypes: a heroic young man fighting for the Revolution and his teenage love during the civil war which followed the Bolshevik takeover.

"Here." Kolchok held out hot tea which he'd brewed in his mess tin over a low fire of twigs and small branches. It had quite a kick. "Vodka," grinned Kolchok. "Put hair on your chest."

Cheslav frowned but accepted the drink willingly. Then he handed the tin back and asked, "How long?"

"Until we go forward?" Kolchok shrugged. "Make the most of it." He peered quizzically at Cheslav. "Nervous, boy?"

Cheslav said nothing for a moment. He looked around him; everyone seemed so relaxed. He nodded and accepted the offer of the mess tin once more. While he sipped, Kolchok rooted in his backpack, brought out a bottle and tipped more vodka into the tea. "Have some courage," he urged and then took a large swig directly from the bottle. Wiping his mouth with the back of his wrinkled hand, he quoted, "'Vodka isn't tea; you can't have too much of it.'"

Cheslav smiled; he'd heard the saying many times since he'd joined the army. "I suppose," he said, nodding to the platoon, "they're used to this."

Kolchok peered around and shook his head.

Cheslav went on. "I mean, they're veterans. They've been in battle before. Proper battle. It's like that proverb: a wet man fears no rain."

Kolchok shook his head again and took another swallow from the bottle. "That's rubbish, boy. They're just as nervous as you are."

"But they've been through it, most of them. I haven't. They're battle hardened. I'm not, and they made me a corporal. *I'm* supposed to lead *them*."

Kolchok sighed, a long, low sound of irritation with a foolish child. "Listen. Battle doesn't harden anyone. You learn a few wheezes, a few dodges. How to stay alive, how not to take risks. That's all. Frontoviki get scared too. Maybe more than you babies, all right? We know what's coming, boy. We just learn not to think about it." He chuckled ruefully. "Most of us."

It was one of the longest speeches Cheslav had heard Kolchok make and he was grateful for the old man's solicitude. Kolchok rarely bothered.

"You'll do all right," he said and reached out to pour more vodka into the mess tin.

Mrs Boldt mostly stayed in her chair knitting, sometimes getting up to turn on the radio. There was no news, only music, and she said nothing more.

The Schleys went back to their apartment, but returned in the afternoon. Ida and Mathias sat around the table, playing cards with Klara. Skat was their favourite.

Axel arrived later that morning with two loaves of bread and announced, "The office has been closed for the day." He said no more but joined the group at the table and they all played doppelkopf.

At first Walter sat morosely on his camp bed, thumbing through the film magazines his mother kept for him in her tin trunk along with her memorabilia. Later he pulled out a copy of Goethe's novel *Wilhelm Meister's Apprenticeship*. Goethe was not his favourite – he found it too difficult to get into – but it had been his father's and he valued it for that. Fabian had given it to Walter when he'd left for the Front, and inside had written: 'To Walter. Find your way as Meister found his.' Walter had never finished the book, despite starting it several times. Now he sat and leafed through it, then held it and stared into space.

Tanya had played cards at first, going a few rounds of elfern with Mrs Körtig, but tired of it, so then the old lady joined the table and they switched games once more, this time to endless rounds of German Bridge. Tanya started on her own copy of Goethe, this one *Faust*. It had been a gift from a man she'd dallied with insincerely some years before. She'd tried on several occasions to get into it but, like Walter, found Goethe inaccessible. He was too depressing, and finally, after struggling for a while, she switched to a selection of poems by Heinrich Heine. A Christianised Jew, his works had been burned on the Opernplatz by the Nazis when they came to power in 1933. Tanya approved of him, and this was one book they had *not* burned. She'd disguised it inside covers she'd removed from a copy of Ernst Jünger's semi-autobiographical war novel, *Storm of Steel*, a book that the Party approved.

Outside the artillery fire waxed and waned, but it didn't end entirely. Tanya ignored it and read:

I had a lovely homeland long ago.
The oak trees seemed
So tall there, and the violets blew so sweet.
It was a dream.
It kissed me in German, spoke in German

(You'd scarce believe
How good it sounds) the words: I love you true!
It was a dream.

Much better! She settled comfortably into her old chair, determined to while away the day with dear old Heine.

At midday Leonid was still waiting in the wet trench. The timetable had called for them to move forward hours before, but they hadn't. The searchlights came on, went off again, came on and went off. Dawn came and still the company waited, and waited. Across the Oderbruch a dismal scene unfolded: soldiers moving forward slowly across waterlogged fields; motor vehicles and horse carts stopping and starting on the causeway roads. Artillery burst all around them and machine gun fire flickered here and there. Figures fell; vehicles puffed into flame or jerked to a halt.

The covering bombardment continued, rising and falling in intensity, churning up the German positions, wreathing the Oderbruch and the Seelow Heights in smoke and dust, and over it all aircraft flew singly and in groups, dropping bombs and firing their cannon.

Chuya did the rounds of the company. "It's a mess." He faced Leonid and Agranenko in the trench, puffing his pipe, sounding like a man commenting on a football match. "The major told me that the Germans pulled out of the frontline trenches *before* our bombardment. All we've done is churn up the ground and make it even more impassable. They've really fucked it up."

Leonid glanced at Polyanski who was staring impassively at Chuya's back. He couldn't have been pleased with Chuya's criticism, but he'd not said anything; not in front of more junior ranks. What he would do when he returned to Battalion HQ and saw Major Zeldin, the battalion commander, might be a different matter.

Chuya shook his head. "So we wait." That was all he said before he carried on down the trench to the next position, Polyanski still trailing him.

Agranenko went to explain it all to the platoon and they made themselves comfortable as they could, sitting and lying along the parapet. They slept, they smoked, they talked; mostly they slept. Leonid read a bit, tried to write a letter to his brother, but couldn't settle to it. Finally, he too tried to sleep, and, after a long time tossing and turning, listening to the sounds of combat, he closed his eyes, but not for long. Less than an hour had passed when he was awakened by the squeak, rattle and rumble of armoured vehicles. Down the road past the trench came a column of tanks, low and broad with oversized turrets. 34s, he thought. He counted a dozen or more, and then came lorries and armoured cars, then more tanks, altogether over sixty of them. Leonid was puzzled: these must be part of Zhukov's tank reserve, supposed to be held back until infantry units like his had broken through the German defences.

"Things not going to plan," observed Agranenko. "But then, they usually don't."

Leonid nodded as another group of tanks passed along the churned-up roadway. The sight of tanks usually cheered an infantryman's heart, but Leonid was not cheered.

By late afternoon Chuya was back, this time without Polyanski. "We're moving up to the first line of trenches. They've been cleared." He looked towards the Seelow Heights, a low shadow along the horizon. Across the plain explosions continued to burst, but now much further forward. "You'll need to move smartly. The Fritzes can see everything from up there. They're dropping shells right on top of our boys."

He turned to face them. Leonid and Agranenko exchanged a brief glance: they knew about the artillery, had been watching it all morning. Move smartly? wondered Leonid. Through that mud? How? But all he said was, "Yes, Comrade Captain."

Chuya smiled grimly. "Don't worry, Leonid Stepanovich. They're going to hit the bastards with another barrage. Should keep their heads down while we get there." He nodded at Agranenko and then ambled away like a morose bear.

It was a few minutes' work to muster the platoon. This wasn't done the way Leonid had been taught back at the academy:

> At the order of the platoon leader, the squad leader gives the command "Prepare for assault", and after the soldiers have loaded their weapons and prepared hand grenades, at the order of the platoon leader the squad leader gives the order "To the assault – march."

Instead Agranenko went to each of the corporals, told them what was happening and let them get on with it. They were frontoviki, after all. Leonid did nothing at all.

The platoon shook itself out into a long line with Agranenko and Leonid in the middle. On either side the other platoons of the company moved into positions along the parapets. Beyond them were other companies of the battalion, and no doubt beyond them, Leonid surmised, were other battalions in the regiment.

His stomach knotted and his mouth went dry; it always did whenever combat was near. He swallowed half a dozen times and hoped his fear didn't show.

They lay flat for several minutes until, with a throbbing roar, a gaggle of brown and green single-engine aircraft passed low overhead. Leonid recognised them, and Agranenko nodded when he called out, "Stormers." Leonid watched them go with pleasure. The *Stormer*, the Ilyushin ground attack aircraft, was the backbone of Soviet aviation. It was armoured and carried a respectable set of cannon and bombs. As he watched, more flew over to his right and left, and even before they had reached their targets, artillery shells began to explode all along the base of the Seelow Heights and across the plain ahead. He hoped that this bombardment would be more effective than the first and the sight of it lifted his spirits. Fear, however, still cramped his gut.

Then Agranenko raised his hand and stood up; the platoon stood with him. Whistles blew on either side and they all began to walk forward. No one ran: it had been made very clear to Leonid during his basic training that running was for the newsreels. To run would exhaust you before you got anywhere near the enemy, and there was the danger of slipping and the formation losing cohesion. It was only in the last few tens of metres that you might sprint. Running would, in any case, have been impossible in the mud. The wet soil clutched at Leonid's boots and made him stumble as all were stumbling around him.

They moved into a lunar landscape: there were craters everywhere. Some were small depressions in the ground, others deep pits large enough to hold half the platoon. They moved around them, reforming the line as they did so. Then they found the remains of forward dugouts: earth mixed in with shattered wood, split sandbags and tangled barbed wire, all churned into the ground by the intense shelling. It was the remains of the German forward positions.

They passed bodies too, some in pieces. None were German, and Leonid tried not to look at them.

He estimated that they were over halfway to the first German trench-line and might get there before anyone shot at them. All of the shelling seemed directed well ahead of them and he hoped it would stay that way. With luck they'd get to the trench without anything worse than a muddy walk.

"Oh, fuck it."

It was Agranenko's curse that drew Leonid's attention to the wide strip of murky water stretching to the right and left in front of them. It was wide and looked deep, but on the briefing map at HQ it had been indicated as nothing more than a narrow drainage ditch.

"You can jump over it, Comrades," Major Zeldin, the battalion commander, had reassured his assembled officers.

No you can't, thought Leonid, looking at it with dismay.

Agranenko sighed. "Time to get wet." He sounded very unhappy; Leonid knew that he hated to get wet feet. Leonid hated it too, and they both stood for a few moments, staring at the ditch. On either side of them, the platoon halted with them. One man, however, did not; he carried on plodding through the mud, and when he reached the water's edge he plunged straight in without a pause and thrashed his way forward.

Leonid recognised him: Private Rybczak, always prepared to press on. He watched the water creep up Rybczak's legs until it reached his hips, and then it went no further.

Rybczak turned and beckoned, then pressed on. No one moved. He was almost at the other side when suddenly he lost his footing and disappeared completely below the surface. He emerged seconds later minus his field cap and spat out slimy green ditch water.

Agranenko grinned. "Going swimming, Vladlen?"

Rybczak said nothing. He glared at Agranenko, pulled himself out onto the far edge and stood up. He held his rifle upside down to let water run out of the barrel, and Agranenko laughed.

Several of the platoon joined in and suddenly the mood lightened; everyone surged forward, wading across with weapons held above their heads. After a moment's hesitation, Leonid followed Agranenko into the water. It was deeply cold and the mud on the bottom was almost liquid. His calves ached with the effort and a couple of times he almost fell, but he made it.

Agranenko helped him out. "I hate wet feet," he muttered.

Leonid was searching for an appropriate reply when he heard the howl of approaching shells. In a second he joined the platoon on the ground. He pushed his face into soil rancid with mulch and froze, listening to the *whoosh* and *thud* of shells behind him, feeling the ground vibrate. Wet feet were no longer important. Then, as quickly as it had begun, the shelling stopped. Cautiously he raised his head. Agranenko was already back on his feet, and with him the platoon. Leonid scrambled up, the last to stand.

"Quickly," Agranenko called out, "before they get the range."

Leonid nodded; the Germans would have seen the fall of shot, and would no doubt be adjusting their aim. The platoon moved on as quickly as the ground allowed, but they'd barely gone a hundred metres when once more shells began to burst, this time on the very spot they'd just vacated. Leonid dropped down once more, twisting his head to watch plumes of soil erupt from the ground and jets of water splash upwards from the ditch. When this too ended, they lost no time in closing the remaining short distance to the abandoned German trench.

It was undamaged. Agranenko tapped the trench's revetted walls as he came to join Leonid. He was wheezing; they were all blown by the dash through the mud, and Leonid felt bands of pain across his ribs. The platoon slumped all along the trench.

"Untouched," Agranenko observed. "Well, that's better for us."

Leonid nodded. He stepped up onto the firing step and looked towards the Heights. It was not a comforting sight. Much was obscured by smoke, some deliberately laid as a screen by artillery covering the attack. Some, however, came from burning vehicles – lots of them. Not too far away an aircraft lay with its nose buried in the soft ground, tail in the air, red stars on its broken wings.

Flashes and puffs of smoke and earth covered the plain in irregular clumps, marking the forward edge of the fighting. It was well short of the Seelow Heights. Slightly beyond it Leonid thought he could make out the canal which was supposed to be the objective for that morning. With a sigh, he dropped back and turned to face Agranenko.

"Now what?"

"I suppose we wait for orders. There's a dugout we can use. More comfortable."

Leonid straightened his coat and cap and followed Agranenko, water squishing in his boots. He noticed that most of the platoon had taken theirs off and were drying their feet with whatever they had to hand.

A short distance along the trench they came to a blanket hanging down the wall. It covered a low doorway, beyond which was a very comfortable place indeed. The sides and ceiling were planked between heavy beam supports; more planks formed the floor. Against one wall were bunk beds, and in the centre a table made of planks laid across empty crates. There was a small iron stove in one corner, the chimney pipe leading out through the wall, and it was still warm. The occupants clearly must have been in a hurry to leave for they'd left behind two dead rabbits hanging from one of the beams.

Leonid joined Agranenko on the lowest bunk to empty his boots and change his socks, a parting present from his mother. Agranenko, he noticed, used regulation footcloths. They were savouring the feel of their feet once more dry when Chuya and Polyanski, as dirty and dishevelled as everyone else, came in. Leonid leapt to his feet and saluted; Agranenko was slower.

"Sit down." Chuya waved Leonid back to the bunk and propped himself against the table, pulled out a pipe and filled it from a rather ornately decorated German pack of tobacco. Chuya was fond of German tobacco, and the company had an unwritten rule that he was to get any that was found; less, of course, a share for the finder. He didn't speak until he'd lit the pipe, something which took three attempts with his German lighter, and Leonid wondered if it had got wet. Chuya's greatcoat, he noticed, was damp below his thighs; so was Polyanski's.

"All right." Chuya puffed out smoke and finally looked satisfied. "We're here. Timetable's shot, though, and we're well behind." He went on to explain that all the tanks had achieved was to clog up the roads, and they'd got in the way of the specialist units, such as the engineers, who were supposed to bridge the main canal ahead of them. "So we wait until they've sorted themselves out." Chuya frowned at his pipe, which had gone out already, and began the elaborate ritual of relighting it.

Leonid felt relieved. He was drained and doubted that he could summon up the energy to move forward. He glanced at Agranenko, who too looked tired.

"How long do we wait?"

Chuya puffed smoke into the air, examined it, again seemed pleased with the result. "I don't know. It'll be getting dark out there soon. The fighting up ahead is still heavy. It might not be until dawn."

Leonid nodded. He could hear the sound of shelling even in the dugout and feel the occasional vibration. Now and then a trickle of earth drifted between the ceiling planks.

Polyanski spoke for the first time. "If we try hard enough we might catch up with the timetable. We need to make a big effort."

Chuya glanced at him irritably. "Yes, well first let's get ourselves reorganised. And we need orders from Regiment." He looked pointedly at Polyanski, who met his gaze but said nothing.

Chuya stood up. "Make sure that you're ready to go in at short notice." He came forward and Leonid caught the faint aroma of alcohol; Chuya was known as a heavy drinker. Chuya nodded to him, then to Agranenko, and left.

Polyanski followed him and then turned at the doorway. "We're almost on the Heights, Comrades. We've broken the back of it. It should be a simple matter of just pushing forward. I think we'll get orders to tonight. The Party will expect your best effort. For Stalin and the Motherland!"

Automatically, Leonid straightened. He should say something positive, he supposed, but Polyanski had already breezed out, leaving the blanket to swish back into place behind him.

"Right," Agranenko muttered, "a simple matter. Push forward. For Stalin and the Motherland." He sat back on the bunk and fumbled in his tunic pocket for a cigarette. "Marvellous."

Leonid said nothing.

THREE

Chuya was right and Polyanski was wrong. Orders didn't come until well after dark and they were simple: wait until dawn. Tanks were expected and more support generally, but the timetable had gone to hell.

When the horizon lightened, Agranenko deployed the platoon once more along the trench. Leonid checked his watch. Soon, he told himself. The scene reminded him of films about the previous war against the Germans: soldiers standing with fixed bayonets on the duckboards laid over the mud; small wooden ladders they'd found in the dugouts propped against the trench walls; bodies tensed; faces grimly determined. Chuya stood at the centre of the company line; Polyanski stood next to him carrying a loudhailer; behind him stood Corporal Semyon Kantovski, the company agitator, carrying a furled banner horizontally. Kantovski worked for Polyanski and was diligent in his duties. He was often found doing his rounds when everyone else was resting: he handed out cigarettes, swapped jokes, delivered the vodka ration, larding everything he did with Marxist chit-chat. The company responded well to his obvious sincerity and he was trusted with their troubles: he was the comradely face of the Party. He offered common sense solutions more convincing than Polyanski's official prescriptions. Moreover, unlike Polyanski, he was one of them: a comrade in arms, not a politico.

Kantovski stood with another agitator, Private Abram Moiseyevich, a very different sort. Moiseyevich came from Leonid's platoon, but he often served as a runner for Battalion HQ for he was slightly built and very fast on his feet. Leonid lent him as often as he could for he neither liked nor trusted him; Agranenko was wary of him too. He'd once told Leonid that Moiseyevich, as the old Russian saying had it, 'looks like a young fox but smells like an old wolf.' Moiseyevich was not trusted by the men, but he was trusted by the Party, and that was what mattered.

Polyanski raised his loudhailer and pulled a sheet of paper from the leather satchel hanging from his shoulder. Pausing dramatically, he read from it.

Our darling son, we hope this letter finds you well. Things are hard here. Since the winter we have nothing to eat but last year's potatoes. They are bad.

The Russian was simple, even crude. It's not exactly Tolstoy, Leonid observed and then chided himself. Tolstoy, who idealised the simple pleasant, would not have approved of his disdain, and Leonid idolised Tolstoy.

Polyanski cleared his throat and the loudhailer squealed, then he went on. The letter was nothing like the agitprop dished out to them on a regular basis: no rousing language, no soaring ideals, no Party maxims. It was simple to the point of banality, but all eyes were fixed firmly on Polyanski and his piece of paper, even Agranenko's.

Petya is dead. We are sad but we manage. There is little food. The fascists took it all and burned the house. We hid in the forest. They are gone now. The army came. They too are gone. We have nothing but we are alive and will survive. Stalin be praised.

Leonid smiled: 'Stalin be praised.' It was a religious echo of old Russia which the Party, for all its strivings, had failed to eliminate. To many, Stalin was a new Tsar and therefore holy: his image was often treated like a new icon to be hung on the wall above a flickering candle or worn around the neck. Holy Mother Russia still lived, especially in rural areas well away from Moscow. For many, perhaps most, of the people of the Soviet Union, God still lurked somewhere in the heavens. It was just that God had changed a bit and now there were new saints.

Polyanski's sonorous voice rolled on.

The snow has gone and the rain. We have no seed to plant. We are living in that old log shed in the forest. There are ten of us. We hope to see you again. Your sister died last winter when we ran to hide from the fascists. She was ill and couldn't run. They found her and they beat her and she died. She would not give them what they wanted and they killed her.

The platoon stirred slightly.

Polyanski was coming to the end and his voice rose in pitch, becoming more forceful.

We live to see you again, my son. We live to see Victory Day. Look after yourself. Mama and Papa.

Polyanski held the letter aloft and paused, looked sternly to left and right. "The soldier this was sent to died doing his duty. He died fighting the fascists. And this is why, Comrades." He waved the letter above his head. "Here is why we fight."

Leonid felt embarrassed. What a ham, he thought, but all around him heads lifted slightly, expressions set. He felt the mood rise in the platoon; for himself, he felt nothing. He glanced at Agranenko, who stood next to him with a wry expression.

"Any minute now."

Leonid followed Agranenko's gaze. Chuya was saying something into the field telephone they'd laid overnight. Then he replaced the handset, turned and spoke briefly to Kantovski and Moiseyevich. Kantovski hoisted the banner above the line of the parapet.

Moiseyevich shouldered his way towards them and halted

without saluting. Leonid knew that he should pick him up on the breach of etiquette, but really, here in this place, he couldn't be bothered. Nor did he want the risk of confrontation.

"Tanks are here."

Leonid nodded. He could already hear the clatter of their tracks, and then he saw them: six, one behind the other, passing down the road. They were heading for the bridge which took the road across the canal ahead; an engineer platoon had been labouring all night to repair it. Other engineers had been busy at other crossing points, laying lighter bridges which would take a man but not a tank. He could see them all now: clusters of brown figures along the canal, still busying themselves.

"Prepare," Agranenko called out and the platoon tensed. Moiseyevich carried on down the trench.

Leonid's mouth went dry and for a moment he gripped his submachine gun too tightly. Mortar shells began to burst, laying down a thick smokescreen along the other side of the canal. Then more mortar shells, this time near the bridges: these were Germans. The engineers scattered and threw themselves down. The mortar fire was brief, however, for the smoke thickened and rose rapidly, hiding the bridges from any observer. The tanks accelerated and a whistle blew.

Leonid looked again towards Chuya, who was scrambling up a ladder followed by Kantovski and Polyanski. Kantovski stepped off the parapet, the banner flicking out in the breeze, blowing across the Oderbruch from the Seelow Heights, a bright red rectangle startling against the drabness.

"Let's go," Agranenko bellowed, and Leonid followed him as all around drab brown figures clambered out of the trench. Machine guns set up on their flanks opened fire, long lines of flickering red tracer reaching forward into the grey-white clouds ahead of them. Shells howled overhead. Shaking out into an extended line, the company advanced. They strode forward; no cheering; no shouts.

Then the Germans opened fire once more.

Bullets hissed and whined past Leonid and mortar shells burst again; only a scattering, but Leonid saw figures twist and drop, cut down by red-hot splinters of steel or hissing bullets. None from his platoon yet.

They pressed on, mud sucking at their ankles, stumbling over the uneven ground. The smoke got closer. Then there was a sharp *crack* over Leonid's head and instinctively he ducked. When he straightened, Tajidaev screamed a warning from his left and dropped prone in the mud. Moments later a finger of tracer flickered over Tajidaev's head and meandered towards Leonid; he too fell flat and hugged the ground. The tracer passed overhead and on.

Looking around, Leonid could see that no one was still standing; more tracer weaved red trails here and there; more mortar rounds burst. They'd come barely three hundred metres from the trench, not yet halfway to the canal.

For a while nothing much happened. Bursts of machine gun fire were interspersed with occasional mortar shells, but the Germans lacked proper targets and the firing became desultory and dwindled away.

Leonid wondered whether he should do something, for no one was stirring and he knew they should take advantage of the lull to get on. After all, he was an officer, supposed to lead, but if Chuya and Polyanski saw fit to stay safely down, why shouldn't he? He was reassuring himself with this idea when again Tajidaev shouted something. He twisted his head and saw Kantovski standing in full view with the banner, and with him stood Polyanski, and with Polyanski stood Chuya.

Leonid's heart sank.

The platoon scrambled to its feet.

"Come on, Comrade," Tajidaev urged and got up. He was smiling, actually smiling. Leonid tried to stand, but his legs didn't cooperate and he managed only to raise himself to his knees.

"Comrade." Tajidaev's dark eyes were on him and his tone was urgent.

Leonid turned his face away; his fear was rising, and he didn't want to reveal it.

"Comrade Lieutenant!" Tajidaev was insistent. Embarrassment replaced some of Leonid's fear and he managed to stand. Tajidaev nodded as if encouraging a hesitant child and walked forward, his rifle held across his chest. After a moment Leonid followed him.

The company stumbled across the muddy ground towards the canal. There was no more shelling as they passed into the smoke, thinning by now, and stood on concrete banks looking down at the slimy dark water. The canal looked absurdly narrow to need so much planning and effort.

The smoke was dispersing fast now and Leonid could see figures running across the plank footbridges the engineers had laid down. At the more substantial bridge of wooden baulks, one of the tanks had left the road and was slewed broadside, black fumes drifting up from its rear engine deck. Another was still on the road, but it too was stationary, hatches popped open on its bulbous turret. The others lumbered across the sodden fields ahead, where Leonid needed to be.

It was mid-morning when Tanya went to her apartment to check that all was all right and lock the door, something she did every morning after a night in the cellar, air raid or not. It was the regulation that doors must be left unsecured to allow access in case of incendiaries, a godsend for looters.

It was dim, for the blackout curtains admitted little light. She stared about her in the gloom, checking for damage or intrusion, although what she could do if she had been burgled, she wasn't sure. The authorities had better things to do than hunt for petty thieves. Her glance passed over the little iron coal burning stove; the wooden table she'd inherited from her mother; the not quite matching dining chairs given to her by friends when she'd moved in; the soft two-seat sofa she'd loved to curl up on with a good book of an evening. All in all, it had been a fine place in which to spend her life; she would miss it if it were taken from her. It's no good, she chided herself. This is just depressing me. She left, locking the stout wooden front door behind her. What good it would do if anyone really wanted to break in, she didn't know, but it was something one did.

The stairwell was in pitch darkness; the small windows were blacked out and there was no electric light, for the power had failed again. She made her way down carefully by torchlight, sliding her hand along the smooth old wood of the balustrade. She used to love the staircase with its wood panelled walls and old carpet, faded opulence from before the Great War. Now it was a dark, musty space.

As she stepped down onto the landing below her own, Walter launched himself across her path. It was the bobbing beam of his own torch that warned her to stop just before stepping into his path. He jerked to a halt and his outsized steel helmet clattered to the floor.

This, she thought, is becoming a habit.

Walter picked up the helmet and set it back on his head. "Sorry" was a mumble as he shifted uncomfortably under Tanya's half-amused gaze

He's so thin, she noted, not for the first time. Everything seemed too big on him: his grey-blue overalls; his lace-up ankle boots; the helmet sitting on his prominent ears.

"I must go," another mumble as he turned awkwardly away, his canvas shoulder bag snagging the ornate balustrade. She watched in silence as he untangled himself and clattered away.

In the cellar, Ida sat talking quietly with Mathias. Tanya wondered whether she should mention that Walter had gone out, but they must know that. He was often out with the Security and Aid Service, the SHD, helping to clear up bomb damage, so she just nodded at them and sat down in the alcove where Mrs Körtig was laying out playing cards on a small folding table. They played a lot together and, thanks to Tanya, Mrs Körtig had become quite an expert at the Russian game of preference. They also played backgammon or dominoes, but cards was their favourite shared pastime.

All of the cellar dwellers had some hobby or interest to help while away the time. Boredom was more of a problem than fear, for time spent in the cellar far exceeded that during which bombs were falling. Often no bombs fell at all during an alert, yet they must remain underground once the sirens sounded. No one was allowed out.

Mrs Boldt was knitting as usual. The clicking of her needles was a sound Tanya had come to associate with the cellar. Another familiar sound was the People's Radio: Mrs Boldt never seemed to tire of listening to it, but it was silent now, the power being off, as it often was. It did have a dynamo, but it was hand-cranked and Mrs Boldt couldn't knit and turn the handle at the same time.

Tanya pulled the blanket across the alcove and took out from her coat pocket the book she'd brought from her apartment. She saw the look of curiosity on Mrs Körtig's face and held it out to her.

Mrs Körtig turned it over carefully in her hands, nodding approvingly at the book's fine binding. Then she opened it. "A Russian Bible?" She was looking intently at a beautiful reproduction of a medieval saint underneath half a page of ornate Cyrillic script.

Tanya shook her head. "No. A missal. My mother's." She felt a pang: her mother used to sit, as Mrs Körtig was sitting, quietly contemplating the book. Memories crowded in on her.

She thought of her girlhood amongst the Russian bourgeoisie and former aristocrats who lived in Rue Vaugirard, Daru, Pierre-le-Grand, the Place des Ternes and, appropriately enough, the Rue de Neva. They had visited others in outlying areas like Issy-le-Moulineaux, Vincennes and Boulogne-Billancourt, but they themselves had lived in poorer quarters. Although the younger daughter of a well-off banker in Saint Petersburg, her mother had brought no wealth with her. She'd been forced to take work as a wages clerk at the Renault automobile plant in the Quai D'Issay, where many of the workers were fellow émigrés, and rented a small apartment in a predominantly Russian tenement across the River Seine from the plant. By day her mother checked invoices and filled out ledger books in a brown little office surrounded by an odd mix of the daughters of Russian nobility and French working-class girls. She had come down in the world, but Tanya's mother tried to maintain standards. As she'd done in Saint Petersburg, she would receive visitors or take Tanya to see friends, playing cards and drinking tea, and in between she liked to sit quietly, praying, her missal resting on her lap as now it rested on Mrs Körtig's.

The old woman's voice intruded on Tanya's reverie. "I'm sorry. What did you say?" Tanya smiled at Mrs Körtig.

"I said that it's very lovely." She handed it back to Tanya.

"Yes." Tanya stroked the leather cover. "Mother sent it to me when the really heavy bombing started in '43."

"She's in Breslau, isn't she?"

Tanya nodded sombrely and Mrs Körtig looked sympathetic. Breslau had been under siege by the Red Army for over two months; Tanya had heard nothing of her mother since then. Mrs Körtig leaned forward across the table and patted Tanya's hand briefly. "It'll be all right, m'dear," she murmured. Then she picked up the pack of cards and began to deal them out. "Everything will be quite all right."

"We should get under cover over there." Agranenko pointed to scattered scrub ahead which thickened into a dense neglected mass. Beyond it the ground began to rise in a slope which steepened further on to become the Seelow Heights. Leonid nodded his acceptance. He was lying with the platoon in a field beyond the bridge. It was open, bare of cover, and mortar and artillery shells were dropping sporadically all along the line of the canal behind them. Not many, not accurately, but enough to make it too dangerous to stay. Anyway, they weren't supposed to stay; other platoons, other companies were already getting up and resuming the advance on either side. More waited across the canal.

He got to his feet, and Agranenko beckoned to Moiseyevich who was lying a few metres away. He told Moiseyevich to find Captain Chuya and tell him what they were doing. Moiseyevich trotted away, Agranenko signalled the platoon, and they all followed him at a rapid walk. Now and again a burst of machine gun fire wandered over their heads or a few explosions burst, but none were near enough to worry about.

"Over there." Agranenko gestured at an old orchard off to one side. The gnarled fruit trees, planted in straight lines and unkempt from neglect and ragged undergrowth, filled the space between them. Agranenko halted the platoon within it while he and Leonid went to the front edge, crawling the last few metres. Ahead and above them was a steep slope which ended in more trees. It glistened with damp, and halfway up what looked like barbed wire was strung between upright wooden posts. It was too far to see what condition it was in, but they did make out what seemed to be craters in amongst the posts, some of which leaned at odd angles.

"As far as I can make out, the bastards are over there." Agranenko pointed beyond the wire and squinted. "Machine gun nest, there..." he pointed to another mound "...and there." Leonid nodded: he'd already spotted both of them. "And there's something *there*," Agranenko pointed to a third mound further up the slope just in front of the trees, "but I don't know what." Leonid nodded again, but he hadn't spotted *that* one.

Agranenko chewed his lower lip and grimaced. "My suggestion is that we wait, Comrade Lieutenant. That wire looks difficult." He smiled mirthlessly. "But we'll need to clear it somehow."

Leonid suppressed his own smile: 'suggestion'. It was a word Agranenko used often, but they both knew it was more, and Leonid followed him, sliding backwards into the cover of the orchard.

Leonid had hardly settled himself when Moiseyevich returned, panting and red-faced. Chuya too had decided they should wait, he told them, and was going to request more support before they tried the slope.

Wants to get at them now, Leonid noted, looking at Moiseyevich's disappointed face. He usually did: he never seemed content except when he was killing Germans.

Moiseyevich had yet to grow a proper moustache and acne sometimes sprouted around his soft mouth, making him seem the boy he was, but his appearance was deceptive. On the dway Leonid had arrived at the platoon, Agranenko told him that Moiseyevich had been with partisans in the Ukraine when they came across him. He had been keen to join them, and Chuya was glad to have him; the partisans had told him Moiseyevich was a good fighter, and why. On the day of his bar mitzvah the previous year, the partisans said, the politsai, paramilitary Ukrainian police collaborating with the Nazis, had joined the celebrations at his home, uninvited. Moiseyevich had been outside washing and spotted them coming. He'd had no chance to sound a warning, but had run to hide. They'd raped his mother, his grandmother and his younger sister. Afterwards they'd shot them, and his father and older brother too. Then they set fire to the house and left.

Moiseyevich joined the partisans. He killed informers; he killed collaborators; he killed nationalists; he killed Germans; and, of course, when he found the politsai who had come to his bar mitzvah, he killed them too.

Polyanski too was glad to have him, for Moiseyevich was dedicated to the Party, swapping Yahweh for Stalin with the ferocious zeal of a bitter convert. But although Moiseyevich was valued, no one really trusted him, least of all Leonid. That shouldn't have mattered; Moiseyevich was only a private soldier and Leonid was his lieutenant, but of course it did matter, for the Party had much confidence in Moiseyevich and, Leonid knew, little in him.

He made a point of sending Moiseyevich back to Chuya with their assessment of the ground ahead: anything to get rid of him.

Leonid and Agranenko lay in the wood, savouring the opportunity to rest. Amongst the trees, the platoon settled itself comfortably and did the same. But it was a short rest; after barely thirty minutes, squealing and rattling through the trees heralded the arrival of tanks. Leonid twisted his head and saw their turrets ping above the scrub at the rear of the orchard: 34s, like those that had got across the canal with them, and Leonid wondered if they were the same. If so, where was the fourth?

A figure scrambled out of one of the turrets and came to squat by them in greasy black overalls. "Senior Sergeant Kolesnikov." He grinned, teeth surprisingly white in a grimy face. "Any other way up there, Comrades?" he asked, jerking his head towards the slope.

"Junior Lieutenant Barakovski and Senior Sergeant Agranenko." Leonid shook Kolesnikov's very oily hand.

"All right for infantry," Agranenko shook it too and then wiped his own on the grass, "but you'd better judge for yourself."

Kolesnikov followed them forward, and after perusing the slope for a while, shook his head. "Not much chance of getting my children up *that*. Too steep, too slippery, and those trees at the top look too dense."

Leonid was disappointed. He had been hoping the tanks might lead them and clear a way through the barbed wire.

Kolesnikov pulled a crumpled off-white pack out of his breast pocket, extracted a cigarette and lit it. "I can give you covering fire, though." He held out the packet: 'Juno', it said on the front in gold letters under an ornate crest. They each took one and Kolesnikov lit them with a small silver petrol lighter engraved with a German eagle. "Not bad." He examined the crest on the packet. "There was a whole case full of them in a Fritz lorry." He tucked the packet back into his breast pocket and drew in the aromatic smoke with great relish. "Better than makhorka." He chuckled, then looked serious. "You tell me when we're needed, Comrades," and he slid away, cigarette dangling between his lips.

Agranenko watched him go. "Jolly fellows, tankists," he murmured, and then hummed the first few bars of a tune.

Leonid smiled ruefully: he knew the song, from the movie *Tractorists*. "'The armour is hard and our tanks are fast,'" he said softly, "'and our men are full of courage…'" Agranenko opened his mouth as if to say something and then closed it again when Chuya's voice called to them from the tanks. They scrambled back to join him. He was talking to Kolesnikov; with him were Gushenko and Turkin, who commanded numbers One and Three platoons, standing amongst a scatter of immature blossoms. One of the tanks had tucked itself in so closely to the trees it had half pushed over a fine old cherry. For some reason, Leonid found that annoying.

Chuya's round pockmarked face was red above his moustache

and he was breathing heavily; he was a stout man and easily showed any exertion. "Comrade Kolesnikov's told me the problem." Chuya nodded at the tank commander.

"Yes, Comrade Captain." Leonid cleared his throat nervously. He thought that Chuya smelled even more strongly of drink than he usually did. "We, uh, were just wondering what to do about it."

Chuya's thick bushy eyebrows rose and his almond-shaped eyes narrowed. "Wondering?" He sounded incredulous. "No wondering, Lieutenant. Major Zeldin wants us up that slope. We can't wait for your *wondering*."

Leonid and Agranenko glanced at each other. "But..." Leonid said.

"But?" Chuya cut him off truculently, his eyes narrowing further.

"There's a belt of wire, Comrade Captain."

Chuya turned his gaze onto Agranenko, seeming irritated by his intervention. "It was supposed to be shelled."

"Well, yes, it's been shelled, but..." Leonid trailed off as Chuya turned his gaze back on him.

"But?"

"It looks intact."

"Looks? Has it been shelled or not?"

"Well, yes."

"Then there'll be gaps." Chuya looked at Agranenko, who stared back impassively, and then cast his gaze quickly around the group. No one seemed prepared to challenge him, and he grunted as if it was the end of the matter as far as he was concerned. "So, Barakovski," his gaze came back to rest on Leonid, "the sooner we start, the sooner we *get on*. Regiment wants no more delays." He glanced irritably at his watch. "Major Zeldin want us up that slope." He looked at Gushenko and Turkin. "All right, I'll go forward with the other platoons. You," he jabbed his forefinger at Leonid, "follow. The machine gun squad will cover us from the orchard."

Then he looked at Kolesnikov. "We'll cover you from over there." The tank commander pointed to the left-hand edge of the orchard.

Chuya nodded. "Move, then."

They all saluted him and turned away. As they did so, Gushenko caught Leonid's glance, raised his eyebrows and shrugged. Nothing more needed to be said. They all knew Chuya, the stubborn peasant: there was no arguing with him when he'd been drinking.

Leonid saw the doubt on Agranenko's face as they returned to the platoon.

"The wire?"

Agranenko nodded. Leonid knew what he was thinking: shelling *might* have cleared paths through the wire, but all too often it simply broke it up a bit without making it any easier to traverse. A lot depended on the nature of the ground, the density of the shelling and the size of the shells. The only sure way to clear wire was with wire cutters: a slow business, and lethal under fire. The tanks flattening the wire would help, although it would still leave strands to trip the unwary, but they wouldn't have even that.

Gushenko's and Turkin's platoons deployed along the edge of the orchard and into a line with Chuya between them. Kantovski stood next to him with his banner. The machine gun squad duly set up their weapons, and the tanks coughed and spluttered into life and drove out from behind the orchard. Beyond them Leonid could see men and equipment from battalions, some under sporadic fire, none moving. Are we the only ones going forward? he wondered nervously and bit his lower lip.

Chuya blew a whistle and the two platoons moved forward with him into the open, the red flag fluttering over Kantovski's head.

"Come on!" Agranenko turned, shouted and waved to their own platoon and they followed the flag up the slope.

All was quiet. In the distance were sounds of fighting, but not here. Leonid kept his gaze fixed on the belt of barbed wire. Time seemed to pass very slowly, and then Kolesnikov's tanks opened fire in rapid succession. Three brown explosions blossomed a few hundred metres away, one on each of the mounds. Nothing happened. Again Kolesnikov's tanks fired, striking the mounds and throwing up gouts of earth. Again nothing happened. Leonid relaxed slightly. That should do it, he reassured himself.

Then a huge flash of flame burst out of the furthest mound. Leonid felt the air compress above his head and heard a dull *clang* behind him. Everyone ducked. A large smoke ring puffed lazily out from the mound, widened, thinned and disappeared within seconds. Suddenly Leonid heard a noise like the ripping of thick fabric and two lines of tracer flicked downslope, but not from the mounds. Instead they came from clumps of shrub to their left and right. The mounds are decoys, Leonid realised with a sinking feeling and heard Agranenko swear. Gushenko and Turkin began to run, their platoons following them as the machine gun fire moved amongst them, jerking some backwards off their feet or twisting them like puppets on strings to fall, thrashing about, on the muddy grass. The squad in the orchard fired back, sending its own bursts of red up towards the source of the fire, but Gushenko's and Turkin's platoons continued to fall.

Then one of the probing fingers of red found Kantovski and he fell, the banner tumbling to the earth. Chuya bent to pick it up and Agranenko broke into a trot with a shout of "Come on!" Leonid and the platoon ran after him as another flash burst from the mound, another smoke ring billowed out and another tank's death-knell sounded behind. Almost at the same time, two exploding shells tore up the ground under the smoke ring.

Chuya struggled up the slope, red-faced and panting. He was leading now, for the platoons wavered: some stopped to fire; some looked behind them. Then Chuya was hit, toppling backwards, banner in hand, to lie still. The two platoons stopped then, turned and ran back down the slope, Turkin and Gushenko running with them.

Leonid hesitated. Go on; go back; what should we do?

Agranenko did not hesitate. He spun around and called out, "Back! Get back!" Then he waved towards the orchard, and within seconds they were all fleeing pell-mell. Leonid could see Kolesnikov's tanks. Two sat with smoke drifting from the edges of closed hatches;

the engine deck of one flickered with small flames. As he ran towards the trees, he heard a third round burst from the mound behind him and the third tank lurched, throwing up sparks from its turret. He could smell hot metal, diesel and something like burning rubber as he passed the stricken tanks, but he paid no attention as he dashed into cover. Behind him machine guns chatted briefly, and then suddenly they fell silent.

Walter turned into the little street and stopped: it was alive with figures, some uniformed, some not, some shouting orders, most silent. He'd passed many such scenes, but until now had not been directly involved himself. His only contribution in the SHD thus far had been sweeps for incendiaries after the bombers had passed, searching back alleys and courtyards with the other boys, extinguishing them with sand carried in a small four-wheeled hand cart. It was tedious but easy; this was another matter.

The street looked like a demolition site: wrecked apartment buildings; a rubble-strewn strip of cratered tarmac. Many walls had fallen away to expose interior rooms like open-fronted dolls' houses; the walls that remained were cracked and sagging. A broken gas main flamed in a crater like a volcanic vent; in another, water bubbled like a spring. The air smelled of smoke and brick dust.

"Amees," Friedrich Jürgs said from behind him.

Walter turned and nodded his agreement. Friedrich was commander of their SHD detachment, and he was right: it was an American attack, not British. 'Amees' fused their bombs to detonate on impact so much of the explosive energy travelled horizontally. They shattered façades, toppled streetlights like trees in a gale, and turned vehicles on their sides. British bombs often exploded after penetrating the ground, sending out a shockwave like a small earthquake. Buildings collapsed completely and lengths of roads fell in and turned into trenches.

"Five hundred kilogrammers." Walter ventured an opinion.

Friedrich nodded. "Yep. Guess so. Big ones, anyway."

Walter glanced upwards. "The light will be going in a few hours." The late afternoon sky was still bright, but it held the promise of evening.

Friedrich peered about him, spotted a man in the uniform of an SHD officer and strode off to get his orders.

They paired off to work over the rubble. Walter went with Friedrich. They were good friends and liked each other's company, although they were very different in many ways. Friedrich was outgoing, sociable, self-confident: a natural leader. Walter preferred his own company; he was happier experiencing life through books and movies, but there were things they had in common. Both loved the countryside and, before travel had become too irksome, would take buses or trains out of the city at weekends and on their holidays to walk and explore. They loved jazz music – a secret love, for the Nazis had banned most of it as nigger kike music – but Friedrich's beloved older brother loved jazz, and that was enough for Friedrich. When his brother was sent to the Eastern Front, Friedrich had taken possession of his record collection. It was a point of pride to keep it safe. He and Walter often hid in the shed at the bottom of the Jürgs's long urban garden with a gramophone. It was well away from any houses, but even so one of them always stood at the shed's window, keeping an eye out while they listened to Duke Ellington, Earl Hines, Count Basie, Josephine Baker, Louis Armstrong and many others.

Walter had taken his lead from Friedrich in his appreciation of jazz, and he took his lead from Friedrich now. He and the rest of the SHD section pulled away fallen timbers, shifted piles of broken brickwork, moved smashed furniture. They listened at pavement level cellar openings, poked the rubble with long metal rods, and found nothing.

During sweaty pauses, Walter sat and watched the other rescuers, and he watched the civilians picking over the rubble and occasionally pulling out possessions: books, clothes, a baby carriage, some bedding. He saw only one body, lying very still under a dusty bed-throw.

When the light began to fail the senior SHD officer came to tell them to go.

"What about torches, sir? We've some in the cart."

The officer grimaced at Friedrich's question. "In the first place," he said, "we can't show lights after dark, even for rescue. Those damned British will probably be on us again tonight. They usually do when the Amees have been here. And secondly," he paused and cleared his throat, glancing around at the other boys in the detachment, "I don't think it's worth the effort." He raised his hand imperiously to cut Friedrich off. "We've been at this all afternoon and found only one casualty. The street warden tells me the only people in the street this afternoon were herself and an elderly woman. Well, we've found the woman."

Walter glanced at the covered body and his stomach lurched slightly. He hated bodies.

"So, you boys, go home now. You don't want to be out after dark." The officer turned to go, and then, seemingly as an afterthought, added, "Well done."

Still Friedrich seemed about to say something, but Walter caught his eye and shook his head. "Let's go then," Friedrich muttered, and the others followed him out of the street.

For Cheslav, it had been an uneventful day. He and the rest of the platoon had seen no combat, only heard it at some distance, but they *had* seen the results. A stream of wounded had passed them on the road almost constantly, loaded on carts, propped up in American jeeps, filling lorries of all description: Soviet Zils, German Opels, British Bedfords; once even a civilian bus, the Nazi posters on its sides disfigured with Russian graffiti.

Come evening, they'd left the verge down which they'd tramped endlessly and sat along a lane to wait for the cooks to do their job.

"Anything tasty?" Kolchok dropped down beside him, puffing on his pipe. He looked pointedly at the package on Cheslav's lap.

Cheslav shook his head. "No. It's from my brother and he never sends me food."

"Doesn't he eat?" Kolchok asked. "Even officers eat."

Cheslav smiled. He couldn't get used to the idea of his brother being an officer. "I suppose they do," he replied. Carefully he peeled away waxed brown paper to reveal a cloth bundle. This too he unwrapped to reveal a book. As soon as he saw the title, he wished he hadn't.

"That's German, ain't it?" Kolchok knocked the ash out of his pipe and began refilling it without taking his eyes off the book.

Cheslav said nothing.

"You *do* know German, then?" Kolchok lit the pipe and puffed out blue smoke.

"I learned a bit in school," Cheslav muttered.

Kolchok nodded slowly. "Handy."

Cheslav didn't answer. He turned the book over, feeling the old leather cover and sniffing it as their teacher used to do. Mr Gerstein had relished books and kept a small library, but it mostly dated from before the Revolution, and when Gerstein was taken away, his books were replaced by dour Marxist tracts. Gerstein himself was replaced by Sarafanov, a dour Marxist man. Cheslav hadn't known which he'd missed most: the books or his teacher. Both, he reckoned, for in his mind they went together.

"Pretty thing," Kolchok said as Cheslav rewrapped the book and placed it in his backpack. He grinned, showing yellowing teeth between wide gaps. "You fondled that book like it were a girl."

Cheslav reddened.

"What's it about?" Kolchok reached out and gently prodded his knee. "C'mon, boy. I'm interested. What's it called?"

Cheslav paused and then mumbled, "*Little Dorrit.*"

Kolchok frowned. "What?"

Cheslav said it again, then smiled wryly at Kolchok's blank stare. "It's a British writer. Dickens."

"What's a Dorrit?"

Cheslav shook his head. "Not what, *who*. It's a girl's name."

"Ah," Kolchok gestured towards Cheslav with the stem of his pipe, "so it is girls after all."

Cheslav looked away without answering, embarrassed. His gaze fell on a group playing cards nearby. Kolchok prodded his knee again.

"Fancy a game?"

Cheslav shook his head. "Not for me."

"Don't you play cards, boy?"

Cheslav turned back to him and nodded. "Chess, sometimes. Chequers. Backgammon. I like backgammon." It had been the family game. They'd often played it, until Father had gone. Cheslav's stepfather was not a player of games.

"Each to his own." Kolchok glanced at the group. "I love a good game of cards."

Cheslav smiled sadly. He was thinking of the backgammon set his mother had given to him on the station platform when she'd seen him off to the war. He'd kept it safe all through training and during the long move west. Then the platoon had been shelled. It was his first time under fire, and in the confusion he'd lost his pack, and with it the backgammon. Cheslav had replaced the pack, but the set was gone forever. Gone too was a book Leonid had given him when he'd left for his officer training: another Dickens, *Nicholas Nickleby*. It was his brother's favourite.

He turned to Kolchok. "So why aren't you with them?"

"Not want my company, boy?" He blew out more smoke and didn't wait for an answer. "They don't play my sort of game." Kolchok shook his head disparagingly. "I like screw. A real man's game, but the Party banned it. Too Bourgeois. Gambling game, y'see. Not approved." He grunted derisively.

"I wouldn't have thought an Old Bolshevik would let a little thing like approval hold you back," Cheslav observed with heavy irony.

Kolchok shot him a suspicious look and then chuckled. The sound trickled around the stem of the pipe like water across gravel.

"You better believe that, boy! Kolchok the Old Bolshevik." He shook his head dolefully. "Not many of those left now." He stared at Cheslav, and for a moment there was anger on his face. "Those Party arse-lickers have seen to that."

Cheslav was startled. He looked around to see if anyone might have overhead, although they sat well away from any potential eavesdropper.

"Don't worry, boy. Out here precious few give a shit."

Cheslav doubted that was true. Party disciplines had been relaxed a lot in the army, yet political officers remained, and there were enough loyalists to hear such remarks and report them.

"You wanted to know about the book," Cheslav said, suddenly keen to change the subject.

"Sure, Comrade Junior Sergeant." Kolchok chuckled, his eyes sparkling briefly as if to say: All right, talk about something else.

Cheslav smiled thinly. Kolchok only ever used ranks like that disparagingly. "*Little Dorrit*. My teacher told me it was famous, but I've never read it."

Kolchok grunted and spat out a wad of phlegm and partially burned tobacco, then he emptied his pipe and began to refill it.

"I think she grows up in a prison in England with her family. When she's older they all leave the prison, but she goes back."

"Why?" asked Kolchok.

"I'm not sure. Something to do with preferring it to the world."

Kolchok snorted. "Preferring prison? The man who wrote stuff like that should try it one day."

"He died a long time ago."

"Rich, was he?" Kolchok sounded unimpressed. "Only a rich man'd think prison's better."

"I don't know."

"I do. Take my word for it," Kolchok sounded sour, "prison's a hell hole."

Cheslav hesitated. It was obviously sensitive ground, but he was too fascinated not to ask. Kolchok rarely spoke much about the old days, but when he did it was worth listening.

"Were you in prison?"

Kolchok lit his pipe and didn't answer.

"It must have been bad then, before the Revolution."

Kolchok blew out slowly, a thin stream of aromatic smoke. "Not then."

Cheslav was startled. "But…after?" He felt confused. Kolchok was an Old Bolshevik, had met Lenin, fought the counter-revolutionary Whites.

Kolchok stabbed his pipe at Cheslav. "'Curious Varvara stuck his nose in, got it torn off.'" He quoted, sounding angry.

"I'm sorry." Cheslav looked around nervously. "I didn't mean to pry, Comrade." There were some things one never asked about.

Kolchok grunted. "You're a good lad." He stood up and stretched stiffly. "I'm for a game of screw."

Cheslav stared up at him and observed wryly, "I thought it wasn't allowed."

"Not allowed." Kolchok nodded sombrely. "That's right." Then he strode towards the seated players. "Hey, boys, want to play a man's game?"

When the company's demoralised survivors staggered back into the orchard, Gushenko, the senior of the three lieutenants, took immediate control: Leonid and Turkin dithered. He consulted with Agranenko, deployed Leonid's platoon in defensive positions just inside the tree cover, moved the other two platoons, such as they were, further back to recuperate, and organised new sections. The wounded he sent to the rear, their ammunition redistributed. Leonid was impressed by his diligence but not surprised. He'd met Gushenko at the academy; they'd been in the same class. Although Gushenko was only a year or two older might have been more. He had the common sense, the authority, the self-confidence which Leonid lacked. He'd graduated ahead of the class and was waiting when Leonid joined the company, a frontovik already.

The Germans seemed content to leave them alone, save for a few mortar rounds that dropped into the trees, splintering some branches and spreading a smell of apple wood and lilac and cordite, but there was no more loss. Which was just as well, Agranenko observed: One and Three platoons had taken very heavy casualties and were brittle.

Leonid's platoon too was edgy, but Agranenko did the rounds and soon settled them down.

Zeldin arrived, Moiseyevich having been sent back to summon him by Gushenko. He listened grim-faced to what Gushenko had to say. The whole battalion had taken heavy casualties, Zeldin told them. Then he spent quite some time on the field telephone he'd brought with him, cable uncoiling from a drum on a signaller's back. When he finally got off the phone, he was brief and to the point: all along the line the attack had been beaten back and it would be some time before another effort was made. For now, they would hold their positions. Leonid hoped that it would stay that way; he had no inclination to move out of cover again.

Leonid was amazed when Zeldin told him that his platoon was the furthest forward in the regiment; it wasn't something he relished.

"But we'll take the Heights tomorrow," Zeldin promised as if that was what everyone really wanted to hear. Even Turkin, usually demonstratively keen, looked subdued. Zeldin promised reinforcements and confirmed Gushenko as company commander, an announcement they all applauded. When Zeldin left, they settled down, tried to get some rest.

Barely an hour passed before the reinforcements arrived. Agranenko was less than appreciative. 'Clapped out' was his comment when they turned up, for they were some of the former POWs they'd seen in the brewery yard. Still, they looked better than they had the last time Leonid saw them. They'd been issued with new uniforms and proper footwear, although it was a motley assortment of Soviet military boots and German civilian shoes. Every man had a rifle, although again some of these were German.

"Still," Leonid commented, watching the new arrivals settle into their sections, "better than nothing."

"I suppose it's best not to look in a gift horse's mouth." Agranenko sounded resigned.

Dusk came uneventfully. Leonid spent the time sitting within the edge of the orchard, quietly reading *A Tale of Two Cities*. He avoided looking at the slope and the scatter of still bodies. In the distance to either side he could hear sporadic bursts of artillery fire, the occasional chatter of machine guns and the crackle of rifles, the sounds fading with the light.

He was interrupted by Agranenko, who appeared out of the shadows with welcome food. Leonid hadn't felt hungry after the attack, but it was several hours since he'd eaten and the aroma issuing from the two mess pots Agranenko carried made his stomach rumble.

"Here." Agranenko sat in front of him, blocking his view.

Leonid sniffed at one pot: kasha again, but there was something else in it; something meaty in the porridge. He took out his spoon and found that it was surprisingly good and he wolfed it down with relish.

Agranenko too ate quickly and then pulled a bottle out of his tunic pocket. "Your 'Hundred Grammes', Comrade Lieutenant."

Leonid took the vodka gratefully; although the food had perked him up, he could do with a drink.

Agranenko took out a second bottle, sipped it and made an appreciative noise. Then he tilted his head. "Getting quieter," he said. The sounds of firing were now very faint on the light evening breeze. Agranenko murmured something Leonid didn't catch.

"I'm sorry?"

Agranenko smiled and sipped more vodka. "'In the distance the battle thunders grimly on, day and night, groaning and grumbling non-stop.'" He paused, his expression suddenly bleak. "'And to the dying men patiently waiting for their graves...'" he took another sip, "'...it sounds for all the world like the words of God.'" He shook his head sadly, retrieved the pots from the grass beside him and stood up. "I'll post some sentries." As he turned to go, Leonid spoke and he paused without looking back.

"Not Pushkin?"

Agranenko didn't answer; he just shook his head and walked back into the shadows.

*

The lorry stopped abruptly and John Marlow fell against the man on his right.

"*Maria!* Kay pasa?" He pushed John away gently.

"Sorry."

The man shrugged. "Esso estabien." He grinned, teeth startlingly white, his face dark in the dim interior.

Someone further in made a comment. John didn't catch the exact words, but they too were Spanish: everyone in the lorry save himself was Spanish. In fact, the whole convoy of lorries was Spanish. He'd been surprised at that when he'd presented himself at the barracks' parade ground that morning. The Spanish officer to whom he'd shown his papers had been surprised too, but he'd looked at the movement order, nodded, said nothing, just gestured to the lorry.

Since then no one had asked him who he was and no one had volunteered any information. He didn't know what unit he was with, nor where he was going. The day's journey from the barracks had been a slow one, pushing through long columns of refugees, twice backtracking to follow another route but always generally going south and east. He'd been able to guess the direction for he had a good view from his position at the tailgate and could gauge it from the sun. By now they were somewhere well to the east of Berlin, but where exactly he didn't know, and really he didn't care much. He had what he wanted: the opportunity to fight. He'd had to wait a year for it, ever since he joined the SS, and now he was happy to be going to do what he'd come to Germany to do all along: help stop the Reds. He didn't need to know the details, not yet anyway; it was enough that his orders assigned him to Nordland, the SS formation under which he'd been nominally placed at the barracks, and the Spanish, he'd been told, would take him there.

It had been a long wait, a tedious year of intense fitness training, indoctrination, drill, weapons handling, route marches and more route marches. He'd resented it for he'd done it all before, was an experienced combat veteran and just wanted to get on with fighting, but regulations were regulations, and to qualify for the SS, he had to do the training.

The Spaniard sitting facing him stuck his head out of the lorry and called softly to someone John couldn't see. "Hey. Kay pasa, José?"

John didn't hear any reply, but a moment later the man pulled his head back in and, with much shrugging and grimacing, launched into a long explanation to his companions. Several muttered or cursed softly.

When he'd finished, John leaned forward. "What's up?"

The man grinned "Se nos asabo la gasolina," and made a thumbs-down gesture.

'*Gasolina*': that John understood well enough. Someone had run out of fuel. It was a constant problem. Cars, vans and lorries had been replaced where possible by carts; people rode bicycles and horses or walked, for even official vehicles found it hard to get all the fuel they needed.

The Spaniards tumbled out, John with them. It was a pleasant afternoon, the bright sun shining down from a sky which held few clouds. Not exactly summer, but the deep cold of a North German winter had been banished, for now at least. He looked along the line of vehicles where soldiers clustered, talking and smoking, some drinking from canteens. A few had gone to sit under the trees which edged one side of the road, uniforms and weapons incongruous amongst the early spring flowers.

He heard voices deep in animated conversation and turned to see an officer with the rank markings of an SS lieutenant colonel bearing down on him, followed by an SS captain and SS lieutenant. John recognised the colonel, Miguel Esquerra: they'd met briefly in Berlin. So his must be Storm Detachment Esquerra. He'd heard of it; who hadn't? Esquerra and his men had a reputation for toughness, acquired fighting partisans in occupied France with the elite German Brandenburg Regiment.

John snapped to attention and Esquerra seemed to notice him and stopped suddenly. Eyes narrowing, he touched the brim of his peaked cap. The captain, a short, slightly plump man with a thick moustache, asked Esquerra something too quiet to make out. John caught some of Esquerra's words, 'uhn Inglayss', and his own name.

The plump officer smiled at John. "Stand eezy, Marlow. Commandantay Esquerra remember you. He wish know why you here."

John paused. Then, speaking slowly in the way Englishmen do when talking to foreigners, he explained, "I'm here to fight Bolsheviks." It sounded pompous, he knew, but Esquerra smiled when the captain translated.

"I've orders to join Nordland." John fumbled for his papers, but Esquerra waved them away. When this too was translated, Esquerra frowned, said something to the captain, and then, with a nod to John, strolled away, chatting to the lieutenant. John saluted his receding back stiffly, right arm raised.

The captain chuckled. "Here, Marlow." He pulled out a packet of French Gitane cigarettes and a beautifully engraved silver lighter, lit one for himself and another for John. "Kapitan Eduardo Vélez Garrido." He tucked the packet back into the top pocket of his immaculate tunic. "So you go Nordland?"

John nodded. "Yes, Captain Garrido."

"Kapitan Vélez," he corrected and drew deeply on his cigarette. He looked at John for a long moment over his cigarette. "I meet Inglayss in *Espagna*. They fight us."

John glanced away, for a moment embarrassed. "International Brigade?"

Vélez nodded. "*Si*. I speak them when we take Madrid. I say them I fight for *Espagna*. I no political." His smile returned; merriment seemed to sit easily with his round face and gentle black eyes.

John's eyebrows rose a fraction; he couldn't help it.

"You surprise, Marlow?" Vélez drew heavily on the cigarette. "My father and he father, *mi abuelo*, all army." He tapped his chest. "Generalissimo Franco for *Espagna*. So I fight for Franco. For *Espagna*. No political. Tell me," suddenly the sparkling eyes were hard, "why *you* fight?"

John hesitated. "Well, as I said..."

Vélez waved his cigarette impatiently. "*Si, si.* Fight *communista.*" He sucked in more smoke. "All fight *communista.* But *Inglaterra* fight Hitler. *Communista* friends of Inglayss."

John shook his head. "I'm half Swedish. And I fought the Reds in Finland."

Vélez raised an eyebrow, threw away his cigarette stub and lit another. John hadn't finished half of his GGitane, was savouring it slowly; it had been a long time since he'd smoked anything so fine.

"And," John went on, "Father was killed fighting the Reds in Finland after the last war. He was in the army too. The British Army, I mean. In the war."

"Ah," Vélez nodded, understanding, "so now you fight, uh, *en su memoria*. His remember?" Vélez's face lit up once more as if the idea appealed to him.

"In a sense, Kapitan." John felt uncomfortable at this probing. "But it's also what I believe in. Stopping the Reds. It's what this war is all about, isn't it?"

"Ah." Vélez coughed, looked at his cigarette and sucked on it again. "Well, you right. We must stop *communista*. That why I here. Why all us here." He gestured around him theatrically.

John's gaze followed the gesture. The clusters around the lorries were breaking up, men joining others who had already settled under trees as Esquerra and the lieutenant moved down the column, issuing instructions. Some pulled pots and pans out of the lorries, hefted boxes of supplies; others piled up deadfall and lit fires.

"We eat now," Vélez explained unnecessarily. "*El sargento* look *gasolina*. Then we go fight."

John nodded. So they were waiting while an NCO went in search of whatever fuel he could beg, or steal. What a way to run an army, thought John. What a way to run a war.

Vélez smiled at John's rueful expression. "Not worry, my friend. *El sargento* find. And if no, we walk, eh?" He laughed, a surprisingly thin sound from such a stout frame. "We do much that!"

Walk? wondered John. It could be miles.

"Yessir," he said.

Vélez waved his hand at him. "Show paper." He took the movement order, read it closely and then, folding it very precisely, handed it back. "So, Nordland."

"It's because I'm half Swedish. The barracks commandant…"

Again Vélez waved him to silence. "*Si*. Nordland. Many Swedish. I meet in *Roosya*."

John nodded. He knew many Spanish had fought in Russia, members of the Blue Division sent by Franco to help his fellow anti-communist, Hitler. Vélez could easily have met the Nordland Division; the war on the Eastern Front was a multi-national affair.

"You go Nordland, be *soldado* soo-ecko."

"Yessir." He smiled to himself at the memory of that morning. It had all been his idea. He'd returned from a visit to Berlin as part of a propaganda broadcast and found that the other English SS volunteers had been sent away to the west. They'd been happy to go, the barracks commander had told him, but John was not. John refused to go quietly, threatened to take it up through channels, and the commander had offered a compromise. His British Freikorps badges had been swapped for general-issue SS and his movement orders written out on the spot. John had been pleased; now Vélez spoiled it.

"We no go Nordland, Marlow."

John stared at him.

Vélez nodded slowly and looked sympathetic. "*Si*. Nordland that way." He pointed. "We go *that* way." His finger pointing in the opposite direction, he shrugged.

"But my orders…" John began.

Vélez shrugged and waved his cigarette once more. "Our orders." He reached out and gently tapped John's shoulder with his free hand. "No worry, Marlow. You stay us. Plenty fight."

John was about to protest; about to point out that he could hardly pass himself off as Spanish even if they could replace his SS tunic. He didn't speak a word of the language. In any case, he wanted to fight with those he could identify with. Nordland was Scandinavian; he'd fit in well there, and if he couldn't get there, he must try and find another unit he'd feel at home with. However, he kept his reservations to himself. After all, what choice did he have? He was just a private, and the Spanish had their orders. He'd just have to go along and make the best of it.

"Yessir," he said.

FOUR

The day began with tea: thick, black and strong. Agranenko brought it in two steaming mugs. "There was no sugar, but I put in some Fritz brandy."

Leonid took it with intense gratitude; despite his mental and physical weariness, he'd been awake most of the night and needed perking up. It was cold and damp in the orchard and he'd found it impossible to get comfortable, and he couldn't clear his mind of worries about what the day would bring. We'll take the Heights tomorrow, Zeldin had said; not a prospect Leonid relished.

Agranenko sat down with his back to a tree and peered at Leonid pensively. "Thinking of yesterday?"

Leonid shook his head. "Today."

Agranenko lit two cigarettes. "All we can do, Comrade Lieutenant, is take each day at a time and keep going. No point in worrying about it."

Leonid brooded. "Is that all there is to it?"

Agranenko smiled wryly. "It's not worth expecting much." He drew deeply on his cigarette, puffed out the smoke and contemplated the glowing tip. "'There is a muteness, the tocsin bell has made us close our lips. In our hearts, once so ardent, there is a fateful emptiness.'"

"*Blok*." Leonid sipped his tea; the sweetness kicked at him.

Agranenko nodded. "Wise words."

"And is that what you feel? Fateful emptiness?"

Agranenko tilted his head to one side.

"Is that way to keep going? To feel nothing?"

"No man feels *nothing*." Agranenko sighed, tipped the dregs from his mug. "Lieutenant Gushenko, sorry, I mean *Captain*, wants you." He glanced at his watch. "Twenty minutes."

Leonid nodded and stood up, stretching the ache from his limbs. "Right." His stomach rumbled. "Do we get breakfast first?"

"Breakfast? Nothing's arrived yet." Agranenko sounded sombre; he believed in starting the day with a full belly, although many frontoviki advised not eating before combat so as to maximise the chances of surviving a stomach wound. He too got to his feet and then grimaced. He led Leonid on an inspection of the platoon. Some were smoking, others eating whatever they had in their packs. Rybczak was washing and shaving in cold water, using his helmet as a bowl; he was taking a great deal of care about it. Leonid smiled to himself as he passed him; it was such a normal thing to do, here where things were anything but normal.

Tajidaev had tied his Plasch-Palatka rain-cape between three saplings to make a tent. He was kneeling inside it, bare head bowed over a tiny fire of twigs lit outside, murmuring soft words, indistinctly, rhythmically. With his two hands he gathered the smoke towards his face. He didn't respond to their presence, and when Leonid made to speak, Agranenko touched his arm and shook his head silently. They walked on.

"Praying?"

Agranenko glanced backwards and smiled briefly. "Of course, Lieutenant."

Leonid stared at Agranenko's impassive face for a moment and then walked on without asking any more.

John was grateful that they didn't have to walk after all. The sergeant found fuel somewhere, and after a hurried breakfast of rough black bread, cold sausage and ersatz coffee, Esquerra's column resumed its journey down narrow country roads, forcing its way past endless streams of refugees, stopping often. Most of those fleeing past them were on foot, carrying their few possessions in wheelbarrows or little four-wheeled dog carts. Some hoisted their goods on their shoulders or backs. There were few horse-drawn carts and no motor vehicles, save for their own. John sat at the tailgate, studying faces, and saw sullen resignation, despair, sometime blankness. He'd seen refugees before in Finland, and after a while had been unmoved, but these people he had an affinity with. These were his grandmother's people, so like those he'd met at Oma's house in Königsberg when a boy: good people, decent people. He felt for them. He thought of the words of H G Wells. 'It was the beginning of the rout of civilisation, of the massacre of mankind'. They came from John's favourite novel, *The War of the Worlds*. He'd first read it when a small boy; he'd not thought then that he might see scenes such as Wells had so vividly described, and he'd seen worse.

They saw no other military units until near to midday when they reached a junction amongst woodland. A clutch of olive-drab vehicles was tucked under the trees. Some were draped with camouflage netting, others with blankets and crudely painted sheets; many had branches tied to their sides. Soldiers stood amongst them, some smoking and talking. The column halted and Esquerra disappeared amongst the vehicles, accompanied by Vélez inevitably smoking a cigarette.

"Hey, *camarada*. Kay pasa?" a voice muttered in John's ear. He caught the strong smell of wine and garlic as the unshaven Spaniard next to him tugged gently at his sleeve.

"Here," John muttered and squeezed back against the awning to make room.

After a quick look the Spaniard shrugged and resumed his own seat. John laid his head back and closed his eyes; he must have dozed off for the next thing he knew the Spaniard was shaking him awake and gesturing out of the lorry.

Vélez stood on the road, beckoning imperiously, and John scrambled out. He saluted the officer and Vélez smiled.

"Bring your things, Inglayss."

"Sir?"

Vélez pointed with his cigarette to the vehicles under the trees where Esquerra was talking with two others John didn't recognise. "Come," he said and strolled away.

John stared after him for a moment then retrieved his pack and rifle and followed. As he approached the little group he saw that one was an SS captain, wiry and self-assured. The other was an SS sergeant, middle-aged and grey-haired, but stockily fit. He noticed that the symbols on their collars were not the usual twin stylised lightning flashes, but something resembling a swastika with ends curved almost to join in a circle. He recognised it: the sonnenrad, the sun-wheel insignia of Nordland. It seemed that he'd made contact with them after all and he smiled, pleased.

The captain was conversing with Esquerra in fluent Spanish and John came to attention and saluted. Esquerra touched his cap. "Ah, el Inglayss." He nodded to the captain, and without another word strode back towards his waiting column.

Vélez smiled at John once more and then took his cigarette from his mouth briefly. "*Vaya con dios,* Inglayss." Then he too nodded to the captain and followed Esquerra, puffing lazily on his cigarette.

The captain looked at John speculatively for a few moments. "Stand easy." John started, for the captain spoke flawless English with a slightly plummy accent. He sounded just like John's favourite actor, Trevor Howard. The idea amused him and he relaxed. The captain glanced at the sergeant. "Commandantay Esquerra tells me you're English *and* Swedish."

"Yessir. Private Marlow." The captain held out his hand and John pulled out his papers. While the captain was reading them, John quickly explained about his family background. The captain stroked his chin. "I see..." Then he chuckled, and in Swedish observed, "Confusing fellow, aren't you, Marlow?"

John answered in the same language. "I was with the British Free Corps. I want to fight the Reds."

The sergeant spoke for the first time, sounding doubtful. "There were English at Schwedt but I didn't see you there."

John directed his response to the captain. "I was in Berlin for a radio broadcast," and as the captain's eyebrows rose, he added, "And for photographs. Propaganda."

The sergeant snorted. "Radio broadcast? *Photographs?*" His thick accent was vaguely familiar.

The captain chuckled. "You must forgive Sergeant Rask, Marlow. He's from Härjedalen. They haven't heard of radios and cameras up there yet."

John smiled back and nodded: Härjedalen. He used to visit the area on holidays with his Swedish family, walking, fishing and picnicking. Rask's solid frame and broad stolid face with its wind-roughened high cheeks and brown eyes reminded him of many he'd seen there: reliable but unimaginative peasant stock.

Rask looked at his captain with affectionate exasperation.

"I met Major Esquerra in Berlin." John nodded towards the lorries on the road. "They took some pictures of us shaking hands for *Signal*." The captain and Rask both nodded their understanding: *Signal* was a popular military photo magazine. Everyone in German uniform knew *Signal*.

"And now you want to fight?"

John nodded. "I *asked* for Nordland."

"Well, we need everyone we can get." He returned John's papers with a wry smile. "This isn't Nordland."

"But..." John glanced at the captain's collar.

"Oh, *I'm* Nordland, so is Rask here, but this is Storm Detachment Berg. We were formed yesterday from a composite training battalion. We've got all sorts here: Swedes, Danes, Finns, Norwegians, even a few Germans. And now an Englishman." He smiled. "A real *pittipanna*."

John smiled wryly: *pittipanna* was a Swedish dish using up any old leftovers, a bit like the bubble and squeak he'd loved in England.

"You should fit in well, Marlow." The captain held out his hand to be shaken. "I'm Captain Ridderstolpe. Welcome. Rask, sort him out while I go and have a word with Major Berg," and he hurried away between the vehicles under the trees.

Rask grinned when John snapped to attention and saluted Ridderstolpe's retreating back. "Relax. You're not on parade. We're more informal here." John nodded; he knew the informality of Swedish units, had served with Swedish volunteers in Finland. "Here." Rask pulled out a packet of Junos and lit one for each of them. Then he smiled crookedly. "You'll not be popular with Ridderstolpe."

"Why?"

"He's the adjutant. Does all the paperwork. You're an Englishmen and a Swedish volunteer in German uniform. Think of all the forms!"

John grinned.

"Come on, I'll introduce you to Greger Engberg. His section's mainly Swedish. We've tried to keep guys from the same country together. Makes it easier giving orders, but we've had to do a bit of mixing." He led John towards one of the lorries. "We'll find you some badges. I think I've got a spare somewhere. Try and lose anything that says you're not Swedish."

John nodded; he'd done that already, but there were a few things, like his folio case, he was not prepared to ditch. It contained cuttings from the journals and newspapers which his mother had arranged to be sent to her when she'd returned to Östersund: articles about London; descriptions of the English countryside she'd loved; features about spring and autumn and Christmas in England. She'd put poems in the case too: Wordsworth, Shelley, Keats, and war poets, the ones his father had liked. When cancer had taken her, John claimed the case for his own.

Rask stopped at the tailgate of the lorry and shouted into its shadowed interior, dim in the shade of the trees.

"Engberg?"

"Not here," a voice answered in accented Swedish from amongst the huddle of bodies slumped back against the canvas. Someone was snoring in the background. It seemed familiar. "What do you want, Rask? We're sleeping!"

"You're always fucking sleeping! Come and meet the new recruit."

A tall man levered himself to his feet and ambled forward, rubbing sleep from his eyes and scratching at an unruly mop of curly brown hair. "Recruit? What are you talking about?" John saw several pairs of eyes, open now, peer towards him, pale orbs in the darkness.

"This is Marlow," Rask turned and beckoned John forward, "from England," he smiled wryly, "and Östersund. Sleepy-head here," he turned back to the tall man, "is Olé Hansen from Norway. He's…"

Rask saw the amazed look on Olé's face and stopped abruptly.

"Hello, Olé," John said, "what the hell are you doing here?"

"Well, fuck me! John!" A slow grin spread across Olé's face. "What the hell are *you* doing here?"

Cheslav glanced at Lopakin standing some way off with Senior Lieutenant Bartashevich, the platoon commander. When he was sure that he wasn't being observed, Cheslav paused what he was doing and stretched his back with a groan.

"Painful, eh, boy?" Kolchok too straightened up briefly, laid his bayonet down on the soggy ground and rubbed the small of his back. "I'm too old for this," he sighed.

The platoon was spread out around them on their hands and knees in a line, poking the ground with their bayonets, probing for the mines which the Germans had laid liberally across the Oderbruch. It had been a long, long morning; ever so slowly they'd cleared whole fields, pausing only to ease aching muscles or to lie flat when sporadic German artillery fire dropped close by, but mercifully not close enough to do any harm. The sogginess of the ground helped, sucking in the shells and reducing the effectiveness of the explosive.

"Slow work, eh?" Now Kolchok rubbed the back of his dirty neck and sighed again. "Well, 'dripping water will hollow out rock.'"

"Don't mention water." Behind them, Beridze, the gangly Georgian schoolboy who'd been with the platoon longer than Cheslav, peered up at them from a puddle. Shadows flickered past them and they looked up. Half a dozen single-engine aircraft roared towards the Heights, sunlight glinting on their canopies.

"Third lot in an hour," Beridze observed, pushing himself up. The lower half of his legs were black with wetness.

Kolchok nodded. "The commander is getting serious."

The aircraft climbed, banked and began a long shallow dive towards the dense smoke and dust which lay along the base of the Heights. Cheslav watched them and thought, not for the first time that day, of Leonid. He uttered a silent what? Prayer? Perhaps, but whom or what was he praying to? Since Father had been taken away and Mother had put away the icons, God had not figured in his upbringing. A hope, then. He patted the cardboard key underneath his tunic. He knew how absurd it was, but he was not the only one who'd kept them for comfort or good luck, and despite the rational Soviet regime, many had other icons. Beridze had a picture of Stalin in his top pocket. Cheslav wondered whether Comrade Stalin's picture would deflect a bullet as the image of Saint Joseph, an elderly peasant once had told him, had done for him in the last war. Cheslav had laughed at the idea then, but when he was given his cardboard key, he put it over his heart. He tapped it again.

Lopakin shouted something and Cheslav sighed, bent again to poke the long thin bayonet into the soil, gingerly testing for anything hard that might be buried death. Prod here and there, sweep a small area in front of him, then move on. Prod again, and again, and again move on. His world was reduced to a couple of square metres of wet soil.

Then, *ting*! Something hard stopped the bayonet. He froze and drew breath, and then gently he stabbed in a widening spiral as he'd been taught, moving the bayonet outwards away from the hard object. Within a few centimetres the bayonet struck only softness and he put it down, knelt to feel for the edges of whatever lay buried. Under the squishy mud it was small and irregular. Probably a stone, he thought, but he licked his tongue across dry lips and felt drops of sweat on his forehead. He blew on his chilled fingers and then slowly scraped away the sticky soil with his fingertips; around him the platoon had moved on. The mud parted to reveal a piece of flint the size of two clenched fists and he pulled it out and put it to one side, one of many he'd found that day. The field was littered with stones, pulled out by the platoon as they worked their way onwards. They had found no mines, but there was a first time for everything. He let his breath out slowly and touched the key again; ahead Kolchok grinned back at him.

Not another saying, Cheslav begged silently as Kolchok opened his mouth, but he yawned instead and called back, "I could do with a good sleep."

Cheslav nodded, heard the sounds of a furious battle on the Heights ahead and wondered when they'd next get the chance.

"Don't stop!" Lopakin's voice broke over them. "We haven't got all day."

Cheslav met Kolchok's look and they raised their eyes to the sky in exasperation.

"Keep going." Lopakin squished towards them. "Remember the old saying: 'dripping water will hollow out rock.'"

Not you as well, Cheslav wondered, as he bent to poke at the ground once more.

Eugen Körtig was dead. Tanya wept when she heard the news. She'd convinced herself that she was inured to the loss of neighbours, of colleagues, of friends; that death had become almost banal. Empty spaces in the queues for bread or firewood; missing faces at the tram stop; names which people mentioned no more in conversation. Her reaction to the news about Mr Körtig unnerved her; it was as if a chink of light suddenly shone through a wall she'd thought solid. She'd liked him, but surely that was all. She didn't really know him well, though they'd grown a bit closer in the enforced intimacy of the cellar. Stuck underground for hours on end, day after day, she'd come to appreciate his quiet sense of humour, his rock-solid common sense, but they'd not been very close. She only ever addressed him as Mr Körtig; he only ever called her Miss Klarkova.

There was more to her relationship with Mrs Körtig. It was that perhaps which upset her: the pain the loss would cause the old woman, and the way the news had come to her must have added to Mrs Körtig's distress. A few badly written lines in pencil on a page torn from a school exercise book, folded into a triangle to keep it together: envelopes were scarce. When the mailman had knocked on the cellar door earlier and delivered it, Tanya knew it must be bad news.

Mrs Körtig had waited until the mailman had gone before retreating to the alcove to read it quickly. Blanching, she froze, saying nothing for a few seconds, then she thrust the note at Tanya and climbed the stairs out of the cellar just as the sirens began to howl.

"Air raid warning," Mrs Boldt said from her chair, but Mrs Körtig ignored her and left.

"It's against regulations," Mrs Boldt muttered, deliberately loudly, locking stares with Tanya.

The words of the crumpled paper had been direct and to the point: *Papa died. He was struck by a lorry.* There was more, but it added little. The essence of it was that Eugen Körtig had been killed by accident in a safe rural backwater after surviving the last war on the front line, and months and years of bombing in the city. It was an irony Tanya knew he would have appreciated, but she could not. She folded the paper carefully, laid it on Mrs Körtig's divan and made for the cellar door.

"Air raid warning," Mrs Boldt repeated in a severe tone. The sirens were still wailing but there was no gunfire yet.

Tanya didn't look at her.

"It's the rules, you must stay," Mrs Boldt added as Tanya mounted the steps.

Tanya ignored her and went to look for Mrs Körtig. After all, they *were* neighbours, even if she hadn't really known Eugen at all.

Leonid's anxieties proved to be pointless. When Zeldin reappeared in the orchard it was with unexpected good news: the Germans were withdrawing.

"Koniev's broken through to the south, we've got behind them in the north." Zeldin's tone was weary rather than triumphant as he relayed this news to his orders group. Turkin and Leonid exchanged looks with Safronov, a former sergeant who had had taken Gushenko's place in charge of Number One platoon. Gushenko kept his gaze on Zeldin. The unspoken question hovered over them: why the frontal attacks if all we had to do was turn their flanks?

"The Fritzes are still up there," Zeldin waved his hand up the slope, "but they'll not hold on for long. It'll be easy, they're beaten."

Leonid shifted nervously; he'd heard *that* before. Glancing at Gushenko he saw more resolution than he felt himself, but still, suppose the Germans didn't know they were beaten? He kept the question to himself.

Zeldin went on to outline his plan: One and Three platoons leading, Leonid again following. It sounded familiar, but this time there was to be substantial artillery preparation.

And this time Chuya won't be leading us, Leonid acknowledged. Thank God, or some such.

Much to Leonid's surprise, it went pretty much as Zeldin promised. They waited in the orchard for several hours. "Give the bastards time to get out of the way," Agranenko observed. Then, shortly before noon, the slope above them erupted with explosions. For over half an hour shells and rockets rained down on every possible German position, and bombs dropped from waves of aircraft who then circled to strafe with cannon and machine guns.

When the time came to walk up the slope, that was all they did: walk. No one shot at them. As they passed the tumbled bodies which had fallen so quickly the previous day, the ease of it struck Leonid as bizarre. Somehow it seemed wrong, but he didn't voice his thoughts.

There was no pause as they plodded upslope, save for Agranenko who picked the Red banner from Chuya's twisted corpse. He rolled the silk around the pole, handed it to Moiseyevich and told him to take it back to Polyanski. As the boy loped away, it was Agranenko who voiced hidden thoughts, quoting in an even voice, 'All riddled by bullets, the crimson silk reminds us of steppe winds, of their dismal groan; wrapped in its folds, in chill silence our dead on the sharp-edged stones lay prone.'

Leonid stared at him. "I don't know that one."

"Kulchitsky. *The Red Banner.*"

Leonid followed Moiseyevich's progress back down the slope and didn't know what to say.

Agranenko smiled grimly and spoke on. "Well, it ends: 'It will flutter in triumph, streaming out in our final battle to end all strife! It will rise above earth like a flaming dawn, a symbol of homeland and love and life.'" He looked at Leonid with a wry smile. "Let's get on, Comrade Lieutenant. We're being left behind."

Leonid watched Moiseyevich pass the following troops and head towards Polyanski, standing with Zeldin in the little orchard. Well, it ends, he mused. I hope so, and he turned to follow Agranenko forward.

It took a little while for John and Olé to explain things to Rask, and a little while longer to catch up on things themselves, sitting in the wan sunlight under the trees, sharing cigarettes with the rest of the section, waiting for orders to move. They were still deep in conversation when Greger Engberg returned.

"Well, who have we here?" He listened for a moment to Olé's opening words and then waved him to silence. "All right, all right. It can wait. We're moving." And John saw that all along the line of vehicles orders were being shouted, sending men scurrying.

It didn't take very long after they set off for John to realise that the suspension had gone on the old Opel Blitz. Greger leaned forward from his place on the bench opposite, gripping a stanchion to stop himself swaying too much, and stared quizzically into John's face. "English and Swedish, then?"

"I'm half English." John met Greger's gaze steadily.

Olé interjected from his seat next to Greger. "His mother's from Östersund."

Greger nodded but didn't take his eyes from John's. "All right, but even so, why are you here?"

"For the same reason as us," Olé said irritably. "To fight the Reds."

Greger shook his head. "A bit late for that."

The words stung and John opened his mouth to issue a sharp rebuff, but again it was Olé who spoke. "John's done plenty. We were together at Salla."

Greger turned to him. "He can answer for himself." He smiled slightly at John. "That's where you two met?"

John nodded and Greger's smile widened, then he held out his hand. "So. Welcome, John Marlow." His eyes narrowed. "If you're Swedish we'll have to find another name."

A thin dark-haired youth sitting on the other side of him from Olé spoke for the first time since John had arrived. "You at Salla? You fight with *Sisu*?" He spoke bad Swedish, but John recognised the accent: the boy was Finnish.

"No." Once again it was Olé who answered. "Colonel Dyrssen's battalion."

"I was in the Swedish Volunteer Corps," John explained.

"So," Greger smiled at him, acceptance in the expression, "how?"

"I met Dyrssen at a fundraising dinner for the Swedish Finland Committee," John explained softly. "My mother was involved with it. Look." He pulled out his folio case and extracted a piece of fabric embroidered with an emblem.

"The Four Brother Hands," said Olé quietly. "Finland's cause is ours."

Greger nodded. "Welcome, Comrade."

The Finnish youth tapped his chest. "Kaarle Olav-Poika Isokyrö-Kylästä." He looked very solemn for a moment and then grinned. "Kaarle." Then he became solemn once more. "My brother die Salla."

John looked at Kaarle and remembered other Finnish boys and men, those he and the rest of Dyrssen's battalion had helped relieve on a grim freezing February day. He saw again their staring eyes, shabby clothes, worn-out weapons, exhausted bodies; desperate defenders ground down by relentless attacks, they'd only just held. He caught Olé's eye and remained silent. Finland had fought a good fight against the Soviet invaders, but many lives had been lost, and in the end the Reds had won. He didn't know what to say. Is this the same? he wondered, and suppressed the doubt.

Olé seemed to guess what was going through his mind. "It was good we went to Finland, John, and it's good that you're here now."

Kaarle grinned once more and nodded vigorously.

"Yes." Greger held out his hand, palm down. Then Olé reached across to grasp his wrist, and Kaarle grasped Olé's. John nodded; he understood, and in turn he took Kaarle's wrist. Greger completed the ring by grasping John's: it was a living copy of the badge. For a moment they looked at each other in silence.

Leonid's platoon reached the Seelow Heights near dusk. There'd been no more resistance coming up the slope and the only Germans they found were the remains of bodies too ripped apart by the intense bombardment to be worth carrying away. They'd picked their way with increasing confidence past smashed bunkers, ripped up trenches and torn wire. It seemed bizarre to Leonid: such stiff opposition at first, so many losses, and then a stroll uphill.

At the top, he found a busy scene. A road lay along the edge of the escarpment and already it was thick with traffic. At the top, they found a small half-ruined farm set back from the road and took it over. Food arrived from the company, the platoon bedded down and Leonid and Agranenko went outside to stand by the road, smoke and watch proceedings quietly. In the distance to the west, Leonid could see flashes of gunfire, hear the rumble of artillery, but it was nothing compared to the previous two days.

Their peaceful moment was broken when four tanks clattered to a halt on the road by them, blue smoke hanging above the engine decks, hatches on the turrets open, the head of each vehicle's commander projecting outside. Like Kolesnikov's, these were 34s, but they had turrets twice as big and much longer guns. A short stocky figure jumped off the lead tank even before it came to a halt, looked around, saw them and marched purposefully towards them. Behind, the tank crews scrambled out and stood about, lighting cigarettes or relieving themselves on the verge.

The figure removed its padded tank helmet to reveal the broad grease-smeared face of a woman of middle years, her short dark hair streaked with grey. "Comrades," she bellowed in a voice deeper than Leonid's. She snapped off a perfunctory salute towards Leonid, which he, startled, neglected to return. Then she punched him on the shoulder, not gently.

"Trofimova," she said, "senior sergeant," and grinned, revealing off-white teeth heavy with dark fillings and several gaps. Leonid introduced himself and Agranenko. Trofimova grinned again when she heard which battalion they were with: the one she'd been trying to find all day, she told them. Her tanks had been assigned to support their attack on the Heights. Seeing their faces, she explained that it had taken her the best part of fourteen hours to get across the Oderbruch. Most of her battalion were still who knows where. "Lost," she commented nonchalantly as she rolled and lit a cigarette, "or stuck in the fucking traffic. Or the fucking mud. No room to bring the whole battalion up in one go. We split. Supposed to meet here." She sucked noisily on the cigarette, coughed heavily and spat at their feet.

Leonid told her about Kolesnikov's tanks and what had happened at the bottom of the slope. Trofimova frowned when he described the mound and the smoke ring.

"Fucking Tiger," she said. Then she shrugged.

Agranenko pursed his lips; he seemed to disapprove of her language.

"It'll be easier in Berlin," Trofimova asserted, slightly more quietly.

"Easier?" Agranenko seemed a little querulous. Leonid knew

that he didn't take to loud, bombastic people and considered that women should be quiet and demure. He turned his head away to hide his brief smile.

"Fritz tanks," Trofimova waved her cigarette, "meant for open country. Fuck all use up close. Your boys can get alongside one with a Molotov or a satchel charge in the city. Then *bang!* No more Fritz."

Agranenko sounded testy. "We *boys* have to get close enough in the first place, Comrade!"

Trofimova grinned again and briefly placed a hand on Agranenko's shoulder. He grimaced. "We've lost enough men trying to get 'up close and dirty', Comrade." Trofimova's grin faded. Agranenko turned to Leonid. "With your permission, Comrade Lieutenant, I'll check on the men." He sounded remarkably formal; he even saluted, something he almost never did. Leonid returned the compliment tardily as Agranenko strode stiffly away.

Feeling awkward, Leonid turned to Trofimova. "Are you staying with us now that you've found us?"

"Don't know. Gotta talk to your battalion commander."

"Major Zeldin?"

"Is that his name?" She spat out fragments of tobacco, dropped the stub of her cigarette by Leonid's boot and started to roll another. He pointed down the grey ribbon of road leading south. The roughly ploughed fields on either side of it were becoming crowded.

"That way. HQ's by a farm with red barns."

Trofimova nodded her thanks and then held out her hand. She had a grip like a vice and her palms were horny.

"See you in Berlin!"

Leonid watched her stomp off down the road and observed, If anyone is likely to get there, you are. He wondered if he'd get there himself, but then drove that fear away and went to find Agranenko.

He found him sitting by one of the fires the platoon had lit inside a decrepit barn, carefully located under the remaining portions of roof. It still didn't pay to take too many risks with the Luftwaffe. Although they were beaten, they didn't all seem to have realised it.

There were still occasional forays by small groups or even solitary aircraft; it seemed that was all they could manage now.

In the barn, the platoon clustered around the flames, some sitting, most lying down. There was little chatter. Agranenko sat off to one side by himself, as he usually did, his back to a crumbling wall. He beckoned with the bottle he'd been dirking from. When Leonid had seated himself, he offered it. It was rum, labelled 'Stroh'. Leonid sipped: it wasn't bad. The bottle was a third empty, and it wasn't a small bottle.

Leonid peered speculatively at his sergeant and returned it. Agranenko didn't seem drunk, yet, but it was unusual that he was drinking much at all.

"She's gone to see Zeldin."

Agranenko swallowed more rum. In the gloom his eyes looked like dark sockets in a skull.

"She's keen," Leonid added.

Agranenko snorted and Leonid didn't know what more to say. Perhaps he should leave Agranenko alone. He was starting to get up when Agranenko spoke.

"I knew most of them well."

Leonid sat down again abruptly.

"Chuya was a fresh lieutenant when I met him, like you." He drank. "Well, perhaps not like you." He stared into the fire. "So many, so quick."

Leonid knew he was thinking of the slope, of those dead and those who might die.

"It's worth it, though, isn't it?"

"Is it?" Agranenko handed him the bottle and Leonid took a bigger swallow before passing it back.

"What do you mean?"

"Good stuff, Lieutenant." Agranenko tipped the bottle right back, then placed it carefully by his feet. He smiled ruefully. "I suppose, to stop those bastards. I could tell you tales, Comrade Lieutenant. I really could. Yes, it's worth it," but he sounded morose.

Leonid waited.

"We liberated a POW camp," Agranenko said after quite a pause. "Back end of '44. Filthy place. Bodies all over the place. Been left for days. The huts were full of the dead and the living, too many." He paused to light a cigarette; his hands shook slightly. Leonid was startled; he'd never seen Agranenko like this.

"Walking skeletons. Never seen anything like it. The smell!" Agranenko reached for the bottle again, but then seemed to think better of it and withdrew his hand. Instead he sucked deeply on the cigarette. "There weren't many left alive, and most of those that were didn't stay that way. I was in Chuya's platoon then. He did his best, but there were so many."

Leonid shook his head when Agranenko lifted the bottle and offered it. He peered at it and once more put it down.

"We cleared out the bodies, cleaned up the living, fed them, those that could eat. Burned the camp. There were guards. Ukrainians. We shot them."

"Yes. I know the collaborators…"

"Red Army men they'd been. Gone over to the Germans when they got taken prisoner and done a deal. They were complete shits, *complete shits.*" Agranenko had finished the cigarette already and threw the remains into the fire. The he picked up the bottle. "The things they did. Some of the prisoners told us. Things you could never believe." He looked momentarily at Leonid, his eyes vacant, then he took a long swallow from the bottle. "Chuya shot the first one he saw after we went into the hut. Pulled out his pistol and *bang!*" Agranenko raised his forefinger to his forehead, just above the nose, and cocked his thumb as if his hand were a gun. "He wasn't the same after that. Drank too much." He stared at the bottle and upended it: a single drop fell out. "It was the betrayal, the way those guards treated their comrades." He stared moodily across the barn to the fire, then he curled up on the ground and said no more.

Leonid and then sat back and stared at the dark sky through the holes in the ruined roof and remembered, remembering. Betrayal, yes. When his father had been taken away, Leonid too had wanted to kill; to do away with those in the village who'd denounced his father: people he'd grown up with, neighbours, comrades. Yes, he understood. The enemy was evil, but it was worse when those supposed to be on your side turned on you. Memories crowded in.

He looked down at Agranenko and then at the empty bottle and wished he had a full one.

FIVE

Artillery muttered faintly on the still, cold air like the distant drumming of many feet on a wooden floor. It reminded John of going into school assembly. He shivered; he'd thought that Salla had made him indifferent to the sounds of battle, but clearly it hadn't. His stomach clenched slightly. He had a sudden urge to relieve himself and clambered over the side of the open-topped half-track in which he sat and let loose a relieving stream onto the road, steaming in the chill morning air. They'd been despatched shortly before the sun came. Simple recce, Rask had said. They'd not driven more than a couple of kilometres from Detachment Berg's overnight resting place when they came to an unmarked crossroads and Rask had decided to halt to find his bearings.

He stood at the front of the vehicle, frowning down at the map draped over the pintle-mounted machine. As he eased himself, John stared out across the ploughed fields which lay all around. About a hundred metres away an 88 sat behind a triple thickness of sandbags. It was a gun designed to shoot down aircraft, but its barrel pointed horizontally eastwards at the low line of woodland and the gunfire.

"Ten minutes," Rask bellowed back, scrambled out and set off towards the gun.

The section tumbled out to ease cramped limbs, light cigarettes, and emulate John's self-relief. The half-track's driver, a stocky, scar-faced red-headed SS lance corporal, came to join him on the narrow road. He nodded casually to John. "Sundberg."

John nodded back. "Marlow."

"Babies." Sundberg stared at the 88 and shook his head disapprovingly.

A group of teenagers stood by the gun; they wore the two-piece blue-grey tunics and round peaked cloth field caps common to many sorts of support units, but they must be Hitler Youth Flak Helpers, John realised. He'd seen a lot of them; most of Germany's anti-aircraft guns were manned by boys such as these, older men having been sent to fight at the Front. Now it looked as if these boys too would face it. They seemed so young and that saddened him. He watched one of the boys step forward and give a formal salute to Rask as he clumped up to them though the clinging sods. The sergeant did not return it.

"Trouser shitters," Sundberg snorted. When John looked hard at him he added, "Soon as they see a real live Ivan they'll do it in their pants. Fucking crazy. Kids like that. Haven't got a hope. A bunch of wet-arsed babies." He had a thick accent like Rask's. John wondered if Sundberg too was from Härjedalen and frowned.

"And that fucking gun," Sundberg continued angrily, "look at it. Every Ivan for miles will see it. Stuck out there on its own. Then one shell and *boom*. Fucking murder." He paused, and in a softer murmur said, "Same age as my kid brother. Thank the fuck *he's* back home."

John looked at the group around Rask again and nodded. That's where they should be, he thought gloomily. Maybe it's where I should be. He offered Sundberg a cigarette.

The opposition have been busy overnight, Tanya observed as she passed the group of girls vigorously scrubbing the wall of the building opposite her apartment block. She changed the word in her head as she walked by. There'd been precious little opposition to Hitler, and even less since the abortive attempt to kill him the previous July, vicious repression had seen to that. Dissenters there were, and those who disagreed, but opponents? The girls were from the BDM:

the *Bund Deutscher Mädel,* the League of German Maidens. Intense in that determinedly teenage way, they'd removed virtually all the lettering from a long swathe of brickwork, but as Tanya passed them unnoticed one sentence still remained. Painted crudely in thick red letters it said: 'Hitler leads us to ruin. Refuse to fight!' Tanya smiled ruefully to herself as a girl in a long brown overcoat set to work on it with a brush and pail of water. Everything was ruined already and the fighting would soon be over, whatever Hitler wanted.

She turned right at the end of the street and saw a man in a cassock ahead of her: Father Kazintsev, the local Orthodox priest; *her* priest, although she seldom went to church anymore. He's out early, she thought. Doing his rounds? Or perhaps he, like she, was on a shopping expedition. It'd become a national obsession, rushing from one shop or street market to another, following rumours and announcements of fresh deliveries. Before the war, Tanya had shopped for pleasure. It was her weekend treat to visit the great department stores: Wertheim's, Hermann Tietz, Kaufhaus des Westens, and there was lovely Karstadt's on the Hermannplatz, next to it the huge ice cream parlour where she'd loved to spoil herself.

The stores had all been so beautiful with elegant display windows full of books and chocolates, crystal-ware and silver, fine clothes and shoes. Now the windows were boarded up, the stores closed, but long before that had happened, Tanya stopped visiting them. The stores had been Jewish owned, and although they'd continued when their owners had emigrated or disappeared, she'd felt guilty and stopped going. After Wertheim's was aryanised and renamed AWAG, she'd never set foot in it again. Visiting the stores, experiencing their wealthy elegance, had been a way of recalling the life she'd shared, albeit very briefly, with her father, but the Nazis had spoiled it for her and she'd never forgiven them.

She followed Kazintsev at a discreet distance. She did not want to speak with him for it had been too long since she'd attended his services. She wondered if he was going to the same grocery as she was and hoped not, but she could not put off her trip. There had been a delivery of soap, Mrs Boldt told them that morning, the Hitler Youth on the bicycle had informed her so. Real soap. Mrs Boldt of course didn't need to go and fetch it, the boy brought her Party entitlement, but the others would have to visit the shop. For such errands, one of them often would go for all the others, and today it was Tanya's turn.

Would Kazintsev fetch his own soap? She dearly hoped not, and she was lucky, for instead of carrying on at the next corner he turned down the street which led to the church. She waited for a few moments to let him get well ahead and then passed the turning in a hurry, keeping her face turned away from the square across which Kazintsev was striding. There was a group of BDM scrubbing walls here too. So busy, she mused, like proper little hausfrauen. She remembered a rhyme she'd read in the *Berliner Zeitung* shortly after Goebbels became propaganda minister; part of his campaign to promote German womanhood:

> Take hold of kettle, broom and pan,
> Then you'll surely get a man!
> Shop and office leave alone,
> Your true life-work lies at home.

She snorted derisorily at the sentiment; she'd been a successful, independently-minded professional woman before the war and the article in the *Zeitung* had infuriated her. She'd stopped buying it, but the rhyme had stuck with her. She looked at the girls and snorted once more. A successful, independently-minded professional woman she'd be again, she determined, and hurried on to find soap.

When Rask returned from his conversation with the flak crew, he ordered the half-track back to the calm, pretty little village where they'd left the detachment.

They found upheaval. It was obvious from the thin pillar of greasy smoke rising above the rooftops that something was wrong long before they clattered into the cobbled square. One of the detachment's Opel lorries stood in the centre, its tyres flat, oily flames flickering in fits and starts from underneath a discoloured bonnet. On the pavement nearby two bodies lay beneath blankets under the watchful eye of three unarmed Hitler Youths, incongruous in shorts and white knee socks. The oldest came forward as Rask scrambled out. As John dismounted behind him with the others, his feet crunched on broken glass from the shattered windows of the nearby houses. While Rask spoke to the boy, John examined the walls. They were pockmarked and cracked; small lumps of brick and plaster were scattered on the ground. It looked like cannon or machine-gun fire. Aircraft, he realised.

Rask confirmed John's guess – "Just some passing Ivan" – when he came back from speaking with the boys. "Major Berg's moved to a wood nearby." He glanced at the blanket-shrouded forms. "Arvidsson and that Danish lad. Can never remember his name." His tone was neutral, the matter-of-fact voice used by soldiers long used to death. None of the other men showed any reaction. "There were a couple of wounded too." Only now did his tone shift. "One of them was Hansen," he said sympathetically and looked at John. "They'll be at the aid post."

John felt his heart flip over.

"What about those?" Sundberg pointed.

"They'll bury them." Rask nodded at the boys.

"Useful for something, then."

"Shut up, Staffan," Rask sighed, "just for once."

They left immediately and found the rest of the detachment under the cover of a pine wood a couple of kilometres outside the village. Rask jumped off the half-track as it passed a red cross painted onto a white bed sheet strung between two trees and waved to John to follow him.

Down a short track, further back amongst the trees, they found the aid post: a fancy name for an open sided tent in which a fat corporal, helped by a private, probed, swabbed and bandaged the torn flesh of a trooper laid on a trestle table. John didn't recognise any of them. The corporal was much younger than John, yet he had an air of authority that would have sat well on any grey-haired consultant in a fancy clinic. Despite the blood and mud all around him, his boots and uniform were immaculate, but his long apron was not.

"That's Kurschat," Rask said, and then added sotto voce with a grin, "we call him Butter." John noted the big man's girth and couldn't help grinning back, but their grins faded as they knelt by the other wounded man lying on a stretcher nearby. It was Olé, his head heavily bandaged leaving only his eyes and mouth uncovered. His eyes were closed and his chest rose in the slow, regular movements of deep sleep. The red-edged brown cardboard tag tied to his collar bore the words: 'head wound, hospital.'

"He's completely out," Kurschat called over without looking up from his task. "Morphine." He stood back, nodded to his assistant and walked over to them, wiping his hands on a filthy towel.

"I think he'll be all right." Kurschat looked down impassively at Olé and at John. "But it's a head injury and should be looked at by a proper doctor." He grimaced. "Rules." He sounded as if rules weren't something he really cared about much. "Transport's coming from the local hospital. It's not far. You can take him back on it." Rask looked at him, and he added, "We need some supplies. You can fetch them."

Rask hesitated for a moment and then nodded. "We'll not be moving for a bit. All right."

"See if you can get some morphine, bandages, that sort of thing." Kurschat ran his hand through dark hair, thicker than regulations normally allowed. "I'll give you a list." He sighed and turned back to the table where the private was tidying up.

As they walked down the track past the column, Rask lit two Junos. "He wants to be a chef."

"Chef?"

Rask nodded. "Butter. His uncle's got a restaurant in Königsberg. After the war he's going into partnership with him."

"I used to visit Königsberg when I was a boy," John said quietly, taking one of the cigarettes. "My grandmother was fond of shopping. We'd have lunch. I wonder if we ever went to his uncle's place."

"Possibly," said Rask. "Butter's family have always lived there. Everyone went to eat there, it seemed."

John pictured Kurschat swathed in chef's whites. It was a disconcerting image: joints of bloody meat, bottles of sauces and kitchen cutlery instead of wounded men, disinfectants and medical instruments.

Rask might have guessed what was in John's mind for he grinned broadly. "Worrying idea, isn't it, Butter in a kitchen."

"How did he end up in Berg?"

"Nordland picked him up in Courland. Was in a field hospital that got bombed. No more hospital, so he came along with us. We needed a medic and they let us keep him when we got out." He looked at the stub of his cigarette, threw it away and pulled out the packet again. "He's a survivor." Rask took another Juno. "He survived a lot. The boys reckon he's good luck. So do I." He looked at the cigarette, seemed to think better of it and put it back in the packet, which went into his top pocket.

"You like him, don't you," said John.

Rask smiled briefly. "He saved my life once. Ran forward when I got hit, patched me up under fire. Should have got a medal. A *really* good medic. Not an aspirin Jesus like some of them: a pill and a pat on the head."

John saw Greger up ahead and waved to him. Then a thought image struck him and he grinned broadly.

"What is it?"

"Oh, I was just thinking."

Rask raised his eyebrows at him.

"I'm trying to imagine," said John, "Butter *running* to rescue you."

Rask stared at John for a few seconds and then they both laughed.

We have become dusty monuments, Tanya told herself as she looked along the queue. The people reminded her of the mime artists she'd seen in the Théâtre Déjazet in Paris on a visit with her mother: still silent grey figures. She fretted; she wasn't made for standing in orderly lines; she was Russian, a mixture of impulsiveness and caution. To the Germans, order came naturally; not to her.

She was bored. The authorities used to provide entertainment and freelance buskers worked Berlin's myriad queues, but not anymore. She stood and fretted, waiting for the shop to open. She pulled out her copy of *Only a Woman*, Hertha Pauli's book about Bertha von Suttner, the radical pacifist. Von Suttner had been the first woman to win the Nobel Peace Prize and Tanya had long admired her. She'd brought the book with her to while away the time, tucked safely into a paper sleeve taken from an approved novel; she'd read Pauli's book before, but it was one of those that could be read and reread and still seem fresh.

Suddenly Tanya had something to look at. Boys in assorted uniforms began to arrive singly and in groups. They came from both directions, some marching, some ambling, but all heading for the same point: the high double wooden gates which opened into the courtyard of the corn merchant opposite. At one point she believed that she saw Walter Schley in a column wearing Hitler Youth dark blue. She almost called to him, but then thought better of it. Suppose it *wasn't* Walter? Or suppose that it *was*? What good would it do? Whatever was going on, clearly it was official.

The boys stopped coming, and an open-topped red car drove past and through the gates. In it sat two occupants: Party men, brown uniforms and plenty of braid. A Hitler Youth came forward as it drew to a halt and met them as they got out. Much heel-clicking and stiff-armed saluting followed, and the boy led the men away out of sight.

An army lorry arrived next and parked outside the gates. The driver alighted when a group of boys approached, but he did nothing more than unhitch the tailgate and stand to one side, looking bored and smoking as the boys unloaded boxes and canvas sacks and carried them into the courtyard. By now the queue was all eyes and a murmur of speculative chatter broke out sotto voce.

It dried up when the lorry drove away and the boys closed the gates behind them. Tanya had hardly got back into her book, however, when she was distracted by what sounded like a rather long speech in the courtyard. Try as she might she could not make out the words. Suddenly there was a youthful cheer and, not at all indistinct, three heils. The gates reopened and out marched the boys; no one was ambling now. They moved in columns of threes, each carrying a weapon and some carrying boxes between them. They sang 'Jugend Will', the official Hitler Youth anthem, and streamed down the road past the silent queue eastwards. How beautiful they look, Tanya wondered, watching them pass: fresh faces, neat uniforms and they carried themselves so well in the self-assured proud way teenage boys could display. But as the sound dwindled down the road, she remembered another song sung by boys just like these and felt sad: 'Hänschen Klein', a popular folk song, and one whose words she knew well:

> Little Hans went alone
> Out into the wide, wide world.
> Staff and hat suit him well.
> He's in such good spirits.
> But his mother cries so much,
> For little Hans she has no more.
> But look! the child
> Changes his mind
> And quickly he runs home.

She remembered another time she'd heard it; remembered a train to summer camp in the early, hopeful days of Hitler's regime. Walter had been on that train, and Tanya had been with Ida and Walter's father to see him off. It had been a jolly occasion, despite Ida's natural anxieties, with smiles and laughter and the chatter of the boys boarding; chatter which had been transformed into song. Now tears pricked her eyes, and then she was annoyed with herself for her misplaced sentimentality.

The two brown uniformed Party men came into view once more, this time on their own, and got into their red car. Moments later it swept out and away, followed by the lorry, leaving the courtyard still and empty.

"Ah," said the stout woman in front of Tanya; it was the only word she'd uttered. She had hair dyed an odd shade of russet brown, and all morning Tanya had been noticing the white roots.

Why bother? she wondered, especially as the regime officially disapproved of dyed hair; disapproved, in fact, of women using any cosmetics at all. It wasn't illegal, but it was regarded as un-German and much frowned upon. How peculiar woman can be, she observed. She herself would never allow such misplaced vanity to overcome prudence.

The woman's voice caused Tanya to pull her gaze from the departing vehicles and she saw that the grocery doors were now open. A sigh ran along the queue and it began to edge forward. Thank God, she thought, for her legs ached and she just wanted to go home. All thought of Walter went from her mind as she contemplated the prospect of soap. She tucked Pauli's book back into her string bag and fumbled for her ration book, but she was to be disappointed, for just as the stout woman got to the shop, the door closed once more. The woman cursed, crude words jarring with her respectable appearance, but there was nothing to be done. Tanya saw the shopkeeper hanging a sign: 'closed'. He stared back at her impassively through the glass panel of the door and she turned away with sinking heart. The queue broke up and wandered away in different directions, some muttering amongst themselves.

It was as Tanya turned to go that she felt a hand on her arm. "I thought that all grocers were fat." Klara was standing behind her, smiling.

Tanya smiled back: the shopkeeper was gaunt, thinner than she was herself. She nodded at the doorway. "Too busy selling it to eat it, I suppose," she said.

Klara's smile vanished. "No luck?"

She shook her head and then frowned. "I'm sorry. Were you in the queue? I didn't see you."

"I was near the front."

Tanya looked at her: she was wearing a long grey raincoat, a man's Tanya realised, and her hair was tucked up under a turban.

Tanya remembered that turban, but hadn't realised whose head was under it.

Klara looked at the closed shop door and, after a moment, pulled a coarse grey slab out of her hessian shopping bag. "Here."

Tanya looked down at the soap for a moment and hesitated.

"Please."

Tanya still hesitated and politeness overcame her want. She shook her head. "No, I couldn't, but thank you."

"Oh, please," Klara insisted, holding the soap up higher. "Do take it. We *are* neighbours, after all."

Still Tanya hesitated, so Klara opened the top of Tanya's bag and dropped in the soap. "There. I insist. We have plenty."

"Thank you."

Klara beamed and then nodded across the street. "Well, and what do you make of *that*?"

Tanya looked around her to make sure no one else was within earshot and shook head. "I don't know." She hesitated: should she ask Klara if she too might have seen Walter? But then she thought better of it.

"Well perhaps it's best not to pry." Klara hoisted her shopping bag. "I'm going back now. Walk with me?"

Tanya nodded and Klara slipped an arm through hers. They strolled away from the little grocery, but Tanya couldn't resist casting a glance into the courtyard. She wondered if it had been Walter after all, and whether she should mention it to Ida when they got back. But perhaps it is best not to pry, she told herself.

Walter tramped through the dreary side streets. Had Miss Klarkova seen him when he arrived? He thought not, and positioned himself behind one of the taller boys when they marched out to ensure that she didn't. He didn't want 'that woman' interfering; it would be too embarrassing. Anyway, he was determined to go with Friedrich.

They'd stood together and listened to the usual stuff from the Party official: Fatherland; honour; Führer; family; courage; Red beasts: stirring words made dreary by a dreary man. The speech failed to move Walter, but most of the others, including, to his surprise, Friedrich, seemed enthused. Then he and Friedrich were given a crate of beer bottles full of a mixture of petrol and soap, each with a taper glued to the top, and attached to the side a friction strip like one found on a box of matches. Molotov cocktails: ironically, they were named after the Soviet foreign minister. The idea was to peel off the friction strip, rub it on top of the taper to ignite it, and then throw the bottle. Theoretically, when it smashed on impact the petrol inside would also ignite, and not before. Theoretically.

Some of the other boys were paired off and given boxes of rations to carry, but not many. Waxed-paper packages of ammunition and rifles, an assorted collection, clean and well-oiled but obviously old; the corporal handing out the weapons from the back of the lorry couldn't tell them what they were, or how to operate them, but Rolf, of course, knew. Before the war his father had run a gun shop, and firearms were the only things which really interested him. He was narrow shouldered, short-sighted, and his diffident manner was almost feminine at times. It would have led to bullying, but his knowledge of guns bought him, if not comradeship, then a grudging toleration. Friedrich and Walter had *Lebels*, he told them.

"Made in the same workshop," he said, and pointed to the date stamped on the stock: 1892.

The Lebels chafed Walter's shoulder as he marched along, the rope handle chafed his hands, and his boots chafed his feet, but he was singing when they turned a final corner and saw a group of dreary warehouses ahead. The road ran between them and crossed one of Berlin's numerous small canals on a narrow bridge. Either side of the near end was a wall made of oil drums around which half a dozen elderly Volkssturm clustered, wearing a mix of civilian and army clothing.

Walter fell out along with Vogel's section while the rest of the column marched on across the bridge, down the narrow street, passing between tall warehouses on the far side of the canal and out of sight.

"What now?" Friedrich rubbed his hands together and winced, watching Vogel stride over to the group of Volkssturm and speak to a grizzled old man in an army greatcoat who had stepped forward to meet him.

Walter shrugged. His own attention was on the red Mercedes which had appeared behind them and was approaching at speed: the same car that had brought the Party officials into the courtyard. Walter looked at the two men inside. They ride, we walk, he noted resentfully and eased the pressure on his feet. Fat golden pheasants!

But Friedrich was admiring. "540K," he said and Walter had to smile: Friedrich was such a car buff.

As the Mercedes halted by the bridge, Vogel ran up to it and saluted the man who earlier had made such a bad speech. He didn't return the courtesy, didn't even get out of the car, but thrust a piece of paper at Vogel, said something very brief and then tapped the driver on his shoulder. Vogel had to stand back quickly as the car turned in a circle and drove back the way it had come, leaving everyone staring after it.

Vogel looked down at the paper, read it slowly and then held it up. "Gather round," he shouted. The boys immediately clustered by him, but the Volkssturm didn't move. Vogel threw them an irritated glance and then announced in his pompous way that State Youth Leader Axman had issued a proclamation. He read it out slowly.

> There is only victory or annihilation. Know no bounds in your love of your people; equally, know no bounds in your hatred of the enemy. It is your duty to watch when others tire, to stand when others weaken.

Walter tried to catch Friedrich's attention, but it was fixed firmly on Vogel. 'Your greatest honour is your unshakeable fidelity to Adolf Hitler.' Vogel stopped abruptly and looked around with that dramatic air he always affected when he was trying to play the leader, and which Walter found so hammy. "Heil Hitler." Vogel snapped off a salute and they all responded, again save for the Volkssturm who just glanced at each other. For a moment no one moved and Vogel seemed uncertain what to do next, then the grizzled old man in the army greatcoat stepped alongside him.

"Good morning." He smiled thinly. "Zugführer Fenstermacher." The equivalent of an army lieutenant, he sounded more like a schoolteacher. "You boys store your kit in there." Vogel frowned, but said nothing as Fenstermacher pointed to the nearest warehouse: a low cement-block construction with a corrugated asbestos roof. He turned to lead the way, but nobody moved until Vogel nodded, and then they all followed Fenstermacher inside.

It was a long dusty space. Near the door was a collection of makeshift beds assembled from rolled-up coats, blankets and assorted kit bags. To the left rifles were stacked against the wall, and next to them was a small pile of tubes with bulbous heads. Seeing the *panzerfausts* Walter felt a little less unhappy at the idea of defending the bridge, but only a little. He shivered in the chill, damp atmosphere.

"That do?" Fenstermacher pointed to the other end of the shed and Vogel nodded. "When you've settled in, we'll get some food sorted." Fenstermacher looked around, smiled thinly and left.

"Not a bad billet." Rolf laid his things next to Walter's and Friedrich's in the corner they had claimed for their own. He usually tried to bed down with them. Unlike the others, Walter and Friedrich were prepared to put up with him, at least most of the time.

When they'd finished sorting themselves out, the three boys went to find the promised food. An oil drum stood apart from the barricade, this one not full of sand as the others were, but instead a fire burned merrily within it. Walter noticed that a ring of holes had been punched around the bottom. A fat man was stirring the pot which stood on two metal rods laid over the flames.

"Hungry, boys?" The man didn't smile as they strolled up, but his voice was friendly. They nodded, and he held up his ladle to let a thick gelatinous brown goo fall back. It smelled vaguely of laundry.

"Good stuff. Stick to your ribs. Finest boeuf bourguignon. You won't get better at the Adlon." He stared at them, still unsmiling, and it took Walter a moment to realise that he was making a joke: the

Adlon was Berlin's finest hotel, and before the war had a reputation for superb cuisine. "I'm Thalberg. I do the cooking. You clean your own mess kit and you'll take turns washing the pots like the rest of us. I'll detail you later." Walter wondered what Vogel would think about *that*, but he kept silent and just nodded. "Come back in about half an hour with your friends." Thalberg went back to stirring the stew slowly and with great concentration.

They turned away and went to explore their surroundings. "Boeuf bourguignon, my arse," Rolf muttered when they were safely out of earshot between the nearest two sheds. "Lorelai, more like." They nodded their agreement: Lorelai was a nickname given to any food the composition of which seemed as mysterious as the mythical creature of the same name. "'You won't get better at the Adlon. Stick to your ribs,'" Rolf mimicked. He often did this, and it was something which didn't always endear him to his comrades, but he was good at it and now they laughed.

Then they stopped abruptly as a man said sarcastically from behind them, "Having fun, Walter?"

They turned and Walter's mouth opened in surprise. Standing with Vogel was Mathias and he had a face like black thunderclouds. Vogel's wasn't much better, and Walter's stomach lurched.

"That's my nephew." Mathias turned briefly to Vogel and then back to Walter; his eyes were like flint. "Get your things, boy."

Walter hesitated, and before he could say anything Vogel spoke. "I give the orders here." His nostrils flared: always a bad sign.

Mathias returned his gaze and narrowed his eyes. "Not to me, you don't." To Walter it seemed at that moment the air turned frosty.

"You three, get lost." Vogel jerked his head back towards the bridge.

Mathias reared up and glared at Walter. "Did you not hear what I said, boy?"

Walter felt his mouth go dry and peered at his boots. Rolf seemed about to say something, but Friedrich grasped his elbow and pulled him back a pace.

"Just who do you think you are?" Vogel stepped between

Mathias and the boys. Neither man said anything for a moment, staring at each other. Walter felt Friedrich's grasp on his arm, turned and followed Frederic and Rolf further down between the warehouses and around the end of one. Behind him an argument raged; he couldn't make out the words, but he could discern the tone.

"All right?" Friedrich asked, leading them to the door of their shed, where he stopped.

Walter shook his head. "What's he doing here?" He looked at the bridge where the Volkssturm were peering in the direction of the raised voices. Fenstermacher, who seemed to have crossed the bridge for some reason, was hurrying back across it. Walter heard Mathias' voice, loud and clear between the sheds.

"…spent two years in Poland fighting the Ivans. *And* six months in the Ukraine fighting partisans, and I'll be damned if I'm taking orders from a mucker-out like you!"

Walter looked at Friedrich in alarm as Mathias emerged into the open, followed by a red-faced Vogel. He stopped as Fenstermacher strode up to him and bellowed, "Enough!"

Walter was startled; he'd not thought volume like that could emerge from such a skinny frame. Mathias and Vogel halted and turned towards Fenstermacher, who stared at them as if they were six years old and they looked away for a moment. Then his eyes fell on Walter and he beckoned, a quick jerk of his forefinger. 'You, boy', it said, 'come here.' Walter glanced at Friedrich, but it was Rolf who spoke.

"Go on. You'd better."

Reluctantly Walter joined Fenstermacher as he stood facing Mathias and Vogel. By now the rest of Vogel's section had come out of the shed and clustered by the door with Friedrich and Rolf, watching. The Volkssturm hovered by the bridge.

"Old men and kids." Mathias seemed to have recovered his poise and coldly waved his hand, first at Fenstermacher's Volkssturm and then at Vogel's Hitler Youth. "You haven't a hope of stopping the Reds. You'll just get them all killed. I was in the last lot, I know what I'm talking about."

Walter got a sour look from Mathias as he hurried up.

"It's his duty!" snapped Vogel, but much of the fire seemed to have gone out of him.

"Enough, I said." Fenstermacher spoke softly. "I got this" he locked gaze with Mathias as he reached into his coat and pulled out a dark metal cross "at Passchendaele. First Class." Then he stared at Vogel. "Yes, you know about duty, boy, but I know a bit more and so does this man." He turned to Mathias sympathetically. "Look, it's no good getting angry about it, my friend. We've been ordered here and here we have to stay. You know that." He replaced the medal and touched Mathias' sleeve. "You understand. Even if you do take the boy away," he laid his other hand briefly on Walter's shoulder, "they'll come and get him again and you'll both be in the shit."

None of them were looking at Walter.

"I won't leave him here." Mathias kept his gaze on Fenstermacher. "He's my nephew. He's just a kid." Then he did look at Walter.

"Uncle!" Walter felt himself flush, whether with anger or embarrassment he wasn't sure.

Fenstermacher sighed. "Have you asked him what *he* wants?" The question seemed to startle both Mathias and Vogel.

"He's under orders." Vogel sounded puzzled, as if the concept of what Walter wanted was irrelevant, as indeed, Walter knew, it usually was.

For a long moment Fenstermacher said nothing, and then he turned to Walter, tilted his head and raised his eyebrows. "Well?"

Walter glanced nervously at Mathias and then back at the shed and the boys watching them. He saw Friedrich staring at him and he knew what he was expected to say.

"I want to stay," he muttered; he felt that he could say little else. It was easier, less humiliating to do what was expected of him. Anyway, he thought, Fenstermacher's right. If I go home with Uncle Mathias they will come for me. And for him too. He glanced at his uncle's angry face and for once did not avert his eyes when Mathias caught his look.

Fenstermacher nodded. "All right." He turned to Vogel. "That's settled." When Vogel seemed about to say something, Fenstermacher raised his hand. "Settled."

Vogel stared at him and then shrugged. Without looking at Mathias, he walked away towards the waiting Hitler Youth.

Mathias sighed. The anger seemed to have been replaced with dull resignation. "I'm staying."

Walter stared at him.

Fenstermacher smiled wryly. "Very well." He nodded. "You can join my section. We'll find you a rifle and an armband."

Mathias shook his head. "I'll take the rifle," he jerked his thumb at Fenstermacher's sleeve, "but no armband."

Fenstermacher shook his head in irritation. "You have to have one. Without it, you're just a civilian carrying a gun. Ivan will shoot you."

Mathias sorted. "You think they won't shoot me anyway?" He looked at Walter and his eyes were sad. "Shoot us all?" Then he turned his gaze away.

Fenstermacher again touched Mathias' sleeve. "All right," he said softly and turned and walked towards the waiting Volkssturm. Mathias stared after him, and then, without looking at Walter, followed.

Walter watched him go. "All right?" He turned at the gentle question and found Friedrich standing behind him, concern on his face.

Walter shrugged.

It was nearly an hour before John heard cart wheels. He went outside the field station tent, where he'd been sitting smoking, and saw a small farm wagon rattling up the track. The horse looked clapped-out; the driver, an elderly man puffing on a pipe, even more so. He wore the short woollen jacket and dark trousers typical of farmers all over Germany, but on his left sleeve was a Volkssturm armband, and on his head was a soft grey pillbox-shaped field cap, the type worn by German soldiers during the previous war. He drew the cart up alongside the tent and stared silently down at John with expressionless eyes sunk deep into a brown crinkled face.

Kurschat came out of the tent to stand next to John. He jerked his head forward in welcome at the old man. "Fürst." Then he jerked it back towards the interior of the tent. "One for the hospital."

Fürst nodded back and didn't move. Instead he began languidly refilling his pipe, and Kurschat tapped John gently on the shoulder and took him inside. John helped Kurschat lift Olé by his blanket into the back of the cart while Fürst looked on, smoking. When they were done, Fürst picked up the reins without any warning and jerked the cart into movement. John had to scramble to get on as he swung the cart around to face down the track. Settling himself next to Fürst, he glared at the old man, but still received no response. Fürst remained silent for virtually the whole journey down the road, now empty and silent, only venturing an occasional grunt when John tried to draw him into conversation. After a while John gave up, and instead settled for listening to the *clip clop* of the horse's hooves and the distant rumble of artillery, smoking an occasional cigarette and watching the flat pretty landscape passing. Here and there they passed men and boys in the fields, sitting or standing about foxholes and trenches doing what waiting soldiers did: smoking, eating, sleeping, or just staring eastwards. Some of those near the road called up questions as they passed, but John had little to tell them and Fürst didn't speak; didn't even acknowledge their presence.

Once, when the cart lurched across a particularly wide pothole and Olé let out a soft groan, John clambered into the back to check on the wounded man. He found Olé still completely unconscious and apparently none the worse for being bounced about.

After about an hour they came to a crossroads by a decrepit farm and turned onto a long, low causeway. Across it lay a barrier of oil drums filled with earth, staggered such that vehicles had to make a sharp right-angled turn to pass through. The barricade wouldn't stop an armoured vehicle, but anything lighter would have to slow down, and men would be unable to run through it for barbed wire had been looped between the drums. Trenches had been dug into the fields by it.

On the other side of the barricade was a 'Spanish rider': a long pole set between cruciform wooden beams, also wreathed in barbed wire. One end of it was fitted with a cart wheel which enabled it to be swung rapidly into place across the gap in the barricade, pivoting on another oil drum to which it was chained. This drum had a wooden post driven into the top with a board nailed to it, to which was attached a white poster saying in bold red letters: *'Panzerfausts and German soldiers are stronger than Red tanks! Heil Hitler!'*

The trenches were unmanned and there were no guards, but as they passed the farm John saw horses in the yard with rifles and sabres dangling from their saddles. Short swarthy men stood about them in German Army uniforms wearing round black fur hats.

Fürst spoke for the first time. "Cossacks," he muttered between teeth clenched about the stem of his pipe. "Ivans. *Hiwees.*"

John was startled and craned his head to look again as they passed. He'd heard about '*hiwees*': Red Army POWs who opted to do menial work for their captors in return for an easier life, but these were fighting men.

They clattered on towards the village John could see beyond the farm, the cracked tarmac of the road changing to cobblestones as they entered it. The cart rattled and shook alarmingly as they clattered past half-timbered houses, some with thatched roofs but most with the red tiles so characteristic of this part of rural Germany. Olé's head lolled with every bump, but his eyes remained closed and he made no sound. John clutched the bench beneath him to steady himself.

They came to the centre of the village, a small square fringed with old trees. On the corners, where four streets led in and out, the trees were half cut through near the base, ready to be dropped. Sandbags were piled up against the houses at ground level, obscuring the lower windows. Standing around by them in small groups, doing nothing much, were more soldiers, but these were all German. A corporal waved them down a side road towards a long, low stone building set back behind a waist high wall, which evidently once had railings to judge by holes along its top. They passed through one of two wide gaps in the wall and halted next to large double wooden doors. Carved into the crumbling stone lintel above them were the worn words: 'Völkische Hauptschule' and the date: '1869'.

Fürst scrambled down awkwardly. John saw how he moved his right leg; it didn't bend at all. Fürst noticed his gaze and tapped it. "Wood. Verdun."

John glanced at the ancient field cap on Fürst's head and nodded. "I'll get someone." He dismounted and headed for the school entrance while Fürst limped to the wall and sat down to puff on his pipe, his leg sticking out in front of him.

Before he could reach the doors, they banged outwards and a middle-aged orderly wearing a grubby white apron over a combat uniform emerged and halted in front of him. He peered past John at Olé. "Bring him in," the orderly commanded tersely and turned to go, but stopped when John raised his hand.

"I'll need help."

The orderly looked at him and then Fürst, his glance taking in the projected leg. He nodded and together they lifted Olé gently out of the cart. They left Fürst, his pipe finished, fixing a leather feed bag over the horse's muzzle and carried Olé on his blanket through the doors and down a long corridor. At the far end were more double doors, held open against the walls.

An army nurse stood in front of them in a blue-grey blouse and light grey skirt, a Red Cross armband on her left sleeve. Even in the gloom John could see that she was young and very petite: six inches shorter than he was, slender with blonde hair and a round face. Her voice, when she summoned them to follow her, was light and musical; her accent was Norwegian. She turned and they went past a hand written sign taped to one of the doors: 'Admissions.' Next to it was another: 'The darkest hour comes before the bright dawn. Herr Doctor J Goebbels.' John couldn't help smiling at the banality of it.

Beyond lay a small hall, with polished plank flooring and an elegant hammer-beam ceiling. The long space was crowded with wooden dining tables, the sort with folding metal legs. Down one side of the hall were half a dozen half-panelled doors clearly leading into classrooms. It reminded John of his primary school in London. It even had the same sort of admonitory plaque at the far end above a small stage, proclaiming in large gothic script, '*Ein Reich, Ein Volk, Ein Führer.*' John wondered what message had adorned the wall previously; in his school it had been, 'Expect Great Things from God; Attempt Great Things for God.' Below it had been a board listing the names of all those former pupils who had died for King and Country in the Great War. There was no such list here.

All the tables were empty and scrubbed white, and by each was an empty metal fire pail. On the stage and on more tables lining the walls were rolls of bandages, metal dishes, towels, an odd assortment of knives, and other implements that didn't look to John like surgical instruments.

They loaded Olé onto a table and the orderly fingered the brown tag tied to one of his buttonholes. "Burn." He began gently to undo the buttons.

"The usual," the nurse said. "Strip and wash first, please." She took the bucket and turned to John. "Are you staying?"

He nodded. "For a bit. Just to see he's all right."

She nodded back and handed him the bucket. Then she pointed to a door to the left of the stage. "Be useful, then. Hot water, soap, flannel and towel please."

Through the door he found a small changing room: washbasins and benches and iron wall hooks for hanging clothes were set at child height, low enough for young arms to reach. He paused for a moment, memories of his school in Stepney rising up. The smell of carbolic soap stirred them too; there was a stack of it at one end of the benches, the rest being covered in an assortment of thick towels and flannels. He helped himself and filled the bucket awkwardly from a tap set above a sink not designed for the purpose. Inevitably he slopped water on the floor and felt absurdly anxious lest some irate teacher burst in to admonition him.

Back in the hall, he found that the nurse had finished undressing Olé, and John was embarrassed at his friend's stark white nakedness on the table. Then he felt foolish for feeling that way. The nurse was matter-of-fact, taking the things from John and, with the orderly, gently wiping and dabbing.

John stepped back, feeling awkward, and was about to suggest that he go outside for a smoke when suddenly the nurse stopped. She was staring at the mulberry-coloured birthmark on the inside of Olé's left thigh. Her eyes widened and her free hand went to her mouth. John and the orderly looked at each other in surprise, and as they did so, Olé opened his eyes. He stared up at the nurse, blinked and smiled weakly.

"Mimmi," he croaked and half raised his hand. No one moved, then Olé's hand flopped back and he was once more asleep.

The wet towel fell to the floor; the orderly stepped forward.

"Mimmi?"

She shook her head and threw a bewildered, questioning look at John.

"Olé Hansen," he confirmed, "it's Olé Hansen."

She stared at him, then went to Olé's grubby clothes, folded neatly nearby, and took the tag laid on top of them. She peered closely at the script and for a moment closed her eyes. Then she put it down and went to lay a forefinger gently on Olé's cracked lips.

"*Ya, dyer er mai,* Olé," she whispered. Then she took his hand. "It's all right, Kurt." She smiled at the orderly. Then she looked at John. "Emilie Olafsdatter. Mimmi."

"John Marlow."

"*Ya. Enyelsk.* Olé told me." She held out her free hand, and in English added, "Pleezed to meet." Then she reverted to German. "You can go, Kurt." She squeezed Olé's hand gently and stroked his hair.

Kurt nodded. "I'll be in the storeroom if you need me, Mimmi." He headed for the door to the left of the stage, glancing back once at John.

When he'd gone, Mimmi smiled at John. "I met Olé in Oslo." She shook her heard wonderingly. "Hospital. After Olé was wounded in Finland, when they sent him home."

John remembered that wound: a splinter from a grenade. "He seems to make a habit of it," he muttered ruefully with a lopsided grin.

Mimmi smiled at John again, gently detached Olé's hand from hers and, fetching a blanket from one of the tables nearby, tucked it around him. Then she gestured for John to follow her to a small desk against one wall near the stage. She sat in one of the two folding canvas chairs which faced each other across it and invited him to sit in the other. For a moment she sat quietly, looking over at Olé, and then she seemed to gather herself and turned to John. Slowly, with frequent glances at Olé, she explained that she'd been a nurse in the military welfare hospital near the Akershus Fortress. When Olé was discharged from there and went back to work at his father's small garage, she'd transferred to another hospital to move in with him, but it didn't last.

"He was bored." She smiled sadly as she came to the end of her tale. "After the Germans came, he joined the SS. He'd been in the National Union anyway. Did you know that?"

John did. Olé had shown him his membership card the previous day when they were catching up on each other in the lorry. It didn't surprise him: Vidkun Quisling's far-right party was precisely the sort of organisation to appeal to Olé, just as Mosley's fascists had appealed to John.

"And you?" John asked.

"Me? I didn't want to lose Olé. I told him that wherever he was, I would be too." Her voice had more than a trace of wistfulness in it. "I volunteered as a nurse to join Norge. Became a Front Sister. We were in Russia together." She smiled ruefully. "We were only separated when he was posted to that training outfit. I didn't expect to see him again so soon." Her eyes moistened and she looked down and then wiped them on her sleeve. "He's been through a lot, you know."

"I expect you have too."

She shrugged.

"What will happen now?"

She sat back, took a deep breath and was suddenly the brisk nurse. "He'll be seen by the doctor. Then I expect they'll send him to Berlin to a proper hospital. We can't deal with his injuries here." She glanced across the hall once more.

"And you?"

"I have to stay here." She stared at John for a moment and then she was soft once more, wistful. "But please God, it'll be over soon."

John frowned. "We're not done yet."

She reached across the table to where his hands lay folded in front of him and tapped them. "If the Reds don't manage it, the Amees will. Nothing's going to stop them now. Better that it ends soon." She held his gaze. "We can get back together then, back home."

John didn't know what to say. He felt that he should rebuke her, should tell her not to be so defeatist, but he too glanced at Olé, naked under his blanket, and the words stuck in his throat.

A door banged and Kurt came into the hall with two steaming tin mugs. "Coffee. If you can call it that." He held one out to John, who shook his head.

"Not for me. Thanks." He stood. "I really have to go." He looked down at Mimmi. "I'm supposed to collect some supplies."

Kurt snorted and put the mugs on the table. "Supplies? Of *what?*"

Mimmi's tone was more sympathetic. "I'm sorry, John." She sipped her coffee and grimaced. "I don't know anything about that. We're very short."

"It was supposed to have been arranged." John felt a tinge of annoyance; surely they could spare something.

Mimmi shook her head slowly, a sad gesture of empathy.

Kurt was more explicit. "We're using torn bed sheets for bandages, half our medicines we got from the local vet and we're down to our last carton of morphine."

"Can't you spare *anything*?"

"Sorry." He didn't sound as if he meant it. "Anyway, I can't give out anything without a requisition form. Have you got one?"

John almost laughed. Stalin was at the gates of Berlin and still they wanted forms. Kurt must have seen the incredulity on John's face for now he sounded sheepish.

"Look, it's not me. If I let you just take stuff, I'll be in real trouble. You said an arrangement had been made. Why not see Doctor Zimmerman? He's in charge."

John nodded. "Right. Where is he?"

"I'll take you." Kurt drained his mug.

John smiled at Mimmi. "Take care of yourself."

She nodded. Then she stood and came around the table to kiss him briefly on his cheek. "You take care too," she urged. He smiled awkwardly.

As John followed him, Kurt grinned. "Lucky you. It's been a long time since a pretty girl kissed me."

John glanced back to where Mimmi was now standing once more by Olé, holding his hand, and felt sad.

Cheslav and Janko clattered down the rickety wooden steps into the cellar and found a long, low vaulted room. It was gloomy, lit only by the light from the door behind them and a row of very small windows set high along the wall. Below these was a long row of large beer barrels, each over a metre wide. Janko grinned at the sight, but when he turned the tap on the nearest nothing came out.

At the far end of the cellar, coal was piled against the wall. A few dusty slatted crates of the sort used to carry vegetables, two rusty old spades, a pick and a mattock lay nearby. Janko inspected the wall behind the pile of coal and pointed out that it was cleaner and newer than the other walls.

"Might be something behind it," he muttered, his eyes glittering at the prospect of hidden loot. They cleared a space and Janko hefted the pick. He spat on his palms and took a few experimental swings in the air, then drove it with great force into the exposed patch of wall. Sparks and shards of brick sprayed outwards and Cheslav stepped back hastily. After a couple more blows, Janko had made a hole as large as his hand and he began levering out the rest of the bricks using the handle.

"What's going on down here?" Lopakin clattered down the steps followed by half a dozen others.

"Found something." Janko levered out a large chunk of bricks and mortar, put down the pick, lit a match and peered inside. "Well, this is a nice find, Comrade Sergeant." He grinned and stepped back.

They all crowded forward, and by the light of Lopakin's torch Cheslav saw a small space. The back wall was lined from top to bottom with shelves thick with bottles, jars and stone crocks.

"Someone's been busy." Kolchok sounded appreciative of the bounty.

They stepped back as Janko hefted the pick once more. It was the work of a few minutes to knock out a hole big enough to let him scramble in and pass out the contents of the hidden store. Jars of pickled beetroots, gherkins, red cabbage, pickled cheeses, some tins and packets emerged and were shared out at Lopakin's direction. Each man got something, and some were set aside for those of the platoon not present.

Kolchok received a stone crock and jerked the cork lid off with his bayonet. The pungent smell of sauerkraut filled the cellar. He walked away, happily shovelling handfuls into his mouth. Others crammed themselves, but Cheslav carefully placed the two jars of pickled mixed vegetables he was allocated into his backpack.

Lopakin put the food he'd set aside into one of the empty crates and he and Janko carried it upstairs. The others followed, contently munching, but Kolchok stayed behind, pushing sauerkraut into his mouth as he walked along the line of barrels, placing his ear against each and kicking it.

Fascinated, Cheslav stood and watched and then stepped forward. When Kolchok kicked the fifth barrel he frowned, looked at Cheslav and then at the top of the steps, where Lopakin had reappeared and was watching them. Kolchok laid his hand on the barrel.

"Something here."

Lopakin tilted his head sceptically.

"I did a spell in a brewery, Comrade Sergeant." Kolchok sounded irritated. "You tap barrels to see whether the beer is ready. You develop an ear for it. This one's different to the others." He went along the rest of the row testing each, and when he'd finished he came back to the fifth. "Yes. Just this one." He went to get the pick. "Could be food. Or someone hiding."

Cheslav hefted his rifle. Certainly the barrel was big enough to hold a man; two or three, for that matter, and the farmhouse above the cellar had only recently been abandoned. When the platoon broke in they'd found the kitchen stove alight and the heavy iron kettle near it still hot.

Lopakin came down to stand to one side with Cheslav, slipping the sub-machine gun from his shoulder. Cheslav suddenly felt nervous. He'd heard stories of fanatical SS or Hitler Youth appearing from hiding, throwing grenades and shooting; suicidal, but some seemed to prefer to die fighting.

"Go ahead," Lopakin nodded.

Kolchok swung the pick and split the end of the barrel with one blow, the planks falling with a clatter to the stone flagged floor. An intense aroma of malt wafted outwards. The deep interior was hidden in shadow, but Cheslav could just make out a single dark shape at the back.

"*Hander hock*," Kolchok bellowed in an accent so bad that Cheslav winced. Then Kolchok said more softly, "*Komm*," and beckoned theatrically.

For a very long moment, nothing happened. Cheslav thought he could hear harsh breathing, faint and laboured, but perhaps it was his own. He felt his trigger finger tighten with each passing second, and conscious of it, he eased off the pressure. Kolchok had stepped away from the opening and quietly picked up his own rifle, but he held it loosely, and Lopakin, although he kept the muzzle of his weapon aimed into the barrel, had his finger off the trigger; the *papashay* sub-machine gun could be light on the trigger and might go off by mistake.

Suddenly, the dark shape stirred and a boy emerged, blinking. He was dressed in an army uniform but had no weapons. He squatted on the edge of the barrel, hands raised, frightened eyes darting anxiously between the three of them.

"Out," said Kolchok sharply and jerked his thumb.

The boy dropped awkwardly to the floor, straightened nervously and coughed several times. Cheslav noticed how clean he was. Despite being crammed into the barrel, his uniform was unmarked. Creases were pressed into his serge trousers, his belt and buckle were polished and his boots were shiny. He looks like he's just come on parade, Cheslav wondered. Or is going to a dance. The thought relaxed him and he put up his rifle. "He's harmless." Kolchok nodded and put down his own rifle.

"Take him upstairs." Lopakin slung his papashay, his sub-machine gun, back over his shoulder. "Send him to Company."

Cheslav stepped forward and quickly patted the boy all over. He found nothing of interest apart from his soldbuch: the record book every German soldier carried; that and a bar of Stollwerck chocolate. Judging by the worn appearance of its brown and gold wrapping it might have been pre-war. He hesitated and then tucked the chocolate back into the boy's tunic pocket; he'd not yet reached the stage of stealing sweets from children, and anyway, he had the pickles. Then he tugged at the boy's lapel and they all followed Lopakin out of the cellar, Kolchok and Cheslav at the back.

They ushered their captive into the main room of the farmhouse and Lopakin went to find Bartashevich. The platoon had made themselves comfortable: beautifully upholstered chairs had been pushed together to make beds; wooden furniture had been broken up to fuel a large blue and white-tiled stove which lay against one wall; packs and helmets lay all about; and weapons, those not being cleaned, were stacked along the walls, oily barrels smearing the elegant flock wallpaper. Emptied cans of food and packs of tea lay in a heap in one corner by a gleaming walnut upright piano.

The boy halted, clearly horrified at the sight. Some of the platoon glanced at him, others stared, and a few glared, but no one said anything.

"Here." Kolchok, looking around, shoved the boy towards the door which faced them across the room. Beyond lay a small library and more mess. Someone had pulled all the books off the shelves and thrown them in a heap. Cheslav hated to see books treated this way, and these were particularly fine, bound in leather or cloth. Some even had gilt tooling. A fine old oak desk stood in a corner. "Sit," said Kolchok and pushed the boy gently onto the small chaise longue next to it. The boy slumped down at one end and turned his face away. Cheslav saw tears run, and Kolchok patted his shoulder gently before leaving the room.

Cheslav slung his rifle over his shoulder and wandered around, picking up volumes from the floor and examining them. The titles were all in German, a cosmopolitan selection: Balzac, Kipling, Tolstoy, Goethe, Ibsen, Shakespeare and many others. They reminded him of the teacher that he and Leonid had admired so much at the Factory Apprentice School they'd both attended. A former lecturer, he'd loved books with an indiscreet passion which led him from the renowned Moscow State University to the Gulag Camp at Vishlag when his bourgeois tastes became suspect. Later, he'd been sent to Cheslav's Apprentice School to re-establish his proletarian credentials. Cheslav and Leonid learned a great deal from him about literature, even more than they'd picked up from Mr Gerstein. There were some things not even the dictatorship of the proletariat changed, and one was a Russian's love for the written word. 'Words are life': it was something Cheslav remembered Mr Gerstein had admonished him and Leonid with whenever they slacked in their reading. According to Judaism, it was the Word that gave life to clay and created the world. Mr Gerstein had told them that too.

Looking at the wreck of the library, Cheslav was dismayed. His feelings must have shown, for the boy, glancing at him, muttered, "You hate it too, don't you?"

The boy stiffened in surprise when Cheslav turned to him and said in clumsy German, "Books shouldn't be treated like this." The boy then stared at him and half smiled.

"Where did you learn German like that? It's not bad." Cheslav smiled wryly at the off-handedness of the compliment. He didn't answer and the boy continued wistfully, "This is my home. I've been away though, studying." He met Cheslav's gaze and sat straighter.

Cheslav wondered why the boy, an enemy, a stranger, should tell him this. He sat down on the edge of the desk and, laying his rifle against it, took out a pack of German Aktivs and lit two of the cigarettes. He offered one and the boy nodded gratefully and took it. They sat in silence for a while, smoking and listening to the buzz of conversation and the clatter of activity coming through the open door. Someone started playing the piano badly. Cheslav thought that the tune might be 'Korobeiniki', an old Russian folk song, but he couldn't be sure because the player was so awful. There was much laughter as the player tried several times to get it right, finally swearing profusely, and they heard the piano cover being slammed down. The boy grimaced.

"Russians like music," Cheslav commented wryly.

The boy muttered something inaudible, and then, seeing Cheslav's quizzical expression, said, "That's not music. Well, it *might* be if it were played properly."

"You know music?"

"I'm a music student."

"How old are you?" Cheslav asked him softly.

"Seventeen."

"Seventeen," Cheslav repeated to himself in Russian. He was older than Cheslav had guessed.

The boy sat back and ran his hand through his neatly combed dark hair. "I used to play that piano a lot." Then he chuckled; the sound lacked mirth.

"What's funny?"

"My father, you see. He scraped and saved to get me to the Liszt School of Music. It's in Weimar. The best in Europe." His voice swelled, and for a moment Cheslav was reminded of Leonid. So proud to be accepted for the Apprentice School; proud again when Cheslav joined the same school four years later. "I worked my fingers off on that piano to qualify. My father hated to hear music played badly. Now…" The boy shrugged.

They sat in silence, both remembering, and then the moment was ended by Lopakin opening the door.

"Here's our little hideaway. Behaving himself?"

He didn't seem to want an answer, but Cheslav gave him one anyway. "Yes, Comrade Sergeant,"

Lopakin nodded. "Good. The captain wants him to go straight to battalion. Keep hold of him until I find out where they are." He looked impassively at the boy who looked away, then he left, closing the door quietly behind him.

Cheslav smiled reassuringly. "It's all right." He could hear another dire attempt being made to play the piano and more ribald comments. Cheslav looked at the boy's woeful face and got an idea. "Come on." He ushered the boy through the door.

Gathered about the piano, the platoon were drinking tea and vodka as Beridze toyed with the keys. They all looked at Cheslav as he entered, propelling the boy forward. "This one can *play*, he says."

Beridze stood up quickly, looking relieved. The boy hesitated, not meeting any of the looks he received, some curious, some hostile. Cheslav gripped his shoulder and pushed him to the piano. The boy paused, and then seated himself. He laid his hands lightly upon the keys, ran his fingertips along them with his eyes closed, so gently no sound came. Then he began to play softly, eyes still closed, a medley of slow tunes by classical composers. Cheslav recognised some of them: Tchaikovsky, Shostakovich, Borodin, Mussorgsky.

Clever, he admired, he's playing Russians.

There were one or two snide remarks at first, some muttered

hostility, but after a little while the music worked its magic and everyone fell silent. When occasionally they spoke amongst themselves, they did so in low voices.

Talent, noted Cheslav. He's got real talent.

The boy seemed lost in the music, his eyes remaining closed for the most part, his fingers deftly gliding and dancing across the keys. It was a beautiful sound, meant to enchant, and it did. Sitting in his despoiled home, surrounded by his enemies, the boy wove a spell of peace.

Kolchok came to sit by Cheslav; he too was silent. Then the music began to range more widely; more composers appeared, even some Germans, and then a few tunes which, by their rhythm, Cheslav guessed were folk songs. By now it didn't seem to matter what the boy played; he did it well and everyone listened.

It went on for some time. Cheslav settled himself against one wall and let himself sink into the music. But it didn't last. Low at first, then growing insistently into intrusion impossible to ignore, came the noise of engines and the rattle and squeal of tracks. The boy stopped, his eyes fixed on the window which faced into the farm yard; it was the other side of the house from the road which ran adjacent. Kolchok and Cheslav rose and made their way outside and around the house.

Stretched along the verge on the other side of the road was a column of armoured vehicles, motionless but with engines idling. Kolchok took a swig from the tin mug of vodka he'd brought with him. "Bare-arsed Ferdinands," he grunted. Cheslav smiled at the nickname. They were SU-76 self-propelled guns. They had no turret; based on a tank chassis, their main gun was fixed in a boxy superstructure, which made engaging targets to the side a slow business for the whole vehicle had to be turned. Despite this, their guns were very effective, firing both high-explosive and anti-tank rounds. Infantrymen were always glad to see them, but their crews were not always glad to serve in them, he knew, for their armour was very thin and the superstructure was open-topped, making them vulnerable to anything dropped from above, including shells.

Some of the crews had dismounted and were relieving themselves alongside their vehicles. One made his way across the road towards them. On his dusty, oil-stained black coveralls he wore the rank of senior sergeant and the badges of an artilleryman. Underneath the enclosing padded hat all armoured crew wore, his haggard face was smudged and his dark eyes bloodshot; he exuded an air of exhaustion. To Cheslav he seemed, even before he spoke, brittle.

"Comrades." The sergeant's voice was dry. Kolchok held out his mess tin and the sergeant swallowed the entire remaining contents in one gulp. He rubbed a grimy sleeve across chapped lips. "Fucking excellent," he said. He nodded at Cheslav. "Sebelev."

"Corporal Barakovski." Cheslav stiffened in the approved way. Sebelev grinned at the formality, returned the tin to Kolchok and scratched underneath his hat, revealing coal black hair wet with sweat. "So where's your boss?"

"The lieutenant is at Company." Cheslav jerked his thumb down the road, past the farmhouse in the direction which Lopakin had earlier told him the major and his headquarters' group were to be found.

"Right." Sebelev said no more but turned abruptly and trotted back across the road to speak with another black-clad artillery man, this one wearing officers' shoulder boards. After a few moments, the officer set off down the road and Sebelev re-joined them. "Any more of that vodka, Comrades?" he asked.

"Inside," Kolchok grunted, and Cheslav caught the tone. Kolchok didn't like the artilleryman.

Sebelev seemed unaware. "Lead the way then," he said cheerily and nodded to the house. Then, when Kolchok didn't move, Sebelev strode towards it on his own.

"That one's so far up his own arse he's bent in two," Kolchok muttered and Cheslav grinned as they followed the dusty black figure.

Sebelev had paused just inside, in the hall which led right through the house. Music drifted through a door to the right, the one which

led into the room with the piano. He stopped and turned to them, a frown creasing his forehead.

"What the fuck is that?"

"Piano," said Cheslav. He cocked an ear. "Bach."

"Bach?"

"Bach."

"Fucking Fritz music?" Sebelev seemed outraged.

"A prisoner, Comrade Senior Sergeant," explained Cheslav.

Sebelev said nothing but looked at Cheslav steadily for a moment, then he went in. Kolchok glanced back at Cheslav, raised his eyes heavenward and followed him.

Cheslav decided that he would remain outside and, keeping the door open so that he could hear the piano, he lit another cigarette. As he drew in the soothing smoke, the Bach ended abruptly and Kolchok came out of the room with a bottle and two mugs.

"Comrade Artillerist doesn't like Fritzes at all," he said. Moments later a different tune wafted through the door.

"Tchaikovsky again," Cheslav observed.

"Music your thing, eh?" Kolchok slopped vodka into the mugs.

"Not really. We had a good teacher when I was a boy and he insisted we listen to a lot of the old classics. I recognise some of them, that's all."

"Music's good," observed Kolchok. "My papa, he played the balalaika a treat."

"Do you play?"

Kolchok laughed abruptly. "Hah! Me? No. I listen." The notes of the piano meandered through a melody and Kolchok smiled for a moment. "Papa used to say, 'music knows no country.'" He swallowed more vodka. "He was right."

"What did your father do?" ventured Cheslav cautiously: Kolchok was known for reticence as far as his background was concerned.

"Farmer. Like me." Kolchok's lips twisted in a partial smile. "Good one. We had land and good neighbours, mostly. That was before…"

He didn't need to finish; Cheslav could finish for him: before the Revolution.

"We had land too," said Cheslav.

Kolchok looked at him for a moment and then nodded. "Look at this," he said, jerking his head back around the courtyard. "Big place. Bigger than any in *our* village; bigger even than the landlord's agent. Nice furniture. Books. Barns over there." He jerked his head again. "Maybe cows, pigs, goats, chickens. There's an orchard behind that barn." Another jerk. "What did the Fritzes want from *us?*"

Cheslav shook his head. "I don't know."

They sat down next to the open door with their backs against the wall, and for quite some while sat silently together, sipping the vodka and listening to the music. Occasionally they heard motor vehicles passing on the road, or the sounds of horse-drawn carts. Overhead the sky was a glorious pale blue and Cheslav felt content.

Some of Sebelev's comrades had abandoned their vehicles and lit fires in the courtyard, a couple busying themselves emptying the contents of various tins and jars into one of the fires. Bottles were passed around, but no conversation: they all seemed too tired, and several curled up on the cold cobbled ground, asleep.

The sight of the cooking made Cheslav feel hungry and he was glad when Beridze appeared with some unlabelled olive-green cans, rectangular and round-edged. Kolchok opened one using the small key attached to the top.

"Second Front." He muttered the nickname for the American processed meat called spam. He dug lumps of it out with his spoon while Cheslav splashed more vodka into mugs.

Beridze was in a chatty mood. "He's good, that boy." Beridze liked music. His skill with the panduri was well known in the company; the panduri was regarded as Georgia's national instrument as the classical guitar was Spain's. He'd brought one with him from his home in Georgia and often played it for them, but Beridze was more than just an occasional player. He kept telling them how he hoped to become a music teacher after the war and join Georgia's

National Folk Orchestra, like his father. Panduri. Every time he told them about his ambition, he'd pull out a grimy photograph of a middle-aged man in folk costume.

"After war, I big man with music."

Kolchok snorted and opened another can of Spam. "'Chickens are counted in autumn', boy."

Beridze smiled at the quotation guilelessly, and the sweet sound of the piano drifted down the hall and across the courtyard as they ate and drank and listened.

It was late afternoon before Leonid's platoon moved on. All the routes were heavily congested: men and materiel moving west; prisoners and wounded moving east. When the battalion was finally allocated a road, they could only use one lane of two: returning traffic used the other. By dusk they were only a few kilometres from the Seelow Heights when Gushenko ordered a halt by another farm, this one not ruined. A complex of outbuildings set on cobbled courtyards and linked by concrete roadways surrounded a substantial house. It was the size of Leonid's village and he marvelled at the scale and quality of it. While Agranenko settled the platoon into a barn, which on its own would have graced a collective, Leonid went to explore. Behind the house he found several parked T-34 tanks, the ones with the long guns. Two bare-headed figures in black stood by the rear of one, peering under a raised hatch into the engine compartment. They straightened and turned as he approached; the shorter of the two grinned.

"Comrade," said Trofimova from behind a cloud of cigarette smoke. She was, if anything, even grubbier than when he'd last seen her. Her companion was a taller blonde girl of startlingly youthful and delicate appearance only slightly spoiled by oil smudges across her face.

"Come and have a drink." Trofimova dropped the spanner she was carrying onto the tank with a clang. "Keep at it, Valya," she told the girl and guided Leonid by the arm towards a door in the farmhouse.

Inside it was a mess. Broken jars and boxes of food had been pulled off the shelves of a pantry and onto the floor. Two male tankists were tidying up. "Pigs," Trofimova commented, "wreckers. They could have left some for the rest of us. It's almost counter-revolutionary."

Leonid looked at her, startled, and she grinned. Then she led him across a short hallway into another room, this an office by the look of the filing cabinets. An ammunition box lay on the only desk. A map of the farm was pinned on the wall, boundaries outlined in red.

Careless to leave that for us. Then Leonid dismissed the thought; what difference would it make? The terrain thereabouts was as flat as a pancake and Berlin could hardly be missed, a dark smudge on the horizon.

Trofimova sat on the desk and gestured to the swivel chair behind it. "Here, Comrade." As Leonid settled himself, she flipped up the lid of the box: it was full of tin mugs and an impressive collection of bottles. She splashed a generous measure of amber liquid into one of the mugs, gave it to him and filled another. "To home."

Leonid sipped, but Trofimova emptied her mug in one go and refilled it immediately. "Brandy. French." She drank half of the refill and placed the mug in front of her.

"The battalion's in the other buildings. Major Zeldin's command post is in the stable if you want to talk to him."

"I already have." Trofimova emptied her mug. "I spoke to him earlier. We agreed that your guys don't come in the house."

He raised his eyebrows and then frowned.

She eyed him coolly, emptied the mug and stood up. "Come with me, Comrade."

He followed her down the hall through a stout door and down some steps into a cellar. Lamps on beams and boxes cast a sickly yellow light through fuggy gloom. Blankets hanging from ropes separated the area into cubicles; where the blankets were drawn back, Leonid saw rough and ready beds made up of bales of straw wrapped in more blankets. The cellar was full of women, all, he guessed, in their twenties or thirties, dressed in men's clothes. A couple wore farm labourer's overalls. Some drank; there were a lot of bottles to be seen. Some smoked; the air was thick with the smell of tobacco and the oily stink of the lamps. One woman was making herself up, applying lipstick while a companion brushed her hair. It was a scene of domesticity which jarred Leonid. There'd been a low buzz of conversation when they had entered; it paused and all eyes were on Leonid as Trofimova led him down. Then the conversation resumed, and Leonid realised the women were speaking Russian.

Trofimova led him to a thin black-haired woman in a patched cotton shirt, threadbare corduroy trousers and heavy labourers' boots. Leonid thought that she could be pretty, but her face was pinched, its paleness accentuated by bright carmine lipstick. He saw that her skin had been roughened by wind and there were deep lines of exhaustion around her eyes.

"Tasha." Trofimova smiled gently and inclined her head towards Leonid. "Comrade Barakovski."

"Comrade." Natasha held out her hand and he shook it very gently, fearful that he might snap something.

"Tasha and the girls were forced labourers," explained Trofimova. "We found them locked in here. They were rounded up in," she turned her head, "when was it?"

"Minsk, 1942." Natasha's voice was as thin as she was.

Over three years, wondered Leonid. Three. He couldn't think of anything to say.

"We're going to keep the girls here until we can ship 'em home." Trofimova nodded at Natasha, who smiled weakly back.

Leonid looked around the cellar, tried to smile at Natasha, failed and drew in a deep breath. He could almost taste the weariness.

Trofimova's expression was neutral. "Thank you, Tasha," she said and led Leonid back up the steps.

As they left, Trofimova kept her voice low. "Tasha was the leader. Kept 'em together. She's worn out, poor cow."

"Tortured?"

"No, just worked too fucking hard, and shit rations," she grunted, "like the rest of us." Leonid didn't know whether that was another quip, so he kept quiet. She took him back to the office and topped up the mugs. "They've had a fucking rough time." She looked at him steadily as she drank. "So, you keep your boys away from the house, all right? Zeldin agreed."

For a moment it didn't sink in, and then he realised what she was saying and his face burned.

"Look, Comrade Lieutenant," she shook her head slowly, "no offence, but your guys are just *guys*. I'd bet some of them haven't seen a woman from home for years. And these girls, well they're desperate for a friendly face. They're weak as kittens. No real fight in 'em."

"You're not suggesting…"

She cut off his protest with a wave of her free hand. "I'm not saying your boys *would*, but better not to tempt them, right?"

"They wouldn't touch a hair on their heads," he protested, but as he said it he knew how lame it sounded.

Now she was steely. "Girls get raped all over. Young, old." She shook her head again. "When we got to Germany, the political officer told me that he couldn't give a fuck what our boys do to Germans. And if it's collective, he said, it's socialism in action." She took a deep breath, set her face. "Your guys can do what the fuck they like to Fritzes as far as I'm concerned, but no one touches these girls."

He looked away, unable to find a reply.

She regarded him critically for a moment. Then she sighed, a long, low, tired sound. "We went through a little town on the way here. First big place we got to in Germany. Küstrin. Let me tell you about it."

Tanya and Klara got back to the apartment building just as the air raid sirens began to wail. Tanya didn't relish the prospect of spending another night in the cellar, but she made her way below stairs only to find that the little alcove behind the blanket was empty: Mrs Körtig was not there.

"I'll fetch her," Tanya muttered to no one in particular and headed up the steps past a sour-faced Mrs Boldt.

Outside the Körtigs's door Tanya hesitated; perhaps she should leave her alone. As she hesitated, bombs crashed down in the distance, one after the other, *thump, thump, thump*; eight in all, then silence. She took a deep breath to steady herself and rapped twice. There was no response and she rapped again, calling out, "Mrs Körtig."

"Go away, Mrs Boldt."

Tanya smiled wryly. "It's me, Tanya Klarkova." After a moment she heard footsteps and the door opened a crack. Mrs Körtig peered at her and then stepped back to let her in.

In the elegant living room a man's clothes lay neatly folded and stacked on the walnut dining table. Next to them was a photograph of the Körtigs standing on the steps of a church: he young and serious in a suit; she young and serious in calf-length dress and absurdly flowered hat. A man's shoes were lined up in pairs under the table on the pink paisley Persian carpet.

"The sirens," Tanya said, unnecessarily for their loud wail was still insistent.

Mrs Körtig said nothing but pulled out one of the dining chairs from under the table and sat heavily upon it.

"Please."

She looked up at Tanya, eyes glistening, and then she shook her head slightly and wiped away the single tear the motion had dislodged.

Feeling rather helpless, Tanya said again, "The sirens…" but as she said it they stopped. She pulled out another chair and sat in the sombre silence, facing Mrs Körtig across the stack of clothes.

"I don't know what to do with them." Mrs Körtig gently brushed the suit jacket lying on the top of the pile. "He's very particular about his clothes."

"Why don't you keep them, at least for a while?"

"No. It's bad luck."

Tanya nodded: it was.

"In any case," Mrs Körtig took a deep breath, "he hates waste." She picked up the photograph and looked at it for a moment. Then she took it to the walnut side table which lay along one wall and placed it amongst several others. She turned and attempted a smile. "Tea?"

"But…"

Mrs Körtig cut her off with a wave of her hand. "I am not going to spend the night down there. I shall remain here. You may go."

Tanya shook her head. "No. I'll stay." Then, glancing at the wedding photograph, "If you want me to."

Mrs Körtig nodded. "Tea, then. Come and talk to me while I make it."

Tanya stood at the doorway of the tiny kitchen, hardly larger than a large wardrobe, as Mrs Körtig busied herself about her elderly Bosch stove. As she opened and closed cupboards, extracted a tea pot and tea caddy, cups and tray, she chatted in a low monotone. Not once did she look at Tanya.

"It was a shock, you see. In the last war, I got used to the idea that he might not come home, although I prayed for him every day. But this is so…"

She stopped abruptly, spooned tea and poured boiling water into the pot. Then she pulled a bottle of brandy from a cupboard and set it on the tray with two small and very elegant crystal tumblers. There was an inscription on the side of the glasses, 'June 8, 1913', and a royal crest: an eagle surmounted by a crown. On the bird's breast, a shield with another eagle. How German, Tanya observed. An anniversary of some sort.

She followed Mrs Körtig back to the table as the sirens wailed again, this time sounding the all clear. There'd been no more bombs; not yet.

Some of the crews of the self-propelled guns moved into the farmhouse to join Sebelev, bringing with them a gift: German wine. Bottles liberated, they said, from an old house. 'Marcobrunner', it said on the labels, and it was good. The wine was welcome, but some of the artillerists stayed to drink it and Cheslav wished that they hadn't. At first they were good natured, swapping banter and making suggestions for tunes, but after a while the mood soured and they refused to let the boy stop playing. When he wilted, evidently tired, and raised his fingers from the keyboard, Sebelev slapped his face. Janko intervened but was told to mind his own fucking business. Cheslav wondered about fetching Bartashevich, but officers were nowhere to be seen, and anyway were usually reluctant to intervene in disputes between lower ranks when they didn't directly affect operations. Soldiers' fights were best left to soldiers. There was, it seemed, nothing to be done, and rather than watch the boy's abuse, Cheslav left.

Beridze had lit a fire outside in a bucket around the base of which were punched holes. For a while he, Cheslav, Kolchok and Janko sat quietly, drinking some of the Marcobrunner. Then, one by one, they wrapped themselves in their greatcoats and went to sleep, but not Cheslav. Instead, he fed the fire and listened to the piano and the increasingly raucous encouragement. The notes became more and more erratic and the playing slower. Cheslav was sure that he heard the same piece of Shostakovich four times. Then the playing stopped, and, after a while, Cheslav went anxiously to investigate. After all, he'd been ordered by Lopakin to keep an eye on the boy.

He still sat at the piano, nursing his hands under his armpits. Everyone else seemed asleep or slumped in drunken somnolence; everyone, that is, except for Sebelev. He stood by the piano, swaying slightly, and raised a half-empty bottle in a mock salute as Cheslav came in. The air was sour with sweat, and drink, and fear.

"Play," Sebelev slurred at the boy and prodded him hard. "Fucking play, Fritz!"

The boy looked at Cheslav miserably and he took a step forward, but the glare on Sebelev's face stopped him; that and the pistol lying on top of the piano.

The boy turned back to the keyboard.

"Still going strong, eh?"

Cheslav turned and saw in the hallway the artillery lieutenant who earlier had gone in search of Zeldin.

"Commander?"

"Let's see how long he can keep it up, eh?" The lieutenant sounded jolly as if he was watching a children's party game.

Cheslav frowned. "I don't…"

"It's a bet, Corporal. My men have taken bets on how long he can keep playing. Just a little bit of entertainment. Care to place one?"

"I…"

"Thought not." The lieutenant took off his padded hat and unbuttoned the top of his overall. He stank. "Well, get on with it," he said, smiling at the boy; a smile which sent a chill through Cheslav.

Sebelev held out his bottle, but the lieutenant waved it away and sat down in a nearby armchair, moving several empty bottles onto the floor to do so. The boy laid his hands gingerly on the keyboard and began once more to play, his lower lip gripped in his teeth. Cheslav stared, and then, when the lieutenant raised his eyebrows at him, he left.

How much longer? he wondered, and then what? Suddenly, Cheslav felt very alone.

Tajidaev sat in the barn with Leonid, Agranenko and Rybczak, feeding the fire he'd lit in the metal bucket with very small pieces of fencing. Around them fires glowed in other containers or burned directly on the slab floor of the barn. Leonid smiled at the sight. We're tinkers, he mused. It reminded him of the wandering Roma who'd come to the village each summer in horse-drawn caravans, bartering things they'd made in exchange for food. Theirs was an age-old way of life which suited everyone, Roma and villager alike, but they stopped coming one year and no one knew why. He'd missed them, for he liked to listen to their stories of other places, and he loved their music. His mother too missed them; she liked to consult the fortune tellers, but his father had disapproved. Leonid remembered those days and felt a little sad.

Agranenko deftly plucked lice from the greatcoat laid across his knees and threw them to flare in the fire.

"Bye-bye, little partisans," murmured Rybczak, seated on Leonid's left. Leonid had never been able to work out why they were so nicknamed; partisans were supposed to be on *their* side, weren't they? "Little bastards, eh?" Rybczak smiled morosely. "Still, as the saying goes, 'who wants the heat, must endure the smoke.' No getting around it, the coat keeps *you* warm as well as them."

"Thank you, Comrade," Agranenko sighed, "for those words of wisdom." He stood, shook the coat above the fire and shrugged it on. Glancing at Leonid, he smiled slightly. "We need some ants."

Leonid shook his head in puzzlement.

"Best way to get rid of lice." Rybczak plucked at his own coat but seemed to find nothing. "Put your clothes on a nest. They eat the little bastards."

"I see." Leonid wondered if he was being teased.

Agranenko sat down again. "I don't suppose you have any handy?"

Rybczack shook his head morosely. "No, but I can swap some of my partisans for yours if you'd like a change."

Agranenko shook his head. "Keep them. I'm used to mine."

Leonid smiled, then his smile faded as his glance took in one of the tankists playing cards nearby with Babich and Ivanova. He thought of what Trofimova had told him earlier.

"I always wanted to be a tankist," commented Rybczak, his eyes following Leonid's gaze.

Agranenko snorted. "Steel coffins."

"Better than walking. What do you say, Comrade Lieutenant?" When Leonid didn't answer, he repeated the question.

"Sorry?" Leonid turned his head towards him.

Rybczak and Agranenko looked at him questioningly; Tajidaev poked the fire.

"Sorry," repeated Leonid, "I was thinking."

"Bad idea," muttered Rybczak and reached down to the vodka bottle at his feet.

Agranenko's gaze was still fixed on Leonid.

"It was something she told me. Trofimova." Leonid hesitated for a moment and then felt he had to tell someone. It had been gnawing at him, and perhaps the vodka they'd been drinking would make it easier, so he related Trofimova's tale about the German city of Küstrin through which she'd passed; told them about the looting, the people shot out of hand for no reason, and about the rape.

"I couldn't believe it."

"I could," murmured Rybczak. Agranenko shot him a sharp look. "Look," he leaned forward, "just remember what the Fritzes have done. People want to get back at them."

"Women too?"

"Sure. What do you expect? Fuck 'em." Rybczak sounded amused. When Agranenko stared flintily at him, he shrugged and drank more vodka.

"War is a bad business." Agranenko picked up a chair leg and poked savagely at the fire, a gush of sparks making Tajidaev jerk back. He looked at Agranenko reproachfully.

"But she seemed to approve. Well, maybe not approve." Leonid corrected himself. "She didn't condemn it, and she's a woman."

Agranenko shook his head. "She's a soldier, she's seen things. When she gets home she'll probably have ten kids, grow into a fat babushka, sing sentimental songs and cry over sad stories and puppies, but not now; not here."

Leonid looked into the fire. "You know, when I left her she was washing her face, combing her hair and putting on lipstick like she was at home."

Agranenko smiled. "All women carry lipstick, didn't you know?"

Leonid nodded: he did. His mother would go to remarkable efforts to get it even during the terrible food shortages and despite official disapproval of makeup as un-communist: a bourgeois affectation. She'd wear it at home, away from prying eyes; many women did. Even at the Front women carried lipstick in their packs; it seemed to be an essential part them, of their femininity, and was one of the last things they'd do without. They'd put up with dirt and lice, with being cold and the wet, with daily danger, but they'd *not* do without lipstick.

Rybczak drank from the bottle and held it out to Agranenko,

who took it. and said, "Even Comrade Trofimova likes to remind herself she's not a man."

"Difficult for her."

They all smiled at Rybczak's comment. Agranenko drank some more and held it out to Tajidaev, who refused it so Rybczak took it.

It's fucking freezing here. My arse is cold." He wriggled and frowned. "Any more vodka?"

"Trust you to cheer us up, Rybczak." Agranenko sounded irritated.

"What's there to be cheery about?"

Tajidaev leaned forward suddenly and jabbed with his finger. He seemed exasperated. "You live. Thank gods."

"Gods!" Rybczak was not impressed. "What fucking gods?"

"What mean?" Tajidaev now seemed angry. "What gods? All round you. You stupid? You not see? You grateful you live." It was a long speech by Tajidaev's standards, and for a moment they looked at him in surprise.

"Grateful?" Rybczak's voice was softer, but still there was an edge to it. "Grateful? I was lucky, that's all. Most of the men I was with in that lousy punishment battalion *didn't* live. I did. Nothing to do with gods." He cast about and found another bottle behind him. "Life is shit."

Tajidaev narrowed his eyes. "Life no shit."

"What, then? Why isn't it?" He opened the bottle and drank. Tajidaev looked blankly at Rybczak for a moment, and then suddenly he grinned.

"Horses."

"Horses?"

"Horses."

Rybczak stared at him, then stood suddenly. "Horses!" He stomped away, taking the bottle with him.

Leonid opened his mouth to call after him and then closed it when Agranenko spoke.

"Best leave it, Lieutenant."

"Is he all right?"

"One of his moods. It'll pass."

Leonid nodded, thinking of what he'd been told about Rybczak: sent to a punishment battalion for forging ration cards. He'd been in the Leningrad siege. The son of a Party member, he'd been named Vladlen, short for Vladimir Lenin. He was one of the privileged Party elite, but it hadn't saved him, nor his family whose ration cards were denied entirely after he'd been arrested. Agranenko had told Leonid about them and their fate: ironically they'd starved to death while Rybczak survived the punishment battalion. He's entitled to bad moods if anyone is, Leonid observed silently and poked the fire. "Any more vodka?" he asked.

SIX

Dawn found the detachment tucked amongst the cluster of warehouses around a railway marshalling where they'd arrived just after midnight, and where Major Berg, it seemed, decided they'd gone far enough. It had been a tedious journey to get there, driving for hours along tracks and minor roads, first west towards Berlin, then east, then north and finally west once more. No one seemed to know where they were going or why, and John had begun to suspect that they were lost, or at least uncertain as to their destination, when they finally halted.

When dawn broke, he, Kaarle and Greger went outside to relieve themselves. Parked in the sidings he saw two railway cars in the livery of the *Berliner Verkehrsbetriebe*, the Berlin Transport Company, and on the distant horizon a dark grey smudge which must be the outskirts of Berlin. It was a shock to realise that they'd retreated so far west.

Back inside they settled to a breakfast of sorts, doled out by the cooks from the dustbin on the far side of the warehouse. They'd lit a fire on the concrete floor and were stewing something thick. John picked up his mess tin and went to get his portion. He sniffed at it suspiciously as he settled himself on his pack and tried to get comfortable: it smelled sour and vaguely meaty.

"Lorelai again," he said, and tasting it found it to be bland but not unpleasant. Kaarle grinned at him and John bent to eat.

His head shot up again when a voice snapped out a command.

"Pay attention!" The low murmur of conversation and the clatter of utensils in mess tins died away. Ridderstolpe stood in the doorway, hands on hips. "Comrades, we're short of fuel." Someone chuckled loudly but Ridderstolpe didn't react. "We're likely to be here for a while so make the most of your little holiday." He started to go and then turned back again. "Well it is supposed to be a holiday. It's the Führer's birthday, Comrades."

Sundberg came to join them. "Happy fucking birthday, Adolf," he said, sitting down and pulling out a cigarette packet. He didn't offer it around. "And many, *many* more." The comment was pointed and Greger looked at him quizzically. "Because if this is the bugger's last," Sundberg observed sombrely, "we're all in the shit!"

Greger glanced around nervously. "Keep your voice down."

"Why? Everyone knows we're for it."

John shifted uncomfortably. Sundberg peered at him with narrowed eyes and pursed lips. "You think we're gonna stop those bastards? With what?" He snorted and blew out a cloud of grey smoke which he watched rise languidly.

"They must have something up their sleeve or they'd have sued for peace by now."

Sundberg looked at him sourly. "Miracle weapons? Are you simple?"

"Well…"

Sundberg snorted again.

Greger pulled out his own cigarettes and offered them to Kaarle and John. "What about those rockets, then? London's taken a pasting."

Sundberg shook his head dismissively. "Lot of good that's done. France has gone and the Amees are on their way here. No," he shook his head dolefully, "it won't be long now."

They sat in awkward silence; and then Sundberg, in a softer tone, went on. "You know, I skipped bail back in Sweden to fight the Reds. Join the SS. Save Europe. Now if I go home I'll spend twenty years in some fucking cell. If I stay here, it's Siberia. Or a fucking bullet." He chuckled with real humour as if the irony appealed to him.

"Do they," John cleared his throat, "hate us that much?"

His three companions looked briefly at each other and then stared at him. It was Greger who answered. "If we're lucky, they'll only shoot us."

"I don't understand."

"Don't you?"

"They've got good reason to hate us." Sundberg shrugged.

"Well I know it was a bit rough in the east, but..."

Greger cut him off. "Rough's not the word, John." He and Sundberg exchanged a bleak look, their eyes full of something only they recognised. It sent a chill through John. "If they do to Germany half of what was done there, well..."

Greger contemplated his cigarette for a moment. An awkward silence settled over them. John, feeling too uncomfortable, excused himself and went back outside. He'd just finished another cigarette when Greger came out to join him.

"Can you get back to England?"

"For what? I haven't been there for years, and if Hitler goes down, the Reds and the Yids will be in charge."

Greger nodded sympathetically, lit two cigarettes and gave one to John. "Östersund, then?"

John shook his head. "My stepfather made it clear he didn't want to see me again." He stared towards Berlin for a few moments. "What were you saying in there?"

Greger's eyes were hooded but he answered plainly. "We destroyed the place. Burned villages, shot hostages. We took all their food."

"Well it's war, and you didn't shoot them all." John glanced at the eastern horizon where the sun was lighting the sky in glorious colours above the mutter of artillery, already.

"Good as." Greger smiled grimly. "If you throw someone out of their home in a Russian winter, you may as well shoot them." He shook his head. "And there were other things." John stared at him and Greger's smile faded. "Look, if you survive, get out any way you can. Germany won't be worth living in. And if you have to surrender, don't do it to the Reds. They don't take SS prisoners, not now."

"What if I wasn't in the SS?"

"They don't just kill SS. The army did its bit in Russia. But anyway, how will you pretend? Take you uniform off?" He shook his head again and tapped his armpit. "They take one look at the tattoo and *bang*."

"I don't have one," said John quietly.

"What?"

"I don't have a tattoo."

Greger stared at him and John explained that when the other SS recruits had had their blood groups tattooed under their left armpit, as was the practice, all the British were excluded.

Greger laughed harshly. "Be glad then. You can deny it all."

John shifted uncomfortably. "I'm not sure…"

"Look, John, I know." Greger smiled ruefully and tapped the belt buckle which every SS trooper wore, quoting the words inscribed there. "'My honour is loyalty.' But you don't have to shout about it. Back home, I kept quiet when I was in the NSWP. It didn't mean I was any less loyal to the cause."

"You were in Lindholm's Party?" John asked.

"Yes. I joined in Gothenburg for the elections in '32. Why?"

"My mother joined it in '39."

"Well then, you'll understand that sometimes you keep your head down and your loyalty quiet."

John nodded. Sven Olov Lindholm had formed his very own National Socialist Workers' Party, a mirror image of Hitler's, breaking away from the Swedish fascist movement to do so. The NSWP had not been popular either with its former colleagues or with the Swedish establishment, especially not after Hitler invaded Denmark and Norway. Keeping your head down had become second nature, even if Sweden officially did its best to be friendly with its Nazi neighbours.

"I was an honorary member of Nordic Youth. I didn't shout about that either."

Greger grinned. "Sensible fellow. You know, you might just make it at that. Shit, this is so serious. Let's see if we can find a drink. It's Adolf's big day, for God's sake. Let's make the most of it."

He cast away the stub of his cigarette and led John back inside.

The fire had gone out during the night and Cheslav awoke feeling chilled to the bone. He stretched and stamped life back into his feet as all around him the company roused itself. Going outside he found that it was raining. As he stood and relieved himself against the barn wall, something struck him as not quite right. Then he realised that he couldn't hear the piano and walked across the courtyard towards the farmhouse. At the door, an Asian man in black overalls barged past him with a mutter which might have been an apology, trailing the sour stink of alcohol and sweat. In the hall the air was stale, and staler still in the room with the piano. Sleeping figures in black were sprawled everywhere, the lieutenant in the armchair, collar buttons undone and an empty vodka bottle by his feet. But Sebelev still stood by the piano, bottle in his hand, and the boy still sat at the keyboard. His hands hovered above, moving slowly up and down without touching it. His stared into space, his face a picture of misery. One cheek was bruised, his lower lip was crusted with dried blood. Cheslav noticed a smattering of dark red on the piano's white keys.

Sebelev glanced at Cheslav briefly and then prodded the boy with the bottle. "Play, you little fucker," he grated, a voice raw with drink and tobacco. When he got no response, Sebelev twisted his lips in a ghastly parody of a smile and nodded slowly. "Finish."

It didn't sound like a command, more like finality, and Cheslav's stomach lurched

"Well done." The lieutenant had opened his eyes and stood up unsteadily. He straightened his tunic and buttoned up his collar, brushed himself down, picked up his coat and hat, and then he beckoned. "*Komm, yoonger.*"

Sebelev put down his bottle and hauled the boy up by his shoulder tabs. One of them broke and a button struck him on the chest. He laughed softly at that and ruffled the boy's hair like a fond uncle. The lieutenant nodded briskly to Cheslav and strolled out. Sebelev propelled the boy after him with a lopsided grin. After a moment's hesitation, Cheslav followed. Somehow he felt he ought to; was part of it. After all, it was he who had set the boy to playing the previous day.

The rain had intensified, bouncing now off the empty courtyard. It soaked the two artillerists in the short distance as they marched with their hapless captive between them before turning the corner out of sight behind a barn.

Cheslav stopped. He had felt that he should follow, but when he lost sight of them, somehow the thread that tugged him along snapped. He stood indecisively in the wet, cold rivulets running under his collar and down his back. The air smelled of damp straw and dung from an old midden heap against the barn; of wood smoke from cooking fires and of engine oil. On the road beyond the house he heard engines and a brief shouted greeting. Then there was no sound save the drumming of the rain and a sharp *crack*. He stood, not moving, feeling the rain on his face. After a moment the lieutenant came back into view followed by Sebelev. Cheslav watched them silently as they passed without acknowledging him, the rain falling in sheets.

Leonid slept fitfully and awoke early. As grey dawn crept through the tiny windows of the barn, he pulled out his notebook: it was just light enough. *Dearest brother,* he scribbled quickly, *greetings and best wishes for your good health.* He stared at the page and added, *There is much to tell you.* He wanted to share what Trofimova and Agranenko had told him; they'd sworn an oath as boys to hide nothing from each other, but the letter might be read by some snoop of a political officer. They both loved poetry and sometimes it best expressed what they meant, so now he opened a yellowing creased clipping from the army's official newspaper *Red Star* and wrote: *I know, dear brother, that you will appreciate this poem.* Then carefully he copied out the words of Konstantin Simonov, an officially-approved poet and surely safe enough to pass any censor.

> *Don't be angry if I write*
> *Only just from time to time,*
> *Writing now and then again,*
> *Waiting till another time.*
> *Letters come in many forms:*
> *Some are sick and some are sad,*
> *Brilliant just occasionally,*
> *Far more often very bad.*
> *Letters leave a lot unsaid,*
> *Often are not understood,*
> *Seem to mean more than they do,*
> *Fail to mention what they should.*

He smiled at the underlining he'd put in; it would do very nicely. Then, the ending:

> *Say "It's better that he wrote*
> *Only just from time to time,*
> *Writing now, and then again,*
> *Waiting till another time."*

He added, *Bad things happen in war. But do not worry, I am well.* Then a few banal words of his own about the breakfast preparations going on around him; about a draft of new recruits he'd seen march in behind Polyanski at dusk; about the lilac bush he'd noticed growing at the edge of the courtyard; and he wrote about distant Berlin, now a grey smudge on the horizon. It was something they'd all waited a long time to see, and he wrote how he could now really believe that the war would end. *I am looking forward to celebrating Victory Day with you,* he wrote.

There were things he did not write: his doubts, his regrets, and his hopes that all would be justified by a new world afterwards.

"Hey, how about some chow for the girls then?" It was Trofimova's hearty bellow. He looked up and saw her walking into the barn, grinning. Leonid read his last words once more, folded the letter and tucked it away safely.

'The Fighting City of Berlin Greets the Führer.' Tanya wasn't sure if she found the words annoying or amusing: they were risible. She was queuing once more outside the small grocery shop, for today was the Führer's fifty-sixth birthday and to honour it all citizens were to receive an extra ration. She'd tramped out into the darkness just after dawn, leaving early in the hope of not having to stand in line for too long this time. And so she stood in the rain, head tucked down under her scarf, waiting. Ida was behind her, and behind *her* was Klara. Mrs Körtig had not come, but Tanya had her ration card and knew the grocer well enough for that to cause no surprise: they often collected for each other.

Mrs Boldt hadn't come either: she didn't need to. Her ration issue would be delivered by a Hitler Youth, the grocer's son, riding his bicycle with its massive basket on the front. Mrs Boldt never had to queue. It was, she told everyone, one of the privileges of being a good National Socialist and they should take note.

I spend my life here, Tanya thought, looking behind her at the long queue. 'They also serve who only stand and wait.' She smiled at the words which came into her head. An English poem, wasn't it? Milton? Her boss at the bank had been fond of quoting English writers. He'd studied literature at a London college before the previous war and had liked to parade his sophistication, at least until Britain declared war. After that he'd been careful to quote only approved German writers, but never the Führer. He never quoted the Great Man himself; she'd wondered at that.

She thought of him now; she'd not seen him for weeks, not since that Monday morning when she'd gone in as usual to find a note on her desk saying that he'd had to go to his country home to deal with a family matter and would be back as soon as he could. She was used to his frequent absences on bank business. This time, however, she'd guessed that it might be some time before she saw him again. She felt no resentment at this. He'd been kind to her too many times for her to begrudge him. For a while afterwards she'd gone diligently to the bank, opening his mail, sorting, replying, filing as a good secretary should, but as fewer and fewer colleagues turned up for work, she began to feel that it was pointless. The bank was doing hardly any business: many clients had closed their accounts, and others had become dormant. So finally she stopped going in and instead spent her time queuing.

The shop door opened and it was her turn. She nodded at the woman who came out; they knew each other by sight, another regular in the queues, but had never really spoken save to say good morning or good afternoon.

Inside there was no small talk: the grocer wasn't one for it. Instead he nodded his greeting, took the two cards and clipped the coupons. Then he prepared two packs and handed them to her: stringy pieces of bacon wrapped in waxed paper, small paper bags of brown rice, cans labelled 'vegetables', unspecified, a few ounces of sugar and some coffee beans. Even the grocer, a man not noted for his sensitivity, seemed embarrassed by the meagreness.

Still, Tanya consoled herself as she tucked the items into her bag, at least there's coffee. Real coffee too, not ground-down acorns. It might cheer Mrs Körtig up; it was about the only thing in the ration issue which would.

As she walked back out she smiled at Ida and Klara, and as she strolled away she turned to look back for a moment and felt a pang. She recalled how, as a little girl, she'd go shopping with her mother, and now in her mind's eye she saw the street market on the Rue Poncelet, a short walk from their tiny apartment: the stalls with their canvas awnings; the piles of fruit and vegetables; the vivid colours of the wares and of the clothes of the shoppers. The sound of people haggling, laughing, and scents of the many flower stalls. The impressions were sudden and vivid, but brief. She sighed as she looked at the dreary street and the drab people and wished that she was a carefree girl back in Paris: colourful, sunny, peaceful Paris.

The moment passed.

When she got back she saw a *Kübelwagen*, a small open-topped military car, parking outside the apartment block. A man got out and, seeing her, waved before going into the entrance to the side passage which led to the building's interior courtyard. He was smoking a cigarette in the Russian way, pinched between forefinger and thumb. He wore the field-grey uniform and high boots, long coat and peaked cap of a German officer, but he wasn't German. She knew that. It was Victor Palanevich: friend and comrade of her father during the civil war against the Bolsheviks; frequent visitor to her mother's apartment in Paris. He'd been Uncle Victor then, always elegant and sometimes gloriously overdressed in the white summer uniform of the extinct Semonovsky Guard Regiment in which he and her father had served. Now he was wearing the uniform of a major in the SS; he was still elegant.

"Victor Mikhailovich," she acknowledged when she walked into the passage. He lifted the cigarette from his lips in greeting. "I suppose you've come to check on the champagne."

"Tanya. So good to see you, m'dear." He spoke an aristocrat's Russian with an unconscious air of authority. He always gave Tanya the impression that he knew things would go his way. He moved easily in high circles wherever he was: doors opened for him, paths were smoothed and influence and wealth seemed to accumulate around him. Never too much; never enough to cause comment or provoke envy, but still enough to ensure that he lived well.

"For the birthday party?" He nodded at her bag and then added wryly, "A day of celebration." He turned his face briefly towards the low mutter of sound that was battle, faint but just discernible. "How things change." He turned back and smiled at her in that formally friendly way of his: no real warmth, but just enough welcome.

She nodded agreement. The Führer's birthday had always been a time for Berlin to go mad with celebration: buildings and vehicles draped with bunting; posters on every surface; bands in the parks and on the street corners; parades through the Brandenburg Gate down the Avenue of Victory. It was a public holiday, a time for dinners and parties. Now we stand in the rain on empty streets.

"Not Führer weather," Palanevich observed, peering at the steady downpour.

That too was different. Hitler always seemed to be blessed with good weather on his birthday. She didn't say anything.

"Yes. Just a quick visit." Palanevich fished a key out of his pocket. "I won't be long. I want a quick word with you."

She nodded and watched from the shelter of the passageway as Palanevich hurried across the paved courtyard to steps in one corner which led to the door of a former coal cellar, used as a general store after the block was converted to gas. A few months earlier he'd come to an arrangement with Mrs Boldt. Gladly she'd accommodated the request from the *Herr Sturmbannführer* to allow him to store a few personal items there. Glad also, Tanya had no doubt, for the few gifts that the *Herr Sturmbannführer* was kind enough to press upon her.

Palanevich sent SS troopers late one night to empty the few items of bric-a-brac contained in the store into the main building cellar and replace them with wooden crates. They'd fitted a new stout padlock to which only Palanevich had a key. None of the residents asked questions; he was, after all, an SS officer.

Tanya hadn't asked either, but she already knew Palanevich's fondness for vintage champagnes. He was notorious for it in Paris, and she guessed he'd brought his collection with him to Berlin when he'd moved there a few years before the war.

She watched him disappear into the store and smiled. Victor and his champagne! Troopers would come from time to time and remove a case or two. Did he drink it himself? Were they gifts or bribes, or did he sell them on the black market? She knew he'd been some sort of art dealer in Paris and now was a cultural advisor to the SS, in which role he'd even assisted Reich Marshal Göring, a man who loved art. Rumour had it that the portly, vain and strutting Göring had hundreds of pieces looted from across occupied Europe. He needed someone to help him with them, and Palanevich would be ideal.

This she guessed, but she never asked and he only occasionally told her things.

After a couple of minutes, he came back, carefully locking the store behind him. In his hand he carried a shopping bag which clanked as he joined her. It looked strange in his hands. He put it down carefully and lit a fresh cigarette.

"I'm making arrangements to move out of Berlin."

"I see." She nodded, wondering why he was telling her this.

"I'm afraid things are going to get very difficult." He smiled humourlessly. "I'm not the only one."

"The Führer?"

He glanced around, although there was no possibility of anyone overhearing them; the German glance: automatic, cautious. "Ah, well, that's another matter. He's announced that he intends to remain in the city. What will *actually* happen no one seems to know. Even Göring's in the dark." He blew out a cloud of aromatic smoke and shook his head. "They've ordered *Clausewitz*. That's the plan to evacuate essential ministries and key personnel and put the city into a state of defence."

She thought of the rumble of guns audible above the noise of the rain. "A bit late, isn't it?"

He smiled; now there was humour in it. "Yes. But, m'dear, one couldn't order a state of defence for a city that there was no possibility of the Bolsheviks reaching." He frowned. "The damn fools left everything too late. Idiots." He spat out the last word with uncharacteristic venom; Palanevich usually didn't let his true feelings show this much.

"Can I get out too?" she asked, more plaintively than she'd intended.

He cast away the stub of the cigarette and lit another, waiting until he'd done so before he said very slowly, as if thinking it through, "I will see if I can arrange something. It won't be easy."

"Perhaps I'd be better staying here."

He shook his head. "Tanya, our countrymen are behaving like beasts. They may have cause, who knows? I've heard rumours about what the Germans did back home, and...well, when the Reds break into the city, it won't be pretty."

"Like Nemmersdorf?"

He didn't answer that but stared into the street, craning his neck to peer upwards. "The rain's easing." He lowered his gaze. "You heard what happened to Königsberg?"

She tilted her head questioningly. "What?"

"The Bolsheviks took it ten days ago. Barbaric."

She shivered. Her mother lived in Breslau. It was under siege like Königsberg had been. Breslau hadn't yet fallen as far as she knew, but like Königsberg it would. Barbaric. Tanya felt slightly sick.

Palanevich gently touched her arm. "Your mother may be all right. It's impossible to know." His voice was gentle, his look one of genuine concern. He was a strange man in some ways: sometimes very ruthless in his attitudes and dealing, yet Tanya knew he made large donations to the Church for charitable works. He affected a materialist's cynicism, yet attended the same Church she did, and far more often; he hated the Bolsheviks, yet admired their determination; despised the Nazis, yet appreciated their single-minded self-interest. He didn't have many good words to say about the Americans or the British either, but approved of their achievements. He held many contradictory views; in that, he was very Russian.

She dragged up an appreciative smile for him. "Thank you," she said.

He cast away another stub; the rain was now just a drizzle. "I must go. I'll let you know what I can arrange."

She walked with him to the car and waited as he clambered in.

"I'll send someone for the champagne soon."

She smiled again and watched him drive down the street

and around the corner. As he did so, sirens began to wail. Happy Birthday, Führer, she thought and hurried inside.

Greger made good his promise: he dug a bottle of Doornkaat out of his backpack, but they decided to wait until the evening before opening it. John spent Hitler's special day, like everyone else in the detachment, cleaning his kit, checking his weapon, dozing, eating, dozing again. At one point Ridderstolpe's radio operator, returning from a stint on his set, told them there was a big raid going on. Few of the men bothered to go and see. Greger was one, however, and John another, but after a few minutes of watching little puffs of brown smoke, some silver glints and the occasional spark of light above the distant city, Greger muttered, "Happy Birthday, Adolf," and they all went back inside.

Later, his chores complete, John dipped into a little yellow Penguin paperback book: *Poets of the Great War*. It had been his father's, and his mother had insisted he have it when he went to Finland. He'd read and reread it, committing passages to memory as his father had encouraged him to do with so many books when he was a boy. Now when he held it he felt close to his father; closer perhaps than when the man had been alive.

By the time he'd finished the book, dusk was coming on. He pulled out his folio case and flicked through the contents, selected a cutting, and began reading.

"Good?" Greger looked at him over the fire he'd been brooding into.

John smiled and nodded.

"Read it."

John felt awkward. He was not a brilliant reader at the best of times, and translating a poem from English into German, well that was something else. "Well, it's about..." he began.

Greger shook his head. "No, *read* it."

John shrugged. It was one of his favourites; his mother too had always liked it, and he felt he should do it justice or not try at all.

"I'm not sure my German's up to it."

"Do your best." Greger frowned. "Come on."

John paused for a few seconds and then nodded. He decided to read it as it was written, in English:

> What passing bells for these who die as cattle?
> Only the monstrous anger of the guns.
> Only the stuttering rifles' rapid rattle
> Can patter out their hasty orisons.

John looked up, not knowing whether he should carry on. Sundberg and Kaarle had been chatting quietly: they stopped and listened. Greger nodded encouragement.

John paused; this was his father's favourite passage and for a moment he couldn't continue. Then he coughed to clear his throat.

> No mockeries now for them; no prayers nor bells;
> Nor any voice of mourning save the choirs,
> The shrill, demented choirs of wailing shells;
> And bugles calling for them from sad shires.

He thought of his father: thought of what he'd told John about Flanders and the previous war. and he thought of what he himself had seen at Salla and elsewhere. Anger flared in him, then died. He went on:

> What candles may be held to speed them all?
> Not in the hands of boys but in their eyes
> Shall shine the holy glimmers of goodbyes.
> The pallor of girls' brows shall be their pall;
> Their flowers the tenderness of patient minds,
> And each slow dusk a drawing-down of blinds.

Sundberg looked at Kaarle and shrugged.

Greger smiled. "Thank you," he said. "Thank you." He stood up and went outside.

"What's it about?" said Sundberg.

John looked at him and sighed.

Leonid stood amongst shattered tree trunks and watched Tajidaev perform his funeral rites.

They'd marched up to the wood late that afternoon; luckily the artillery strike had arrived before they did. Lucky for them, but not for others.

As they approached the place, shells had cascaded briefly and viciously onto the crossroads that lay within the wood: an obvious target: a spot where roads converged. They heard the strike, saw earth and fumes billow up above the trees, and then they heard the screaming. It was still going on when they hurried up. They found what was left of a detachment of Cossack cavalry, all dead save for one screaming horse. Dismembered and twisted bodies of men and animals lay scattered amongst the still smoking craters.

Tajidaev ran to the thrashing horse and shot it.

"Ten minutes' rest," Gushenko told them when Leonid relayed Tajidaev's plea. "That's all you get."

So while the company took a break beyond the wood, Tajidaev went about his business. He stood amongst the trees, his back to Leonid, his head and hands raised to the sky, and he chanted softly. He paused, extracted scraps of newspaper from his jacket. Tajidaev couldn't read; he used them for hygiene purposes, Janko once had jokingly remarked. Now Tajidaev rolled some of the paper tightly into a taper, lit it and waved it in circles in front of him. His chant became a song, soft and lyrical. Leonid didn't understand the strange words, but he was moved. Then Tajidaev wept silently, his face still averted, but Leonid knew that he wept.

When the flame went out, Tajidaev crumbled the remains of the paper onto the soil, picked up a handful and scattered it. He turned. "I pray," he said, wiping his face with the back of his sleeve.

Leonid nodded.

"Horses sacred to U'lgen."

Horses? Leonid wondered. He prays for the horses? He looked at the riders, mutilated heaps amongst their butchered animals, and said nothing. Tajidaev picked up more soil and wandered slowly amongst the craters, scattering it over each fallen animal. Some of the platoon, sitting on the edge of the wood, could see him; a few grinned.

Leonid looked on with mixed feelings. Officially the Soviet

Union had no gods, but many of its citizens still believed. They wished to believe, perhaps *needed* to believe; scientific socialism was not enough. For himself, Leonid didn't know what he needed to believe. His father joined in with religion to be part of village life, but in reality he'd been indifferent to it. His mother was an instinctive believer and superstitious with it, full of pre-Christian beliefs which nestled comfortably alongside what she heard in the little village church. Leonid's stepfather was an ardent atheist as the Party required; his faith in Marxism-Leninism was strongly professed: a true believer. When his mother had married his stepfather, she stopped speaking about God. That she'd forgotten Him, Leonid doubted.

He turned and walked back to the platoon. Moiseyevich was waiting for him, but he was staring at Tajidaev. His face held a mixture of puzzlement and contempt, and Leonid was annoyed.

"What do you want, Private?"

Moiseyevich didn't salute. "The Comrade Captain wants to see you."

Leonid looked at him for a moment and then waved him away. "Very well."

Moiseyevich didn't move. Instead he peered past Leonid, his eyes still fixed on Tajidaev.

"*Very well*, Private." Leonid had let the annoyance show in his voice and he regretted it; he didn't like Moiseyevich to know how much he got under his skin. Still Moiseyevich didn't move. Leonid pursed his lips in exasperation. "Did you never see a man pray before?" Now Moiseyevich did look at him and the disdain was evident. Leonid felt anger, whether at Moiseyevich's insolent behaviour or his attitude towards Tajidaev, he didn't know. He snapped, "Did you never pray yourself?"

A grim smile flicked across Moiseyevich's face. "Not since my bar mitzvah, Comrade," he said slowly and walked away.

Leonid stared after him. Not since God let your family die, he realised. Watching Moiseyevich walk away, he felt his anger fade. Then he glanced at Tajidaev and something touched him.

*

Tired and chilled in the dusk twilight, Cheslav huddled with the rest of the company in one of the drainage ditches which ran along both sides of the road. They'd left the farm after breakfast and marched all day without a break. Plodded would be a more accurate word. Plodded past disabled German vehicles and abandoned weapons; past the personal belongings of civilians, much of it crushed by passing traffic; past abandoned trenches and foxholes, shell craters and blasted woods. The road was busy with motor vehicles, carts, towed guns, marching soldiers. Now and then aircraft passed overhead; it was still busy, although not so much.

Cheslav pulled his boots off to let his feet cool and the sweat dry. He wanted only to sleep and didn't care that the ditch was damp and smelled of rot, but sleep stubbornly refused to come, although around him most of the others sprawled unconscious.

In the twilight Cheslav took the brown paper parcel out of his backpack and unwrapped Leonid's gift from its packaging. He stroked the book, feeling the finely-tooled brown leather, pressing it to his face. Then he opened it, felt the thick pages, but it was too dark to read, and when Kolchok approached he bundled it back into the brown paper and tucked it away in his pack. Kolchok was carrying something and Cheslav squinted in the gloom to see what it was.

"Here." Kolchok held out an elegant silver coffee pot. It was covered in some sort of delicate chasing and Cheslav thought he could make out a complex pattern of leaves and branches. He wondered if it was a coffee plant; he'd never seen one, nor a picture of one. He was startled at the incongruity: such a work of art here amongst the dirt and destruction. The aroma was delicious and he pulled out his mug. Kolchok poured a generous measure and Cheslav sniffed it, then sipped it: good coffee; real coffee. He'd only experienced the like once before, when his stepfather had entertained an important visitor from the Party and had pulled out all the stops. He'd been allowed a small sip of the heavenly drink and the taste had remained with him ever afterwards.

He nodded at the pot. "Where did you get it?"

Kolchok said only, "Good coffee, eh, Comrade? Fritzes know how to live well."

Cheslav looked around him, and then suddenly saw in his mind the fine farmhouse, the elegant books, the walnut piano.

"Yes," he said. He saw the boy playing Bach and the coffee tasted bitter.

SEVEN

Just before dawn, John stood outside the warehouse with several others watching an Opel lorry deliver a miscellaneous load of fuel drums and cans of fuel. There were a lot of shouted orders, a lot of rushing about to transfer the fuel into empty tanks, a lot of packing and loading up of kit, and then they'd gone nowhere. Instead, they stood about in the chill damp, doing nothing, saying little. No one seemed to know what was happening. But eventually, they did move, setting off in a column under a dull grey sky. From the position of the pale smudge of the sun behind the clouds, John guessed they were heading northeast again.

After less than an hour, they halted at a crossroads on a raised causeway: a bad location for it would prevent the column getting off the road if hostile aircraft appeared. Sundberg muttered to no one in particular, "Get a fucking move on," and then "Fucking lost, I bet." He pushed between Greger and John to hang out the back.

When the column lurched into motion once more, Sundberg muttered a sigh of relief, "Thank God," and John had to agree with him. He craned his head to peer in all directions at the grey dreary sky, mercifully empty of any aircraft; so far.

Light rain began to fall, obscuring everything, but shortly the column slowed and halted. John stuck his head out from under the awning and peered ahead through the mizzle. It was difficult to see any details at first, but then he made out a cluster of buildings. As his eyes adjusted, he saw a line of oil drums across the road which passed close to a farm; it was a sight he'd seen before. Christ, he realised, we have been going around in bloody circles! Greger caught his eye and shrugged when he told him.

John sat back as the column lurched into life once more. As they drove through the barrier, John noticed that the trenches on either side were now manned. Volkssturm stood miserably in the wet, watching them pass with listless expressions. John looked back beyond the end of the column down the empty road and wondered. It wouldn't remain empty, and he doubted how long the Volkssturm would hold. He hoped that he wouldn't be there to find out. Then he thought of Mimmi in the little school and wondered if Olé was still there, and his hope shamed him.

"Take a break," a colour sergeant shouted when they halted in a street leading to the square. "Stretch your legs!"

John scrambled out gratefully and approached the sergeant with a request.

"You've time," he was told. "Not likely we'll be moving off for a bit, but don't be long."

John hurried towards the school. It was busy now, the hall crowded with wounded, too many for the tables and so some lay on the floor or sat along the walls. A few orderlies and nurses moved amongst them; there was no sign of Kurt or Mimmi, but he did see Kurschat going through the supplies laid out on the stage, setting some to one side under the direction of one of the orderlies. On impulse he headed for the office where Mimmi had taken him, nodding to Kurschat across the hall as he passed.

Olé was sitting on the table, his hand in Mimmi's as she sat on her chair looking up at him. Their heads turned as he entered and John saw that only the crown and the right side of Olé's head were now bandaged. The left was uncovered, one huge red welt.

Mimmi waved him over and smiled; Olé managed a grimace. Then they both stared behind him and he turned to see Kurschat's bulk occupying the doorway.

"I thought you'd be looking for Hansen," he said and beamed

at Mimmi. His eyes, John noted, roamed over her in a way which annoyed him.

John introduced Kurschat to Mimmi, and when she held up her free hand for him to shake, he took it in both of his and, in a gesture absurdly formal, kissed the air above it. She blushed and murmured her thanks, pulling her hand away. Kurschat straightened, beaming.

"She's always been a sucker for good manners." Olé's voice was thick but still recognisable. John prodded him gently in the arm.

"How are you, Comrade?"

"Well enough."

Mimmi snorted.

"I'm fit enough to pull a trigger. I'm not going to be caught in some damned hospital when the Ivans arrive." He stood and pulled his hand free from Mimmi's, using it to steady himself on the desk.

"Don't be an idiot, man," Kurschat admonished gently. "You need to be in a warm bed being looked after by nice nurses." Then he glanced at Mimmi. "Sorry, I meant…" He didn't sound it.

She smiled ruefully and took Olé's hand once more, pulling him down gently to sit. "You know what Doctor Zimmerman told you. What good can you do like this?"

"She's right." John smiled at her. "You'd just get in the way."

Olé looked at Mimmi, smiled wryly and then punched John gently on the arm. For a very long moment he said nothing, staring into space. Then he nodded and closed his eyes with a sigh. He looked all-in.

Kurschat tapped John on the shoulder. "We have to go." He nodded slowly to Mimmi, looked at Olé for a moment and then walked towards the door. When he reached it, he turned. "Good luck."

Olé opened his eyes and smiled at him wearily as he left.

John reached across and shook Mimmi's hand gently. "Take care," he said and nodded at Olé. "You too."

Mimmi stood up. "Don't worry about us. There's transport due soon. We're evacuating the wounded and staff. We'll be well away by the time…" She didn't finish, but instead smiled sadly at Olé.

"Always organising things," he muttered and touched her face.

Kurschat grinned when John joined him in the hall. "She's a real peach, that one. That little *Lysol Mouse* can change my bandages anytime."

"For God's sake, Butter…"

"What's wrong?" Kurschat seemed genuinely surprised. "She's a nice one, that's all I'm saying." He paused, then grinned again. "And not just a looker, if I know women. Just the sort to win a gold Mother's Cross."

"A what?"

"You know," Kurschat explained, "Mother's Cross. Medals for having kids. Five gets a bronze, seven a silver, and for eight, a gold. I wouldn't mind getting a medal for making babies." He chuckled; it should have been a jolly sound, but it wasn't.

"For God's sake," John repeated in a tight voice, "just shut up, will you."

Kurschat looked at him with a slightly wounded expression. Then he turned away towards the stage and muttered, "I'll get my supplies."

John tried to sound conciliatory as he walked away. "Do you need help?" He felt that he'd overreacted, but there was something in Kurschat's manner which seemed oily. His father had been strict about treating women with courtesy: salaciousness annoyed him.

Kurschat shook his head without turning.

"I'll be outside, then."

John met Sundberg hurrying down the entrance hall towards him.

"We're moving out."

"Butter's getting supplies"

Sundberg nodded. "Get on the lorry. I'll fetch him." He hurried into the hall.

A lorry was parked down the street, the interior almost full of boxes and crates, some marked with red crosses. Greger stood by the open tailgate smoking an Aktiv. He grinned when John joined him.

"I thought you'd deserted. Pretty nurses too much for you, eh?" When John's face hardened at the joke, he looked surprised, and then without another word scrambled up. He turned and held out his hand, but before John could take it a sudden howl burst across the rooftops and they froze, staring at each. Suddenly the ground rose up and struck John like a hammer from below, and the next thing he knew he was face down on the cobbles, breathless, stabbing pains in his palms and knees. The lorry juddered wildly above him and the ground bounced beneath him, and his ears rang. He lost his balance, falling flat, the cobbles pressing cold and hard into his face.

He took a deep breath to steady himself as the ground stopped moving, but before he could do anything else, hands gripped his shoulders and he was hauled roughly up to stand facing Greger.

"Move!" John saw the word mouthed, but he could hear only ringing. Greger pulled him away from the lorry, but then the ground bounced again and they fell to the ground to lie side by side in the lee of the adjacent building. Tiles dropped about them and a shadow passed overhead. Then it was gone and all was still once more.

Greger lifted himself to his knees and then scrambled shakily to his feet, holding onto the wall, pulling John up behind him. John swayed and leaned against the building. Putting his hands behind him for support he felt sharpness in his palms, and when he lifted them he saw raw abrasions oozing blood. Somehow it surprised him and he just stared at them.

Greger glanced at him and then looked at the lorry. Holes peppered the canvas awning, the two rear tyres had burst and several of the boxes and crates were splintered. Greger drew in a deep breath and went forward to the cab. He peered in for a second and then reached forward to do something.

John took several deep breaths and straightened. He realised the ringing in his ears was fading; already he could make out the distant sound of an aircraft engine and a dog barking somewhere. Greger backed out of the cab and met his gaze.

"Driver's had it." John looked at him. "No one you know." Then Greger stiffened, his gaze beyond John's shoulder. As John turned he heard a low rumble and saw dust billow along the street. For a moment they turned their heads, eyes squeezed shut, trying not to breathe. Then as quickly as it came, the dust was gone and John opened his eyes.

The school was a wreck. John couldn't see the door for the upper storey had collapsed right across it. A drift of bricks, wooden beams and roof slates covered the small yard and spilled out onto the street. "Christ," he muttered and looked at Greger. Then, "Olé. Mimmi." And as an afterthought, "Butter."

John sprinted forward, but almost immediately, as he approached the rubble, he slowed. A boot was projecting out of it. "Christ," he repeated and began clearing the area where he guessed the head would be. Greger joined him. It was the work of just a few minutes to reveal Sundberg's dusty, bloody face. The empty staring eyes told John all he needed to know and he sat back on his heels. He sighed, and then, after a moment, resumed his work.

This time Greger did not help. Instead he stood up and jerked his head towards the lorry. "Come on!"

John didn't look up. "They're in there!"

Greger reached down and shook his shoulder hard. "Now." Then John did look up at him and his eye caught a group of Volkssturm trotting towards them down the street, past the lorry. One was leaning into the cab just as Greger had done. "We have to go now. *Now*, John." His tone brooked no refusal.

John stood up, suddenly very weary. Nearly the whole upper storey had collapsed, and he felt sick as he imagined its weight crashing down onto the hall crowded with the helpless wounded and their unprotected helpers. He saw Olé and Mimmi, and then he pushed the thought away and took two deep breaths to steady himself. For a moment he felt that he might argue, but he could hear the sound of engines starting. The Volkssturm were already clearing the rubble and he knew that Greger was right: they must go. They were needed elsewhere, and others must see to what was needed here. He spat grit out of a dusty mouth and reluctantly followed Greger down the street towards where Berg was waiting. He didn't look back: he daren't.

*

Mrs Boldt as ever sat in her chair knitting, but she paused at the sound of every distant bomb. Klara had a bath towel wrapped around her head, supposedly protection against explosions. Tanya sat at the table playing cards on her own, patience, for Mrs Körtig was still upstairs. She looked at Ida sitting in her corner, reading a Bible, wincing at the sound of the far-off air raid, and she remembered – her mother in Paris reading aloud each evening from the family Bible they'd brought from Russia. When her mother had remarried and they'd moved to Germany, the Bible was put away, for her new husband was a Lutheran. He'd not actively interfered with her faith and she'd continued to go to church, but only for the high festivals. Tanya hadn't been sorry; certainly she'd liked going to church, seeing the wonderful paintings and carvings, smelling the candle smoke and incense, listening to the haunting liturgies, but she had little personal faith and didn't want to go *every* Sunday.

She recalled of her earlier encounter with Father Kazintsev. She'd first met him when he was a deacon ministering to fellow Russian émigrés in Paris. He was invariably polite, but also a little pompous and self-important: he made her feel that she somehow was not quite up to scratch as far as God was concerned, so she'd been pleased to leave him behind to come to Berlin. When the previous priest at their little Orthodox church on the square had retired, however, it was Kazintsev who'd replaced him. Tanya's none too frequent attendances became rarer. For some reason, thinking of that and of her mother now, she felt guilty. She looked again at Ida and on impulse put down the cards and went to her.

"Would you like some tea?"

Ida glanced up and smiled weakly; she'd been weeping. Should I tell her? Tanya wondered, but then she decided against it. She couldn't be sure it had been Walter she'd seen in that courtyard and why worry the woman with speculation? Then again, she might at least be able to make enquiries. Walter had not told his mother where he was going. Ida only knew that he'd gone to the Hitler Youth in response to a summons delivered by another boy who'd arrived in uniform on a bicycle, and he'd not come back. Nor had Mathias, who had gone to find him. Poor Ida, Tanya thought, no word about your husband, and now none about your son.

Tanya gently touched her shoulder. "I'm sure he's all right, you know. Off somewhere on air raid duties. Everything is so disorganised these days. He'll be back. You'll see. Mathias will find out." Ida looked up at her miserably, but Tanya couldn't meet her gaze and turned away. "I'll get that tea."

When she returned with two steaming mugs, the Bible had been put away. Instead Ida was looking at a copy of a magazine, *Film Kurier*. She put it on her lap and sipped appreciatively.

"He loves films, you know, my Walter."

Tanya nodded: she did know. Every spare pfennig he scraped together went on visits to the cinema, or on magazines and books about the movies. She looked at *Film Kurier*. The boy seems to live for make-believe, she thought, but then, why not? What's so attractive about real life? She considered her own absorption with literature and chided herself silently: 'But do not do what they do, for they do not practise what they preach.' It was one of her mother's favourites, that quote from Matthew's gospel; she'd always intensely disliked double standards.

"He wants to go into films."

"Excuse me?" Tanya forced herself back to Ida.

"I said he wants to go into films. Walter. He's artistic, you know." Ida sounded very proud.

Tanya hid her smile in a sip of tea. "He wants to be an actor?"

"Well, no. Director or something. He wants to make them. I don't really know much about it."

Tanya nodded: Ida was not the best informed of people.

"Yes, very artistic." Ida laid her hand on the magazine. "His father was like that."

"Films?"

"Well, no, they weren't a big thing when we met. Fabian was an assistant in an arts shop. He liked to paint and draw. Watercolours and pencil sketches, you know. He wasn't very good, but he liked to dream. Walter got that from his father too."

Tanya smiled encouragingly: better to let her talk it out than brood.

"We met just after the war, you know, 1920." Ida plucked at her skirt and smiled sadly. "He was a clerk in some general's office and missed the fighting. He felt a bit bad about that, but it gave him time to paint a lot. After the war was over, though, he never seemed to do any."

"Well, with a family to look after…"

Ida shook her head. "He was out of work a lot. Things were hard for a while. He said he couldn't afford the paint and brushes. He was always looking for work and said he had no time to paint, but I think he'd just lost interest." She sighed. "He went back to it in a way, eventually. Sent me cards."

"Cards?"

"Postcards, when they sent him to Russia. Fabian used to send them to me and Walter. Look." She reached down into the tin chest at her feet and pulled out a small dog-eared bundle. She held them out and, after a brief hesitation, Tanya took them. They were official postcards, the sort sent by soldiers on active service. Fabian had written very few words, but each had a sketch: men sitting around a fire; a stand of birch trees; a church with a cupola and three-barred cross; a horse-drawn cart passing between simple huts. She felt a lump in her throat: Russia, there in pencil on white card.

"They're good." Tanya passed them back.

"I wish he'd written more," Ida sighed, replacing the cards in the tin, "but Fabian was never one for words. Walter's the same: not great talkers." She laid her hand upon the magazine. "Artistic, though, very artistic." Two tears rolled slowly down her face.

Tanya felt awkward. "I'm sure there's nothing to worry about," she muttered and then felt churlish. She cast about for better words. "I'm sure he'll be all right." Tanya heard the inadequacy and wished she hadn't said it. "Mathias will look after him."

Ida squeezed Tanya's hand. "Yes, all we can do is pray."

Tanya, looking at Ida's distraught face and listening to the distant sounds of bombing, had to agree with her.

Leonid's platoon was wet, cold and exhausted for they'd had a long march through steady drizzle down a road much broken up by the passage of an army. Sometimes they had to stumble over ploughed fields, pushed off the route by insistent vehicles. Now and again they rested, but only briefly when something up ahead halted them and then not for long. They'd never had enough time to do more than ease packs off aching shoulders and briefly rub blistered feet or relieve themselves onto the ground: they were on the conveyor-belt of war, an endlessly moving column of men, vehicles and animals stretching in front and behind.

"Another hold up." Agranenko cleared his throat as they slumped on the wet raised verge. Gunfire crackled faintly ahead. He frowned at Leonid. "Might be a while, I hope."

Open fields lay on both sides of the narrow road, unbroken by trees or buildings. Columns of men struggled across them. Nearby was the wreckage of an aircraft, a crumpled mass of charred fabric, tangled wires and bent struts. Like a toy someone stepped on, thought Leonid. Parked a short distance ahead of them was a jeep, two wheels on the tarmac. There was one occupant who sat smoking, ignoring the few soldiers standing about it in admiration.

He introduced himself when Leonid and Agranenko strolled up to take a look. "Driver Corporal Nekrasov." Leonid nodded as he inspected the vehicle. Nekrasov must have been proud of it for it was unusually clean and tidy. There was nothing remarkable about the jeep itself, however, one of many American and British vehicles he'd seen. Usually jeeps were reserved for senior officers or specialists and he wondered whose this was.

Nekrasov was slightly pompous when he answered Leonid's question. "A special mission, Comrade. Very important person."

Agranenko looked sceptical. "Who?"

When Nekrasov told them, Leonid tried not to sound surprised. "A *poet?*"

Nekrasov nodded and pointed to a figure walking back from the aircraft.

"Surnachev. Mikola Surnachev," the poet introduced himself when he arrived somewhat out of breath. He was a little stout, perhaps a few years older than Agranenko, wore lieutenants' tabs and smiled easily. He had a distracted air, as of one who had serious matters on his mind.

"So you're a poet, Comrade. *On a special mission?*"

Surnachev grinned at Agranenko and looked at Nekrasov. "Is that what he told you?" He shook his head. "Nekrasov can't read or write. He thinks everyone who gets something published is a Tolstoy or Pushkin. I scribble a bit of poetry now and then. That's all." He looked at Nekrasov with affection.

"My father once told me that in Russia you don't get to be a proper poet unless you're in exile or dead."

Surnachev seemed a little put out by Agranenko's observation and Leonid was embarrassed. Then Surnachev grinned once more. "Yes. So I've been told. Let's hope it's not true." He cleared his throat. "My colonel gets me to scribble a few verses for the divisional paper. We've even managed to get a few bits and pieces in *Red Star*. Ehrenberg wrote to me once, you know." He made the statement with more than a tinge of pride in his voice.

Now Leonid was irritated. Surnachev seemed to think highly of himself, and he wasn't the only one who scribbled verses.

Surnachev turned and cast a long, thoughtful gaze across the field at the aircraft. "My colonel sent me forward to get a better feel for what's going on. I'm writing a piece for *Red Star* about the attack on Berlin." He turned back to them. "Have you been in the thick of it?" He pulled out a pack of American cigarettes and lit one; he didn't offer any, not even to Nekrasov.

"Yes." Agranenko's voice had the neutral tone he used on people he didn't much care for. Surnachev nodded slowly, but Agranenko wasn't paying him any attention. Instead he walked towards the aircraft. Surnachev stared at him, and when Leonid stumbled after Agranenko, he followed them back across the field.

A body lay face down in a mangled patch of wet rush close by the wreckage. It was small, one leg twisted at an impossible angle, the head misshapen. Leonid was grateful that the stained leather flying cap completely hid its contents.

"What a waste. It's almost over. Seems pointless dying now." Surnachev looked at the corpse with detachment.

Agranenko stared about him. "I can't see the other one."

"Other one?" asked Surnachev.

"They have two crew, usually," explained Leonid.

"Women," added Agranenko. "Night witches."

They were silent for a moment, then to their surprise Surnachev knelt, reverently straightened out the body as if arranging her on a funeral bier and crossed her arms over her chest. He sat back on his heels and, reaching out awkwardly, tugged out a handful of the wiry green rush and laid it on the corpse as if it was a posy of flowers. Solemnly he said, "She'll never be older, this child of a soldier, nor welcomed back home with two hands on her shoulders." He stopped for a moment, and then, more hesitantly, "She lies, arms flung wide…"

Surnachev looked away as if seeking something, then more words came suddenly in a rush. "She lies, arms flung wide, what use are our tears? Charred, over her bend the rustling ears." He stood and stared down at her.

For a moment none of them spoke, then Leonid turned in surprise as Agranenko took up the refrain. "She lies like a warrior in the trampled rye. If you meet with her lover…" but then he too stopped.

Surnachev found the final words. "Don't tell him she died." He nodded at Agranenko. "Thank you, Comrade."

For a moment they all looked at each other, then the moment was broken.

"Orders to move," said Moiseyevich and they turned as one.

The boy was standing only a few metres behind them, gesturing to the jeep where Gushenko now stood watching them.

"By the way, Comrades," Moiseyevich added, a half sneer on his lips, "it's not rye, it's rush." He spun about and walked away.

Softly, in a low voice, Agranenko muttered, "Right. Rush." His eyes narrowed at Moiseyevich's retreating back.

Like he's sighting rifle, Leonid observed and the thought made him grin. Agranenko glanced at him, but he didn't elucidate.

"Well, I suppose that's right," sighed Surnachev. "We must speak of reality, even in a poem."

"I know what's real." Agranenko looked down at the twisted corpse. "I don't need him to tell me."

Surnachev shook his head. "I don't know what *you* mean by real," he too looked down, "but the Party calls it 'objective truth.'"

Agranenko looked at him impassively.

"Meaning, I suppose," said Surnachev in a speculative tone, "that we hold the vision of tomorrow in our eyes. Yes, that's it. We're not deflected by what we see around us or by what we've learned in the past. The Party teaches us that we must subordinate the present to the inevitable future. Poetry must reflect this."

Agranenko nodded, saying nothing.

"Well, best get on." Surnachev's lips spasmed, not quite a smile, and he strolled back towards his jeep.

"That sounds like a piece for *Red Star*," snorted Agranenko quietly.

It was not usually something to take much notice of: the body of a German soldier hanging from a tree. Such sights were becoming more common as they advanced. "Encouragement," Bartashevich had observed ironically when the platoon passed its first ad hoc execution: an elderly Volkssturm hanging from a street light in a pretty little market town near the Polish border. A placard hung around that old man's neck: 'Coward. He declined to defend German women and children from the beasts.'

This corpse had no placard to say what his misdemeanour had been and Cheslav wondered if it had anything to do with the earlier fuss.

Some of the platoon had entered the detached house outside which the corpse was hanging; they'd come out very promptly and called for Bartashevich. He spent quite some time inside, and when he came out his face was grim. He'd told Cheslav to prevent anyone else going in, then he'd trotted away in the direction of Battalion HQ.

"What's going on in there?" Kolchok wandered up and offered a cigarette. Cheslav took one and shook his head; the three searchers had gone off with Bartashevich before he'd had a chance to ask them what they'd found.

"Can I take a look?"

Cheslav smiled ruefully at Kolchok but again shook his head. "Boss' orders."

Kolchok shrugged.

"And here he comes now."

Kolchok spun around as Bartashevich strolled up the street, the three who'd accompanied him in tow. They dropped out to join their comrades resting against the houses.

"Comrade Lieutenant..." Cheslav began to ask when Bartashevich approached, but Bartashevich waved him to silence and pulled out a packet of German cigarettes. When he'd extracted and lit one, he nodded at the door behind Cheslav.

"There's a girl in there. Lying on the floor."

They waited for him to say more, but he didn't. Then Kolchok scratched his head. "Dead?"

Bartashevich nodded.

"Lot of dead women about."

Bartashevich nodded again. "It's not a woman, it's a little girl." He sounded unconcerned and lit another cigarette from the stub of the first. "About ten or eleven, I'd guess." After a pause, he added blandly, "Raped."

Cheslav looked at the hanging body and went cold; Kolchok's face hardened.

"About the same age as my little sister. Pretty thing." There was still no emotion in Bartashevich's voice, but the corner of his right eye twitched slightly. Cheslav was surprised; he'd always thought of Bartashevich as cool to the point of iciness. He was dispassionate, a graduate of the Party's special schools: those attended by children of the nomenklatura. Such children were taught to look at the world objectively according to the lights of Marxist doctrine. Emotionalism was frowned upon: the 'New Soviet Man' was to be free of bourgeois sentimentality.

Kolchok and Cheslav looked at each other.

Bartashevich dropped his three-quarters unfinished cigarette and took out a notebook. "All right. You can go." He went inside, closing the door behind him.

"Shit," Kolchok muttered and spat. He picked up Bartashevich's cigarette and sucked on it; the tip glowed briefly and he drew in the smoke with satisfaction. Then he headed off to speak with the three men who made the discovery.

Cheslav walked around the back of the house. He didn't feel like sitting with the platoon yet; he didn't want to answer any questions, and he didn't want to be where he could see the corpse. Behind the house was a little garden backing onto another, neatly tended with a stand of lilac bushes in one corner. Although there were few blossoms, the scent of lilacs enveloped him and for a moment he found himself back in his childhood. His father had loved flowers and took Cheslav and Leonid for long walks through the fields when the wild blossoms sprang up. They would say little, but he would hold out blossoms for them to smell, telling them what they were. The wild poppy was his father's favourite, and whenever he found some he would tell the boys *The Tale of the Scarlet Flower*. Cheslav came to love that story, and even if a poppy was not to be found, he would beg his father to tell it each time they went walking. Leonid soon tired of it, but Cheslav never had. He came to know it by heart:

the wily merchant, his three daughters, the demand for a scarlet flower and the beast that turned into a prince, and how it all turned out right in the end. Fairy tales, he thought and sat down with his back to the house, his gaze on the lilacs: the flower Leonid preferred.

"Thinking?" Kolchok stood over him, looking down. Cheslav didn't answer.

"Doesn't do to think too much." Kolchok followed Cheslav's gaze to the lilacs. "I love that smell." He sauntered over and plucked a twig laden with small early blossoms, held it to his nose and breathed in deeply. Then he came back and held it out. "Here, boy," he said, "cheer you up."

Cheslav looked at him, startled, then took it and smiled.

Kolchok sat down and laid his head back against the rough cobbles of the wall. "Thinking of that girl?"

"Yes. Do you think the German, was it him?"

Kolchok shrugged. "Who knows? Maybe and he got caught."

"Why leave the girl's body, then?" Cheslav fingered the twig on the grass beside him. "Could be our guys caught the German with the girl? Hanged him?"

"Maybe."

"But why leave her there?" Cheslav wondered again. The more he thought about it, the less sense it made. Wouldn't anyone catching the German bury the girl, or at least make her decent somehow? Certainly you wouldn't leave her on the floor as you found her, would you? The idea disturbed him.

"Best not to think about it." Kolchok tapped Cheslav's knee. "Get on with it. 'Life is not a walk through a meadow.'"

Cheslav fiddled with the lilac irritably. "Do you have a saying for everything?"

Kolchok chucked. He reached into his tunic and pulled out a small bottle. "Here, good medicine for sad thoughts, and that's not a saying, Comrade."

The vodka helped a little. "It's just that, well, I know the Germans are bastards, but a little girl?"

"How do you know it was Germans?" Cheslav stared at him. "I saw some of that during the Civil War."

"The Whites?"

"Not just the Whites, boy." Cheslav stared at him and Kolchok shrugged. "Good cause doesn't mean good people."

Cheslav nodded; he knew that right enough. "It is a good cause, though, isn't it? Whatever happens?"

Kolchok licked vodka off his grimy fingers and tucked away the bottle. "That'll do." He stood up and stretched. "We'd best get back to the others." Cheslav scrambled up, and for a moment Kolchok almost smiled at him, a slight lifting of one corner of his mouth. "Good things can come out of a war, as well as bad." He nodded, as if to himself. "Seems to me that things have got better already. The bigwigs in the Party don't throw so much weight about since the Hitler War started. Lots o' people seen a lot o' new things. Won't be the same when we go home." Kolchok reached out and took Cheslav's arm in an iron grip. "All's well that ends well, eh?"

It was one of the longest speeches Cheslav had ever heard Kolchok make. He wondered if Kolchok was right, thought of the little girl and the German hanging from the tree, and hoped so.

The detachment reached the outskirts of the city shortly after midday, driving through the gates of a factory. It was large, the main building extending for nearly half a kilometre. Almost as long was the row of low wooden barrack huts in front of it. The detachment was halted by an officious military police sergeant: Ridderstolpe and Rask went to speak with him. Then Rask trotted back towards them and the sergeant set off towards the huts.

"We're staying," Rask called into the lorry and waved them out. They all sighed with relief: after the pell-mell exit from the village, the detachment had woven its way down secondary country lanes for hours without a break and they were all travel weary. Greger speculated that they'd stayed off the main roads to avoid any more encounters with hostile aircraft, or perhaps to find roads less congested. The main routes had become busy again with retreating columns: everyone seemed to be falling back on Berlin.

"You can have that hut." Rask pointed. "But not that one." Another point. "It's off limits." He turned away to the next lorry in line, but then stopped and spun about when Greger vaulted over the tailgate with a question.

"Why not that one, sergeant? Why the guard?" Standing outside the hut Rask had pointed to was a middle-aged man wearing the distinctive shiny helmet and grey-green uniform of the Berlin Police Force. He carried a sub-machine gun which John recognised as a Bergmann MP 18, dating from the last war. Old, but he knew from his father very effective. The policeman was immaculately clean and John was conscious of his own unshaven face, grimy uniform and filthy boots.

"It's full of *pommes frites*." Rask grinned: it was army slang for Frenchmen. Then he strolled on down the line, calling into more lorries, leaving them to settle themselves in.

Their hut was basic: a long space, open up to the rafters. The plank walls were lined with tiers of simple wooden bunks. There was no bedding and just one lavatory cubicle at the far end. The two iron stoves spaced equidistantly down the middle had no fuel and the huts were cold, but they were dry and no one complained. Dinner, when it came later courtesy of the detachment's cooks, was a surprisingly good thick soup of root vegetables and flour. Afterwards they settled down to sleep, but John needed fresh air and slipped out. He was standing in the deepening dusk, smoking one of his few remaining cigarettes, when the door of the POW hut opened and the occupants shuffled out. They lined up facing it under the steady gaze of the policeman he'd seen earlier: the Bergmann was slung casually over his shoulder. Two more policeman emerged from the hut, these armed only with holstered pistols. One began languidly to call the roll while the second strolled up to John and held up a cigarette.

"Good evening. May I have a light?" He had a friendly lilting voice and twinkling eyes. He was portly with a round rubicund face and handlebar moustache, and suddenly John was reminded of a character he'd seen in a Stepney music hall. It's the bloody laughing policeman, he observed, amused: a well-known stage character with a popular song John liked, and immediately he remembered the opening verse:

> I know a fat ol' policeman, he's always on our street
> A fat old jolly red-faced man, he really is a treat.
> He's too fine for a policeman, he's never known to frown
> And everybody says he is the happiest man in town.

He struggled to suppress a grin and shook the policeman's hand. The policeman didn't offer John his name, and John was relieved; he didn't want to reveal his Englishness to a German policeman. He was too tired for explanations.

Lighting the policeman's cigarette, he watched the roll call. The POWs answered each name listlessly; they looked as if they hadn't had a decent meal in weeks. They were very thin, unshaven, their uniforms worn and much patched, some with boots bound in cloth. Their eyes were deeply sunken, faces sallow and lined.

"Scared of their own shadows," the policeman shook his head, "and I don't blame them." He looked at John and smiled sadly. "They've had a pretty rough time of it."

"I suppose they have."

"Away from home for five years. Hard work and bad food."

"You sound sympathetic."

The policeman nodded. "I had some of that myself. Was in a camp in France during the last lot, and after it."

"POW?"

"Yes. Captured in '16, didn't get home until '20 when they let us all go. I worked on a farm, though, not in a factory. Wasn't treated too badly. Not as badly as these lads, but it was still hard." He looked again at the POWs. "Hard," he repeated.

"What will happen to them?"

The policeman sighed. "God knows. We're to march them to a railway station tomorrow and put them on a train west to a camp.

We'll be away early, I think. No idea when there'll be a train. What do they think they're going to do? Look at them. No fight left in 'em." He threw his finished cigarette away and pulled out a packet: Gitanes. Catching John's glance, the policeman offered him one. "French." John nodded. "I got a taste for them when I was there."

John thought of the French POWs and wondered where the cigarettes had come from: parcels from home meant for POWs usually contained cigarettes. He didn't ask and lit both cigarettes from the expiring stub of his own. "There's a lot of 'em out there, you know: prisoners, guest workers. Now with the Reds coming, no guards on some of the camps, the bombing messing things up, a lot of 'em have run off. There's loads of 'em camped out in the woods. Harmless, mostly. Like this lot." He stared sadly once more at his charges, now shuffling back into the hut. His fellow policemen weren't bothering to watch them but stood to one side, smoking and chatting. "No one bothers them as long as they don't bother anyone else. Some of 'em, though, starting to cause trouble. Steal food, that sort of thing."

John looked at the emaciated prisoners; he didn't think these had the strength to steal from a child.

"I have to go." The policeman held out his hand for John to shake. "Good luck." He smiled again, and then added in a low voice, "Englishman."

John was taken aback. "How did you…"

"Your German's good," the policeman smiled, "but my wife's from London. Stepney. I can tell." He smiled, added in passable but heavily accented English, "*Gin arp, oold jap!*" and walked away.

John stared after him. Stepney? Bloody hell, he thought, it *is* the laughing policeman! He grinned and walked back to the hut, humming the tune.

EIGHT

As the laughing policeman predicted, the POWs left early to catch a train. A watery sun was hardly above the line of hut routes before the dismal column of ragged Frenchmen shuffled away under the uninterested gaze of their police watchdogs. Only John watched them go.

Detachment Berg stayed in its huts, those not on watch, for they had no orders. Rask had informed John and the rest of the reconnaissance platoon that the major was trying to find someone in authority to tell him what to do, but it wasn't easy, it seemed. Meanwhile, the industrial estate was as good a place as any, providing ample opportunity for defence.

They waited, doing what all soldiers do in such circumstances: they dug in as best they could. They erected barricades and sangars between the warehouses and huts using whatever they could find, leaving some areas open through which attackers could be channelled and defenders could retreat. They deployed the detachment's few mortars together amongst a group of small warehouses, well back from the expected direction of attack, and pre-registered chosen target locations. Ammunition was shared out; zones of fire were allocated; weapons were cleaned, checked and rechecked; and that was about all they could do.

There was little food, and Berg ordered that it be cooked and stored, for who knew when they'd find more? John's belly started the day rumbling and it carried on that way, but he got used to it, and after a while he was too busy to notice that he was hungry.

When they were done they settled down to wait, as all soldiers do.

*

It started at dawn: cars crossing the little bridge full of men in suits and gaudy uniforms, well-dressed women and children, all stacked high with baggage. They passed in dribs and drabs, sometimes in twos and threes, but usually on their own.

"Sneaking out down the back roads," Mathias said sourly when a luxurious boxy car roared past. The two platinum blondes sitting in the back turned and blew kisses when Vogel saluted; the two men in gold braid in the front did not.

"Adler Standard 6," Friedrich said. Walter nodded, although he didn't really know, but Rolf's gaze was fixed on the blondes, not the car.

By lunchtime they'd stopped coming. Then three Opel Blitz lorries with SS number plates turned into sight from the opposite direction the cars had come from and pulled up outside one of the locked warehouses. Drivers emerged, SS tabs on the collars of their field jackets. Having relieved themselves in the canal, they stood around smoking. No one felt inclined to ask them what they were up to. Finally, a Kübelwagen arrived and parked behind the Opels. As it passed him, Walter saw a middle-aged slightly chubby sergeant in Luftwaffe field uniform driving and an SS major sitting in the back. Walter thought that there was something vaguely familiar about the officer but he couldn't place it. The Opel drivers cast away their cigarettes and came stiffly to attention, clicking their heels and saluting with upraised arms when the major got out.

After some lengthy orders which none of the boys could hear, the drivers rushed to open the backs of their lorries and followed the major as he unlocked the warehouse and strolled in.

Crates began to emerge, some carried by one man, some by two. One particularly large specimen needed all three drivers, struggling to hoist it into the back of one of the lorries. Fenstermacher and Vogel stood together by the bridge watching; they were not asked to help and they didn't volunteer any. Finally, the major reappeared at the doorway to the warehouse and beckoned his men in.

As he did so, Walter stared and started.

"You know him?" Mathias asked, watching him. "Come on, boy. Spit it out."

Walter glanced at his boots. "I think I saw him with that woman."

"What woman?" Mathias narrowed his eyes and glanced at the warehouse door.

"That one downstairs. That Slav."

"Slav? What are you talking…" Mathias stopped in mid-sentence and pursed his lips. "Tanya? Miss Klarkova?" He stared intensely.

Walter shifted uncomfortably and nodded.

Mathias' lips twisted in disapproval. "Don't call her 'that Slav.' She's a neighbour and a good one." He stared at the door. "You're sure?" Walter nodded slowly.

Fenstermacher had left his place by the bridge and walked up to join them, Vogel trailing behind. "I wonder what that's about."

Mathias set his face, glanced at Vogel and turned. "Let's find out." He strode towards the lorries; Walter, Rolf and Fenstermacher looked at each other in alarm.

"I wouldn't…" Fenstermacher called out softly, but Mathias ig-nored him. As he passed the Kübelwagen, Mathias nodded to the Luftwaffe sergeant still sitting in the front and then peered into the back of each lorry in turn. When Mathias returned, Fenstermacher raised his eyebrows enquiringly.

Mathias rubbed his chin. "Officially marked."

"Marked?"

Mathias looked pensive. "Party insignia and *Reichsmarschall des Großdeutschen Reiche* written all over. Fat Hermann's loot, I'd guess."

Vogel looked annoyed and seemed about to say something when Rolf spoke up. "I think they've finished."

They turned to see the major locking the warehouse doors and the three drivers shutting up their lorries and clambering in. When the major got into the Kübelwagen, Walter saw the sergeant say something and the major glanced towards them. Then the Kübelwagen lurched into life, turned and headed back the way it had come, followed by the lorries. They watched in silence as the vehicles passed; this time the major nodded at them with a supercilious smile.

Mathias pursed his lips as the groups of vehicles turned out of sight.

"Who was *he*?" asked Friedrich.

Walter shook his head.

Breakfast was not as good as dinner the previous evening; a chewy concoction of unidentifiable tinned meat, rubbery vegetables and lots of salt was doled out shamefacedly by the cooks when they left the hut to fetch it just after dawn. John wiped the inside of his mess tin with a grey slice of long-life bread. He sighed; he liked his food, an interest belied by his lean frame. A kipper between the eyes, his father used to call him. His mother had worried and tried to fatten him up, but she'd failed.

Greger peered into his own empty tin, shook his head sadly, looked at Kaarle and shrugged.

"Not exactly the Savoy, is it." John tucked his tin away, still hungry. "Not even Lyon's Corner House." Seeing Greger's puzzled expression, he explained. "The Savoy Hotel in London. Used to do great lunches. Still does, I suppose, war or no war. It's where the toffs eat."

"Toffs?"

"Rich people."

"Rich. *Toffs*." Greger leaned back against the hut outside which they were sitting and chuckled. "Toffs." He repeated the word several times.

"And there's Lyon's Corner House, a big café. Lots of people go there. My mother and I used to eat there whenever we went up west. Sorry, I mean when we went to the West End of London. She liked shopping. Not," John added ruefully, "that we could afford to spend too much after Father died."

Greger lit a cigarette. "Meatballs with dumplings. We had it every Sunday for supper when we went to see Grandmother."

John nodded: he knew the Swedish passion for the dish. "Fish and chips," John observed wistfully. "Every Friday night Mother would send me to fetch fish and chips. We'd have it with bread and butter. Father loved it."

"Baked lutfisk. With a cream sauce." Greger smiled.

John nodded. "Yes."

Greger looked puzzled. "You had *lutfisk* in London?"

"No." John grinned. "You don't get dried fish in England. Not like in Sweden. When I was in Östersund, I loved it. Christmas Eve especially. *Lutfisk* and cream sauce, and pancakes."

"With lingonberry sauce!" Greger licked his lips extravagantly.

"And rhubarb with custard. My father loved rhubarb." John's stomach was rumbling.

"Mine too," observed Greger, "the old bastard."

Seeing Greger's expression, John felt it was better to let that remark pass.

"*Laskeereeaska.*"

They looked at Kaarle: he was staring wistfully into space. "What?" they exclaimed simultaneously.

"*Laskeereeaska.*" Kaarle grinned. He pretended to roll something out. Then he made a sizzling noise through his teeth. Greger and John looked at each other, puzzled, so Kaarle repeated his actions.

"Oh, bread. Or a pancake?" John frowned.

Kaarle nodded. "*Ya.* Bread and, uh, *Koskenkorva.*"

John knew *that* word: they'd had a lot of it at Salla to keep out the cold. "It's a spirit," John explained to Greger, "like vodka."

Greger was amused. "Typical Finn: bread and alcohol." He tucked his mess tin away. "I wish Butter was here; he was a good cook."

John studied Greger's sombre face and knew it wasn't Kurschat's cooking that he missed. Then John thought of Olé and for a moment felt sombre. John glanced at Kaarle's puzzled face as he felt the gloom. This won't do, John chided himself, brooding. His father would have chided him.

He prodded Greger's knee. "Have you ever tried jellied eels? With mash and liquor?" When Kaarle and Greger stared at him he chuckled and began to explain.

*

They'd entered the suburbs of the city early that morning, the companies and platoons moving on parallel streets. What struck Leonid most were the smells: acrid brick dust tickled his nostrils, the ammonia of ruptured sewers caught at his throat and the sweet stench of buried bodies soured his mouth. He caught the aroma of hot pork fat as he and the platoon picked their way down a rubble-strewn street lined with fire-gutted roofless houses. The damage was, from the look of the craters, the result of a massive bombing attack, but it wasn't recent: there were no fires, not even any smoke, and no corpses. The pork tugged at his memory and he was back in his early childhood, his mother standing at the stove stirring a large iron pot, making lard which she would pack into crocks to keep in cold storage. The smell of cooking pork fat, the crackling of which he was allowed to chew once the rendering was done, was a childhood comfort, but this smell didn't comfort him. Who had burned here?

He scanned the buildings around him and looked through the empty doorway of the nearest ruin. There was little left save blackened baulks here and there where the thicker roof timbers had partially survived; all else was ash. Even the floor had gone, burned through and collapsing into a cellar space choked with unrecognisable debris. He walked to the door-less frame. The stink was stronger here and his eyes watered a little. He shook his head at Agranenko who stood on the opposite side of the street, watching him, to indicate that all was clear, and the platoon moved on.

Fifteen minutes later they halted again, this time not for a smell but for a noise. They'd passed beyond the ruins into streets of neat German houses. All was still except for a woman's voice howling despair and terror: an ugly, desperate animal sound. Leonid couldn't make out any words.

They turned a corner and a strange sight met his eyes. Red Army soldiers were waiting patiently in line, half a dozen of them, weapons held casually. They were lined up outside a handsome house: white plaster and red brick, grey tiles and wooden shutters around the windows. The door had been smashed in. From inside came the voice, but none of the queuing men seemed disturbed. They just waited, some chatting, most silent. One or two glanced around as the platoon passed them, but no one left the queue.

Leonid hesitated and Agranenko spoke softly. "Best not."

A soldier emerged from the house. He was expressionless, as if he'd just paid a visit to the quartermaster or the field post office: a man who'd completed satisfactorily his personal business; nothing of importance, though. The queue shuffled forward one space as another soldier went inside to take his turn.

Leonid and the platoon moved on.

Later, when the company paused to rest, Agranenko came to him with some black bread and a piece of hard German cheese. They sat and ate it together.

"Nothing to be done about it." Agranenko said it impassively, watching Leonid brood.

"But…"

"It's war." Agranenko was dispassionate. "What is it, Comrade Lieutenant? Feel sorry for them?"

Leonid looked at the ground and ate silently.

"She's lucky: she's alive. In Leningrad the women starved and watched their children starve. *I* watched them starve." Agranenko shook his head. "There are worse things. Here," Agranenko fumbled in his coat pocket and thrust a crumpled piece of paper towards him, "look."

Leonid unfolded it. It was one of the leaflets Polyanski and Moiseyevich had distributed when they'd moved up to start the assault on the Seelow Heights. He handed it back; he remembered the words and didn't need to read them again.

Nor did Agranenko who, as he put it in his pocket, recited them. "'The time has come to draw up the balance sheet of the abominable crimes perpetrated on our soil by the Hitlerite cannibals and to punish those responsible for these atrocities.'"

"Women too?"

Agranenko finished eating before he answered. "They had it coming to them."

"Do you really believe that, Sergeant?"

"In Leningrad, it was terrible."

Leonid nodded. "Yes. We heard about the starvation, the bombardments, the…"

"You heard?" Agranenko interrupted gently. "You see…" He reached out and made as if to grasp Leonid's arm, but at the last moment he pulled back. Suddenly his voice was intense. "You see, it wasn't what they did to us. We starved, froze, bombs and shells blew us to bits, but it wasn't that. It was what they made us do to each other…" He trailed off and seemed suddenly very tired.

Leonid looked away. He'd heard rumours, they all had: people eating their pet animals; boiling their leather belts; scraping the wallpaper paste from the wall; hunting rats. There were other rumours: graves opened; corpses vanishing off the streets before the official clear-up teams could retrieve them for burial.

'What they made us do to each other…' Leonid didn't directly experience the terrible famines in the countryside, but he knew the rumours. Food was taken away by officials to feed the cities, leaving those in the country to starvation, malnutrition and the diseases it brought. They were left to other things too. No one ever used the word 'cannibalism': it was officially forbidden. In the town which became Leonid's new home the children played a game in which one group took the part of a Requisitioning Brigade; another group would play bourgeois speculators, hiding the grain needed to feed the people. They were always caught, of course, tried and *sent away*. Leonid and Cheslav's mother and stepfather had argued about it, she forbidding them to join in, he encouraging them to. They wouldn't say why they differed, but Leonid and Cheslav knew anyway. And they remembered their father being taken.

Leonid looked at Agranenko staring into space. What was he seeing? What was he remembering?

Agranenko caught the look and smiled, but there was terrible recollection in it and no joy. "Akhmatova caught it, like she always does:

> No one wants to help us
> Because we stayed home,
> Because, loving our city
> And not winged freedom,
> We preserved for ourselves
> Its palaces, its fire and water.

Agranenko shook his head. Leonid turned back to his bread and cheese.

Tanya and Mrs Körtig amused themselves by talking about food. Each was a keen cook: they often swapped recipes and cooking tips as now it was a way to pass the time. Mrs Körtig's uncle and aunt had been celebrated restaurant owners in her childhood town of Pillau and much of their skill had rubbed off on her. In particular, she'd learned the secret of making wonderful stöllen.

Mrs Körtig sat comfortably across from Tanya in the curtained-off alcove and regaled her with long descriptions of lazy Sunday afternoons spent sampling her aunt and uncle's wares and watching the eclectic mix of seasonal tourists and local residents who kept them in business. Mrs Körtig had quite a talent for satirical description.

In turn, Tanya described her mother's cooking; how in the heart of Paris she'd converted meagre provisions into fine Russian food. "She didn't miss a festival," Tanya explained. "Kept all the holy days and never skimped. We always had guests, mainly other émigrés. She was well known for her hospitality."

Mrs Körtig nodded approvingly. "You can't do better than lay out a good meal for people."

"Well, she went to the Smolny."

"The Smolny?"

"The Smolny Institute for Noble Maidens." Tanya smiled at the pomposity of that. "Cooking was de rigueur."

Mrs Körtig smile back. "Quite right too."

"Sometimes after church on Sundays we'd go to others for dinner." Tanya wistfully recalled those days: elegantly dressed men and women, witty conversation, but instead of caviar and champagne,

Niello silverware and Kornilov porcelain, it had been fish paste, workingmen's wine and cheap white tableware. Tanya sighed. "We'd dress up and Mother would get out her jewellery. She managed to take some with her when we left Russia. She sold most of it, but she kept her wedding ring and a pearl necklace my father gave her when I was born."

Mrs Körtig leaned forward and patted her hand sympathetically.

"And her cook book." Tanya stopped as a wave of sadness washed over her. "She gave it to me when she left Berlin. I still have it: *A Gift to Young Housewives*."

Mrs Körtig smiled. "Elena Molokhovets."

"You know it?"

"Yes, m'dear. It was all the rage when I was a girl. A classic."

"Yes, it is that. A classic." Tanya sat back and stared at the ceiling. "I remember that once we held a dinner for a prince. Mother took all the recipes from that book. It was her Bible."

"A prince!" Mrs Körtig sounded impressed.

Tanya looked at her ruefully. "Nothing to boast about, really. There were a lot of Russian princes in Paris; mostly they had titles and no money. I can't remember his name." She paused. "It was the anniversary of the Tsar's Birthday. Well, the birthday he *would* have had if he'd still been alive. The men all wore their old army uniforms. Mother looked her best, I had my flowered dress on. A friend brought champagne and salmon; it was the first salmon I remember having. A whole fish, covered in cucumbers and gherkins and hard boiled eggs." Tanya stopped and shook her head sadly. "Salmon. I can't remember when I last had salmon."

"Nor me. Now it's black bread and potatoes. And sauerkraut. We mustn't forget the sauerkraut." They smiled at each other. "It sounds like a wonderful meal."

"Yes," replied Tanya simply, "it was."

"Who was the generous friend?"

"I beg your pardon?"

"He brought the champagne and the salmon."

"Oh yes. Victor. Victor Palanevich, a friend of Papa's. They served together in the army. Fought against the Reds later. He came to Paris after the Revolution." She stopped, then added bleakly, "Papa didn't."

Mrs Körtig said nothing but patted her hand again.

"Victor was a sort of uncle," explained Tanya, "was good to us in Paris."

"Forgive me for asking," said Mrs Körtig, "but is he the officer who…"

"Stores things in the coal cellar? Yes." Tanya was disconcerted; Mrs Körtig's astuteness sometimes caught her by surprise.

"And he likes champagne."

"Oh yes," Tanya chuckled, "he likes champagne."

"I like a drop myself, m'dear. At least, I used to." Mrs Körtig looked down, primly folded her hands on her lap and sighed. "But bread on the plate is better than cake on the shelf."

Tanya nodded. "It's a true saying, but now and again wouldn't it be nice if we could have just a little cake?"

"Or salmon and champagne."

They paused a moment and then Mrs Körtig frowned. "What happened to it?"

"What?"

"That place your mother learned to cook."

"The Smolny Institute for Noble Maidens?" Tanya sighed. "Victor Palanevich told me the Bolsheviks turned it into Party headquarters."

Mrs Körtig stared at her and then they both laughed. What an absurd world, Tanya noted.

The company had halted in the middle of a ploughed field. Cheslav sat on his pack up, examining jeeps parked under a stand of trees a hundred metres away. There were so many about these days. He could see the Soviet red stars but he knew they were American. Half the army's motor transport seemed to be from America. Once officially derided as the great capitalist enemy of the working classes, now America was a partner in the fight against the fascist beast. The irony was never lost on Cheslav.

The small lorries parked by the jeeps were unfamiliar. They were squat with engine cowls like the snouts of pigs, metal cabs, canvas awnings enclosing the backs. Scattered along the edge of the copse, with nothing like the parade ground neatness of the newsreels, were mortars and boxes of mortar rounds, some open. The mortar teams sat or lay about, and clearly were not expecting to do much for a while for they were cooking, shaving and playing cards. One was sitting on a chair next to a wind-up gramophone and a woman's voice sang across the grass.

"Ruslanova. Nice."

Cheslav glanced at Kolchok who had come to sit next to him and nodded. It was Lidiya Ruslanova all right, a popular pre-war singer of folk songs. Her words were clear on the still, chill evening air despite the rumble of vehicles and the clatter of men and horses passing along the road on the other side of the field.

For a moment they listened in silence, but then Kolchok joined in, a surprisingly melodious sound emerging from his weather-beaten face:

…my Valenki, my Valenki
Oh, they are worn and they are old.
My Valenki, my Valenki
Instead of bringing me gifts
It is better to mend my Valenki…

Kolchok broke off and cleared his throat. Cheslav was amused; how typical of an old peasant to be moved by a song about boots! Valenki, made of knee-length thick felt, were warmly proof against the deep and bitter Russian snows and much valued by any peasant. Cheslav had worn them himself regularly, at least before his family moved to the town where the gritty wet slush made leather boots more practical, if you could get them.

Someone else was singing now; a young man's voice, wistful, rising from amongst the mortar men. It was not as good a voice as Kolchok's, but Cheslav could hear the emotion in it. More men joined in.

The words affected Cheslav as they'd affected Kolchok, who once more had found his voice. The song was about more than boots. Cheslav listened to the beautiful words, the lament of a girl who cannot go out into the bitter winter to find her true love because, being poor, she has no Valenki. But eventually, despite the cold, she goes to him anyway. Ruslanova and the mortar man sang together:

> …judge me by
> the power of my love:
> For during the frost I went barefoot
> to my darling…

The record came to its end with a hiss and silence fell for a moment, then came a sudden burst of laughter amongst the mortar men nearest the gramophone.

Cheslav turned back to the booklet he'd been reading. Kolchok pulled out his pipe and began to fill it. "More, who was it, Dockens?"

Cheslav shook his head. "Dickens. But not this one. Just some poems." He waited, hoping that would satisfy Kolchok and that he'd be left alone to read. He wasn't.

"Go on, then." Kolchok looked at him expectantly. Cheslav tried not to let his annoyance show; he opened the cardboard covers and read aloud. Kolchok's face relaxed into soft pleasure.

"That's good," he mumbled, teeth clenched around the stem of his pipe.

"What is?" Beridze walked up to them, chewing a piece of black bread, Janko in tow. Without waiting for an answer, they sat next to Kolchok. Janko seemed drunk, as he often was.

Now Cheslav really *was* irritated. It was bad enough that Kolchok had intruded; at this rate half the company would soon be here, but there was no helping it. He knew the next poem mostly by heart and hardly bothered to look at the page:

> Flimsily dexterous
> The droplets go
> The Spring let sketchily
> Darts to and fro.

As he recited, Cheslav watched their rapt faces. Leonid liked to say, "Scratch a Russian and find a poet." The idea cheered him as he went on:

> While I
> A rock that's well past my prime
> Feel helpless to guess one thing:
> Just why this inanimate little spring
> Is moving faster than I.

Cheslav paused. Janko laughed appreciatively and pulled a half-empty vodka bottle out of his pocket. "Hear that?" He pushed Kolchok's knee and the old man gave him a flinty-eyed look. "'A rock well past my prime...'" Janko took a mouthful of vodka.

Kolchok frowned. "Another," he said.

Cheslav turned the pages.

> "Wait for me and I'll come back!
> Wait with all you've got!
> Wait, when dreary yellow rains
> Tell you, you should not..."

Janko nodded, silently mouthing the words: Simonov's poem was well known and loved. When Cheslav finished the poem, around them men chatted and laughed, someone played a mouth organ while the road rumbled and clattered and in the distance guns barked, but they sat in a pool of companionable silence. Then Kolchok held out his hand for the book, and while he flicked through the pages, Cheslav explained.

"It's an official collection of war poetry. I brought it with me from the depot."

Kolchok handed it back and nodded. "Good."

Watching him turn the pages, Cheslav realised that Kolchok couldn't read: he'd held the book upside down.

"You reading one," Beridze urged Kolchok.

"I'll read another one," Cheslav said hastily, but to his surprise Kolchok shook his head.

"I'll do one." He sat back and stared into space for a moment, and reciting rhythmically in a sing-song lilt, he quoted another Simonov poem, *Smolensk Roads*:

> Remember, Alyosha, the roads of Smolenshchina,
> Remember the rain and the mud and the pain,
> The women, exhausted, who brought milk in pitchers,
> And clasped them like babies at breast, from the rain.

Like a bard in the old days, wondered Cheslav, and he was entranced by the performance as Kolchok went on with no hesitation or breaks. It was a long poem, but no one stirred. When Kolchok came to the last verse, Cheslav noticed Janko turn away to wipe his sleeve across his eyes.

> I'm proud that the mother who bore us was Russian;
> That Russian I'll fall as my ancestors fell;
> That going to battle, the woman was Russian,
> Who kissed me three times in a Russian farewell!

Kolchok ended and looked around the group, smiled briefly and began refilling his pipe.

"You sad old bugger." Janko shook his head slowly. "Let's have something jolly." He pushed Beridze's shoulder. "Get that thing of yours."

Beridze smiled: he liked to play. He disappeared towards the platoon's cart, parked a few metres away, and returned with his panduri. Sitting cross-legged, he tuned the strings for a moment and then began to play. Cheslav watched as Beridze's long thin fingers glided across the sound box, drawing out an exquisite ripple of sound. Beridze closed his eyes, and as the melodies wafted into the air, Cheslav too closed his eyes, letting himself be caught up. In the music he saw the dry dusty plains and river valleys of Georgia; he smelled the summer forests, heard the tinkle of goat bells and the singing of women as they went about their work; and above it all he saw the snow-capped mountains of the Caucasus. Cheslav had never been there, but Beridze had described it all many times and now it was here in the sweet playing of a young soldier.

When Beridze finished, Cheslav opened his eyes and saw Bartashevich and Lopakin standing to one side. All around many of the platoon and mortar crews were standing too, still and silent.

"Now something jolly," Janko hiccupped and Kolchok glared at him.

Walter gazed across the brazier at Friedrich and saw that he was brooding. Rolf sat between them, seeing nothing: he was not the most observant of boys as far as people were concerned.

"Odd, wasn't it?" Friedrich met Walter's gaze with a rueful smile.

"Odd?"

"That bit with the lorry and those boxes. Your uncle was very angry."

Walter grimaced. "He often is."

"Bit of a Red, isn't he?"

Rolf's question disturbed Walter. Sure, Mathias had been a Trades Union man before the Führer had abolished Unions; he'd been a Social Democrat before the Führer had abolished Social Democracy; but he wasn't a Red. Walter shook his head.

"Someone told me your uncle might be on the police watch list."

They stared at Rolf. Walter too had heard that; Vogel had made a point of telling him a few times. "He disagrees too much," Walter said, glancing across the fire at Mathias who was sitting by another brazier with some of the Volkssturm, smoking his pipe.

Friedrich grinned. "You too."

"Me?"

"Yes, you." Friedrich's grin faded into a concerned frown. "You may not think so, but people can see when you don't agree with them. You've a glass face. My mother used to say that 'glass face shows everything.' Best not to show too much, all right?" He too glanced at Mathias and added softly, "Especially now."

"Why?"

"Remember Schenck?"

Walter's eyes widened slightly and he nodded. He remembered Schenck all right: he'd been the unit leader when Walter first joined. A stern, proper young man, he'd been popular with the younger boys for his fairness and generous encouragement; he believed that loyalty ran down as well as up. It got him into trouble during a Führer's birthday parade, Walter's first with the Hitler Youth. One of the older boys had the honour of carrying the Company Banner during their march past local officials. The banner caught on some low branches. It had been picked up quickly, but that didn't stop one very fat and pompous official from berating the banner carrier afterwards: he'd slapped the boy's face. Schenck, outraged, had stepped forward and protested forcefully. Shortly afterwards, Schenck's call-up papers had been sent to him early and Vogel took over. Schenck never came home again and rumour had it that he'd been sent to a concentration camp, but no one dared to ask.

Walter shifted uncomfortably. "Schenck was different."

Rolf shook his head. "It's dangerous to cross them."

"I don't."

"No," agreed Friedrich, "but your uncle does. Can't you say something?"

"To Uncle Mathias? You're not serious!"

"He's your uncle. Arguing like he does, well it's not safe."

Walter shook his head in irritation at Friedrich. "I know that! *He* knows that! Anyway, we don't talk much. No." He heard the anger in his voice and controlled it, spoke more gently. "I *can't* talk to him. It'd only make it worse." Walter glanced again at Mathias who was grinning at something one of the Volkssturm had said. For some reason that irritated him even more. "It's no good, Friedrich. Mother always said he and Father were alike in one thing: they'd never learned how to keep their mouths shut. If they think something's wrong, they say so."

Friedrich nodded slowly and Rolf said, "He's a good man. I can see that, but so was Schenck."

"Good?" The word startled Walter. He pondered it for a moment: he'd never really considered Mathias to be *good*.

"Yes." Rolf was emphatic. "He came to find you, didn't he? And he stayed to look after you."

"I don't need him to look after me!"

They both looked at Walter intently for a moment, and then Friedrich murmured, "I wish I had someone like him looking out for *me*."

Walter didn't reply to that, but looked away for a moment before staring pointedly into the fire. They said no more. Instead they sat together quietly as the shadows lengthened and listened to the comforting crackle of the flames as out of the shadows came the occasional sound of a vehicle, the intermittent murmur of distant artillery fire and the low drone of conversation around the bridge.

NINE

Boredom: the soldier's lot. John's father had tried to explain the waiting to him when he was a boy, the long periods stuck in miserable conditions in the trenches of Flanders doing anything they could to alleviate the tedium. John had not really understood. He had been too young; to him, boredom was immediate. Boys have a short attention span, but they also forget quickly. It wasn't until he was at Salla that John really understood what his father had meant by how boredom ground a man down worse than the shelling. Ennui: the listlessness and demoralisation of having nothing to do but wait, and wait, and wait. For a soldier it was made worse by knowing that what you waited for might be something dreadful, but you couldn't know what.

At Salla he'd know men eventually cast away their weapons and desert because of it; they were fine in the fighting. He'd known men take foolish risks because of it; they'd been cautious in combat. But waiting through mud, rain, the same endless routines of watching was too much. Some men got into fights, their nerves frayed by it. Others got drunk on whatever they could find or brew for themselves. They had done that in Flanders too. "You're never bored when you're sozzled," John's father had told him, and as long as the men were capable of pulling a trigger, he and his fellow officers had tolerated moderate inebriation.

Here there was no mud, they were warm and there was no shelling; at least none nearby.

They waited.

*

To Leonid, the fire station looked beautiful in the bright morning light. Built of grey stone blocks, it had tall mullioned windows and square towers at either end topped with copper cupolas, green with age. There were double wooden doors in the centre of the façade. Once solidly elegant, they now lay across the cobbles in splintered pieces, the stonework around them pitted and scarred, and all those beautiful windows were shattered. Inside, instead of gleaming red fire engines there were the twisted remains of an anti-tank gun and its dead crew.

The station occupied one side of a small square at the end of the narrow road down which the platoon had advanced. Trofimova's tank stood at the entrance to the square, one track unfurled behind it like a strip of ribbon. The other two tanks sat in a side alley. The platoon was standing about them as Trofimova explained it all to Agranenko and Leonid.

"*Crack*, comrades. Split the fucking track. Just like that." She grinned and added wistfully, "Good shot. Used my last HE to finish the bastard, only AP left now."

Leonid nodded. Armour-piercing rounds, were solid slugs of steel designed to kill tanks; they were useless against buildings for which you needed high-explosive. The route the platoon had followed all morning had been marked by many wrecked buildings, evidence that Trofimova's platoon had been liberal with their HE. Tankists were notoriously aggressive and disinclined to give the Germans the benefit of the doubt. With no HE left, she obviously expected the platoon to clear the building from which, she said, there'd been some rifle fire. Leonid contemplated the prospect gloomily. They'd trained for such an eventuality, but they weren't well equipped for it. They had neither explosive charges nor fuel for flamethrowers; the battalion had by now used up its allocation of both. He looked back down the road to where Gushenko stood watching him. Behind him the company waited, and behind them no doubt the battalion. For all Leonid knew, the whole of the Red Army was lined up waiting for him to *do* something: his was point platoon. He stared at the fire station and pondered.

It was a pretty setting, despite the debris. There were trees in front of the four storey buildings lining the other sides of the square, all narrow windowed and narrow gabled with decorative eaves. It was peaceful. Artillery fire rumbled intermittently, but it was distant and the loudest noise nearby was the call of a songbird nesting in one of the trees, or perhaps under the eaves. He couldn't pinpoint it; he thought that he recognised the loud *tsee, tsee, tsee* of a blue tit. At another time, in another world, he'd have been glad to stroll across the square or sit outside the closed and shuttered café on the corner. He and Cheslav might drink tea and talk about books, girls or music.

"So what's the plan?"

Engelina's rumble cut across his daydream. He looked at Agranenko, who nodded to him, and cast his mind back to what he'd been told in the academy, which wasn't much: 'stone buildings with enemy nests of resistance are destroyed with mortar and cannon fire, their occupants with hand grenades.' The mortars would be no use at all, whatever the book advised, and Trofimova's cannon could do little more. More useful was the briefing the battalion's officers and senior NCOs had had from a major sent from division the week before the assault across the Oderbruch. He was a veteran of Stalingrad, the battle they called 'The academy of street fighting'. Leonid had paid close attention; he pulled out the sheet of notes he'd taken and, under Agranenko's amused gaze, read them slowly, ignoring Trofimova's muttered, "It's not a fucking schoolroom."

"'Use artillery and tank guns to fire explosives direct at the building beforehand,'" the major had said. "'Use heavy weapons such as machine guns and anti-tank rifles to provide covering fire. Get inside fast and use sub-machine guns, grenades, entrenching tools, knives: anything you can use in limited spaces. Rifles are no good.'" The idea of using a knife or shovel made Leonid squirm.

The major had stressed they should avoid moving across open

spaces and being spotted. "'Sneak up. Take covered ways. Use roofs, back alleys, cellars, and use satchel charges to blast holes in walls to get in.'" Leonid looked across the brightly-lit open square surrounded by close-packed houses and grimaced. At least they had plenty of hand grenades.

He looked once more back down the road. Gushenko had been joined by Polyanski and Zeldin. Clearly his superiors were getting impatient. He turned to Agranenko and laid out his plan. To his surprise Agranenko made no changes and sent Moiseyevich to fetch the anti-tank section. Their long barrelled heavy rifles mounted on bi-pods fired a solid slug twice the diameter of a normal bullet. They could provide covering fire, shooting into the upper windows where the rounds hopefully would bounce about inside, chopping things up or at least keeping heads down. Half the platoon would rush the building with an assortment of weapons under Agranenko's command. The other half, with all the platoon's light machine guns, would provide covering fire and backup.

It was as much as he could do; it seemed simplistic, but it worked like clockwork.

When all was ready, Agranenko shouted, "Go!", the covering group opened fire and the building was rushed. There was no resistance at all.

"Bastards have slipped away," commented Trofimova as Agranenko and his men stormed past the wrecked gun. Leonid hoped so, but it seemed an eternity until Agranenko reappeared and waved him over.

"Empty," he confirmed. Agranenko glanced back at the tumble of bodies inside the broken doors. "Mostly." He lit a cigarette. "Hope they're all as easy."

Leonid too looked at the broken anti-tank gun: for that crew, it had *not* been easy. He hoped it had been quick. He nodded, lit a cigarette of his own from Agranenko's, and then walked into the square. Catching the scent of lilacs, he saw a tree beginning to blossom. He heard the songbird again and a tiny blue and white shape darted and swooped above his head. His gaze followed as it wheeled and ducked around the square and then away over the rooftops towards the distant shellfire, and he smiled.

Tanya found it hard to concentrate for long on anything much: the crash of shells outside was too distracting. Sometimes one or two exploded at a time; sometime a sudden burst; sometimes close; usually distant. Tanya tried to read, then talked with Mrs Körtig, played cards with her and with Axel and Klara. She tried to talk with Ida, but Ida was too morose, preferring to sit and leaf through Walter's things, or just sit, staring listlessly into space. Tanya ignored Mrs Boldt completely.

The block warden spent her time cranking the handle on the radio in search of news, but it was sparse and unhelpful, comprising bombastic generalisations: 'stiff resistance'; 'staunch heroism'; 'holding the enemy'; 'determined to make the Bolshevik Beast pay.' Mostly, however, the radio played light dance numbers or operettas. Tanya heard 'The Merry Widow' twice before midday. It was Hitler's favourite, but did they have to broadcast it so often? The second time Axel made her laugh. The operetta, he told her over the game of skat they were playing with Klara, had been written by one of the Führer's fellow countrymen, Franz Lehár. She knew that, but she didn't know that Lehár's wife Sophie had been a Jewess before she converted to Catholicism. Axel told her that Hitler was so taken with Lehár's work that, almost as soon as he'd become Chancellor, he issued a decree making her an honorary Aryan. Tanya chuckled and earned herself a glare from Mrs Boldt.

Near noon she suddenly wanted to wash but had no water: they were conserving it to drink for the mains supply had failed and it was too dangerous to go outside to the standpipe. Her scalp itched, her skin itched and she felt so grubby. If only I could have a proper bath, she thought. She sighed and picked up the book she'd been reading by the dim light from the window. The cover said it was a collection of poems by an approved Nazi poet, Hanns Johst. In fact, she was reading *Buddenbrooks* by Thomas Mann, who most certainly was not approved.

When the Nazis came to power and started banning writers, people bought cheap copies of approved works, removed the covers and used them to camouflage forbidden publications. Tanya had quite a few, but just why she'd hidden Mann inside Johst she wasn't sure: she didn't really like Mann. She'd protected Mann's book only because he was an important German writer and because she objected to being told who she could read, but bringing it to the cellar had been a mistake. She'd forgotten how much Mann irritated her and she again laid the book down.

Mrs Körtig whispered from her chair, "Here we go," and nodded at Mrs Boldt, who yet again laid down her knitting and went to the radio. After the initial hiss and crackle, she found a jolly little tune, vaguely familiar to Tanya: something from pre-war days. A folk tune, the sort of thing the Nazis highly approved of. Suddenly it stopped halfway through a bar and a very self-important announcer instructed listeners to stand by. Mrs Boldt raised her hand imperiously and told them all to listen, quite unnecessarily for they were already doing so.

Even Ida paid attention when a beautiful tenor voice began to sing 'Germany Land of the Faithful', a well-known SA marching song. Tanya had heard it many times before in the streets, sung badly by strutting columns behind raucous brass bands. Its lyrics had been written as a deliberate appeal to every German's sense of Heimat: feeling for place and community, a sense of belonging. The Nazis used Heimat well. It was such a common song that Tanya knew most of the words, although she didn't want to. This time it was well sung, and when it was done a new voice took over: Goebbels. He confirmed the gravity of the situation, but then he spoke, as he often did, of the struggle with world Jewish bolshevism; of the subhuman beasts threatening the German people from the east. He welcomed a chance for a final showdown which would lead inevitably to the triumph of Germany, of German values.

At this, everyone except Mrs Boldt and Ida looked at each other in astonishment; Mrs Boldt smiled quietly and nodded her head. Ida covered her mouth with her hand and turned away; Tanya imagined she saw a tear run down her face.

Goebbels went on in the same vein for a while. He used a phrase he'd used before, after the terrible German defeat at Stalingrad: 'Now, folk, rise up and storm break loose!' It was an old rallying-cry from the Napoleonic wars and seemed absurdly melodramatic to Tanya. Finally Goebbels told them that the Führer would stay at his post in Berlin, fighting alongside his people. The radio played the National Anthem and Mrs Boldt stood; after a moment's hesitation, so did the rest of them, except for Ida who remained sitting, her head turned to the wall with her eyes still closed. Mrs Boldt glanced at Ida but said nothing. She looked almost happy; everyone else looked resigned.

When the music ended, they sat in silence.

Then Mrs Körtig reached across and patted Tanya's leg. "Would you like some tea, m'dear?" She glanced at Mrs Boldt, knitting once more, a smug look on her flushed face. "I think we could all do with some."

Walter was bored. It was a problem for everyone and morale was sagging. There was nothing to break up the tedium of waiting by the bridge except to play cards, read, eat and sleep. An occasional civilian vehicle drove across the canal, now and again pedestrians passed through the barricade carrying bags or pulling carts, but they were off the main roads in a rundown industrial suburb with few houses and saw very few people.

They felt completely isolated: they had no radio, there were no telephones and none of those passing could tell them what was going on save that the Reds were close and getting closer. In the distance they heard spasmodic rumbles of artillery fire or the crash of exploding bombs. Now and again aircraft passed overhead, but never low enough to be identified. Fenstermacher sent a couple of his section along the canal to find out who held their flanks. They found similar mixed groups of Volkssturm and Hitler Youth at the crossing points on either side with the same orders: hold. They also found a police station and used its telephone to call the district office. No one answered so they rang every one of the police list of nearby headquarters. Most didn't answer, and those that did told them the same: obey your orders; stay put.

The world closed in. Mathias was no comfort.

"Sit around, freeze your arses off and then pee your pants when something finally happens. That's soldiering for you," he commented after one of Rolf's frequent complaints. Everyone grumbled, and they became less and less certain about what they were doing there; even Vogel was diffident when asked about it, although he insisted that orders were orders, they had a duty to perform, and no, they *couldn't* pop back home for a bit. It was a refrain that satisfied no one. The grumbling continued; some of the boys even began to backchat Vogel, a risky undertaking at the best of times and one Walter did not join in.

Things were not improved when finally they did encounter a friendly military unit, although friendly was not the term Walter would have used. He was finishing the latest game of skat with Rolf and Friedrich when Thalberg shouted "Alarm!" from his watch post over the bridge and came running back across it, puffing and red-faced: he was a fat boy. After a moment of confusion and uncertainty, they grabbed their weapons and ran to their positions behind the barricades or amongst the surrounding buildings. Men in uniform could be seen coming down the approach road on the other side of the canal.

Walter tensed, but almost immediately Mathias said, "It's all right. They're ours," and stood up the better to see across the pile of builders' sand against which he'd been sitting.

Everyone watched in silence as the column passed. Walter was shocked. They moved like dejected civilian refugees, shuffling along with no order. Their Luftwaffe field uniforms were stained and disarrayed. Few carried weapons and all were wounded, some helped by their less damaged comrades, others ambling along on their own. They looked completely exhausted, bloodshot eyes staring from haggard faces. To Walter they seemed like figures from a ghost story: an army of the dead. He saw no one in command, and although Vogel ran up and down barking questions, few spoke to him. Those who did mumbled replies he didn't pass on. Eventually he gave up and stood with the others, watching them stream down the road further into the city. After they'd vanished from sight, Vogel didn't move for a while, nor did he speak; and nor did anyone else.

Leonid saw Trofimova again later that day when he came out of a battalion officers' briefing. Further up the road, where her tanks were, she and Agranenko stood smoking. Her crew were sitting on the engine decks doing the same.

She slapped him on the shoulder when he approached. "So how did it go?"

"Go?"

"Your sergeant told me you've been in a meeting."

Leonid nodded.

"So, where next?"

"We wait."

She stared at him. "Wait?"

He nodded again. "Regiment wants to reorganise, and there's a canal up ahead. Major Zeldin wants to wait for the engineers."

She spat out tobacco and snorted, "Shit-trampers", the slang for boots and the infantry who wore them. She sounded impatient, but then, she usually did.

"It's orders."

"Fuck, boy," she'd rasped disdainfully, "orders? The only order I know is to get ahead and kill fascists. Know your Simonov?" She stubbed out her cigarette against the side of the tank and dropped the butt onto the floor, lit another. "'Then kill a German, make sure to kill one! Kill him as soon as you can!'"

Agranenko raised his eyebrows.

"Wassa matter, Comrade Sergeant? Think I don't know a verse or two?" She laughed, the cigarette in her mouth bouncing up and down; the sound came out like a cross between a cough and a sneeze. "'We Bolsheviks have hearts forged from steel.'" She grinned and spat flakes of tobacco.

"Simonov again."

She nodded at Agranenko. "'Gunner Poliakov'. Hey, Karabai, waddya think?" She looked up.

Lifting their gaze, they saw a face tanned by steppe winds and the intense sunlight of Asia peering down at them from the turret. He showed brilliantly white teeth. "Yes. Steel."

"Fucking steel, right? Like Comrade Stalin, *Man of Steel*." She dropped her second butt onto the floor and wiped her mouth with the back of her hand. "I need a piss." She strode away.

"*Heart vee Kruppshtahl…*" Agranenko shook his head at Trofimova's back. Leonid stared at him.

"Motto of the Hitler Youth," he explained. "Swift as greyhounds, tough as leather, hard as Krupp steel." He glanced up at Karabai who was clambering out of the turret.

"She quotes Poliakov to everyone; he is one of her favourites." Karabai dropped lithely to the ground and fumbled in his breast pocket. He held out a yellow-white box, carved in beautiful geometric patterns. Inside were several ready-rolled cigarettes and Leonid took out two, handing one to Agranenko.

"An heirloom. My father gave me it when I left for the Front." Karabai spoke Russian slowly and carefully as if it was a foreign language. He sounded archaic, formal, like a man from a previous age: not at all proletarian. He took a cigarette for himself and tucked the box away.

Leonid nodded his thanks, lighting the three cigarettes in turn.

"Every man in our family gives one to his son to mark his transition to adulthood."

"A cigarette?" asked Agranenko.

Karabai shook his head irritably. "No, my friend." Leonid

noticed that he used the old Russian term; he did not say *comrade*. "No, in the old days it held sherbet. Travellers used it to sweeten their water."

Leonid and Agranenko smiled.

"Now," Karabai explained, "I use it to keep cigarettes in." He wrinkled his nose, blew a cloud of smoke into the air. "Sweetens the air." He peered at them intently through an aromatic cloud. There was something spicy in the tobacco, Leonid could taste it on his tongue. "Do not be too hard on Comrade Trofimova. She was raised in an orphanage. She did not know her mother. She began work when she was five years old. She was proud of it. Her father was at the *Trëkhgornaya Manufaktura*. He was one of those who manned the barricades in 1917. He was executed by the Whites."

"I see." Leonid was impressed. The *Trëkhgornaya Manufaktura* was a textile factory once owned by a rich aristocratic family. Occupied by its workers, it was stormed by the authorities and all the ringleaders shot. The *Trëkhgornaya Manufaktura* was an icon of communism; its martyrs were new saints.

"Her family were her comrades at the factory where she worked making tanks." Karabai smiled sadly. "She went with it east when the factory was evacuated in 1941. She put all her savings into a workers' fund to help buy *him*." He slapped the tank very hard with his free hand. "She got the idea from *Komsomolskaya Pravda*."

"Oh yes," said Agranenko, thinking for a moment, "There was a series in it about a worker who drove the tank he made straight out of the factory into battle." He sounded sceptical.

"*Letters to Mother?*" ventured Leonid and Agranenko nodded.

"When he was sent to the front," Karabai touched the tank again, "she went too." He stopped, puffed on his cigarette a few times. "Our commander was killed in him. She was his driver. She took over when it happened, got us out of danger. They let her keep the platoon afterwards." He pulled out the carved box, opened it and looked at the contents, then replaced it in his pocket. "I smoke too much," he observed and leaned back against the tank. "It was hard on her. Commander and she were together, you see. They were close." When Agranenko looked quizzical, he added, "*Very* close."

Leonid felt surprised. Somehow he could not imagine Trofimova to be that much a woman. It was too absurd: she was wholly worker; wholly soldier; wholly *comrade*. That she might be something more to a man seemed bizarre. Then he thought of the women in the cellar, and he thought of the makeup.

"She's not got much patience. All she wants to do is kill Germans."

I know someone else like that, Leonid told himself. He caught the look on Agranenko's face and guessed that he too was thinking about Moiseyevich.

Then Agranenko smiled wryly and nodded past Leonid's shoulder. "Here comes Heart of Steel."

They turned to see Trofimova stomping towards them, face set. "All right," she announced when she reached them, "we're going forward."

"But..."

Her eyes narrowed. "We're going forward."

Agranenko shot Leonid a warning look.

"*But* is a word for paper pushers." She nodded brusquely at Leonid and Agranenko, and then clambered onto her tank followed by Karabai. She heaved herself onto the turret and scrambled inside. The other crews, seeming to take their cue from this, did likewise. Three engines coughed into life.

"Shit," said Agranenko under his breath, then he shrugged. "She's not a woman, she's a force, a tempest in the night."

More Simonov, Leonid realised as the three tanks lurched down the road. He watched them go with some trepidation.

Will we ever get back to normal? Cheslav wrote to Leonid as he watched the vehicles leave the field, pulling their mortars behind them. *There are German prisoners on the road, a long column, hundreds. Grey figures like cows going to milking. Do you remember how old Bachmeier's cows used to follow him?* Cheslav paused and reread his words, musing.

Bachmeier, their neighbour in the village, had been a morose man. He'd lived alone, his wife dead long before Leonid or Cheslav were born. Only his younger sister had much to do with him, taking time off from caring for her husband and children to cook and clean. Some in the village believed him 'touched', 'apart', for he didn't speak much except to his cows.

Cheslav and Leonid would watch Bachmeier tend them, treating each as if she was a person. Sometimes he'd give the two boys a drink of milk straight from the pail, warm and creamy. Sometimes, after church, he'd beckon to them when he thought no one was watching, reach into the small bag he wore at his belt and bring out thick slices of cold grebel: fried bread dough drenched in sugar. At other times he'd give them small honey cakes. He'd wink, unsmiling, and they'd hide the food to eat later when no one was watching. One Christmas Eve, as they waited after mass for their mother to finish her conversation with the priest, Bachmeier gave them each a bag of small cakes powdered with sugar white like the snow. They'd loved the unfamiliar spicy-hot taste when they ate them in secret, snuggled up together under the blanket on the big stone stove.

The following spring Bachmeier was taken away, his cows lowing mournfully for lack of milking until someone fetched them for the collective farm. There were no more secret treats, for Bachmeier never came back, but they remembered him and would speak of him with fondness.

Cheslav watched the German prisoners. Will anyone remember them? he wondered sadly.

We are here for a while, he wrote. *The roads are full and we have orders to wait. The men are lighting fires, washing, cooking, sleeping. You know how it is. I'm sharing a tent with Kolchok.* Cheslav snorted at what he'd written: tent! The two men's rain-capes buttoned together and strung on a length of rope between cut branches driven into the damp ground. It was standard practice and gave a degree of shelter, but he'd rather not have been sharing with Kolchok. *I hope he washes today*, he wrote and grimaced. Then, glancing towards Kolchok where he sat smoking with Beridze and Janko, Cheslav's grimace turned to a wry smile. The three men were laughing at something Kolchok had said, Beridze rocking back and forth, his young face aglow with delight. Kolchok slapped Beridze's knee. Cheslav looked at the old man's seamed face and thought, He's like a character from Tolstoy. Gerasim in *The Death of Ivan Ilyich* perhaps, or Platon Karataev in *War and Peace*, or like one of the peasants back home in the village. But Tolstoy's peasants were embodiments of his ideals, unlike Cheslav's villagers.

"Good and bad and indifferent; mostly indifferent," his father had said of their neighbours. Real people, not symbols.

Cheslav watched Kolchok talking and wondered what it was about. He rarely spoke this much. One of his stories from the old days, Cheslav mused. Folk wisdom. His father would have snorted at the idea. On impulse, Cheslav put the letter away and went to join them.

"There's a remedy for the little buggers," Kolchok was saying as Cheslav approached. He glanced up and carried on without breaking stride. "Old pig fat. Rub it on. Keep the buggers from biting."

Beridze, seeing Cheslav's puzzlement, explained. "Midges."

Oh, thought Cheslav, right, and nodded.

"Keep everyone else away too," snorted Janko and held his nose mockingly.

Kolchok stared at Janko for a moment. "Clean dirt's fine," he said, "healthy."

Cheslav exchanged a rueful glance with Janko: clean dirt! At home, they'd washed daily and bathed at least once a week. Not everyone in the platoon, however, aspired to Cheslav's standards. They knew to keep their weapons in good order, and Bartashevich's daily inspection of hands and faces and the white linen bands inside their collars ensured they all washed what was visible; and to be fair, Cheslav knew that most would strip off and wash the rest now and again. Kolchok's personal hygiene was, however, a bit of a joke in the platoon, but Kolchok, for all his oft-expressed disdain for 'dandies', in reality appreciated Cheslav's determination to stay clean and tidy, even if he didn't copy him. Like many of the older soldiers, he regarded good personal grooming as a sign of kultura, of being a gentleman, words they would not use in front of a Party member, but it was how they felt.

"What's this about midges?"

"He was telling us how wonderful it was, back then." Janko glanced around him, but he was relaxed; there were no officers nearby. "Going hunting with the toffs. Midges an' all. Who'd have thought it? An aristocrat sleeping rough, away from his nice big house and servants." He sounded disbelieving.

Kolchok looked irritated. "What do you know about it, boy?"

Janko grinned and shook his head.

Kolchok prodded Janko's knee hard with a gnarled brown forefinger. "Listen. The master's son might have been a dandy but he could ride a horse, shoot, live in the forest when you were still on the potty. Don't think they were all softies. Not like you city boys."

Cheslav smiled.

"All gone now, though."

Janko nodded. "Good thing too," and then seeing Kolchok looking at him, "I mean, there were a lot of bad things, back then."

Cheslav thought of his stepfather's creed: progress *was* communism, and he had to agree in part. "There were a lot of poor then. You know that, Kolchok."

"Things got better after the Revolution."

Kolchok looked unimpressed with Janko's observation. "You think so?" Then he chuckled.

"What is it?" Janko looked at him warily.

"A joke I was told once by a good comrade. A Party member." Then, seeing their expectant faces, he sighed. "All right, I'll tell you." He cleared his throat. "So, a little girl comes home from school and her grandmother asks what she did that day. The girl tells her they learned about progress. 'When we reach communism, Granny,' she says, 'the shops will be full. There'll be butter and meat and sausage.

You'll be able to get anything you want.' The grandmother nods and smiles and says, 'That's good, just like under the Tsar.'" Kolchok's face was solemn but his eyes twinkled.

Beridze looked uncertain, but Janko looked uncomfortable and after a moment he stood up. "I'll, uh, get some tea," he said, his eyes averted, and he walked away.

Kolchok shook his head at Janko's retreating back. "But it's a good joke," he protested softly.

Cheslav smiled at him ruefully, but he said nothing and knew that it was one scene he'd not relate to Leonid, at least not in writing.

They heard them before they saw them, faint and indistinct at first but quickly growing louder, a noise like fingernails on a blackboard coming from beyond the bridge. Then sounds like chains dragged across cobbles and short metallic bangs, and engines. Walter's mouth suddenly was dry, his stomach lurched and he lost control of his bladder for a moment. He felt the shame and fear like a solid lump deep in his gut. Mathias' face was unreadable but his complexion was sallow, Rolf licked his lips repeatedly and Friedrich seemed strangely detached, as if he was trying to guess the make of the approaching tanks as he would a car.

Fenstermacher shouted, "Take cover!" and everyone stirred suddenly, running behind the barricades and between the warehouses. Walter's group took up the position they'd been allocated towards the rear, lying flat behind the stack of building sand where Mathias liked to sit. He saw Fenstermacher cross himself.

Vogel ran up, "Tanks," and Mathias looked affronted that Vogel felt the need to tell him. "Hold your fire until ordered," he snapped and ran back to the barricade.

Watching him go, Mathias shook his head slowly. Then he stiffened, peering past the barricade down the approach road the other side of the canal. "Here they come."

Walter squinted. At the far end of the road where it turned a bend, something squat and green hove into sight.

Mathias said calmly, "Keep your head down, boy."

"Are they Ivans?"

Mathias didn't reply.

Two tanks swung behind the first.

"T-34s, I think." Friedrich frowned.

"Not ours?" Rolf's voice had risen an octave or two. "You're supposed to be able to smell them," he added.

"Smell them? What do you mean?" Again, Mathias sounded irritated.

Rolf flushed brick red. "Um, well one of the Volkssturm told me that Ivan tanks smell of real petrol. Ours smell, well, like a doctor's surgery."

They all stared at him for a moment and then Mathias snorted. "You mean like Ethanol?" Rolf nodded in embarrassment. "So what do we do? Sniff like a dog around a bitch on heat?"

Rolf looked crestfallen. "Well, I was just told, that's all."

They watched in silence as the tanks closed in on the bridge, the leader swinging its turret slightly from one side to the other as if scanning, and Walter saw red Cyrillic lettering on the side of it, clear enough through the grime. That's it then, he realised and his stomach knotted again.

"Little fools!"

Walter stared at Mathias, who was leaning forward, lips pursed. He twisted his head to follow the direction of Mathias' gaze and saw two Hitler Youth doubling forward, crouched low below the bridge's parapet, carrying something. The tanks stopped. From where they sat the boys might be out of sight, but surely not for long. For a long moment, it seemed an eternity to Walter, the tanks sat with engines idling, the air shimmering above their engine decks. Nothing else moved until suddenly a hatch on the turret of the lead tank clanged open. The distinctive padded helmet of a Soviet crewman appeared followed by black-clad shoulders. The crewman raised binoculars for a few seconds and then the tank lurched forward.

"Come *on*," Mathias urged.

The two boys had reached the far end of the bridge and, as if hearing him, they stopped. One stood up in full view, raised what could only be a *panzerfaust* and tucked it onto his shoulder, all in one fluid motion. A jet of flame shot backwards over the canal and a small flash burst on the turret of the tank. Almost immediately it slewed around, sparks spraying up where the tracks ripped the cobbles. The tank's long gun threw off more sparks as it scraped along one of the nearby buildings, ripped off a drain pipe and sent it clattering, first across the turret and then along the cobbles to drop with a splash into the canal. The tank buried itself in the building, half collapsing the wall, bricks cascading down. Flames leapt out of the open hatch for a few seconds like gas jets on a stove. When they died down the crewman had vanished. The tank's engine coughed, died, and silence fell.

The second boy on the bridge leapt to his feet and struck his companion on the back. Walter could see that he was laughing.

"Move, you idiots," Mathias muttered. They heard Fenstermacher calling the boys back.

The other two tanks began to back slowly up the road. As they did so, the one at the front fired a short, precise burst from the machine gun in its turret, and as both boys turned at Fenstermacher's summons, they twisted and fell. The *panzerfaust* fell to the ground, rolled to the edge of the canal and, like the drainpipe, dropped in with a splash.

Two figures scrambled out of the turret of the disabled tank and dropped out of sight behind it. Without any command being given, everyone started shooting at the tanks. Bullets whined from the cobbles, cracked shards from the walls and shrieked off steel armour. Fenstermacher called to them to stop wasting bullets, but either they couldn't hear him or didn't want to.

The two crewmen who'd disappeared behind the tank emerged further up the street, dashing from side to side, but in turn each twisted and fell out of sight. Yet the firing carried on, and only when the remaining two tanks vanished back around the far corner did it finally fade away and stop.

Walter looked uncertainly at Mathias who shook his head, drew in a deep breath and, in a matter-of-fact tone, observed, "No infantry." He seemed amazingly calm.

Walter turned to Friedrich, who was staring at the tumbled bodies of the two boys on the bridge. His face was chalky white and oily with sweat; his eyes had sunk deep in dark sockets. Suddenly he dropped to his knees, doubled over and clutched at his stomach with both hands. He heaved in short violent spasms and spewed out yellow bile.

Walter, shocked, averted his gaze. He heard Friedrich retch three or four times and then cough. Without turning his head to look at him, Walter asked, "You all right?"

He got no reply and kept his eyes on the bridge.

Mathias spoke gently. "Leave him alone."

They watched silently as the disabled tank began to burn. Tiny flames like those of badly trimmed candles puffed out here and there along the seam where the turret fitted into the hull. Some merged into bigger flames and ran as thin rivulets of fire over the hull, onto the top of the tracks, over the wheels and down to puddle on the cobbles. A solitary thin streamer of greasy dark smoke wafted up from the open turret. Friedrich spat to clear his mouth.

The row started when Diederich came to the door of the cellar late that afternoon. They all knew him: he was their caretaker. He and his wife lived in a tiny ground floor apartment in the courtyard, but Mrs Boldt refused to let him in. Worse, she refused him the water he asked for and turned him away dismissively.

"We're not having any communists in here," she snapped at Tanya's protest, closing the door on his crestfallen face.

The others looked at each other, puzzled.

"He's not a communist, for God's sake."

Mrs Boldt snorted at Tanya and sat back down in her armchair and picked up her knitting. "So you *would* say."

"I beg your pardon?"

"Protecting him, are you?" Mrs Boldt looked at her slyly.

"What *are* you talking about?"

"You stick together, your lot."

Tanya looked at her in puzzlement for a moment. In amazement realisation dawned, and then anger. "You're not seriously suggesting that I'm a communist?" Tanya snapped. "You know very well that my father was killed by them. They took all we had and Mother and I had to leave Russia. Your suggestion is offensive." Mrs Boldt shook her head dismissively. Tanya was ice cold. "And it is a stupid accusation. Stupid, even for you."

Mrs Boldt reared her head, her nostrils flaring. She stood and took two steps towards Tanya, grasping her knitting in one hand, pointing an accusing finger with the other.

"How dare you," she spluttered, "you, you…" She seemed to grope for words, then found them. "You damned *Slav*!"

Tanya glared at her and flushed.

"Coming here, bringing your damned Bolshevik ideas. Jews and Slavs, contaminating good Germans!"

"I am *not* Jewish." Tanya spoke coldly.

The silence in the cellar was arctic. Then, as Mrs Boldt appeared about to speak again, Mrs Körtig stood up from the table where she'd been playing skat with Klara and Axel. "Please," she began to admonish.

"Do not interfere!" Mrs Boldt's voice was now almost soprano, quite unlike her usual throaty bark. She turned towards Mrs Körtig and glared. In her chair, Ida looked distressed, biting on the knuckles of one clenched fist, eyes wide like a frightened child. Tanya knew that Diederich and Ida had always got on very well; the caretaker and his wife had sometimes looked after Walter for her.

"That's enough." Axel stood suddenly; Klara looked up at him in alarm. He didn't raise his voice, but Mrs Boldt lowered her eyes and turned back to her chair.

Tanya felt a soft touch on her arm.

"Come away, m'dear," whispered Mrs Körtig and guided her gently into the alcove.

"Damn woman," Tanya muttered as she sat in her chair.

"Diederich a communist. What rubbish!"

"Actually," Mrs Körtig said very softly as she pulled the blanket across the opening, "there *was* something." Tanya looked at her in astonishment. "A few years ago." Mrs Körtig settled on the divan and lowered her voice. "The Gestapo called him to an interview. Nothing came of it in the end."

"It's absurd," Tanya murmured, but she'd been taken aback at the mention of the Gestapo.

Mrs Körtig shook her head. "He might have been one, you know. After the last war, when he got back from the Front, he was involved in those demonstrations in '18 and '19."

Tanya frowned. She supposed it was possible. Germany was a hotbed of dissent and confusion at the time and people drifted in and out of political movements, looking for hope, looking for stability. Even veterans like Diederich, unhappy with Germany losing the war, looked for radical solutions. Some sought them on the right, some on the left.

"Diederich told Eugen about it." Mrs Körtig smiled sadly. "So proud of doing something, he was. Went to the rallies, but Mr Boldt found out about it and the landlords told Diederich he'd lose his place here."

They would be unhappy, realised Tanya: the landlords were a notoriously reactionary family. They never came to the apartment block, but they kept an eye on their tenants through the Boldts.

"I don't think he was really political." Mrs Körtig sighed. "He just wanted to protest. A lot of people did then, but I don't know if many were truly what you would call *political*."

Tanya nodded. She could understand that Diederich might have a past, but for Mrs Boldt to start raking it up and claiming now that he was dangerous was nonsense. Since Tanya had known him, he'd always been quiet and reliable; nothing was too much trouble, and his wife was a pleasant little mouse of a woman who hardly said a word. She shook her head at Mrs Körtig.

"It's absurd," she said again.

"Yes," agreed Mrs Körtig. "Many things are these days."

*

When it happened late that afternoon, it happened fast. Suddenly and with no warning a torrent of shells tore up the ground, splintering the huts, some of which collapsed. The vehicles parked at the far end of the row of huts took a direct hit, and in moments several of the detachment's precious vehicles were on fire.

John, Greger and Kaarle hugged the ground where they'd been sitting halfway down the row outside their hut as explosions burst all around. Someone screamed briefly amongst the huts. The bombardment was short and they scrambled up, but then came the buzz-saw sound of machine guns; the crack of rifle shots; shouts and the *crump* of grenades. A few stray rounds hissed past them and they threw themselves down again. Greger however scrambled to his feet after a moment and dashed forward between the huts in the direction of the firing.

They waited, prone, rifles pointed expectantly in the direction he'd gone. The sound of combat dwindled quickly to the odd desultory shot, and they stood once more and eased the safeties back on their rifles. Behind them men ran around amongst the vehicles, trying to quench the flames of those that burned; from one lorry came the pop and crackle of exploding ammunition and it was given a wide berth.

Greger reappeared and gave a thumbs-up sign. "Stopped them cold." He stared at the mayhem amongst the lorries and shook his head. "Just some infantry." But almost as soon as he'd said it, the firing broke out once more, and through the noise came the squeal and clatter of tracks.

John heard the cough of engines starting behind him and turned to see Berg's surviving vehicles accelerating away, taking the first turnings they could between the huts to get out of sight.

"Cover quick," Greger yelled and pulled John between two barrack huts still standing as a pair of tanks drove into view, one behind the other, men in brown amongst them. Berg scattered into cover.

Everyone opened fire without any order being given. Some of

the enemy fell; the rest ran into the alleys either side of them or tried to squeeze behind the tanks. The lead vehicle lurched backwards and burst into flame as a *panzerfaust* roared. The second didn't hang about but reversed rapidly out of sight, driving over a comrade crawling to get out of harm's way.

For a few moments, all firing stopped again. Then someone shouted, "Back," and back they went, dodging from one hut to another, moving in bounds as they'd been taught: one section of a platoon covering while another retreated.

It set the pattern as they fell back amongst the warehouses, workshops and office blocks beyond the main factory building. At first the enemy pursued them recklessly, infantry following as tanks charged forward, but after losing two more tanks to Molotov cocktails they changed tactics. Instead, they sent in their infantry first and the tanks held back, providing covering fire. Men were expendable it seemed.

Despite bodies littering the ground, they kept coming. The detachment didn't try to hold them off; instead, they made brief stands, pouring on fire from automatic weapons and rifles, then falling back when the enemy paused momentarily, slipping away before they got too close.

One desperate charge did make contact, forcing a vicious hand to hand fight. Men wielded rifle butts and bayonets, and John saw Ridderstolpe in the thick of it, standing calmly as men swirled about him, picking off targets with his pistol as if on a range. Greger laid about him with a short-handled entrenching-tool, its blade honed to razor sharpness. Kaarle used a *puur-ka*, the short bladed Finnish hunting knife he carried on his belt, and John was shocked at the manic gleam in the boy's eyes. Twice John saw Kaarle, a feral grin on his baby face, calmly knock aside a thrusting Soviet rifle with his hand, run in close past the bayonet and plunge the *puur-ka* repeatedly into a hapless soldier.

It was a relentlessly grim, exhausting retreat: a matter of sudden ambush, sudden death, sudden withdrawal. Most of the death was the enemy's for they attacked with reckless determination. But no all the bodies left behind wore brown. Now and again a grey-green form lay amongst the dead and dying. One of them was Rask's, the sergeant cut down by random shot as he sprinted with the rest of them to the next position. John didn't know it until Greger told him, grim-faced, as they lay panting for the next probing rush. Greger said it dispassionately; and John took it dispassionately. He would feel it later. This was not the time for feelings.

The enemy kept up the pressure and the detachment was glad when they reached the far edge of the factory site and found themselves the other side of a concrete perimeter road amongst the bombed-out ruins of workers's homes. Twilight was falling fast, shadows deepening quickly between the wrecked buildings. It was then that the tanks pulled back and the brown infantry became shadows in the fading light, slipping away.

Suddenly they were left alone.

Ridderstolpe did the rounds, detailing groups to occupy those houses which faced the site across the road. John, numb with fatigue, slumped down in the first floor room he'd been assigned with Greger and Kaarle. He pulled off his helmet, letting his sweat dry in the cooling air, his legs trembling.

"Drink." Kaarle proffered a bottle of brandy. John felt as if every bone and muscle ached, but he eased himself up and gratefully took the bottle.

"That might be it for now," Greger mused from the window. He turned to face them. "The Reds hate moving around in the dark. I don't think they'll stir much."

John went to the window and offered the bottle. "I don't blame 'em." Outside, the shadows had thickened into deep gloom. The moon was not yet up and little could be seen, save here and there, over distant roofs, the flicker of fires.

Greger took a sip of brandy. "Good." He swallowed another mouthful and passed it to Kaarle. "Best settle in. I'll take first watch."

The twilight deepened and turned to deep night. Rifles cracked, machine guns chattered, tank guns barked, but all in the distance and not many. Now and again they heard the boom of a few artillery rounds, sometimes the very distinctive noise of a *panzerfaust* rocket, but the sounds dwindled to single rifle shots and the *whoosh* and *pop* of illumination flares. Once they heard the *putt-putt-putt* of one of the biplanes flying to and fro, looking for targets, and made sure that they cupped their cigarettes in their hands. Another time a dog barked somewhere: an anxious, hopeless sound. John recalled what Greger had said and prayed that the enemy would stay safely in their positions for the night. He was deeply tired, too tired to sleep, and he doubted he could summon the will to fight again so soon.

John took second watch, and as Greger and Kaarle curled up together for warmth, their rifles by their sides, he stood at the window, watching the occasional pulse of light from distant flares: white, red, green, blue. His father had often told him of the sometimes beauty of the battlefield, and now, despite his exhaustion, his hunger, his nagging fears, something in him was stirred.

"How lovely," he murmured, and carefully within cupped hands lit another cigarette.

Walter leaned on the barricade and stared at the tank. Smoky blue-yellow flames still licked around the base of the turret. More flames flickered out of the hatch, illuminating a column of greasy smoke within which sparks flashed. It had an eerie beauty. Even at this distance he could smell the acrid fumes and taste something unpleasantly metallic. He hawked and spat but it did little good. He was deeply tired and his eyelids felt as heavy as lead, but he couldn't sleep for it was his watch. He glanced at Friedrich and smiled wanly. Friedrich grimaced wearily, eyelids drooping then snapping back open: it was his watch too. Mathias and Rolf lay nearby, curled up together on the greasy cobbles. Walter peered into the gloom, trying to see the bodies of the fallen boys, but they were invisible and he was glad.

There'd been a lull after the tank's destruction and some discussion about fetching the boys. Mathias thought it not worth the risk;

neither boy had moved or made a sound since they'd fallen and they must be dead. Vogel demurred, demanding that his guys be brought in. He and Fenstermacher were still debating it when the enemy had rushed the bridge again, this time infantry who'd got quite close in the gloom of dusk by crawling behind the dead tank then running pell-mell when they'd passed it. At the end of the road one of the surviving tanks had reappeared, and peppered the barricade with machine gun fire, but not for long, for as soon as the infantry got up they blocked its line of sight and it stopped for fear of hitting its own men. The rush carried some of the attackers onto the bridge, drab brown figures running forward with loud cries of *urrah*, and everyone opened fire. A couple of the attackers fell immediately and the rest melted away as quickly as they came, and that was that. The tank's machine guns opened up once more, firing over the heads of the retreating infantry who ran doubled up back down the road. It all seemed to happen so quickly, and lying behind their pile of sand, Walter, Friedrich, Rolf and Mathias had not even fired a shot.

They waited for another attack, but dark came on quickly and the enemy didn't return. Across the city the sounds of small-arms fire and explosions dwindled, and around the bridge all was quiet save for a faint crackling from the tank. Mathias relaxed. Ivans, he'd said, didn't like to attack at night, and anyway, cities were bad places to fight in the dark. After a while, Fenstermacher had ordered them all to stand down, leaving Walter's group to take the watch.

"Still awake?"

Walter turned to Thalberg as the man wandered up with a small tin milk pail. He grinned down at Mathias and Rolf. "Sleeping beauties. Tea." He tapped the tin and looked the tank over while Walter and Friedrich helped themselves. The tea was lukewarm, for the braziers had all been extinguished earlier to avoid illuminating the area for any opportunistic sniper, but it was very sweet and helped Walter blink away his fatigue.

"Good shooting, that was." Thalberg jerked his head.

Walter nodded. He imagined the two dead boys and felt glum.

Friedrich nursed his tin mug as if trying to extract some warmth from the cold metal.

"What's happening?"

Thalberg shrugged. "Dunno. Fenstermacher reckons we're all right till dawn." He picked up the pail. "But stay alert."

As he waddled away, Walter watched the tank cook slowly. Over the faint crackling sound of burning he heard popping as if balloons were bursting in the heat. The smoke eddied and reformed; the sparks flickered and whirled, dull colours in shades of grey.

It really is quite beautiful, Walter wondered. I wish I had a camera.

TEN

The sun was not yet up, just a pale lightening of the sky above the rooflines. Leonid struggled to see the bridge clearly, even with the help of Gushenko's binoculars. The dead tank blocked a lot of his view and the Germans were keeping themselves out of sight. Good discipline, he thought, but then they are German. He smiled ruefully. It had been axiomatic at home: Germans were systematic, Slavs impulsive. At school, such sentiments were regarded as bourgeois and nationalist and were discouraged, but they all believed them nevertheless.

"See anything, Comrade Lieutenant?" Leonid glanced behind him. Agranenko held out one of the two mugs of tea he was carrying. Behind him he could see that the cooks had arrived with breakfast; it was a welcome sight for he felt famished.

Leonid took the mug and sipped gratefully. "Nothing."

Agranenko scratched at his blue chin thoughtfully. Still unshaven, noted Leonid with some surprise.

"I was speaking with Captain Gushenko just now. He says we'll try the bridge just as soon as the flamethrowers arrive, and Safronov's platoon is looking for a way over further up." Leonid nodded and put his mug carefully on the ground, taking another look at the bridge. It was the immobilised tank that posed the major problem. Although the bridge was narrow and the barricade of oil drums well arranged, with proper support a determined rush should carry them across and amongst the defenders before they could get off too many rounds.

As he stared at the tank he noticed something odd: underneath it the roadway was a pale whitish-yellow.

"Maybe a tank could push it forward into the canal?"

"Hmm." Agranenko sounded unconvinced. "Maybe, but there's a risk it will jam; it's pretty tight." He glanced back down the road towards the company cooks gathered around their fire. "We'll be eating soon."

Leonid didn't feel hungry.

"Feeling unhappy about attacking again?"

Leonid didn't answer but went back to studying the bridge and the far bank of the canal.

"Someone's got to do it." Agranenko held up a green packet. Lucky Strikes was written on it, black inside a red circle; American, but the words puzzled Leonid. He took a cigarette gratefully and sniffed it: the smell was rich, aromatically pleasant. The smoke dispelled the unpleasant stink from the tank.

Agranenko tucked the packet away. "Got it off a dead Fritz." He smiled grimly, drew in a lungful.

"It seems an easy way to get killed. We should wait for Safronov to outflank them." Leonid was thinking of the first pell-mell rush, shot down in moments.

"Maybe, but there are lots of flanks, lots of bridges. Someone's got to cross them. And there are worse deaths to risk than being shot." He stared at the tank. "I never understood how anyone could drive around in a steel box waiting to fry like bacon."

Leonid glanced at the tank, still smouldering and pushed away the images that Agranenko's words conjured in his mind.

Agranenko shook his head. "Let me tell you a little story. During the siege in Leningrad we went out on patrols. Even people like me from HQ. They needed everyone they could get, and anyway my boss thought I should get some combat experience. Well, one night we ambushed a German tank. One of those little box things, a Mark II. Tin can on tracks, twenty mil pop gun, three-man crew. They used them for recces. Fast, but it burns well, we discovered.

Molotovs." His lips twisted but it wasn't a smile. "Two of the Fritzes got out, but one didn't. One of the Fritzes ran back. That tank was burning by then but he got back onto it. He dropped a grenade in. We took that guy prisoner. He was out of his head. Burned hands, a mess. Crying, but it wasn't the burns. Turned out the guy stuck in the tank was his brother. Odd that, isn't it? Two brothers in the same tank."

Leonid thought of Cheslav and his heart sank.

Agranenko's eyes flicked away from Leonid's for a moment. He dropped the cigarette, now a stub, onto the ground. Then he asked, "See the white stuff?"

Leonid nodded, staring at the patch under the tank once more. "Yes. Some sort of oil, I suppose. Or maybe scorching?"

"Fat" was all Agranenko said and walked towards the waiting fires and breakfast.

Leonid felt sick, and he knew that what Agranenko had said was right: frying like bacon. Suddenly the idea of breakfast did not appeal.

Friedrich nudged Walter. "I heard something." He pointed across the canal. They stood with Rolf behind the oil drums at the end of the bridge taking their turn at watch, but they could see little. "There." Friedrich sounded edgy.

Walter squinted into the gloom but nothing showed itself.

"Did you hear it?" asked Rolf.

Walter frowned, shook his head; he heard only the noises of spasmodic distant firing. Friedrich looked at Mathias sitting nearby with his back against the drums, eyes closed, mouth half open.

"Should we wake him?"

Walter hesitated. He didn't want to risk waking Mathias for a false alarm, then he *did* hear something: a voice, low, plaintive. He and Friedrich looked at each other.

"Sounds German." Friedrich sounded puzzled.

Walter shook his head slowly and the voice came again; a light voice, wavering, the rhythm German but the words indistinct.

And then their eyes widened. "He's alive!" they exclaimed simultaneously and Mathias woke up.

"What's going on?" He stood, rubbing sleep from his eyes with one hand, grasping his rifle with the other.

"Someone's calling."

"One of ours," added Walter. He'd been out all night still alive and they'd not known it. Perhaps he'd been unconscious, had only now come to. Walter hoped so: the idea that the boy might have been lying in pain and fear just a few metres away made him feel sick.

Mathias stared at Walter. The voice came again and he nodded, turned and went to awaken Fenstermacher and Vogel. The three men crouched behind the other row of drums, talking in low voices, glancing now and then across the bridge. Then they came to join them.

"So someone's alive." Fenstermacher scanned the far bank.

Walter and Friedrich nodded.

Vogel muttered, "We should get him back." Then, frowning at the doubt on their faces, he added more forcefully, "We have to."

Mathias pursed his lips in his sceptical way that Walter knew only too well. "They might be waiting for us to do just that."

"We *have* to," Vogel repeated. "We can't leave him out there." No one would meet his angry glare. "If you won't go, I will." He sounded disdainful.

Then, to Walter's surprise, Mathias nodded. "Yes. I suppose we have to."

Fenstermacher opened his mouth, then closed it again.

"Let's get on with it." Mathias sighed as if agreeing to do something only mildly inconvenient.

Walter looked at him, then across the bridge to the wreckage and the bodies and felt a grudging admiration. Mathias was critical, awkward, always finding fault with Walter, but he'd come to look for him; had stayed with him despite the danger. Now he was offering to help a stranger, someone who was Walter's comrade, not his, and Walter began to feel a little ashamed of himself.

"I'll go too," he said.

Mathias shook his head. "No, no you won't." He sounded annoyed, as with a child who has no idea of what he's saying but wishes to appear clever in front of the grown-ups.

Walter flushed crimson. Fenstermacher touched his arm gently and smiled. "A fine sentiment, young man, but we have enough volunteers. Best not to send more than we have to."

Silence lay between them for a moment; then it was broken by another plaintive cry.

"Well? Why are we waiting?" Vogel demanded, but to Walter he sounded less sure now, as if it had begun to dawn on him just what it was he was about to do.

Mathias flicked Vogel a look of irritation. Then he caught Fenstermacher's eye and turned to Walter with a softer expression and gripped his shoulders.

"It'll be all right," he said gently, "it'll be all right."

They were wondering what to do about Ida. She'd left just after dawn. All night she'd kept looking through Walter's magazines and board-games, taking them out of the little trunk and then putting them back again. When Mrs Körtig tried to get her to sleep, she'd reacted sharply. Ida had been insistent that she had to go and find her boy; she'd go to the police, she'd said. Or to the local Party office. Once she even asked Mrs Boldt if she'd make enquiries for her, but Mrs Boldt told her she was mad, then Axel shut Mrs Boldt up. After Mrs Boldt's sarcasm, Ida didn't say any more but just sat, looking haggard.

A few times she made as if to leave, but what was the point, they asked her, of going out at night? She'd get lost; it was too difficult. Anyway, there was a curfew for civilians. How would getting herself locked up help Walter? The authorities would let him come home soon, they told her; it'd be over soon, they told her. And so they'd pressed reassurances upon her, and each time they'd done so, she stayed.

But at dawn she pulled on her overcoat, put a hat on her head and walked out. Tanya had considered trying to force her to stay, but in the end let her go. After all, as Axel observed, what else could they do? Walter was her son and she had every right to look for him. So Ida left.

They sat in silence, playing cards, trying to read or sleep. Mrs Boldt kept scanning the radio but there was little to hear, and then even that was taken away. Radio Berlin announced that it was closing down and the People's Radio became just a Bakelite box. For a while Mrs Boldt wound the handle and twiddled the tuning knob, but except for static, there was nothing coming through on any band apart from the BBC and Radio Moscow, both of which she skipped over quickly.

"So, that's it then," commented Klara to no one in particular when Mrs Boldt finally gave up and went to sit in her armchair, staring listlessly at the ceiling.

"No more music," sighed Mrs Körtig.

No more speeches, realised Tanya. She wasn't sure whether she was sad or glad. Berliners called their radios Goebbels's snouts, but it seemed to her that he'd had less and less to say. As Germany's situation became increasingly desperate there'd been fewer speeches and more entertainment.

"I shall miss the Jarosekas Quartet most." Mrs Körtig sounded wistful.

Tanya smiled and nodded; the Lithuanian music group was a favourite with her too. "And Willi Bendow."

"Yes." Mrs Körtig sighed again. "Do you remember that night?"

Tanya looked at her for a moment and then realised that she was referring to a time two years before when Tanya had gone with the Körtigs and a few of her bank colleagues to celebrate her thirtieth birthday. After a pleasant but rationed dinner, they'd all gone to see *Bendow's Colourful Stage*. The cabaret had been wonderful; they'd hardly stopped laughing at Wilhelm Bendow's irreverently satirical routines, and for a while they'd all been able to forget the times. And when the three of them returned to the apartment block, the Körtigs had invited her to share some wine they'd put aside for better days. Over their last two bottles of pale-red pre-war Spätburgunder they'd listened to the Körtigs's record collection of Bendow and his comedic partner Paul Morgan. She'd felt closer to the Körtigs afterwards.

And yet we never did it again, she mused.

"Where is Willi Bendow now?" Mrs Körtig asked. "He was still on the radio after they closed the theatres last year but I wondered if those were recordings. Has anyone seen him lately?"

Tanya sighed and shook her head briefly. Bendow had made his reputation before Hitler came to power, mimicking famous beauties of stage and screen. Zarah Leander, Marlene Dietrich and many others had been fair game. His camp performances were very risqué, but not an uncommon style on the Berlin cabaret circuit: Tanya had seen similar at the Kadeko and the El Dorado. Such humour was sharp and suited Berliners, but had eventually been too sharp and many venues were closed down. Those that survived did so because they'd changed to programmes of approved popular music. Several performers fled abroad, but Willi Bendow adapted and stayed. *Bendow's Colourful Stage* had even become a favourite with Party members. It was then that Tanya, with great regret, stopped going: she'd felt uncomfortable sitting amongst the Party uniforms, listening to watered-down performances which were not a patch on Willi's original work.

"You're all talking as if there'll be no more radio," piped up Mrs Boldt, dropping her gaze to face them. "It's temporary. They'll be back on as soon as they've sorted things out." She looked sternly at Tanya as if daring her to disagree. "It'll be fixed in no time."

"They said they were shutting down," snorted Axel. "There'll be no more broadcasts. At least not German ones."

"What do you mean not German ones?" Mrs Boldt snapped.

"Good God, woman!" Axel snorted. "Don't you understand anything?"

Mrs Boldt glared at him and he glared back. Both opened their mouths to speak, but Klara put her hand on Axel's arm and he subsided and turned his gaze away.

"Everything will be sorted," Mrs Boldt asserted. "The Führer has promised."

And when, pondered Tanya, was the last time you heard the Führer promise anything? As far as she was aware, no one had heard Adolf Hitler's voice for nearly three months, not since his annual speech to mark the anniversary of his coming to power. Since then there'd been plenty of reports in the papers or on the radio of what the Führer had said, but the man himself was unheard. The great speech maker had fallen silent. Other leading Nazis had continued in the public eye. Goebbels in particular had been very visible, touring bomb-damaged areas, meeting angry, bewildered, frightened people. He'd earned a grudging respect from even the cynical Berliners.

As if she'd settled the matter, Mrs Boldt smiled and nodded and picked up her knitting.

Mrs Körtig looked at the silent radio and said very softly, "He used to love listening to Willi, you know."

Tanya knew that she was talking about Eugen, but she didn't think it wise to say so for Mrs Körtig's eyes were moist. Instead, with a cheeriness she really didn't feel at that moment, Tanya suggested another game of preference.

Just over fifty men remained in Detachment Berg, little more than a large platoon. Tired, filthy, many wounded, they marched on into the city all day. They tramped empty roads, skirted unmanned barricades, scrabbled across rubble and paused now and again, but never for long enough to get a proper rest. Finally they turned a corner into a narrow cobbled way and saw a barricade stretching between the tall old apartment blocks which lined both sides of the street, behind which men were waiting with weapons. It was well made: three chest-high timber boxes filled with rubble were arranged in a two forward, one back, chequer pattern. Passing through the gap between the forward boxes one had to swing around the box behind. Across the front of the barricade were *hedgehogs*, each made of three steel beams about five feet long, welded together at the centre to make a six pointed three dimensional star. It looked to John as if a giant child had been playing a game of jacks, but these weren't meant for play. Hedgehogs wreaked havoc with vehicles, causing them to belly, wheels or tracks lifted helplessly off the roadway, or jamming running gear.

At the order to halt, John gratefully lowered his makeshift yoke to the ground and sat, nursing his aching shoulders and feet. Greger sat next to him with a groan as they watched Ridderstolpe stroll forward.

John looked at the defenders and realised that these were not men: none looked more than sixteen. They wore dark bell-bottom trousers and open-necked tunics over shirts striped in pale blue and white; their circular sailors' caps had two dark-blue ribbons hanging down. Naval Hitler Youth, he realised. They carried old-fashioned looking sub-machine guns with wooden stocks which John recognised as Italian Berettas, and through the gap in the barricade, where Ridderstolpe stood talking with the boys, he saw a beer crate. He doubted it contained refreshments.

"Jesus. Look at those little darlings." John turned his head at the sound of Weber's voice, dismissive, exasperated. The orderly was carefully lowering a large first-aid box from his shoulder. He no longer wore his white tunic, and his battledress, like everyone else's, was filthy.

"Very pretty," agreed Greger.

Weber shook his head dolefully and sat down next to John. "Boys in sailor suits. They're too young. What have we come to? They should be home with Mama."

Greger frowned at Weber. "They're doing their duty."

Weber smiled at him in conciliation. "Just a soldier's joke."

John shook his head; he was angry and wasn't sure if it was because Weber had been so dismissive or because he was right: the boys *were* too young.

Greger lit a cigarette and looked at John with a rueful smile. "You English."

"What do you mean?"

"It upsets you?" He gestured to the boys.

"Well..." John murmured and trailed into silence.

"You think it's a game? That you can't play until you're old enough?" Greger shook his head; he sounded exasperated. "It's not *cricket!*"

John felt stung and was about to retort when he looked again at the beer crate and held his angry words back. Molotovs: they must be. He'd once seen boys no older than these using them at Salla where the fighting had been desperate. The boys there hadn't played by any rules. They'd given no quarter and received none; had in fact been worse than their elders, devoid of moderation in the way only the very young can be. He reached into his pocket for his own cigarettes and lit one from Weber's pipe.

"Play up! Play up! And play the game!" he sighed. Weber looked quizzical and John explained. "A poem, about a boy's first experience of battle. By a guy called Newbolt." He stared at the Hitler Youth and blew out a cloud of smoke.

Greger stood and stretched his legs. At the barricade Ridderstolpe was beckoning. John settled his rifle and the dangling ammunition boxes across his weary shoulders and lurched to his feet with a helping hand from Weber.

"My father loved it." John recalled his father reading the poem to him and smiled sadly. "But he said war is not a game."

Weber exhaled a cloud of blue smoke and hefted his first-aid-box. "No." He looked at the boys by the barricade; this time he sounded sad.

Leonid was completely at a loss. It was definitely a boy's voice, very young, one of Agranenko's 'immortal kids', suffering and perhaps dying slowly. It could be Cheslav, he thought. He felt he ought to do something, but what?

Agranenko lay on the cobbles at his feet, peering around the corner of the building using a shaving mirror tied roughly to a bayonet. Unlike most of the platoon, he never fixed it to his rifle.

"They're up to something," he said and pushed himself stiffly upright, brushing mire from his filthy trousers. He held out the makeshift periscope.

Leonid took it. The cobbles dug into his knees and elbows as he knelt to peer at the bridge. There was something white moving above the low wall of oil drums. He glanced up.

"Flag of truce?" It wasn't really a question, but Agranenko nodded slowly anyway.

Leonid scrambled to his feet. "Have we got a white cloth?"

Agranenko stared at him. "It's too dangerous. You can't trust those bastards."

"It sounds like a boy out there. Just a boy." Leonid was thinking of the corpses scattered by the Fritz 88mm gun in the field they had seen on the road from the Heights.

"Just a boy…" Agranenko began, but he didn't finish. He shook his head.

"We have to do something." Leonid. It could be Cheslav. The realisation hardened his resolve.

Agranenko looked at him steadily for a few more seconds, then turned and walked back to where the platoon sat waiting. Leonid trailed behind feeling less certain now.

Agranenko beckoned to Tajidaev and sent him inside one of the houses to find something they could use as a truce flag. When he emerged a couple of minutes later, Tajidaev was clutching a small white bundle. With a grin he shook it out and held it to his loins: it was a woman's frilly knickers. A couple of the nearest men guffawed; someone whistled appreciatively.

"Quiet!" Agranenko snapped, but his lips twisted slightly in amusement.

Tajidaev lifted the kickers to his nose and sniffed appreciatively. Even at this distance, despite the stink of dust and smoke and sweaty unwashed bodies, Leonid smelled lavender.

Agranenko took back his mirror and went to lie once more by the corner. Leonid and Tajidaev followed.

After a few minutes, Agranenko stood once more. "There's a Fritz on the bridge."

"I should go and speak with him." It was something Leonid felt he should say.

"Too dangerous, Comrade Lieutenant. Let me go."

Leonid considered this for a moment. "Can you speak German?"

"What?" Agranenko smiled. "I learned a bit at school. *Genug um sich soo.*"

"Schoolboy German." Leonid smiled wryly. "*Deesas gespreck vird zeener mussen airvackzun.*"

Agranenko said nothing as he separated the mirror from the bayonet and attached the white knickers instead. Leonid took it, turned away, but stopped when Agranenko said, "Wait a moment," and trotted back to the platoon. Leonid watched him send the light machine gunners into the building above the canal where he'd put them during the previous rush for the bridge. I should have thought of that, he chided himself.

"I told them to stay out of sight unless something happens," Agranenko told Leonid on his return. They looked at each other, nodded and Leonid reached out with the makeshift truce flag, waving it. He licked his lips, suddenly very dry, took a deep breath, stepped into the open and walked slowly towards the wrecked tank, flag held aloft. In the middle of the bridge a lone German also held a white flag aloft. Leonid felt clammy, sweat on his face. His stomach churned. As he stepped gingerly over the twisted corpses of the two dead crew he heard footsteps behind him and turned his head.

Agranenko strode up. "I'll stay behind the tank." He held his rifle low to keep it out of sight.

Leonid nodded. He walked to the near end of the bridge and stopped; the German advanced slowly. He looked well into middle-age, wore civilian clothes and was unarmed. Of course, Leonid realised and glanced down at the revolver still strapped to his belt. By rights he should have taken it off, but the German didn't seem to mind.

Standing facing each other, they lowered their flags and spoke slowly.

"A truce," said the German. "To get the boy."

Leonid nodded.

"He's just a boy. He's wounded. He won't be doing any more fighting."

Leonid hesitated; Polyanski and Gushenko would want their tongue. "We'll look after him," he said.

The German shook his head. "He's just a boy," he repeated.

Now it was Leonid who shook his head. "He's in uniform. He fought."

The German looked away, then back again. The boy's voice rose in a low moan, wordless but pleading, and Leonid glanced to where he lay in the lee of the parapet, doubled up in a foetal position, clutching his stomach, a dark pool of blood around him. The boy shifted slightly and a feeling tugged at Leonid. It was his turn to look away.

"All right," he said, "we won't shoot. You don't shoot. You get the boy but you clear out."

The German shook his head once more; he seemed resigned. "We have orders."

"So do we, and if you don't clear off we'll blow you off the bridge. Then you *all* will die. Take the boy and go home. Hitler's finished. You know that. Go home."

The German hesitated, looked back across the canal, and for the first time Leonid noticed there was a figure squatting behind the parapet at the far end of the bridge, a boy in Hitler Youth uniform, no doubt like Agranenko keeping a wary eye on proceedings.

"We can't go home."

Leonid stared at him, thought, You are home. We're not, and suddenly his mood hardened. He remembered where he was, why he was there. We didn't ask to be here. We'd like to go home but it's because of you that we can't, and a good many never will. He wondered if Cheslav would be one of those never to go home. At that idea he stiffened, let his arm drop, the white cloth hanging limply alongside his brown greatcoat.

"Your choice," he said.

The German stared at him, seemed to sense the change in mood and his shoulders slumped a little.

"We'll take the boy," Leonid said. "It's that or he stays there." He was surprised with himself. He met the German's gaze and the man looked away once more, sighed, shook his head sadly.

"I'll tell my commander." He didn't sound hopeful.

Leonid nodded brusquely.

As the German walked back across the bridge, white flag trailing by his side too, he shook his head at the figure behind the parapet, then he said something Leonid couldn't hear.

Leonid turned and began walking back to the tank, and a flash of sparks erupted from the cobbles in front of him. A ricochet whined away; a rifle barked from behind him. He spun around, dropping the truce flag, and saw the German shouting at the Hitler Youth who now was standing on the bridge. His rifle was pointed at Leonid and he was reworking the bolt.

Leonid froze, heard Agranenko shout, felt a bullet pass by him towards the Germans, saw them duck down. Shouting broke out across the bridge, then the light machine gun Agranenko had placed in the warehouse began to fire and Leonid ran.

Cheslav had begun to wonder if they'd ever catch up with the fighting. They didn't leave the copse of trees until mid-morning, and even then their march was more stop than start, but shortly after mid-afternoon they entered the city's suburbs and Cheslav began to feel that they were getting somewhere.

It was beautiful: widely spaced roads lined with two, three and four storey houses. There were allotments, orchards and gardens, all well-maintained. There were few signs of war: an occasional crater from a stray shell or bomb, here and there abandoned equipment, but ahead he heard the rumble of artillery and saw thin columns of smoke and dust.

As they penetrated further into Berlin, the cityscape changed. Denser blocks of housing appeared, an occasional railway line and more damage. Some buildings had obviously been the focus of resistance: they gaped open, a few still burned. There were barricades here and there, sandbag and timber bunkers, coils of barbed wire. They passed corpses, military and civilian, of both sexes and all ages; they passed dead horses, wrecked cars and smashed carts. Then the first casualties passed them, going the other way on foot and in carts. They saw no German prisoners.

Mid-afternoon they tramped into a square on which stood a small church. It was set back from the pavement behind a low wall, the top of which bore the marks where iron railings once had been. The building was a plain box with no tower or steeple; only two narrow windows of stained glass bearing biblical texts and a small stone cross at the apex of the roof betrayed its nature.

As the others sprawled about, opening rations and smoking, Cheslav went to look at it; more than that, he was drawn to it. He was surprised with himself. He'd thought that when Father went and Mother remarried all that was done with. At their new home after all, instead of Catholic images of saints and martyrs, there'd been pictures of workers and peasants; instead of tracts condemning sins and extolling virtues there were condemnations of class privilege and exhortations to collective life. The Holy Corner where his mother had once prayed to a picture of the Virgin Mary and Baby Jesus became the Red Corner with an official print of Stalin flanked by Lenin and Marx. There had been no churches.

Now Cheslav faced the church door and remembered. As his eyes wandered over the fine carpentry, his mind wandered through the memory of Sundays at the little village church; the holy days; the gatherings in the open air around an altar table; processions around the fields, vestmented priest and acolytes, lantern, crucifix, banners and incense leading the way.

He reached out and touched the wood of the church door, running his fingers lightly across the varnished surface. He was tempted to push it open and go inside, although the battalion political officer had decreed that they should not enter such places; he could hardly remember what one looked like and wanted to see. He glanced about him; no one seemed to be watching, but perhaps it was not worth the risk.

He closed his eyes once more and let the wan sun play upon his face. He wondered what Leonid would do; he doubted that Leonid would waste time on God. Leonid had not seemed to miss Him at all. It was one of the few subjects on which he and his brother disagreed substantially.

"Thinking again, Barakovski?" Cheslav was roused out of his musings by Lopakin's high-pitched voice. He opened his eyes and looked down the steps at him. Lopakin's face bore a friendly smile. Although he often teased Cheslav about what he called his bourgeois intellectualism, his barbs usually were gentle. Lopakin respected education, as many Russians with his peasant background did. He could barely read or write and Cheslav often helped him with the platoon's paperwork.

"We're going." Lopakin walked up the steps and looked at the two hands carved into the curved lintel over the door. They were clasped in supplication, and over them were words painted in red: *'Oh Gott, wo kann ich mich verstecken vor deinem Geist? Wo kann ich fliehen vor deinem Angesicht?'*

Lopakin stared at them. "I wonder what it says?"

Cheslav shrugged.

Lopakin stared for a moment more and then turned away, repeating softly, "We're going." Across the square the platoon were gathering themselves together.

Cheslav followed him down the steps, but he looked back at the words for one last time. He did know what they said, of course. The words were from Psalm 139, one of his mother's favourites:

'Oh God, where can I hide from Your spirit? Where can I flee from Your presence?'

They disturbed him.

*

Walter sat with Friedrich behind the oil drums; he felt drained and helpless. Mathias lay where they'd dragged him a moment before. It had all happened so quickly: the rifle shot, the short burst of machine gun fire, the shouting, then silence. Walter had seen Mathias run back, fall, and in the following silence he had, without thinking, run to him. As he'd grabbed Mathias' lapels he'd realised that Friedrich and Rolf were with him, and together they'd hauled his uncle back into cover. Walter had had no time for terror, but now he did and he had to squeeze his arms across his chest to calm his violent shivering. Vomit rose in his throat; he forced it back down and drew several uneven deep breaths. Friedrich knelt next to him, very still, eyes closed, white faced, his hands clasped together in front of him. Walter reached out and gently squeezed them. Friedrich opened his eyes and smiled feebly at Walter, and then at Rolf who sat with his back to the oil drums, his eyes closed.

Walter looked about him. Thalberg, who'd earlier brought them their tea, was kneeling by Mathias, gently opening his greatcoat, jacket and shirt. Beyond him, crouched low behind the barricade, Fenstermacher and Vogel also knelt. They faced each other, red-faced, snapping and hissing like quarrelling geese. Walter heard angry words that cut across each other in a confused jumble.

"…no right to fire…"

"…doing my duty…"

"…flag of truce…"

Walter heard the word 'coward' quite clearly. He and Friedrich looked at each other in dismay, and then disgust.

Suddenly there was a pause as if Fenstermacher and Vogel had to draw breath at the same time.

"He needs a hospital," Thalberg said matter-of-factly and sat back on his heels. He looked at them; they stared at his red-stained hands in silence. "Bullet in his side. I can't find an exit hole." Thalberg took a field dressing out of his pocket, unwrapped it and stuffed it inside Mathias' clothes. Mathias opened his eyes, his face haggard with pain, and Walter went cold.

"Here." Fenstermacher crawled forward with a flask. Behind him Vogel stared fixedly over the bridge where nothing now moved. The wounded boy had fallen silent.

Fenstermacher held Mathias up as Thalberg helped him drink and then gently lowered him. Mathias smiled at him weakly, struggling as if to say something, but Fenstermacher hushed him and Mathias closed his eyes.

"I'm getting too old for this," Fenstermacher said wistfully to Walter and sat next to him. Vogel stared sullenly at them. As Fenstermacher pulled out his pipe, Thalberg extracted a packet of cigarettes from his voluminous overcoat and offered it to them. Walter shook his head, but Friedrich accepted with relish.

"You're allowed, you know." Fenstermacher looked at Walter with amusement as Thalberg tucked the cigarette packet back into his pocket. "If you're old enough to fight, I think you're old enough to smoke, don't you?" Then he looked at Mathias and he became serious. "He's badly hurt."

Walter nodded and Fenstermacher explained that there should be a small field hospital about a kilometre away. "Should be an easy trip unless Ivan's got behind us, which I doubt. I don't think they're over this bit of the canal yet or we'd know it right enough." He looked glum. "Won't be long, though," he added. He looked over the bridge and blew out a puff of smoke.

"Why did Vogel shoot?"

Fenstermacher shook his head at Friedrich's question. "I don't know." He blew out another cloud of smoke, seemed about to say something else, but Thalberg spoke.

"You need to get going." He glanced down. "I think he's passed out." Mathias lay very still, pale white face showing no sign of life, but his chest moved up and down gently.

"All right." Fenstermacher tapped his pipe against an oil drum to empty it and tucked it away. "You two," he pointed at Walter and Friedrich. "You know how to rig a stretcher from your rifles, do you?" They nodded. "Very well. Go." He looked across at the warehouse from where the machine gun fire had come earlier. "We'll cover you. I'm not taking any more chances." As Rolf helped Walter and Friedrich put together their makeshift stretcher, Fenstermacher detailed several men and boys to aim their rifles at the windows. He ignored Vogel pointedly; so did everyone else.

Gently Thalberg helped Walter and Friedrich roll Mathias onto the stretcher. Everyone was careful to keep their heads below the level of the oil drums. Then, doubled over, they carried Mathias away from the bridge at a trot. Walter expected that at any moment bullets would fly, but nothing happened.

Leonid felt awkward as he briefed Gushenko and Polyanski.

Gushenko said nothing, but Polyanski was pert. "You know the orders. Who gave *you* permission to have truces?"

Gushenko raised his hand. "No matter, Melor Egorovich," he said mildly, "no harm was done and that Fritz hasn't gone anywhere. We'll get him later."

If he's still alive, observed Leonid. By the look on his face, Polyanski was having the same thought, but he said nothing more. It was, Leonid knew, a sign of the times. Once Gushenko would automatically have deferred to Polyanski, but after the early disasters of the Nazi invasion, the authority of political officers over military commanders was much reduced. Party control had been deemed less important than beating the Hitlerites.

Leonid wondered how long that would last when Hitler finally was beaten, but seeing that Gushenko seemed to be at least nominally on his side, he felt able to speak. "What now, sir?"

Gushenko sighed. "Battalion wants that bridge." He looked at Polyanski who nodded. "All right, Lieutenant, return to your men. Best get a bit of rest, I'll let you know."

Leonid's salute was returned sketchily by Gushenko; Polyanski just nodded.

When they were out of earshot, Agranenko said gently, "Don't take it to heart, Lieutenant."

Leonid shook his head. "I'm not."

"Mistakes happen."

For a moment Leonid was annoyed. What mistake did he think Leonid had made? "You think we were shot at by *mistake*?"

"I don't know." Agranenko stopped and looked back at Leonid. "Someone too eager. Sees you walking away, gets angry. *Bang*. Fires without thinking. It happens."

"Their man had a white flag." Agranenko said nothing and Leonid continued. "I mean, it's their boy lying out there. They were trying to get him back. Now they won't." Leonid paused, drew in a breath. "Probably dead by now," he added sadly.

Agranenko reached out as if to lay his hand on Leonid's arm but jerked it back. Leonid looked at him in surprise; it was so unlike Agranenko's carefully-maintained personal distance. Agranenko smiled wryly and Leonid returned the smile. He was about to say more when Agranenko cocked his head to one side and sighed.

"Now what?" Agranenko was staring past him and Leonid turned to see Moiseyevich trotting up.

"Now what?" Leonid echoed softly.

Moiseyevich came to a halt. "Flamethrowers are here," he said.

The hospital was exactly where Fenstermacher had told them it would be, not far, but it took Walter and Friedrich some time to get there. Mathias wasn't light and the cobbles made the going difficult. They had to stop several times to rest, and they had to make a detour, a wide one it turned out, when they found their path blocked. An aircraft had smashed into an apartment block and lay smouldering amongst a jumble of rubble and furniture and household goods. The charred wreckage was so blackened and distorted that neither Walter nor Friedrich were able to say with confidence what it had been, although both prided themselves on their knowledge of aircraft. Walter was convinced that it was German.

"*Messer*," he said sagely. Then, pointing out the remains of two engines added, "Me 110 night fighter."

Friedrich demurred. "Soviet PE-2 dive-bomber."

They argued the finer points of the aircraft's identity all the way to the hospital, which turned out to be a five storey yellow apartment block, the large Red Cross flag hanging down its façade making it obvious. That and the civilian bus pulled up outside with several walking wounded being helped out by the elderly driver. Walter and Friedrich tried to follow them through the arch in the centre of the building, but they were stopped by an officious soldier standing to one side of it. He was young, not much older than Walter and Friedrich, but his face was old. He ignored Walter as he tried to explain and pulled back Mathias' greatcoat to see for himself. Then he waved them through with a dismissive flick of his hand. Not once did he speak.

"Did you see his decorations?" Friedrich asked as they walked through the short passage. "He had an Eastern Front Medal and a Kuban Bridgehead Shield."

Walter nodded, although he'd noticed only the small bronze-coloured shield. He'd been distracted from noticing anything else by the soldier's left ear: half of it was missing.

The passage took them into a courtyard across which lay an open double-door. There was a strange smell in the air, a mixture of disinfectant and scent. It took Walter a moment to notice the mature lilac tree beginning to blossom against one wall; an ornamental stone bench sat underneath it. He smiled at it, and then, when the scent brought thoughts of his mother, his face fell and he hurried on through the doors. Next to them was a very smart brass plaque with the words: 'Institute for Veterinary Medicine'.

Walter and Friedrich stopped and looked at it in surprise. Then a voice called to them.

"In here!"

Beyond the door a middle-aged orderly in a stained white jacket stood in a linoleum-floored wide corridor which smelled even more strongly of disinfectant. Wounded men and boys in various uniforms sat all down one side of it on folding wooden chairs. They followed the orderly into a second corridor, this one lined with trestle tables on which lay more wounded.

"Put him here," the orderly told them and gently they eased Mathias onto an empty table. He didn't stir, nor open his eyes; he just moaned once, softly.

"Bullet wound," Water said and licked his lips.

"Left side," added Friedrich.

The orderly said nothing and pulled away the layers of clothes, then gently eased off the field dressing. It was sodden, crimson, and Walter and Friedrich looked away.

The orderly pursed his lips. "You can go now." When Walter hesitated, he snapped, "Back to your unit."

"His uncle," said Friedrich.

The orderly hesitated and then smiled briefly at Walter. "All right, lad," his voice was softer now, "wait down there." He pointed the way they'd come and turned back to Mathias.

Walter and Friedrich disassembled their makeshift stretcher and found two unoccupied chairs between an elderly Volkssturm and a young SS trooper in a mottled camouflage jacket, a dented steel helmet under his seat. The trooper seemed to be asleep, his head tilted back against the wall, blond hair streaked with dried blood. The left side of his head was covered with a wad of lint tied in place by a bandage. The Volkssturm was smoking, and beyond him a man in fire brigade overalls sat with his hands clasped between his knees, rocking slowly. He seemed uninjured.

On the wall opposite someone had tacked up the front page of a broadsheet newspaper. It was a copy of *Das Reich*, dated two days before: 22 April. Walter was surprised that the newspaper was still being published and went to look. Under the banner headline 'In National Self-Defence' was a large photograph of the Führer in conversation with the head of the SS, Heinrich Himmler. Behind them stood another man, obscured and difficult to make out. Someone had written on the newspaper in red ink, marking one side of the photograph with the word 'Yes!' The article was by Reich-minister for Propaganda and Enlightenment, Joseph Goebbels. As he read the opening lines, Walter felt a curious mixture of anxiety and hope:

> The war has reached a stage at which only the full efforts of the nation and of each individual can save us. The defence of our freedom no longer depends on the army fighting at the Front. Each civilian, each man and woman and boy and girl must fight with unequalled fanaticism.

Friedrich came to stand next to Walter.

The article was well written, playing on everyone's fears for the future. It spoke of death and torture, of destruction and enslavement, but then the article changed tone. It spoke of the power of resistance, of the need to hang on and so win through. One phrase in particular struck Walter and his gaze returned to it when he finished reading: 'only the hard path leads to freedom'.

Friedrich's face was pale. "Did you read this?" he asked, his finger pointing to a line near the end of the article where Goebbels derided the defeatists, the doomsayers who he claimed were crawling out of the rubble as Germany faced its final battle. He made great play of the instinctive power of the German people to defend those they held dear.

Walter whispered aloud the words under Friedrich's finger. "'A fourteen-year-old lad crouching with his bazooka behind a ruined wall on a burned-out street is worth more to the nation than ten intellectuals who attempt to prove that our chances now are nil.'" He felt a strange thrill of pride: he was fourteen himself.

"It's all shit." They turned to see the wounded blond SS trooper staring at them. He repeated, "Shit."

Walter was startled. "What?"

The trooper snorted, "Shit." He spoke with an accent Walter couldn't place: German, but not a Berliner; nasal and harsh-sounding.

Friedrich and Walter stared at him. Walter was starting to feel angry. Who *was* he? He was in the SS; he shouldn't be talking like that!

The trooper smiled at him grimly. "I just spent three months retreating." He sounded angry. "I got this," he tapped the ribbon of an Iron Cross, Second Class, pinned to a buttonhole of his grimy jacket, "at Küstrin. They fucked us. Now Küstrin's Russian. Forget fighting to the end." He bit his lip, his anger faded and he sounded very weary as he repeated softly, "It's all shit."

Friedrich shook his head. "No." He walked down the corridor towards the open door, the SS trooper's gaze on his back. Then the trooper stood and gently took hold of Walter's chin, as Walter's father had sometimes done. Surprised, Walter jerked his head free and cracked it on the wall behind him. At the sound the man in the fire brigade uniform raised his head. He stared at them with a blank expression, his eyes distant, before he lowered his head again and resumed rocking.

The trooper smiled wryly. "Listen, kid," he said, "I fought three fucking years. We almost beat 'em, but almost ain't enough. Go home. It's done with."

Walter didn't know what to say. He saw Friedrich disappear through the double doors into the courtyard, then he turned his head at another voice.

"Listen to him," urged the elderly Volkssturm. He pointed at Walter's feet. "See them?" It took Walter a moment to realise that he meant Walter's canvas ankle gaiters. "Retreat wrappings, those are. When we got 'em in '18 we knew it was all up. If they can't afford proper boots, it's all up. Scraping the barrel." The trooper nodded and the Volkssturm continued, "We'd run out of everything: bullets, shells, food, but the French and British had lots. And then the Americans came in. We had to give up."

"But we didn't give up," expostulated Walter. "We were stabbed in the back!"

The Volkssturm looked exasperated, as if he was dealing with a particularly stupid child. The trooper looked more sympathetic. "Sure," he said, "we know that. Fucking Jewish bankers and the rest. Traitors. My dad fought that war and he always said we could 'ave won." He glanced at the Volkssturm who looked away. "But this is different." He paused and touched the lint wadding on his face. "You see," he licked his lips, his eyes taking on a faraway look, "we did things. In Russia. 'Ad too. Well…" He fell silent for a moment, looking over Walter's head at the article, then murmured, "They ain't taking *me* prisoner." He looked again at Walter. "Fuck off 'ome, kid." He turned, paused, turned back. "Get rid of that fucking uniform." Then he sat down, closed his eyes and rested his head back against the wall.

"You heard him." The Volkssturm's tone was gentle, grandfatherly.

Walter shook his head. He considered other words he'd just read in the article: 'In 1918, we gave up at the last minute. That will not happen in 1945. We all have to see to that.' And he said to the Volkssturm, "We have to fight. My father…" He hesitated, and then he said, "He was there too, when we gave up."

"Was that your father you brought in?"

"No."

The Volkssturm held his gaze for a moment and then shook his head. "Go home, boy."

Walter glanced at the trooper but his eyes were still closed. He walked towards the double doors, and as he did so the medical orderly appeared at the end of the corridor and beckoned.

He ushered Walter past the trestle tables and through a door into a white-tiled examination room where Mathias lay on a long wheeled table, draped in a blanket, only his head showing. Walter noticed that his clothes were neatly folded on a chair to one side, his boots underneath. Standing by Mathias was a man in a long white coat, looking like any hospital doctor, but he wore polished jackboots. The man had a kind face under blond hair; his eyes were vivid blue. He seemed young, no more than mid-thirties Walter guessed, unlike the orderly who was very middle-aged and looked it.

On the walls of the room were charts of animal physiology and cupboards full of what Walter assumed to be veterinary medicine. The bizarreness of it struck him and he remembered something Mathias had once told him: 'doctors are only in it for what they can get out of it. Most of them are damned useless. If you fall sick, get a vet.' Walter looked at his uncle lying now on a vet's examining table and had to fight the urge to giggle. Then he noticed that the middle of the blanket bore a dark stain and he felt that he wanted to weep.

"Hello." The man smiled. "I'm Herr...sorry, *Lieutenant* Lang." He paused, looked uncomfortable, his smile fading. "I've done all I can. He was badly wounded, I'm afraid." He spoke excellent, precise German, but there was something odd about his inflections: a little *too* formal. Lang wiped his hands on a paper towel and dropped it into a bin under the table. "The bullet did some damage. I had to take out quite a bit." Walter's stomach lurched. Lang touched Mathias' forehead. "No fever signs yet. Good." Then he turned to the orderly. "Get some Sulphanilamide." The orderly nodded and left briskly. "That's a sterilising drug to clean the wound," Lang explained. Walter knew that already but didn't say so. "All we can do now is keep the wound clean, let him rest and hope that he pulls through."

Walter nodded. Then, perhaps encouraged by the man's friendly manner, asked, "You're not a Berliner, are you, sir?"

Lang smiled at him. "Does it show?" The orderly returned with several paper packets which he began to tear open and Lang walked to the door. "Come along. Let's go outside for a bit. I could do with some fresh air."

Walter followed past the trooper, eyes still closed; past the rocking fireman and the Volkssturm, who ignored them. Outside they found Friedrich sitting on the bench; he too ignored them.

Lang pulled out a yellow cigarette packet labelled 'Lande Mokri Superb'. He offered one to Walter. "Do you?" and when Walter shook his head, he smiled. "Good. Bad habit." Then he pulled out a small cigarette lighter, flicked the top up and ignited the wick. When he'd drawn in a lungful of smoke, Lang coughed slightly. "I'm not from Berlin, no. Actually I was born in England. London."

Walter was startled. An Englishman?

Lang chuckled softly. "Don't be surprised, young man. I'm Volksdeutche."

Walter nodded slowly: Volksdeutche: those of German blood living abroad. Many had come home when the Führer had summoned them. There'd been a Volksdeutche in Walter's Hitler Youth section, a shy boy from Romania. A bit of a dullard, physically underdeveloped, his poor performance in training had been made worse by his execrable German. At first they'd had difficulty in understanding him and he them, but after a few weeks of merciless ribbing he'd learned enough to get by and the teasing eased, although it never really stopped until the boy reached eighteen and left for Russia.

Lang spoke slowly, staring into space as if remembering. "I was studying at Guy's in '38 when Papa decided we should come back to Germany. That's a medical school in London." Walter nodded. "Then," Lang took another puff on his cigarette, "they called me up in '43. I didn't go to the Front, thank God. I was training to be a specialist, you see. Pathologist. That's a…"

"I know what a pathologist is," said Walter, who had seen numerous detective movies. "You're a police doctor."

"Police?" Lang laughed. "No. That's a forensic pathologist. I'm a clinical pathologist. I was interested in diseases. They sent me to a research lab."

"Oh," Walter said, but in his mind was, all this man does is research diseases and now he's treating the wounded. Maybe a vet *would* be better.

As if reading Walter's mind, Lang chuckled. "Don't worry," he reassured, "I've had a lot of surgical training. And," he added grimly, "a lot of practical experience recently." They watched two civilians with Red Cross armbands carry a stretcher across the courtyard and through the double doors. Lang threw down the stub of his cigarette.

"I'd better get back to work," he muttered, smiled at Walter once more. He seemed about to say something else but a voice carried across the courtyard.

"Excuse me, Herr Lieutenant."

They turned to see the orderly standing in the double doors. His expression was neutral but there was something in the intense way he met Lang's questioning gaze that made Walter's stomach lurch. He felt a stab of cold when the orderly shifted his gaze to him and took a step forward. He was checked by Lang's gently hand.

"No. You wait here. I'll be back shortly."

Lang followed the orderly into the building and, despite the officer's words, Walter started forward after them but again he was checked, this time by Friedrich's gentle instruction.

"Don't. Sit here with me."

Lang was as good as his word. It seemed that he had hardly left when he returned; the orderly wasn't with him,

Walter and Friedrich stood as Lang walked towards them. He had that carefully neutral expression doctors wore when they had difficult news to impart and Walter didn't need to hear him say, "I so sorry."

It was Friedrich who answered. "He was all right just now."

Lang shook his head, extracted and lit another cigarette. After a pause, he held out the packet and they took one each lit them from Lang's.

"He seemed all right." Lang frowned speculatively. "But one can never tell. I'd guess his heart. He wasn't young."

"He wasn't old." Walter was surprised at the tremor in his voice when he said it; and was more surprised when he felt tears prick his eyes. He blinked them back.

"No." Lang smiled sympathetically, the professional smile of a doctor. "But he wasn't young, and injuries like that are quite a strain."

Walter said nothing but stood with the cigarette burning uselessly between his fingers, staring at the lilac blossoms. His mind was blank.

Lang reached inside the pocket of his lab coat. "Here." held out his hand. "My brother sends them to me through the Red Cross in Switzerland." He smiled ruefully. "He works for them in England, you know." He saw the grief on Walter's face and looked away briefly. "He decided to stay with Mama." Walter glanced down and saw two foil rectangles, each with a brown paper wrapper around the middle. Walter took them. Printed on them were the words: 'Cadbury's Dairy Milk Chocolate'. English words. Enemy words.

Lang smiled once more, very briefly. "I am so sorry," he repeated.

Then he said, "Good luck," and walked away.

Walter looked down at the bars. Then he gave one to Friedrich, who smiled the old, warm smile they'd always shared.

"Thank you." For a moment they looked at each other, and then, draping his arm around his friend, Friedrich said, "It's time to get back."

Later that day, as the sun was setting, Leonid sat by the dead tanks and watched the platoon picking over the German positions. He wondered how to describe it to Cheslav. He should keep it simple: Cheslav hated long-winded stories. "Don't wander like a lost cow," he'd say. "Get to the point." And in truth there was little to say. He sucked thoughtfully on his pencil and stared across the canal. It looked like a scene from a movie: grey figures moving in the fading evening light; shadows cast by the flames of a warehouse burning fitfully; bodies sprawled in the awkward, stiff poses of those surprised by their own deaths. Many were black and charred, and one or two still smouldered.

Beyond he could see nothing in the deepening shadows, but he could hear the rest of the company clattering in and out of buildings, checking for more defenders. There seemed to be none. He bent his head to the notepad on his knees and wrote: *Agranenko got the flamethrowers onto the roof of the warehouse this side of the canal.* He formed the words carefully in the gloom, squinting to make them out. *Safronov found a way across further up and hit them from the flank. Then the flamethrowers opened up. The Fritzes hardly got off a shot.* Leonid paused; the words were too dry, too impersonal. They seemed detached from the reality he'd witnessed; clinical like an official report or an extract from a handbook: *The Drill for Taking a Bridge,* but it hadn't been a drill. After all the waiting and the worry, the earlier failure, it had seemed effortless, done within moments. They hadn't lost a man: the Fritzes had been too distracted and the billowing clouds of burning kerosene too overwhelming. He'd heard no one cry out, had watched the figures stagger and twist amongst the flames, more images from a movie; images of hell. No sounds save for the *whoosh* of the flamethrowers and the chatter of Safronov's machine guns. He'd expected screaming, but could recall none.

Then the whistles blew, feet ran across the bridge, the stink of burned fuel and flesh, single shots as his men moved amongst the bodies, stilling those that showed signs of life. A few more shots after figures running into the darkness. Leonid wrote it all down calmly, surprised at the steadiness of his hand, his detachment. Maybe he'd feel it later.

"Comrade Lieutenant." He looked up and saw Tajidaev holding out a crumpled piece of brown paper. "I found this on the ground over there." He pointed across the bridge, past the burning warehouse to where the road vanished into shadows between the buildings. Leonid took it, turned it over and sniffed.

"Chocolate," Tajidaev confirmed.

Leonid was curious: the writing on the wrapper was English. Probably nothing, but it might be important. He handed it back. "Take it to Comrade Polyanski."

Tajidaev nodded and disappeared between the tanks down the approach road to where the battalion waited for Leonid's platoon to finish their work.

Leonid looked down at the letter. It was getting too dark to complete it now. Tomorrow, he promised himself and bundled it up with the others. The collection was getting quite bulky. He hefted them in his hand. I ought to post them, he realised, but even assuming that he could get the letters safely back to regimental headquarters, postal services to and from the frontline had been suspended for now. He sighed and returned the letters to his satchel then watched the warehouse burn in fits and starts.

ELEVEN

Walter awoke suddenly and found that it was day and he was sprawled in a little alley. He was struck immediately by his stink: he reeked of petrol, sweat, burned meat and an aroma like that from a blocked drain.

He clawed himself to his feet, holding onto the bricks of the wall against which he lay, and dry retched. Not even saliva emerged and his mouth was painfully dry.

He looked around, bewildered. He couldn't focus his mind, barely recalled running into the alley the previous evening, didn't remember passing out, but one thing was fixed in his mind: an image of his mother, and he set off for home.

The thick dust, dry and acrid, tainted his mouth as he walked. His body was numb and he moved as if in a dream, yet everything was vivid. Time changed; he moved through a succession of scenes, like a slide show. He was only *here* and *now*; yesterday was unimaginably distant and tomorrow inconceivably far ahead.

He drifted past people pushing goods loaded on carts or their backs; past queues by standpipes and outside shops; past men and boys standing at barricades and in sangars, trying to look determined. They all ignored him, and he noticed them not at all. Only once did anyone approach him. As he walked past a group of soldiers drinking outside a bar one stepped forward and held out a bottle, but Walter said nothing and carried on. The soldier shrugged, drank deeply from the bottle and turned back to his comrades.

Walter walked in a daze, seeing and hearing but not taking it in. The distant rattle of gunfire and explosions; the occasional drone of aircraft; the sights and smells of the suffering city: nothing seized his attention. He was going home and that was all that existed for him.

He walked on. It could have been for hours or days or weeks. Time meant nothing.

Then suddenly, he turned one more corner and saw ahead of him the little grocery store facing the yard from which, years before it seemed, they had all set off for the bridge. Memory returned: mustering in the yard, collecting weapons, the speech. Then he remembered the previous evening and stopped dead in front of the gates. Instantly it was so vivid: Friedrich walking towards Fenstermacher; the man's theirs, and then machine guns chattering. Fenstermacher dropping the mug at Walter's feet; someone shouting: was it Vogel? Confusion and noises, lurid yellow flames licking across the canal, the stink of burning petrol, and fear like a physical force. He remembered turning in blind panic, running, Friedrich and Rolf behind him.

Walter looked around in confusion, saw the little grocery shop, saw the gates to the yard, and fear struck him again like a hammer blow, leaving him winded. He *had* to get away; to get home! He ran as he had run the night before, and again he heard Friedrich scream, shockingly clear here and now on the empty street. He stopped and turned as he'd done the night before when Friedrich fell headlong; he saw again Friedrich looking up at him, bloody hands to bloody throat, choking, and on the street behind Friedrich figures crawling on fire. One of them was Rolf. He heard the sound of whistles, the shouts of *urrah!*

Here in the empty street he wrapped his arms around himself and silent tears coursed down his face.

Gently a woman spoke behind him and touched his arm. "Are you all right, son?"

The question made him giggle: 'are you all right?' He was filthy; his face and hands were bruised and blackened; he stank of burned fuel, burned bodies, piss and shit. Suddenly he began to shake and he crammed his hands into his mouth to stop the scream he felt rising. He bit hard and the pain comforted him, then he turned around.

The woman stepped back in alarm. She called over her shoulder, "Liesel!" and looked at him warily. She had a middle-aged careworn face under a worn scarf. Another woman and a girl his own age were standing beyond a cart on which were several buckets and bowls of water, looking at him uncertainly. Then the woman called Liesel came forward and they fussed over him, cooing and reassuring. Liesel pulled off her headscarf, went to the cart, dipped it in one of the buckets, came back and wiped his face and hands, wrinkling her nose. Instinctively he jerked his head away, like he'd done as a little boy when his mother had seen to him. Embarrassed, he froze.

"Better," Liesel said softly. Looking closely at his face, she murmured. "Where is your family?"

He shook his head.

"Go home," said the middle-aged woman.

Blankly he stared at the girl by the cart. She looked away and so did he.

"Go home," the woman repeated softly and gently pushed him.

Liesel touched his arm. "Do you know where it is?"

He nodded. "It's not far." And he turned and walked away.

It took him another two hours to reach the apartment block. On the way, conscious now of his condition, he found another empty alley, stripped off his trousers, eased off his foul underpants and threw them into a corner. He did what he could to clean himself with his neckerchief. When he emerged onto the street, barely cleaner, still no one took any notice of him.

Finally he turned a familiar corner and stopped dead. When he'd left the cellar, the street had been undamaged, but now there were craters everywhere along the tarmac and amongst shattered paving stones. Two of the fine Wilhelmine iron streetlamps he'd always admired stood at crazy angles. One of the buildings, not his own he was relieved to see, had lost its roof, shattered beams showing to the sky. He realised that there wasn't an unbroken window in the street.

The ground glittered and glass crunched as he stumbled forward. For a moment he thought of Kristallnacht: the night seven years before when every Jewish shop window had been broken. Peacetime.

A woman sat on the steps to his apartment block. It was his mother, waiting for him, and his heart lifted. He walked forward quickly.

"Mama," he croaked.

The woman raised her head and she was a stranger, young and looking ancient. She stared at him with dull eyes from a haggard face. She stood up unsteadily, holding onto the door frame for support.

"Please," she said in a low voice that conveyed such pain it cut through Walter's own misery. Instinctively he stepped forward, but she shrank back and he stopped. "Please," she repeated. "Help me."

Leonid had no time to finish his letter. He had only just awoken, and with Agranenko was watching the platoon enjoy a meagre breakfast in one of the warehouses when Moiseyevich bustled up. He pulled out a small notebook and, like a clerk reading off an inventory, told them the company's order of march, who would follow whom, how heavy equipment was to be allocated and when they'd leave. To Leonid's relief his platoon would bring up the rear, for once.

As Agranenko watched Moiseyevich leave, tucking his notebook back into the pocket of his greatcoat, he shovelled a couple of spoons of the steaming porridge he'd been eating into his mouth. "Quite the little writer."

"Writer?"

Agranenko smiled at Leonid sourly. "He puts a lot into that notebook of his, always jotting something down."

Leonid stared at the doorway through which Moiseyevich had left. Come to think of it, he *was* always writing things down. "What?" He raised quizzical eyebrows at Agranenko.

"The usual." Agranenko's eyes were bloodshot and there were deep lines of strain around them. "Everything he thinks is anti-Soviet or lacks real proletarian commitment, I'd imagine." Agranenko shovelled in more porridge.

Leonid nodded. He knew of course that Moiseyevich was a committed communist and no doubt passed things on to Polyanski. It was, after all, a time-honoured way for the Party to keep an eye on things. At battalion level and above the deputy commander for political affairs sat alongside the combat commanders. At lower levels in the chain of command, the Party encouraged the formation of cadres whose activists played a key role in maintaining what was officially known as political awareness. There were lectures and discussions about the latest news, political theory and political self-awareness classes. Leonid thought of them as toeing-the-line classes. Ordinary soldiers like Moiseyevich were officially encouraged to take the lead in such sessions; unofficially they also were informers. Some took their monitoring duties more seriously than others, and Moiseyevich was a dedicated Party hack.

"He writes a lot about you, I think."

Leonid shifted uncomfortably. "Writes what?"

Agranenko shrugged. "Who knows? The little shit writes a lot about me too, I'd guess." He smiled sourly. "What the hell, Lieutenant? He watches us, Polyanski watches him, someone watches Polyanski. And over it all sits Glorious Comrade Stalin, Father of the People, keeping his beady Georgian eye on all his children."

Instinctively, Leonid looked around to make sure no one was listening. No one was, of course. They were too busy eating, washing, cleaning weapons.

"I wonder if they think it works."

"Works?" Leonid didn't grasp Agranenko's meaning at first.

"All this control and taking notes and political education. Do they really think it makes men fight better?"

Leonid looked around again. Clearly Agranenko was tired, and perhaps the strain of the past two days was starting to have an effect: he was becoming indiscreet.

"'A willing horse needs no whip,'" Agranenko quoted softly. He smiled ruefully at Leonid. "Most of these men" he gestured around him "have been through hell, or seen it. Homes burned, families and friends killed, raped, tortured. No amount of preaching comes close to that. They just want revenge, not communist heaven."

Leonid nodded again. "They want to get back at the fascists all right. Who wouldn't?"

"'Kill the German,'" quoted Agranenko, "'this is your old mother's prayer.'"

"'Kill the German,'" Leonid murmured, "'this is what your children beseech you to do. Kill the German…'"

"'This is the cry of your Russian earth. Do not waver. Do not let up. Kill.'"

Leonid thought of the bodies the platoon had collected and laid out by the little bridge: old men, young boys, many unrecognisable but still German, and he felt sad for the first time since they'd crossed the canal. "Is that all you think there is to it?"

Agranenko smiled wryly and touched his arm. "Don't worry, Comrade Lieutenant. I'm all right." Then he sighed. "Better get the guys together. Moiseyevich will be back if we don't move out soon."

"With his little notebook."

Agranenko grinned at him.

Detachment Berg finally stopped at a small bridge across a deep railway cutting, a natural dry moat too steep and deep for tanks and probably too much for men on foot, unless they had ladders. The road was narrow, passing between three and four storey apartment buildings. There were defenders there already; John saw a couple of men standing on the near end of the bridge and recognised Captain Vélez.

When Ridderstolpe brought them to a halt they slid to the ground, resting their backs against the nearest buildings.

"This is it, you think?" Greger nodded at Ridderstolpe who had gone to speak with Vélez. He sounded infinitely weary. "We staying here?"

"I hope so." John smiled wearily, licked his cracked lips and spat out dust. His feet and shoulders ached.

Kaarle, sitting on the other side of John, peered at the bridge. "Here?"

"God knows," John answered.

"He come." Kaarle nodded, and John turned his head to see Ridderstolpe walking back towards them. Behind him Vélez had lit a cigarette and was watching. He caught John's eye but didn't react.

"All right, gentlemen," Ridderstolpe announced to his group, gesturing for them all to stand, "we're joining Esquerra for the moment. This is where we stay for now." That brought a rash of smiles: fighting was preferable to endless retreat.

"Good a place as any," muttered Greger as Ridderstolpe led them across the bridge. As they passed, Vélez kept on watching as if weighing them up, but, despite John passing within metres of him, he still showed no reaction.

They halted on the other side of the cutting and John caught his reflection in the undamaged plate-glass window of a small grocer's shop against the bridge. What he saw startled him. Like all the others he was covered with dust and soot, his eyes glittered like glass from a haggard face and he looked much older than his thirty years. He doubted he'd have recognised himself; it was not surprising that Vélez had ignored him.

Greger slapped him gently on the shoulder and grinned. "Pretty sight, eh?" He lifted his helmet, ran fingers through his greasy hair and shook his head. "I could do with a bath."

"Me too." John wriggled: he hated being dirty, and grit had got in everywhere. What he wouldn't give for hot water and soap!

Ridderstolpe watched them squirm and a brief smile played across his lips. "You gentlemen will have plenty of time to clean up. We're well back here and should get a bit of rest. Corporal," he turned to Greger, "your post is in there." Ridderstolpe nodded towards the grocer's shop. "Settle in and then report to me for further orders. HQ is *there*." He pointed further up the road to a building on a corner where the road became a T-junction. Greger nodded and Ridderstolpe went to detail-off more of his men.

They had to break into the shop, smashing the glass panel in the door to get at the catch from the inside. It was bare: there was no furniture and even the light bulb had been removed from the ceiling. When he tried it, Kaarle found the till empty.

"You'll be lucky," chided John and they all grinned at each other before Greger led them through the door behind the counter into a short hall. To the left another door led into a small yard, empty save for a brick hut which turned out to be a latrine. Across the yard was yet another door. Back inside, steep narrow stairs led up from the far end of the hall onto a small landing.

"This'll do nicely," Greger commented when they walked into a room overlooking the bridge through a single glassless window framed by dusty blue curtains. The room was empty save for a very worn old sofa, thick with grit, and a battered table with four chairs, equally filthy. Pale patches showed on the walls. On the far side of the room a curtained doorway revealed a tiny alcove with a sink.

Greger gave a grunt of satisfaction when he tried the tap and cold water flowed from it.

"Still working?" observed John in surprise.

"Probably a tank on the roof." Greger reached to turn off the tap. "Best conserve it."

"We should boil it before we drink it," John said, but Greger shook his head.

"We've plenty to drink." He leaned his rifle up against the wall, pulled off his helmet and began to undo his webbing. "I'm gonna have that wash!"

Someone tapped on the door to her apartment and Tanya opened it reluctantly: she'd come to be alone for a while and resented the intrusion.

Mrs Körtig looked at her uncertainly. "Excuse me. May I come in?"

Tanya hesitated. "Well…"

Then she nodded and led Mrs Körtig down the hall. She stopped halfway and turned when Mrs Körtig, closing the door behind her, said softly, "Walter's back." Mrs Körtig nodded at Tanya's surprised expression. "He looks terrible. Filthy. He's been in the thick of it. He was asking about Ida."

Tanya grimaced.

"I had to tell him."

"How is he?"

Mrs Körtig shook her head. "I left him sleeping in Mathias' apartment." She paused and then added, "I gave him some of Mathias' schnapps. I hope that was all right…"

Tanya smiled and nodded.

"But really he needs something to eat and I don't have anything. I wondered if you might have a little something here. I don't want to go down to the cellar for it."

"Yes. I might have something."

Mrs Körtig trailed her to the kitchen. "Actually, there's someone else."

Tanya turned again.

"There was a woman with him."

"A woman?"

"Yes." Mrs Körtig shook her head. "You'd best come and see."

When she led Tanya into Mathias' apartment she raised her finger to her lips and nodded towards Walter, dimly visible in the gloom on the large wood and leather sofa Ida had brought with her when she and Walter had moved in. It was, Tanya recalled, terribly comfortable.

"I put her in Ida's room. I didn't think she'd mind," Mrs Körtig whispered apologetically, leading Tanya into a bedroom.

A woman sat on the edge of the bed. The blackout curtains had been drawn back, and in the pale sunlight Tanya saw that her clothes were dusty and her face bruised and puffy. She stared at them with such anguished eyes that Tanya had to look away.

"M'dear," Mrs Körtig murmured. She went to pat the woman's shoulder, but pulled her hand back when the woman flinched away. Mrs Körtig glanced at Tanya. "This is Monika Eberhardt."

Tanya nodded. "Let's get you tidied up." She held out her hands, but Monika ignored them and levered herself awkwardly to her feet. She grimaced and touched her breasts briefly.

"Are you hurt?" Then Tanya felt foolish for asking, and muttered, "Yes, of course you're hurt."

Monika looked down at herself. "I want to wash." Her voice was a strained whisper, a ghost's voice.

Tanya began again to reach out, but stopped herself and let her arm fall. "I'll get some water."

When she returned with a bowl and soap and clean towels she found Monika sitting on the bed once more and Mrs Körtig hovering awkwardly. She laid one towel on the floor and placed the bowl on it; a second she laid on the bed with the lump of ersatz soap, grey and greasy. She wished she had the real thing, but her supply of that had been used up long before.

"Please," Monika said softly, "may I be alone?" Her German was well-educated, her accent Berlin.

Mrs Körtig and Tanya looked at each other and Monika once again touched her breasts.

Mrs Körtig frowned. "M'dear, I think you should let us help."

Monika shook her head.

"Please," Tanya urged.

They stared at each other for a moment, Monika seeming stubborn. Then suddenly she seemed to deflate; she licked her lips, her shoulders sagged and she nodded once, a weary jerk of her head.

Mrs Körtig and Tanya began to undress her but stopped when they saw Monika's pale white breasts. They were covered in angry red and ugly blue welts, and there were other marks, unmistakable.

God in heaven, Tanya realised, aghast, *she's been bitten.* She knew then what she was seeing. Goebbels' propaganda machine had spent the previous six months bombarding everyone with stories of atrocity, of rape. The hapless East Prussian village of Nemmersdorf had been recaptured from the Red Army the previous October and then the cinemas and newspapers had been full of dreadful images: traumatised women weeping into cameras as they blurted out incoherent tales; contorted bodies on the ground, clothes in suggestive disarray; wrecked houses and scattered possessions; grim-faced liberators. 'This is what happened', the reports told them. 'This is what will happen so fight to the death; it's better than falling into their hands, into the hands of the Slavs.' She looked at Monika. 'This is what will happen to your loved ones, to you if you let them in.'

I'm one of *them*, she told herself and felt sick.

Mrs Körtig stared at Monika's breasts and then said in a calm, matter-of-fact voice, "I'll fetch some more schnapps." As she reached the door, she added without turning her head, "And some Vaseline."

For some hours Cheslav and the rest of the platoon had slipped and stumbled slowly through the wrecked suburban streets without meeting any resistance, but it was hard going. Some roads were clear, but many were half-hidden by rubble or blocked by barricades and cut down trees; some had been torn up by bombs and shells. Many of the streets were festooned with white flags. The buildings were empty or contained women and children: there were no men, no boys and no resistance.

None that is until suddenly they were shot at in a narrow street chocked with uncleared brickwork. This street had no white flags.

Two men fell wounded and the rest of the company ducked into cover in doorways and passages. It was Kolchok who cleared the way, leading a group at a run while the rest covered him. They threw grenades in the door, charging inside. More shots, shouting, silence.

"Kids" was all Kolchok said to Cheslav when he came back out. He spat dusty phlegm and shook his head. "Little fools."

They marched on, leaving the two wounded bandaged and propped up against a wall for the company orderlies to deal with.

They were not shot at again that day. They took a few prisoners, anxious elderly Volkssturm and a couple of sullen, frightened Hitler Youth, and sent them with a single escort back down the column. Then, as the afternoon shadows lengthened, they emerged from the sprawl of houses onto a wider road running alongside a small sports field and were ordered to rest.

Cheslav sat thankfully on a low wall which ran down the pavement on the opposite side of the road from the field. Behind it the houses were all bombed out. His feet ached abominably and he longed to take off his boots, but he dared not. He didn't know how long they'd be here, and if he took his boots off there was the possibility he'd not get them on again for a while.

Sitting with the others, he sipped water and looked across the road. The field was covered by wooden barracks, burned-out or collapsed. Moving down the road past them to the rear was a shuffling forlorn group of prisoners guarded by just two men. No more seemed needed, for the prisoners were old and listless.

Cheslav commented disparagingly on their age as they passed. Then he reddened, remembering Kolchok was sitting next to him, but Kolchok only chuckled.

"The old fox gets the chicken; the young fox gets the snare."

"It don't matter how old you are." Beridze was sitting beyond Kolchok. "My grandfather told me that it's *heart* that matters."

Kolchok patted him on the shoulder. "Your grandpa was right, boy. Heart, but an old head helps." Cheslav looked at him, thinking of the verve with which he'd cleared the house earlier, and nodded his agreement. Kolchok lit an inevitable pipe and eased off his boots, then wriggled his toes in the cooling air, the foot cloths wrapped around them dark with sweat.

Cheslav was wondering if it was in fact all right to take his own off when a large black dog with a tan tail and ears leapt over the wall beside him and ran up to sniff at Kolchok's feet. Kolchok jerked them back, startled. Beridze laughed and held his hand out, then someone whistled and the dog bounded back across the wall and into one of the gaping houses.

Cheslav spun his head to see half a dozen soldiers grinning as they walked out of the ruins, papashay sub-machine guns over their shoulders, long poles in their hands. One of the poles ended in a loop of wire and was connected by a long cable to a box on a soldier's back. Around his throat dangled a pair of earphones.

Sappers, approved Cheslav. He'd seen such troops before, but not with dogs. He watched the animal sniff around the sappers as they slipped over the wall and sat themselves along the verge and pulled out canteens.

"He likes your feet, Comrade," a sergeant called from where he sat on the wall. The dog bounded back to Kolchok. "He likes interesting smells."

Kolchok frowned and Beridze leaned forward and fondled the dog's ears. Then he knelt and stroked the dog, grinning and twisting his face away when the dog licked it.

"Boys and dogs," muttered Kolchok gruffly, but he too reached out, allowing one hand to be sniffed cautiously.

"Yours?" Cheslav asked and the sergeant nodded. He slipped off the wall and came to join them.

"Cheslav Barakovski."

"Ilya Pyriev." The sergeant shook Cheslav's extended hand, looked down at the dog and smiled. "We use dogs for finding booby traps and Fritzes. Pretty handy at it."

Beridze fumbled in his pack and pulled out half a loaf of black bread. He held it up, tilting his head to one side questioningly. Pyriev nodded and Beridze carefully broke the bread and fed a piece to the dog who by now was showing great interest in it. The dog's tail thumped appreciatively and they all grinned.

Cheslav made a decision and slipped off his boots. He looked at the sappers who by now were all sprawled on the grass, eyes closed, equipment spread about them.

"Hard going?"

Pyriev nodded and rolled himself a cigarette. Kolchok reached across with his pipe for him to light it. "Thank you, Comrade." He drew in a lungful appreciatively. "The Fritzes laid lots of mines and booby traps." He contemplated the cigarette thoughtfully.

"Mine detector?" Cheslav nodded at the box and the pole with the loop of metal lying on the ground alongside the sapper who'd been carrying it.

Pyriev nodded again. "Don't spot 'em all, though. Only the metal ones. Fucking fascists have some in wooden boxes. Need the dog for that: he's good at it." He looked at the dog and a brief, tight smile creased his face. "Flowers are a fucking problem, though."

"Flowers?" Cheslav wasn't sure he'd heard right.

"Sure." Pyriev pointed with his cigarette. They twisted to see a couple of lilac bushes pushing stubbornly through a scatter of brick below the broken and sagging wall of the house behind them. Their colour was vivid against the dull red of the rubble and the green of the spring grass.

"Coming up all over the place. The scent throws him off."

Cheslav looked at the dog sitting adoringly at Beridze's feet and nodded. "I'd noticed the scent."

"Even with the stink," Kolchok muttered through teeth clenched around the stem of his pipe.

"Yes. Makes a nice change." Cheslav smiled at Kolchok, and Beridze nodded absent-mindedly, still playing with the dog's ears.

Pyriev didn't smile; he drew one last time on his cigarette and threw away the stub. "I hate fucking flowers now." He shrugged a little apologetically, then nodded a farewell to the three men and walked back to his sleeping team. Beridze watched the dog wistfully as he trotted after his master.

Cheslav shook his head. Hate flowers? He loved them. He and Leonid often would gather wild posies for their mother when they were boys. She'd put them in a bowl of water, thank them formally, kiss them both tenderly and give them a treat: a biscuit or a piece of bread. On impulse he stood and went to kneel by the lilacs. Kolchok and Beridze were watching him and he felt a little awkward, but he reached out to touch them and sniff his fingers. Then he took out *A Tale of Two Cities*, carefully broke off a small stem of blossom and tucked it inside the front of the book. Returning it to his pack, he sat on the wall and wriggled his aching toes. Neither Kolchok nor Beridze made any comment.

*

The fire was small, just enough to keep Leonid's toes warm. He sat as close to it as he could in the yard of the carpet shop they'd occupied when Gushenko decided once again to halt for the night. It was a small space, three sides enclosed by the windowless backs of buildings; the fourth was a high wall with a double wooden gate leading to an alleyway. Around Leonid some of the platoon were sleeping, curled up on rugs they'd found in the shop.

He was glad to ease his feet. It had been a long day tramping along in the rear of the company, tiring and tedious: stop, start, stop, start.

Once a runner had come back down the line. "The lieutenant says to wait a bit while we check it out," he'd told Leonid. 'A bit' turned out to be quite a long time; up ahead the crackle of small arms seemed to go on and on. Leonid had been glad that the delay hadn't been his fault this time. Eventually they'd got going again, passing a barricade with a few dead Germans and one of their own from Second Platoon. It had been the pattern for the day: move a bit, wait for resistance to be cleared and streets made safe, move on again. There were many obstacles to be overcome: barricades made of rubble or improvised from trams turned on their side; steel hedgehogs wrapped in barbed wire; cut down trees and earth-filled oil drums. The resistance was patchy, but still it slowed them. Grenades thrown out of windows; snipers on rooftops; bursts of fire from the barricades, usually found abandoned when they got to them. Delay and more delay and the occasional casualty.

Leonid's platoon stayed at the rear and he lost no men; not that day at least. Then night came and no one wanted to advance in darkness, not even Polyanski.

Leonid wrote: *We're holed up in a carpet shop. Mother would love it.* He smiled to himself. She liked good needlework; rug weaving had been her father's occupation. He'd died long before Leonid was born, but his mother had kept a few of Grandfather's rugs: large flower patterns woven into thick wool in bright reds, pinks, blues and greens against black. The ones they'd found in the shop were different: bright colours certainly, but no black and the patterns were geometric. Persian, Leonid ventured a guess. The men had been impressed and taken them as bedding.

Fine work, he wrote to Cheslav. *Better than Grandpapa's.* He looked up. Even above the firelight he could see a few stars coming out. He set pencil to paper once more:

It's midnight outside and the candle-flame's dying.
The stars glitter high in the sky.
You're writing a letter to me and you'll post it
To a war-town address far away.

Simonov's words were so apt, but then they usually were. He looked up at the sound of the back door to the shop opening.

"Comrade Lieutenant." Agranenko was carrying two mugs, and as he set them and himself down carefully, Leonid smelled vodka. He smiled: it was very welcome.

"Writing again?" Agranenko stretched his feet out to the fire. "Another writer."

"Like Moiseyevich." Leonid sipped the vodka: it was hooch, home brewed *samogon*, but it would do.

"Hardly." Agranenko grinned ruefully and pulled out a full bottle, which he was careful to place well away from the heat. He drank deeply; he was doing more of that, Leonid had noticed, but then they all were.

Agranenko stared into the fire and drank again, topped up his mug. "I wanted to be a writer."

Somehow Leonid wasn't surprised.

"It was what my father wanted." A note of bitterness crept into Agranenko's voice. Leonid said nothing. "He was an *intellectual*." He made it sound unclean. "A Professor of Literature at Petrograd Imperial University." Agranenko paused and smiled quietly at Leonid's quizzical expression. "Yes. It was before the Revolution.

My father married late. I was his only child." He topped up both their mugs. "I didn't really know him. Mother died having me and my father, well, he wasn't very Bolshevik. They took him away when I was ten."

Leonid wondered why Agranenko was telling him all this, but it seemed tactless to interrupt.

"I was brought up in an orphanage."

Leonid shifted uncomfortably: Soviet state orphanages were soulless places. He'd known a few who'd been brought up in them; there were a lot of orphans, it seemed. Then, Agranenko told him, his luck had changed. Weeks after he'd been discharged from the orphanage he got temporary work in the famous Petrodvorets Watch Factory, cleaning the latrines.

"I was spotted by Alexander Voznesenski." Leonid noticed that the note of resigned bitterness in Agranenko's voice changed to one of wonderment.

"Who?"

Agranenko looked at him, bleary-eyed and irritated. "Who? *Who?* Rector of the University, that's who!"

Leonid waved at him to keep his voice down.

Agranenko smiled sourly. "Rector of the University," he repeated. "Brilliant man, Comrade Voznesensky. Economist. Real Marxist, not like…anyway, I wrote some poetry for the factory newssheet and someone showed it to one of the lecturers she knew. *He* showed it to Voznesensky and I was invited to sit an exam. Then…"

"Why?" asked Leonid, and wondered again why Agranenko was telling him this. How much vodka had his sergeant been drinking? The idea disturbed him.

"Why what?"

"Why did they let you sit the exam?"

Agranenko looked at him ruefully.

"Oh. That. Well, he liked to take on ordinary people. Not just…" He looked away as if slightly embarrassed.

"Not just privileged children of Party members. Like me."

Leonid said it for him. "I'm hardly that. My stepfather sorted some things out, that's true. And arranged for me to go to a Factory Apprentice School and then to a Higher Technical School. He did it for Cheslav, my brother, too, but I had to work for it. We had to pass exams and all that."

"Not everyone gets the chance, Lieutenant. Not in the land of proletarian equality." Agranenko poured more vodka into their now almost-empty mugs.

Leonid wondered whether either of them should drink more, but he was past the point of worrying and took a deep swallow. "What did you study?" he asked.

"Russian Literature." Agranenko placed his hand on his chest and made a mock half-bow.

"Like your father." Leonid's voice was low and soft. Emotion welled up in him; perhaps it was the vodka.

Agranenko blinked. "You know," he said, "every Russian has a poet's soul. That's what they say."

"Yes. That's what they say. I'd like to be a proper poet."

"It's occupation that pays well. You'd end up cleaning latrines in a factory." Agranenko coughed and drank. "Better. I kept working at the watch factory." Then he smiled at Leonid with real warmth. "What do you want to write poems about?"

What do I want to write about? wondered Leonid. He asks just like that.

There was a long pause while they sipped; outside the sound of distant gunfire and explosions was dwindling. They heard the *putt-putt-putt* of night witches in their little bi-plane, looking for Germans to kill.

"I want to write about suffering."

"Suffering?" Agranenko stared at him. "Suffering? You want to write about *suffering*? I can tell you about suffering."

Leonid took more vodka.

Agranenko looked through him into the distance. "I saw a lot, and I lived it."

"I saw what the fascists did to people too." Leonid felt a little irritated by Agranenko's tone.

"You can write about something if you see it, but you won't understand it unless you experience it." Agranenko shook his head. "Not really. You won't feel it. Tell me, what do your family think about you wanting to write?"

"They don't know about it. Well, only Cheslav."

"Your brother, then. What does he say?"

Leonid considered for a moment. How could he explain? And should he? Leonid and his brother had always been very close, especially since their father had been taken away. They loved and cherished their mother: she cared for them. Yet they didn't confide in her as much as they did in each other. How could they? She'd married a man who was one of *them*: one who'd torn up their lives and those of everyone they knew. She'd done it to protect them, but the brothers felt that they could really understand only each other.

"He wants me to do it."

Agranenko snorted. "Hmmm. 'It's easier to build castles in the air than on the ground.'"

"That sounds like a quote."

"An Englishman." Agranenko sounded amused. "Someone called Gribben, I think."

"Was he a writer?"

"Historian. And a writer."

"How do you know him?"

"My father didn't just teach me about Russian literature. He believed in a wide education." There was a tinge of pride in Agranenko's voice.

Leonid nodded and told him how his mother had attended classes in the Workers' Reading Room in Bradander; how his father had objected to what he saw as their blatant political propagandising and to the long distance she had to travel. Eventually the classes were closed during the famines because of poor attendance, but by then his mother had developed a taste for books, so her husband read to her, using books her boys brought her from Gerstein's library and the few in the priest's house. When the church was closed, these were hidden under Gerstein's floorboards. Leonid and Cheslav took over the role of reader when their father was sent away.

"Mother used to write to Father telling him what we'd read to her," Leonid explained to Agranenko. "He liked to know."

"You heard from him?" Agranenko sounded surprised.

"Yes. Letters were allowed," said Leonid.

"Where was he?" asked Agranenko softly.

"The second time they sent him to Svobodny to work on the railways. He managed all right at first, but then we heard nothing, and later they sent us a letter saying he'd died of natural causes."

Agranenko nodded. "Yes. They do."

They stared at each other for a moment, and then Agranenko raised his head. A cluster of star shells was bursting above a wall in the distance. "So beautiful," he murmured.

"We stopped reading to mother then," Leonid said softly. "She didn't want us to anymore."

Agranenko picked up the bottle and emptied it into Leonid's mug. "Better get another." He went into the carpet shop leaving Leonid staring up into the sky where the star shells were sinking slowly to earth.

As the afternoon lengthened, John had been drawn to the window by the unmistakable sound of marching men. Greger and Kaarle joined him when he beckoned to them. They stood for a while in silence, watching a long column of men marching in formation down the road and across the bridge. Some wore Wehrmacht uniforms, some Luftwaffe. John's mood lifted at the sight: they seemed fresh and well equipped. Many carried *panzerfausts* as well as rifles; there were plenty of machine guns and he saw several mortars pulled in dog carts. They seemed so confident; some of the passing platoons even sang. John joked about it at first, but then, after Kaarle and Greger went back to their game of German whist at the table, he joined in with the singing, sitting on the windowsill, keeping time with a lit cigarette. He was halfway through a croaky rendering of 'Argonnerwald' when Greger spoke up in exasperation.

"For God's sake, John."

Kaarle grinned.

John twisted his head towards them. "I like music," he complained plaintively.

Greger laid his cards down and snorted, "So do I. And I particularly like that song so please shut the fuck up!"

John looked pained and was about to retort when the singing vanished under the squeal of tracks. He looked again out of the window and smiled with grim satisfaction.

Greger and Kaarle looked at each other.

"Now they get it," Kaarle observed when he came to the window. Greger, standing by his side, nodded.

A column of tanks had approached the bridge and was clattering across, men moving hastily out of the way. It stretched back out of sight beyond the T-junction. John noticed that Ridderstolpe stood at the turning, watching.

Greger nodded. "Good."

John began counting. By the time the last tank crossed the bridge he'd reached twenty, more tanks than he'd seen in one place since Finland, and they'd all been Russian. Most of those passing were Mark 4s: an old boxy model, but still effective in experienced hands. There was also half a dozen of the newer Panthers, lean and angular with a very long gun. But it was the last two which brought a whistle of admiration from Kaarle: huge, twice the size of the Mark 4s, with a massive gun emerging from a lozenge-shaped turret.

"King Tigers!" Greger leaned out of the window. "Give the bastards hell!" he shouted, but no one could hear him above the roar and screech. The Tigers barely fitted onto the bridge and the second one across caught the top of the parapet with its front edge, sending a length of brickwork down onto the railway line.

Kaarle grinned.

"Impressive sight, eh, gentleman?" They turned to see Ridderstolpe standing in the doorway, puffing on a cigarette. For the first time in ages he seemed relaxed.

Greger saluted. "Yessir. Very."

Ridderstolpe came to watch the last of the column pass: a collection of horse-drawn wagons oddly out of place behind the tanks. "Battlegroup Werner, I'm told." He peered briefly through the window and then turned to face them. "The remains of two divisions and a lot of Luftwaffe."

"What's it for, sir?"

A wry smile flickered across Ridderstolpe's face at Greger's question and he flicked the stub of his cigarette out of the window. "We're mounting a big push at last light." To John, he sounded as if he was announcing something of little matter: a casual affair like a visit to the cinema or an evening at the dance hall.

Greger, John and Kaarle looked at each other.

"To buy time, sir?"

John's question brought a frown to Ridderstolpe's face. "Time for what, Marlow?"

"Well…" John cleared his throat. "Back in Berlin they said there might be talks…" John paused when Ridderstolpe shook his head dismissively. "With Churchill and the Yanks, I mean."

Ridderstolpe's frown deepened. "I'd heard something like that too. But it's just a rumour, Marlow. There's no deal as far as I know. There's still fighting in the west."

Kaarle's face fell and Greger nodded grimly. John pressed the point. "But sir, it was more than a rumour. An official in the Ministry told me. And Goebbels…"

"It's just a rumour, Marlow." Ridderstolpe grimaced. "Get used to it. Churchill and the Yanks are not going to do a deal. There's no last minute reprieve. We keep fighting. That way we buy time for the women and children to get out. And anyway…"

He didn't finish, but John guessed that what he'd been going to say was "…anyway, what else is there for us to do?"

"Maybe Yanks get here before Reds?"

They all stared at Kaarle who blushed and shrugged.

"Maybe," muttered Greger and caught John's eye.

Ridderstolpe looked out of the window once more. "Good lines of sight here," he said speculatively. "I'll send up some more ammunition." He turned for the door, and just before he opened it he paused and, without looking back, added, "Good luck," but there was no feeing in the words, and nothing else was said before Ridderstolpe closed the door behind him.

TWELVE

A cold, damp dawn woke Cheslav. He'd slept fitfully, wrapped like everyone else in his greatcoat, the company sprawled between the wall and buildings in untidy groups of men. His bladder was full.

Somewhere nearby Kolchok muttered loudly, "Is that all it's about?"

Cheslav raised his head and peered blearily at the nearby fire around which Kolchok faced Janko, puffing on his pipe.

"Don't you hate them, then?"

Cheslav sat up with a groan: his back ached, his feet were cold and his mouth tasted foul. He reached for his canteen and swilled out his mouth. Kolchok didn't answer, but instead inclined his head towards Cheslav.

"Good morning, Comrade."

Janko nodded a greeting and turned his gaze back on Kolchok. "So why do you fight?" He shovelled food from the pot on his lap into his mouth: it looked like kasha and the sight made Cheslav's stomach rumble. With another groan he levered himself blearily to his feet and saw the company mobile cooker, where two cooks, white aprons incongruous over stained uniforms, ladled out breakfast to a straggling line. He reached for his mess tin.

Janko grinned at Kolchok. "Love of the Motherland?" Even with a mouth full of buckwheat porridge he managed to sound sarcastic, but then he usually did.

Kolchok shook his head again and tamped the bowl of his pipe, which had ceased to smoke, sucked contemplatively, then tapped it against the sole of his boot. He quoted Simonov slowly:

> If you cherish your mother, who fed you at her breast;
> If you have not forgotten your father, who rocked you in his arms,
> Then kill a German, make sure to kill one! Kill him as soon as you can!
> Every time you see him, make sure you kill him every time!

He refilled the pipe. "Is that all there is to it, Janko?"

Janko snorted and scraped his spoon around the pot: he wasn't one for poetry.

Cheslav wondered what had started it. It was usually Janko: some sarcastic remark, a crude aside. Kolchok rarely bothered responding, but sometimes the corporal got under his skin, as he sometimes got under everyone's skin, and then Kolchok would let fly. Kolchok usually had the right words; Janko usually ignored him. He did so now, staring across the fire but saying nothing, showing no expression, just eating slowly.

Kolchok turned to Cheslav. "No answers, eh? And what do you think, boy? Is comrade Janko here right? He says the only thing is getting back at the Fritzes."

Cheslav contemplated Kolchok's words. "We have to beat them, sure. And they must be punished." Kolchok lit his pipe with a brand from the fire; his gaze didn't waver, but he showed no expression. Cheslav shifted uncomfortably; he badly needed to pee, but he couldn't leave it like that.

"Things will be better after the war. It's why we fight." He knew it was a lame thing to say, but he couldn't find anything better and his straining bladder distracted him.

Janko snorted dismissively, but Kolchok nodded encouragement. "Go on."

"Well, I mean, look at us here. Things are much easier in a way. Well…"

"Freer?" Kolchok smiled ruefully.

"Yes."

"And you think it'll last? After the war?"

Janko looked around cautiously.

Cheslav nodded and took a step towards the ruins. "Well it has to. Once it's all over."

Kolchok shook his head and exchanged glances with Janko who grinned back. Cheslav flushed slightly, feeling affronted. He'd thought that Kolchok might agree with him, but it seemed now that he and Janko weren't too far apart after all.

"Look, I know the system's got its faults, but it stands for something good."

Kolchok nodded. "It did. What we fought for in the Revolution, boy that was good. Getting rid of that Tsar was good." He looked at Cheslav and shook his head. "Trouble is, we've got another one. You think he's going to be any different after we get rid of Hitler?"

Janko frowned.

"Well…" Cheslav began, but then turned away suddenly as the pressure in his bladder became insufferable. "Got to go," he gasped.

After a meagre breakfast of tinned bread and lukewarm coffee in the front room of the grocer's apartment, John shared a cigarette with Greger and Kaarle and watched the column stream back across the bridge, only it wasn't a column anymore. It was a disorganised stream of men, shuffling along, dirty, dishevelled, many wounded. There were no tanks. No one was singing this time and Greger stared at them gloomily.

"Christ."

John felt depressed. What now? he asked himself. He was still contemplating the sight when Greger grasped his arm and pointed to three tanks which had appeared behind the retreating men.

"What?"

For a moment John's heart lifted: some of the tanks had survived, obviously. Then Kaarle said, "Reds."

John didn't understand at first: it was difficult to make out the exact shape of the tanks for they were festooned with bulky bundles. Then he realised that they were mattresses: extra protection.

"See?" Greger pointed at the figure standing upright in the turret of the lead tank. John nodded. "See his head?"

"Bugger." John raised his rifle: the figure wore the characteristic padded helmet of Soviet tank crew. Kaarle too took aim and let off a shot; the figure ducked back into the turret.

For a moment all was terribly still. Heads turned amongst the retreating men and the tanks accelerated. Panic broke out and the column scattered, surging across the bridge. The tanks raced forward, their machine guns spraying the windows of the buildings. They took no notice of the fleeing men who bolted up the road and out of sight; not one stopped to fight.

From other windows, rifles opened up and a solitary machine gun sent flickers of tracer towards the bridge. The lead tank rumbled forward, sparks erupting from its front. As it passed the last building on the far side before the cutting, a small flaming object flipped out of an upper window. It landed on the cobbles and liquid fire spread in front of the tank. Another Molotov flew out, bounced off the mattresses on the tank's turret and disappeared over the parapet and into the railway cutting, but a third flipped out of the window of the building on the opposite side and broke across the rear deck of the tank as it lurched between the parapets of the bridge. Instantly, fire puffed up and then disappeared inside. The tank coughed, lurched and stopped. Hatches banged open and a struggling figure emerged, followed by another. The figures fell, cut down by the hail of bullets spraying off the tank. One fell into the cutting, the other onto the roadway, but a moment later it scrambled up and away behind the burning tank.

The tanks following had halted, machine guns chattering ceaselessly, and Greger, John and Kaarle ducked down momentarily as rounds thudded against the outside wall. Then the firing stopped. The lead tank was burning furiously now, flames licking up through the open hatches and out of the engine louvres. From inside came the frantic popping of detonating ammunition.

John saw the turret of the rear tank traverse; the gun fired and the window of the building from which the first Molotovs had been thrown erupted outwards in a massive explosion. John ducked again as a brick flew through the window and whirled past his head, smacking off the wall behind him. His ears rang.

"Out," croaked Greger. Without waiting, he rushed for the door followed by Kaarle. John risked one last peek onto the road, saw that the turret of the second tank was turning towards him and flew out of the room and down the stairs. He'd just reached the yard when the wall above his head shuddered and he felt something shove him hard in the back. He fell to his knees, cracking them painfully on the cobbles. Then he felt someone grab his lapel and yank him to his feet. Dust billowed out through the doorway behind him.

"This way." Greger let go of John's tunic and ran across the yard to where Kaarle stood by the door in the wall. Another explosion shook the building as John stumbled to join them in a narrow alley and followed them back to the road.

Greger cautiously peered out and then beckoned. The tank on the bridge was burning steadily now; the mattresses had already been consumed, and the flames billowing out of the engine louvres had been replaced by thick black smoke which swirled about, trapped between the buildings. They could see nothing beyond the cutting, but could clearly hear machine guns firing, rounds hissing down the road; cracking off cobbles; thudding into walls.

"Move," Greger urged and they jogged after him up the street. All along it men tumbled out of the buildings and ran towards the junction where Ridderstolpe stood waving them on, seeming oblivious to the passing bullets. John thought he could hear a voice shouting in Spanish behind him then another explosion. It was as he followed the others past Ridderstolpe that something slapped his left arm hard and he knew he'd been hit.

They slept through the night in the apartment: Walter in his own bed, Monika in Ida's, Mrs Körtig on the sofa. Tanya dozed fitfully in an armchair. Nothing disturbed them until dawn when the distant shelling started again. Tanya fumbled her way past the unfamiliarly placed objects to the window and edged back the blackout curtain. The pre-dawn light made everything look grey and deeply shadowed and she could see little. She dropped the curtain back and turned to Mrs Körtig who had stirred and was sitting upright, a vague shape in the gloom.

"What's that noise?"

The two women turned at the anxious voice and a low flicker of yellow light. Walter was standing in the doorway of his room, holding a Hindenburg lamp on a saucer, wide-eyed and white faced. There was a hint of panic in his voice.

"Just the shelling. It's far away." Mrs Körtig stood and went to him, touched his arm briefly before turning to Tanya. "I'll check on her." She went into Ida's room and Walter took her place on the sofa. His hands, Tanya noticed, were shaking, causing the lamp to flicker wildly, and he almost dropped it when he placed it on the low table next to him.

"Would you like a drink?" Tanya tried to summon a smile but it came out as a weary grimace. "Well, I'll make some for us anyway." But as she stepped towards the kitchen something burst nearby with a sharp *bang*, rattling the window. Walter leapt to his feet as several objects clattered down the roof, knocking over the lamp. From the street below, Tanya heard the sound of shattering tiles.

It was then that Tanya decided they must take shelter. No one demurred; there was no trouble leading them all downstairs. It was Mrs Boldt who caused the trouble.

"Who's this?" She jerked her thumb at Monika as they trooped into the cellar one behind the other. Klara and Axel stared at them.

Mrs Körtig ignored her and led Monika to the alcove.

"Well?" Mrs Boldt tapped Walter's arm as he brushed past and he looked at her wide-eyed for a moment. "Well?" she repeated at Walter's silent back as he headed for the tin trunk.

It was Tanya who answered, standing by the door which she closed before clattering down the steps.

"He found her outside." Tanya gestured at Walter who had sat on Ida's chair and was now busy pulling out his magazines.

"What do you mean *found*?"

Walter looked at her again, anxious and uncertain.

"Leave them alone, woman." Mrs Boldt turned at Axel's intervention and for a moment they locked stares. "Can't you see they've been through it?" He looked sympathetically at Walter and then at Monika, but she didn't seem to notice and Mrs Körtig pulled the alcove curtains.

"This isn't a refugee camp," Mrs Boldt muttered, turning her gaze away with a frown. She sat down heavily in her chair and picked up her knitting, adding sourly, "This will have to be reported, you know. Oh yes."

Axel grinned at her and went back to his seat.

"Does anyone want tea?" No one answered Tanya's question, but she went to make some anyway. As she fussed with mugs and kettle, she looked at Walter. He was going through his magazines one by one, putting them in some sort of order. For a moment he looked up at her, a brief empty look, before lowering his head once more.

She was pouring water into the large coffee pot she used for making tea when she heard Monika's low sob, clear through the blanket: just one, followed by Mrs Körtig's soothing murmur.

Mrs Boldt smiled grimly. "Bolshevik swine. No woman's safe. Those filthy Slavs." She sounded smug and her gaze flicked towards Tanya, then she settled back to her knitting.

Walter looked up at her and then at Tanya. Now his look was intense; his eyes glittered. There was something not quite normal about it and Tanya felt a slight chill. She could see the look in his eyes – 'you're one of them' – and she knew he was thinking of his mother, out there, vulnerable, a woman.

Tanya glared at Mrs Boldt and would have spoken, but Walter stood up suddenly, scattering his precious magazines around the tin trunk. They all looked at him as he stood, hands clenched by his side, eyes bright in a ghastly white face. No one moved.

"Walter," Klara said softly, but he didn't seem to hear, just stood staring at Tanya.

"Walter," Tanya echoed, then she took a step towards him and he recoiled: a simple step, but stiff with feeling. She stopped dead; her stomach lurched.

Then Walter strode across the cellar, and ran up the steps.

As he jerked open the door, Tanya called out, "Walter! Stay here!" She took a few steps after him, but stopped when she saw the look of anguish on his face. Then he stumbled out, leaving the door wide open.

Axel was back on his feet, facing Mrs Boldt. "Damn you, woman, can't you keep your mouth shut?" He came to Tanya, ignoring Mrs Boldt's furious glare, her knitting needles tap-tapping angrily behind him. "Let him be," he said, placing his hand gently on Tanya's arm. "He'll be all right."

But she shook her head and felt tears well in her eyes.

"He'll be all right." Klara repeated softly. "Best to leave him for a bit. He'll be back."

Tanya smiled at her weakly and then gently detached Axel's hand. She went to the steps, but before she followed Walter out she pointed at the furiously steaming kettle.

"Can someone see to that, please?"

"What do you think?" John looked at the group of soldiers Greger had indicated with a jerk of his head. They were standing at one end of a barricade. At the other end a small group of soldiers in German uniforms and camouflage smocks stood in conversation with Ridderstolpe. He shrugged and then wished he hadn't: his arm hurt like the devil under the thick bandages. He winced and moved his shoulder to ease the pain; he'd been lucky, Weber had told him when he'd dressed it after they'd put enough distance between them and the railway cutting to risk halting for a while. It was only a flesh wound, a lump gouged out by a ricochet or a splinter of wall. Nothing serious; nothing to be evacuated for.

"Foreign Legion?" Greger rubbed his chin through grime and stubble.

"Perhaps. They're French, all right." The inflection of the men's voices, a word or two which carried to them, told John that much.

"I heard about a unit outside Moscow in '41. They were some sort of legion?" Greger sounded uncertain. Kaarle, standing next to him, nodded.

"I met a few French in Finland." John turned his gaze to Greger and tried to ease his shoulder. "In the training barracks before we went to Salla."

Greger tugged at his lower lip and nodded. "Well why don't we ask this guy?" He nodded towards the small group again and John turned to look. One of the Frenchmen was ambling towards them smoking while the others carried on talking to Ridderstolpe. He stopped and grinned.

"Good morning."

His German was flawless with a trace of accent John couldn't place. "Bonn jewer," he replied, "bonn mattin."

The Frenchman looked delighted, vivid green eyes sparkling in a dirty unshaven face. "Ah bohn. Voo parlay Fransay. Say trey bee-anne. Kell tennay allay voo?"

John shook his head: the quick-fire French was too much for him. "Jay sweez onglay," he explained apologetically, then added in English, "I don't speak much French." He tapped his chest. "Jay sweez John Marlow."

"Uhn Onglay?" The Frenchman switched back to German. "Can you understand me now?"

"Yes."

The Frenchman extracted a packet of Lande Mokri Superb cigarettes from the pocket of his greatcoat, lit one and handed it to John.

"Thanks. I'm John Marlow. This is Greger Engberg from Sweden and this is Kaarle...just Kaarle. He's a Finn."

Kaarle grinned. The Frenchman touched the peak of his grubby forage cap in a casual salute.

"I'm Alain Sabaev. We" he gestured back to his comrades "are the Thirty-third Waffen Grenadier Division of the SS." He handed the cigarette packet to Kaarle. "Very German. As we're French, we prefer to be called Charlemagne."

He grinned again; it seemed to come easily to him. John couldn't help smiling back: Sabaev's apparent good humour was infectious.

"Is this all of you?" John glanced along the barricade.

"All of us that got through before Ivan closed the ring."

"We're surrounded?" Greger, having taken the packet from Kaarle, extracted a cigarette and returned it to Sabaev.

"Pretty much. I suppose that you could find a way out if you wanted to, on your own." Sabaev exhaled slowly through his nostrils. "And you're…?"

John explained about Berg. "Espanyalineyen too," Kaarle added when he'd finished, pointing at two men sitting listlessly nearby, one with a heavily bandaged face.

Sabaev looked puzzled.

"Spanish," John translated. He told Sabaev a quick tale about Storm Detachment Esquerra, the canal bridge, their pell-mell rout. "We lost touch with Esquerra after that. These two ended up with us."

Sabaev nodded. "And now you've found Charlemagne. Quite a mix, eh? French," he tapped his chest, "Swedes, Finns." He jabbed his cigarette at Greger and Kaarle. "Even the damned English." Sabaev grinned at John.

"Thanks."

Greger chuckled. "Even the French."

Sabaev frowned and seemed about to retort, but John intervened.

"What brought you here?"

Sabaev ground out his cigarette on the barricade before answering John's question. "Family business. What brought you?"

"I want to stop the Reds." He knew it sounded pompous and grinned sheepishly when Sabaev raised his eyebrows. "All right. Maybe family business, too." He explained briefly about his Prussian grandmother, his father, his Swedish mother and Finland.

Sabaev nodded. "Papa and I were in the PPF."

John understood and explained it to Greger and Kaarle: the *Parti Populaire Français* was a French fascist movement before the war. He'd met a couple of PPF men in London when they'd come to a conference of European fascists.

"After they let me out of camp in '41, I joined the LVF." Sabaev extracted the Lande Mokri Superbs, lit another for himself and passed the pack around once more. "That's the *Légion des Volontaires Français Contre le Bolchevisme*." Sabaev chuckled. "Another mouthful."

Greger nodded. "I was in Lindholm's party," he explained.

"*Svenska Socialistisk Samling?*" John knew them. "Swedish Socialist Unity," he explained to Sabaev. "It's modelled on Hitler's Party." Greger frowned at that and John added, "In its basics. It's Swedish National Socialism, not German."

"I didn't think it was right, leaving the Reds to attack Finland." Greger smiled at Kaarle. "Our neighbours. More 'family business.' That's why I joined the Samling."

Kaarle grinned approvingly. "All fight Reds."

Greger and John nodded their agreement.

Sabaev smiled ruefully. "I hope you're right." He hesitated for a moment, his smile faded, he became sombre and opened his greatcoat. "Look." There were two medals pinned on his field jacket; he handed one to John. Hanging from a light green and black striped ribbon was a bronze-coloured Maltese cross. At its centre was an oval surrounded by a laurel wreath: it contained an eagle holding a shield divided into three vertical bars with the word *France* across the top. Turning it over, John saw more words in capitals: *CROIX DE GUERRE LÉGIONNAIRE*. He passed it to the others.

Sabaev handed him the second medal. This one was black, an oval attached to a ribbon by a clasp in the shape of a German helmet. The ribbon was red with white and black striping. On the medal was another eagle, superimposed on a branch, clutching a swastika in its claws. On the reverse side, over a crossed sword and branch was the engraving 'Winterschlacht Im Osten 1941/42'.

"I got them for the same reason." Sabaev retrieved the medals from Greger, who'd been peering at them both intently. "This one," Sabaev held up the bronze cross, "I got from *La Patrie* for fighting Bolsheviks in Russia. This one" he held up the black oval "I got from the Fatherland for fighting the Bolsheviks in Russia." He smiled sourly. "Now I'm fighting the Bolsheviks in the Fatherland and maybe soon I'll end up fighting them in *La Patrie*. If I get back at all." He shook his head. "Whether we stick together or not, the bastards will win."

Kaarle and Greger looked at each other and then Greger snorted. "But we'll take some of the bastards with us."

Sabaev flashed his grin once more. "Yes, my friend, we'll do that at least." But to John it seemed that the grin was forced and Sabaev's tone held a tinge of resignation. As the medals were pinned back in place, John whispered under his breath. They looked at him and he smiled wryly. Speaking English, he quoted slowly:

I have a rendezvous with death, at some disputed barricade,
When Spring comes back with rustling shade,
And apple blossoms fill the air.
I have a rendezvous with Death,
When Spring brings back blue days and fair.

John did his best to translate, unsure if he did the poem justice. Then he explained, "Seeger, an American. He fought in the Foreign Legion in the last war."

Sabaev, pinning his medals back onto his tunic, nodded. "Another man in someone else's fight." He closed his greatcoat. "What happened to him?"

John looked at him sombrely. "He died on the Somme."

"Dumb," Moiseyevich sneered as he walked up to Leonid and Agranenko. They were standing by Trofimova's tank on the bridge across the railway cutting. Charred mattress flock lay about their feet; the stink of burning was in their nostrils. Mercifully Trofimova's corpse had been removed from where it had lain smouldering until the bridge had been secured. Karabai had come back for it after his escape from the flaming wreck. The remains of the other two crew members, if there were any left by now, were still inside: the residual heat was too great to retrieve them. Leonid could feel it on his face and hands, radiating from the metal which was now a strange orange-red colour where the paint had burned off, except around the engine louvres where it was tarry-black.

Agranenko gave Moiseyevich one of the ice-cold looks which had earned him the nickname of 'Grandfather Frost', after the mythical figure who visited children at Christmas with rewards and punishments. It was an appropriate nickname. Moiseyevich pursed his lips.

"Salute the lieutenant," Agranenko said with dangerous softness in a way that said 'don't push your luck, boy.'

Moiseyevich hesitated and then complied. "I beg to report, Comrade Officer," he said, staring past Leonid's shoulder. Leonid saluted back, staring at Moiseyevich's spotty chin. Neither of them meant the compliment. Without looking at either Leonid or Agranenko, Moiseyevich explained in sentences almost insolently terse that Battalion Headquarters had sent orders for them to press on immediately.

"Anything else?" asked Agranenko, his voice still chill. Moiseyevich shook his head. Agranenko made a point of turning to Leonid and asking very formally, "With your permission, Comrade Lieutenant?" Leonid nodded. Then Agranenko dismissed Moiseyevich with a curt jerk of his head. "You can go. Tell the captain we need more ammunition. Any sign of food yet?"

Moiseyevich shook his head and walked off. This time he didn't salute; Agranenko let it go.

"Little shit," he muttered, glaring at the boy's back.

Leonid sighed. "Why can't he at least pretend to be polite?"

Agranenko pursed his lips briefly. "It's his ears that are the problem, not his mouth." He shook his head. "You know what the men call him?"

Leonid inclined his head.

"Polyanski's quiet dog. I beg your pardon, that's *Comrade* Polyanski's quiet dog. You know: 'Beware...'"

"'...a quiet dog and still water.'" Leonid finished the proverb. "Both dangerous." He sighed. "Him and his little notebook?"

Agranenko said nothing for a moment, then he smiled wryly. Gingerly he touched the side of the tank and snatched his fingers away. "Still too hot. He's right, though." He glanced down the road at Moiseyevich's retreating figure.

"Right?"

"It was dumb to charge across the bridge like that. No infantry support."

Leonid nodded. 'Advances straight down the streets are to be avoided', the book said. "I thought she might have learned her lesson at the canal."

"Comrade Chuikov would not be pleased."

Leonid smiled humourlessly. General Chuikov had commanded the victorious defence of Stalingrad and had written a manual passing on the lessons of Stalingrad: useful lessons, battle-winning lessons, life-saving lessons, but Trofimova had ignored them once too often.

"She was impatient, I suppose, wanted to get at the Fritzes." Leonid reached out but held his hand back: the tank *was* still too hot.

Tanya couldn't find Walter. He wasn't in any of the apartments: she knocked on every door, called his name, but it did no good so she went outside. He wasn't there either, nor in the yard. One last place to look and then she might as well take Klara's advice and wait for him in the cellar. She had raised her hand to knock on the door to Diederich's apartment when it opened and the caretaker stepped out, almost colliding with her. He was holding several hessian sacks. They paused, then Tanya lowered her hand.

Diederich glanced behind him and she saw his dumpy wife looking at her anxiously. "Good morning, Miss Klarkova," he said, formally.

She smiled at him: he was always so polite, so deferential, so helpful.

"I'm looking for Walter Schley. Have you seen him?"

Another glance at his wife. "Well, no."

"Were you going out? I wondered if you might keep an eye out for him." Then it struck her: why was he carrying sacks? He looked once more at his wife who nodded, a quick jerk of the head, then he turned to Tanya.

"Actually…"

"Go on, Diederich. You might as well tell her. She can help you carry things." His wife had a high voice and a Silesian accent which Tanya had always found slightly amusing. Now the sound of it made her smile briefly, but Diederich didn't smile. He looked at her with great earnestness.

"The school has been abandoned. People are helping themselves."

She didn't understand for a moment, then she realised he was talking about the old local high school which months before had been closed and taken over as headquarters by the SA and Volkssturm. They kept their stores there.

"Oh." She frowned. "That's looting, surely?"

His face fell, the relaxed conspiratorial expression replaced by wariness. "Well, there's no one there and I was told…"

His wife stepped forward. "It seems a pity to leave it for the Reds." She sounded more confident than he, her look determined. "And we'll be needing the food, I'm thinking."

Tanya hesitated. It was almost certainly illegal, but who knew when more food would become available, and they couldn't eat regulations. She glanced across the yard at the low window of the cellar.

"We should tell the others."

Diederich followed her gaze and this time he was emphatic. "Mrs Boldt?"

She knew he was right, of course: they could hardly explain what they were going to do to her. Best to keep this to themselves. She would think of something to tell Mrs Boldt after they got back, and no doubt she could bribe her with whatever they came back with.

Diederich grasped her elbow. "Come. Now. It won't take them long to empty the place!"

His wife nodded and closed the door, and Tanya followed him out of the yard.

When they turned the corner at the end of the street she saw people hurrying along carrying empty bags and baskets. Others were walking back loaded with tins and packets; staggering under the weight of bulging sacks; dragging boxes behind them. Two elderly women stumbled past them pulling a bed sheet lumpy with loot. How fast rumours spread, she wondered.

At the school they found bedlam. The street outside the wide entrance was littered with broken cartons and smashed bottles; people, mostly women, shoved past each other, going in and out. Those coming out were heavily laden. Clearly the school hadn't been stripped, yet.

Tanya stopped and contemplated the mess, her upbringing revolting against such anarchy: it was stealing, wasn't it? Even though she knew that what she didn't take someone else would, even though she had as much right to the food as anyone else, even though she knew the food would be needed in the coming weeks, she at first recoiled, uncertain. She looked about her: there were no uniforms in sight, no one in authority, but still she hesitated.

Diederich gave her no time to resolve her doubts. He grasped her arm, led her up the entrance steps and down a wide corridor, past more split and trampled boxes. The floor tiles beneath Tanya's shoes were sticky. They passed classrooms empty of desks, offices with nothing in, out the back and across a small playground. No one they passed said anything to them; all averted their eyes.

On the other side they went into what must have been the exercise hall. There were climbing frames fixed to the high walls, two wooden horses, and athletic equipment was stacked at one end. Steel shelving now criss-crossed the hall, half-filled with boxes, jars and packages. It was full of people, pushing, grabbing what they could. Tins clattered down and glass smashed. Tanya froze, but Diederich pushed his way through and she followed him behind a row of emptied shelves to a door set in the back wall of the hall.

"Wait a moment," he said, looking around to make sure that no one was watching. Then he pulled out a key. "I did some work here from time to time," Diederich explained. "I was the night-watchman too for a while." She didn't ask how he still came to be in possession of a key; in Berlin these days one did not ask such questions. He ushered her quickly through the door and locked it behind them.

Beyond it was a treasure trove. Stacked on shelves around a small room were luxuries she'd not seen in years: real Brazilian coffee in tins; French brandy and wine in bottles; packets of Indian tea; boxes of Swiss biscuits; Swedish canned meat.

"Quickly," he said, turning to one of the shelves. In a few minutes, Diederich's two sacks were full and they left, Diederich checking first that no one was outside the door.

They dragged the sacks back through the ruck in the hall; no one took any notice. Once outside, they paused, out of breath. Tanya wondered whether they'd be able to get the sacks back: they were so heavy, but she kept her doubts to herself as Diederich set off for home. They stopped from time to time to recover their strength, the gaps between stops becoming shorter and shorter until finally Diederich, red-faced and puffing, stopped.

"No good," he wheezed, leaning against a wall. "I'm not up to this anymore."

Tanya, herself exhausted, looked at him anxiously. "We'll have to leave one behind," she suggested breathily.

"We're not," he gasped, "leaving anything behind."

"But we can't drag both. It's ridiculous. Between us we might manage one."

He looked at her speculatively for a moment, then, staring past her, he stiffened. She turned, expecting to see uniforms and trouble approaching. Instead she saw a man standing nearby, watching them. He was thin, malnourished-looking, his complexion wan. He wore threadbare overalls with a large white letter sewn on his chest: the symbol for a forced labourer. There were many in Berlin: blank-eyed men and women, shabby, pathetic. This one had the letter P for Polish. Tanya and Diederich looked at him warily.

Then Diederich spoke. "*Vitietch pryacheloo. Ci now oo nam pomotch?*"

The man started. So did Tanya. Polish? she wondered. He speaks Polish that well? She knew that Diederich's wife spoke it: she was Volksdeutche, from the part of Silesia which once had been Polish but was now part of Germany, but that Diederich spoke it well surprised Tanya. She felt Mrs Boldt's suspicions creep into her, and then suppressed her feelings, annoyed with herself.

She waved at the Pole. "What does he want?"

Diederich smiled and began a slow conversation with the man, with many pauses and much pointing and gesturing. All the while Tanya looked around to see if anyone was watching, but there were few people around now, and those that were only glanced at them before hurrying on. Even so she was greatly relieved when Diederich and the Pole smiled at each other and shook hands with an air of finality.

Diederich placed his hand briefly on the Pole's shoulder. "He'll help us, for a share," he said.

Tanya nodded: it was the obvious solution.

The Pole smiled at her and, with a formality that amused her, brought his heels together without sound: he wore broken-down cheap canvas shoes. Then he held out his hand. When automatically she took it in hers, he bent his head and pretended to kiss it.

"Come on then," said Diederich.

They walked on, Diederich and Tanya hoisting one sack between them. Behind them, despite his meagre frame, the Pole carried the second on his back.

They arrived at the apartment block without incident and lugged the sacks into the hall. Diederich extracted an orange box of Austrian Milde Sorte cigarettes from the pocket of his dark-blue caretaker's denim jacket: more loot. He lit three in turn and gave them one each, then he slumped tiredly against the wall while Tanya and the Pole assembled a small stack of tins and jars on the bottom step of the staircase.

"As agreed," she said in German, and then repeated the phrase in Russian, hoping he would understand. Diederich translated into Polish. The Pole made no comment but just smiled, teeth brilliantly white in a weather-beaten face, eyes vividly green under close-cropped black hair.

"Thank you for your help," she added softly, formally, in German.

The Pole took her hand and once more pretended to kiss it. "*Sehrdetch-shineyeh zaprashamee panee,*" he said.

"He says," began Diederich, but the Pole smiled broadly and held up his hand to silence him.

In flawless German, he then said, "You are most welcome, Madam." His smile widened at her look of surprise and his eyes twinkled mischievously. Then he picked up his stack of groceries. "Good luck to you both." He nodded at the astonished Diederich, turned abruptly about and strode down the hall, carrying his reward.

Diederich and Tanya watched him go in silence. As he reached the door, Walter barged in. For a moment the man and boy froze, starting at each other. Walter's eyes gaze flicked over the letter emblazoned on the Pole's clothing and he stepped back.

Tanya took a step forward. "It's all right Walter. He's a friend. He's been helping us."

Once again Walter glanced at the embroidered letter and his eyes narrowed.

The Pole smiled at him, nodded gently and stepped around him. Walter turned as he did so. As if afraid to turn his back, Tanya wondered sadly. Only when the Pole had disappeared into the street did Walter relax and come towards them. As he passed, Tanya reached out gently to touch his arm.

"Are you all right?"

Walter jerked away from her touch and, without looking at her, went into the cellar.

*

Cheslav stood in the dingy cellar looking at the monochrome photograph in his left hand. It was grainy, creased and stained and the light was bad, but he could make it out well enough. It showed an izba: the hut in which most Russian rural families lived. Walls of wood and roof of wood and floor of wood, built around a massive stone stove and chimney. An elderly couple: a skinny man in blouse and trousers with knee-high boots, a peaked cloth cap above his brown creased face, a thick beard, and a stout woman in a calf-length dress, a scarf around a chubby face wrinkled like a prune, stood outside the hut, surrounded by chickens. With them was a young boy, perhaps ten or eleven years of age, a beardless version of the man. Cheslav had seen such families a hundred times, a thousand. The photograph had been tucked into a letter written in German which had been taken from one of the two young men Janko was keeping watch over against the far wall of the cellar. There was no address on the top, just a date: '*XV Mai 1943*'.

They'd found the men asleep under the table which occupied one corner, curled up together under a single blanket. They wore German Army uniforms with peaked cloth forage caps; they had no helmets, no webbing, no backpacks and no weapons: no field kit at all. They had no papers either, except for the letter found in one of the men's much worn high leather boots. Janko had made them take their boots off, and now Cheslav wished that he hadn't been so diligent. At first sight the letter was innocuous, a few lines such as one might read in any of a million letters from parents at home to a son serving with the army at the Front: any front; any army. A letter in German, but one phrase had jarred Cheslav: 'cousin Semyon sends his greetings.'

Cheslav read it again. Semyon was a Russian name. The prisoners didn't look Russian: their faces were plausibly German, but each had on his left sleeve a pale mark where something shield-shaped had been stitched on and then removed. Some sort of badge, he guessed.

"Take 'em to the boss?" suggested Kolchok who was standing behind Cheslav on the stairs down from the street. Cheslav hesitated. By rights they should hand the prisoners over to Bartashevich and Lopakin immediately. They were tongues: potential sources of information, and information was like gold dust, but the value of it dropped rapidly, especially in street fighting where situations changed hour by hour, sometimes minute by minute.

Still he hesitated.

"Well, boy?" Kolchok began to sound irritated. "We should get 'em out of 'ere."

"That's right." Janko sounded belligerent, but then he often did. "Get rid of the bastards."

One of the prisoners started very slightly. Janko's tone held menace, but he spoke in Russian, and a very provincial Russian at that. Cheslav wondered that the German had picked up the underlying threat. Did he understand? Cheslav looked at the photograph closely, then at the prisoners and an idea occurred to him.

He half-turned to Kolchok, making sure that he could see the prisoners's faces, and said loudly, "You know, I think these men were in the Homeland." He held up the picture, adding, "This is a souvenir." He paused to ensure that he had the men's attention. "What do you think they did to this family?"

Kolchok and Janko stared at Cheslav, then at the photograph and then at the prisoners. Kolchok remained impassive, but Janko's jaw tightened and his eyes glittered. When the Germans and Ukrainian politsai had raided his village, Janko had been away with his father, and they'd both returned to find the village aflame, his mother and sisters missing with the rest of the women and girls. The young boys and old men were dead, including Janko's twelve-year-old brother. When the Red Army came to liberate the region a few weeks later, Janko volunteered immediately although he was barely sixteen.

Janko fidgeted with his rifle. The two prisoners looked at him and their fear was palpable.

Good, Cheslav thought. Suddenly hardening the look on his

face and the tone in his voice, he said to Kolchok in clear, precise Russian, "They must be guilty of something. We'll shoot them here."

Kolchok, who knew Cheslav's abhorrence of killing prisoners, looked startled, but Janko grinned and the prisoners' look of fear turned to one of terror.

Cheslav walked towards them. Holding up the photo, he pushed it close to the owner's face. The man shrank away, banging his head on the wall behind him. Cheslav prodded him hard in the chest with his free hand.

"You understand me, don't you?" Switching suddenly to German, he added, "You'd best own up. My comrades don't speak German. I do. Talk to me. You're Russian, aren't you?"

The prisoners looked at each other, then at Janko and Kolchok. Finally the man whose photo Cheslav held whispered to him in German, but not the sort of German Cheslav would have expected to hear in this dark, grubby Berlin cellar. It was the sort of German he'd been brought up with: Volga German.

The prisoner claimed that the photograph showed his family. He gabbled as if desperate to explain. Both men had been called up together, he told Cheslav, friends and neighbours, put into Red Army uniform and then captured almost before those uniforms had lost their creases. Then the Germans had forced them to fight for them instead. A general called Vlasov had visited the camp, where they had been starving, and they'd agreed to join him.

Now Cheslav knew what the pale patches were: missing badges of the Free Russian Army, former Red Army soldiers fighting for the renegade general; traitors to the Motherland; followers of Vlasov. *Vlavsovskii.* At agitprop meetings they'd been told to look out for the Free Russian Army and their insignia: a red-edged white shield with a thick blue cross of Saint Andrew across it, the letters POA above.

The pale patches on the prisoners' coats said enough.

"Vlasov," Cheslav murmured and the prisoners lifted their anguished eyes. Behind him Janko and Kolchok stirred. Why did they do it? Cheslav wondered and anger flared in him. Surely they must have known of the terrible things the fascists had done? How *could* they put on these uniforms? But then he thought of the camps they'd liberated, full of Red Army prisoners no more than skeletons, malnourished and brutalised by overwork and beatings and left to freeze in Russian winters without adequate clothing or shelter. He remembered the famine back home when he was a boy; he saw the long column of dispossessed that had passed through his childhood village and his anger faded.

"They're Russian?" Kolchok joined Cheslav and looked the two men over dispassionately.

Janko's eye's widened. "Fuck," he said and hefted his rifle a few centimetres. "What?" Briefly he glanced between Kolchok and Cheslav before returning a hostile gaze to the prisoners.

Cheslav hesitated, but then he explained. Really, he had no choice.

"You're fucking kidding me!" Janko stepped back a pace and pointed his rifle at the prisoner whose photograph had condemned them.

The man spoke again, pleading with Cheslav in a low monotone: a voice empty of fear, but empty also of hope.

"He says," explained Cheslav, quickly stepping forward to push the muzzle of Janko's rifle to one side, "that he did it to stay alive. He wanted to see his family again."

Cheslav held up the photograph. Janko looked at it and then at the two prisoners. He jerked the muzzle of the rifle away from Cheslav's finger. "I don't give a fuck," he said very softly.

Cheslav looked at him: he could see that Janko would kill them and wondered what he'd do if Cheslav tried to stop him.

"*Bitte*," begged the prisoner whose eyes were now fixed on the photograph of the family he wanted to see again. He sounded so weary.

Now Kolchok pushed Janko's rifle away. "No," he said very gently. He met Janko's glare and stared him out. "No," he repeated firmly.

"Fuck that," snapped Janko, but after a moment he swung his rifle away and walked up the steps.

"Get them out of here," Kolchok said softly.

Cheslav nodded and held out the photograph.

"*Vielen dank, dass sie so sehr, mein freund.*" The prisoner took his photograph, stared at it for a moment and then tucked it into his pocket.

"*Komm.*" Kolchok gestured and they preceded him up the steps. When he reached the top he turned his head back to Cheslav. "How did you…" Kolchok began, then he stopped. "Never mind," he said and followed his two charges out.

Cheslav stood for a moment, looking around the cellar but not really seeing it. He knew what fate probably awaited Vlavsovskii. He saw his father, his mother; he saw others from their village; and he saw Leonid. He recalled of what the prisoner had said to him: 'I wanted to see them again. My father and mother. And I wanted to see my brother again.' Cheslav thought again of that long, sad column passing through the village; and thought again of his father led away. He shivered and wiped tears from his face with his sleeve.

John looked at the scarlet sky and smiled. 'Red sky at night, shepherd's delight': it was something he remembered his father saying often. It'd been true, too: frequently a red sunset *had* been followed by good weather in the morning.

His smile faded as he watched the dull glow above the city. It was not a sunset and the next day would be anything but good. He was sitting with his back propped up against the barricade, Kaarle, Greger and Sabaev alongside him, filthy, covered in dust, bloodshot eyes staring out of grimy grey faces. They'd been there all day, sitting, sleeping; had done no more than clean weapons and eat some meagre rations provided by Charlemagne. They were all exhausted. It seemed now that simply being alive was tiring. John wished that he could blank out his fatigue for a moment. Or forever, he thought. How good it might be just to let go, then he jerked his mind off that track. It wouldn't do; if nothing else he owed it to his comrades to carry on; he owed it to his father.

"Visitor."

John looked in the direction Greger tilted his head. An officer was walking towards them with a slight limp; John noticed that he favoured his left foot. He was dressed like any trooper and was as filthy; had it not been for his officer's peaked cap and the air of authority he carried, his rank might have gone unnoticed. John recognised him: he was one of Berg's, but John didn't know his name. He had a small box tucked under his left arm; his right lay along a bulky rifle with a curved magazine which was slung horizontally from his shoulder on its strap. Storm Rifle 44, John observed. He eyed it enviously; it could be set to fire either single shots like his own bolt-action Mauser or automatically like a sub-machine gun: a handy weapon, especially in street fighting.

The officer stopped by them and they all stood; they didn't salute. He looked at each of them in turn in a way John found annoyingly appraising. "Private Engberg?" His used formal German, the sort one heard now only from landed gentry and elderly Prussian officers.

Greger nodded, rubbed the back of his hand across his cracked lips. "Sir."

"Congratulations."

"Sir?"

The officer opened the box and pulled out a medal with a red, black and white striped ribbon. "Iron Cross, Second Class," he said, "on Captain Ridderstolpe's recommendation." John saw that the box was full of different medals, their multi-coloured ribbons reminding him of his mother's sewing basket.

Greger stared at the medal, took it and blinked.

The officer turned. "Corporal Sabaev?" He accented the name very heavily, drawling the last syllable, a sound more Belgian than French. Sabaev nodded. "You've been awarded an Iron Cross, *First Class.*" Again he rummaged around in the box.

John looked at Sabaev, startled. To get a First Class meant that Sabaev already had a Second, yet he wore no ribbon in his buttonhole as was the custom, and indeed the regulation. Nor had he mentioned it when showing them his other medals.

"Thank you," Sabaev said indifferently.

The officer frowned as he rummaged around. "You don't seem impressed, Corporal."

"I am grateful, sir," but Sabaev still sounded indifferent.

The officer looked up. "Well, I don't have one."

"I'll settle for a cigarette."

The officer stared at Sabaev for a moment, then favoured him with a thin, cold smile. He closed the box and tucked it back under his arm. Then he reached into his breast pocket and pulled out an elegant silver cigarette case with a crest engraved on it.

Of course, John realised, it would.

"Here, Corporal. For acts of valour." The officer flipped open the case, extracted half a dozen cigarettes and held them out. "Turkish. Perhaps the last in Berlin. Heil Hitler." With that he turned on his heel and limped away. When he was out of earshot, Sabaev muttered something under his breath in French, but when John looked at him he just smiled and held up the cigarettes.

"Pour vai-once," he said. "Eel son Turc." They chuckled with him, and sitting they shared four of the cigarettes.

"Excellent," observed Sabaev, sucking in appreciatively. They were indeed good, and John closed his eyes momentarily. If he could just blank out the constant rumble of fighting nearby, he might be anywhere, sitting with friends and enjoying a good smoke.

"Better than a medal," commented Greger. "Even a tin necktie."

Kaarle nodded. John opened his eyes and looked at Greger questioningly.

"Tin necktie: Knight's Cross." Greger tapped the base of his throat and John nodded: it was one of the highest awards the German Army could make. "You know what they say, don't you?" Greger went on, smiling grimly. "After a Knight's Cross, a birch-wood cross."

Sabaev blew out a long stream of smoke then looked closely at the glowing end of his cigarette. "This *is* better." He looked up at the ruby sky for a moment. "Guys who get the tin necktie get the shittiest jobs...sorry, get the *honour* of leading every mission. Once a hero, always a hero."

"It's the same in the British Army," John said softly.

Sabaev nodded.

"My father," explained John, "told me that they had a VC in the regiment in Flanders. He got all the dangerous missions. One day he didn't come back."

Greger grunted.

"Vee see?" asked Kaarle.

"A medal. Like the Iron Cross. More like the Knight's Cross really. The thing is," John sighed, "my father said that the man had wished that he'd never won it. Father spoke to him before he went on his last mission. The man told him that ever since he'd got the medal, he'd felt that he had to show an example, but really he just wanted to keep his head down like everyone else."

"You know what they call suicide missions?" Sabaev tossed away the stub of his cigarette and smiled, blowing smoke out of his nostrils with a look of pure satisfaction.

"No. What?"

"A Knight's Cross job." Sabaev pulled a second Turkish cigarette out of his pocket, looked at it lovingly and put it away again. "You can keep your medals."

Greger nodded. "You know there's a name for guys who want to win them? Knight's Crosses, I mean."

John shook his head.

"Widow-makers. They *so* want to have that damned medal, they get guys killed looking for it."

John tasted the tobacco on his tongue and smiled. Yes, it was better than a medal.

When Palancvich knocked on the cellar door late that afternoon, it was Axel who opened it. He looked surprised, but no more surprised than Tanya. She stood abruptly from the table where she and Klara had been playing cards with him. Mrs Boldt, fruitlessly busy with the radio, looked up and stopped cranking the handle. Tanya saw her eyes widen at the sight of Palanevich's immaculate grey field uniform and her face set into the expression she always adopted when faced with officialdom.

Mrs Boldt stood and raised her right arm. "Heil Hitler." No one copied her.

Palanevich inclined his head graciously. "Yes..." Then he smiled at Tanya and asked, very formally and in Russian, "May we speak in private, Tatiana Ivanovich?" He turned the smile on Mrs Boldt and reverted to German. "Perhaps, Mrs Boldt?" He gestured with his hand towards the door. Then he looked at the others. "If you would excuse us, please?" He stepped back into the hall and everyone looked at Tanya. With an apologetic grimace, she rose and went out. Mrs Boldt followed nervously.

Palanevich was waiting just outside the door; he closed it gently. "I thought that it would be better," he addressed Mrs Boldt, "if we spoke privately."

She looked nervous. "Well, if the *Herr*..."

Palanevich cut her off with a wave. "Please. Just Major." Mrs Boldt snapped her mouth shut and looked surprised. He pulled out his engraved cigarette case and offered it first to Mrs Boldt, who hesitated and then took one, then to Tanya, who shook her head. He smiled, took a cigarette for himself. Keeping to German, he said, "Tanya. You must be surprised to see me."

"Victor Mikhailovich..." She trailed off: she wasn't sure if she was or not. Palanevich had a habit of turning up when she least expected it.

He pulled out his lighter, lit the two cigarettes, puffed appreciatively and then watched amused as Mrs Boldt tasted hers very tentatively and coughed. "I must explain, madam," he said to her, "that I had a mission to escort some items of great value to the Reich out of the city." He paused, puffed on the cigarette again and looked at Tanya. "It failed. The routes out were blocked." Once again he smiled at Mrs Boldt. "I have left the items somewhere safe." He saw Tanya's raised eyebrows and explained to her, "I can't tell you where, but suffice to say the, uh, items are well hidden from the Bolsheviks."

Mrs Boldt nodded. She wore the look of one who is being brought into a great secret and she stood a little straighter, her eyes still watering from the Turkish cigarette.

"And now I must hide myself."

They looked at him in surprise.

"You see, I must retrieve those items once matters here are, uh, settled." He leaned slightly forward towards Mrs Boldt and lowered his voice conspiratorially. "It is a matter of great importance for the Reich. That means I must be, as they say, incognito. For that, madam, I need everyone's cooperation."

Tanya turned her head to hide a grin and supressed it; he was laying it on a bit thick, but it seemed to be working. Mrs Boldt nodded self-importantly.

"I understand, Herr Sturmbannführer. I mean…" She stopped, confused, and Palanevich smiled sympathetically. "We shall be honoured to assist in any way." Her gaze was fixed on his face.

Tanya kept her own gaze firmly upon the wall behind his shoulder; despite her anxieties at seeing him here, she feared she would laugh.

"Yes. *Major*, please." He puffed his cigarette. "That is most kind. Of course I shall endeavour to see to it that no one is inconvenienced, and after…after matters are settled I will make sure the Führer hears of your loyalty."

Mrs Boldt stood straight as a ruler, her chest swelled. "The Herr…the Major is most kind," she simpered and Tanya didn't know which she felt most: amusement or distaste.

Palanevich turned towards Tanya and spoke more plainly. "You understand, of course?" He switched to Russian. "I shall explain more later." He beamed at Mrs Boldt and pulled a heavy key from his pocket. "Now, I need some help to move a few things from the yard." He reached past her and opened the door to the cellar. "Would you be so kind, madam, as to request those two young gentleman downstairs to come to see me?"

She nodded. "But of course, whatever the Herr Sturmbannführer wishes."

As she thumped down the steps into the cellar, Tanya heard Palanevich mutter under his breath, "Major, please!"

THIRTEEN

The shellfire sounded like feet drumming on a wooden floor: a continuous vibrato, half-felt, half-heard, rising and falling. Leonid coughed, sat up and rubbed sticky sleep from his eyes. Agranenko nodded to him across the room of the ground floor apartment in which they'd spent the night. He was kneeling below the glassless window using his steel helmet as a bowl for his habitual start-the-day ablutions. Scrubbed hands and smooth-shaven face made a startling contrast to his stained uniform and dirty boots. Leonid knew he looked just as filthy; they all did by now. Their uniforms were shabby and patched, their boots were scuffed, but their weapons were clean. It was a discipline enforced with vigour by the veterans who knew the cost in lives of a jammed gun.

"Tea." Tajidaev pushed open the door with his shoulder. Leonid nodded to him as he walked to the dining table at the centre of the room, placed two steaming mugs on it and grinned at the litter of empty bottles underneath it. "Food soon." He sloped out, leaving behind a faint aroma like damp straw; they all stank too but no one noticed it much, usually.

Leonid eased himself to his feet; how he ached and, despite the sleep, felt a deep, draining weariness. The tea, sweet and thickly black, revived him a little. He took a large swallow to wash the foul taste out of his mouth and crossed to the window.

Agranenko wiped his face, rose and picked up the mug Tajidaev had left by his side. "Someone's getting it." The rumble was louder now.

Leonid nodded, drained his mug and went outside to empty his bursting bladder. He found some of the platoon in the hall, sipping drinks and chewing cold rations. Tajidaev stood in the apartment doorway and beamed at him. Leonid smiled back before heading to the kitchen; the sink met his need admirably. When he returned he found Agranenko waiting for him with Tajidaev. Moiseyevich was also with them.

"Major Gushenko wants you," he said tersely. "Officers' meeting."

Agranenko frowned at him. Leonid only nodded, but wondered why a meeting? He knew what they were going to do, the same as the day before and the day before that: move forward, clear any resistance, keep going until dark or until they were too tired to stand up, or too wounded to fight, or too dead. Leonid sighed and handed his mug to Agranenko. He brushed fruitlessly at his dusty coat and followed Moiseyevich across the rubble-strewn street into the downstairs room in the apartment block opposite which served as Company Headquarters. Trofimova's remaining two tanks were parked outside it. They were Karabai's now of course, but Leonid still thought of them as hers.

Gushenko, flanked by Polyanski, was standing in front of the company's few remaining officers. Everyone in the room was dusty. We look like bakers, Leonid told himself as he entered. He suppressed the urge to grin; Gushenko didn't like levity in his meetings.

They went through the usual litany: objectives, routes, flanks, timings, enemy forces, own forces, Gushenko using a torn-out page from a Berlin city guide on which he'd drawn in pencil to indicate as he spoke. Leonid only half-listened, but he pricked up his ears when he heard his name.

"Lieutenant Barakovski's platoon will take point with the tanks."

Platoon? he thought wearily. Despite a trickle of replacements which had somehow found their way forward, his platoon was by now well under half strength. He'd reorganised it into two weak squads instead of the official four strong ones, but everyone was making such shifts. The platoon had never been at full strength since he'd joined it anyway. Most of the platoon were newer than he was, aside from a tiny hard core of surviving veterans like Agranenko. Tajidaev called anyone surviving more than a couple of engagements, but really it was random chance at first. After that they had enough experience to make a difference to the odds of surviving. Newcomers died in circumstances veterans might come through completely unscratched, and Leonid supposed that, having survived thus far, he too was now a frontovik, but he didn't think of himself as such.

Gushenko finished his briefing and they waited until the bombardment ahead stopped and the dust it had thrown up settled. Then they moved on as usual, picking their way around rubble, edging down both sides of the streets with the tanks driving down the centre. It wasn't long before they met resistance at an obvious place: a crossroads. Out of the shattered windows at the top of a two storey apartment building a machine gun burred suddenly like a buzz-saw and rifles barked. Rounds struck sparks off the tanks, ricocheted from walls and pavements and whined around them like gnats, yet no one was hit as they ran for cover in doorways.

The tanks halted, quickly firing a round through each of the windows. Their frames burst outwards in turn in a spray of wood and dust and the firing ceased.

Leonid watched it all with tired familiarity. Too easy, he told himself as Agranenko led one of the sections through the front door at a run. Then the faint *crump* of grenades, the *rat-tat-tat* of sub-machine guns, and silence. Tajidaev appeared at the doorway, grinned and nodded. Another assault, another building cleared. Leonid went inside, pushing past his men as they re-emerged. None were missing save for Agranenko and for a moment his heart lurched.

But Agranenko was unharmed. Leonid found him standing on a first floor landing staring into a room. He didn't turn when Leonid approached up the stairs, nor did he respond when Leonid spoke his name, but he jumped when touched and turned with a blank expression. Leonid was startled at how tired Agranenko's eyes were, how empty. He stepped into the room and stopped. Two bodies lay twisted against a wall, dark blood soaking the rich carpet around them; small shapes: boys. Behind a machine gun mounted on a tripod a third boy sat upright on a dining chair, left hand on the top slide cover, right arm straight down by his side. He might have been posing for a photograph. His skin was bloodless white, his uniform dark through the inevitable coating of dust. His eyes were wide open, cornflower blue; his hair a thick thatch of sunflower yellow. He looked to be no more than twelve or thirteen years old. Smile for the camera, Leonid urged silently, but the boy didn't smile and never would again. On the finely chiselled feminine face, the lips were turning grey. Two tiny drops appeared at the corner of the boy's eyes and rolled turgidly down his cheeks. Surely, wondered Leonid, dead boys cannot weep? But they were not tears. More drops trickled from the boy's ears, forming a thin rivulet that ran slowly down his neck and into the collar of his pale brown shirt. Leonid felt a hollowness in his belly and bile in his throat; he swallowed it and reached out to touch the face. Someone spoke German behind him and he snatched his hand back and turned sharply, reaching down to his pistol holster, but it was Agranenko's voice.

He stood in the doorway, hands by his side, eyes fixed on the boy. Anguish flickered across his face and he quoted tonelessly:

Germany,
your sons will
no longer play
as children.

His German was flawless.

Leonid turned from him, unable to bear his look of desolation. By the time he gathered himself and turned back, Agranenko had left him with only the dead boys for company.

Late that morning John was woken from exhausted sleep by Sabaev's prodding toe.

"Eat," he said and pointed to a line forming in front of Weber who stood behind a pile of sandbags. He was ladling something out of an old tin washing tub.

"More Lorelai," murmured Greger from beside him, but he was careful to keep his voice low and lurched eagerly to his feet to be fed.

When it was John's turn to hold out his mess tin, Weber slopped in a thin grey liquid with two unrecognisable bits floating in it. "Sweeties too," he said with no flicker of humour and handed John two small greyish-white tablets taken from a mess tin full of them resting on the sandbags by the wash tub. John stared at the tablets in his hand and Weber grinned. "Go on. Make an übermensch of you."

John grimaced: übermensch. He'd first heard the word on a course of Nazi theory: superman. The next stage of human evolution from the shining Aryan. The thought of himself as super-anything made him smile grimly.

"Pervitin," said Sabaev behind him. "Pep pills, that's all."

John hesitated; his mother hadn't approved of drugs of any sort. She'd been a devotee of folk remedies. "God's natural medicines," she'd call them: potions and ointments made from natural ingredients, most grown in her own herb garden, the recipes learned from her mother, a Dorset farm wife, a throwback to Hardy's mythical Wessex. Chamomile tea for indigestion, insomnia and headaches; chamomile washes for cuts and grazes; elderberry for sore throats and coughs; nettle juice for his teenage dandruff; cabbage juice for his teenage acne. He remembered them all.

"Get on with it." Sabaev sounded impatient. "I'm hungry."

John put the tablets in his pocket and moved back to where he'd left his kit by the barricade. He sat next to Greger and drank the stew: it was too thin to eat. There wasn't much and it didn't taste of anything except water and grease.

Greger grinned at him. "You slept like you had a good conscience."

John nodded; it was a well-known Swedish saying. "In England we'd say 'slept like a dog.'"

"Dormeer sur say durz oray," Sabaev offered, coming back with Kaarle in tow.

They sat for a while in weary silence. Sabaev dozed, curled up in a foetal ball, arms tucked into his chest, legs drawn up. Greger and Kaarle played a desultory game of cards. John couldn't be bothered to do anything except sit watching a group of Volkssturm who'd turned up earlier, one of several such groups which had passed through. For some reason these had stayed; now they were at the other end of the barricade doing nothing much in particular, like the rest of them.

More interesting were five Hitler Youth sitting against the wall of an apartment block further up the street. One had bandaged hands and a thick wad of gauze over half his face. They all looked worn out, pinched young faces white above the grey-with-dust uniforms. The boy with the bandages seemed livelier than the others despite his injuries, talking constantly. John found him fascinating for some reason he couldn't explain to himself; perhaps it was the boy's animation, his hands waving like white semaphores, his head turning this way and that.

The boy caught John staring at him and paused, then scrambled awkwardly to his feet and limped over, announcing in a high child's voice: "Timo Schröder." He knelt down, taking great care that his bandaged hands touched nothing, and settled himself cross-legged facing John.

"Marlow. This is Corporal Endberg, this is Kaarle," Timo nodded earnestly to each in turn, "and Sabaev."

Greger and Kaarle ignored him but Sabaev sat up and pulled out a cigarette. Timo shook his head when he was offered it and winced.

"You don't?" asked John.

"I'm not old enough."

Sabaev laughed, lit the cigarette for himself. "Not old enough? Fuck that! You've been fighting." He pointed at the bandaged hands.

Timo nodded. "Molotovs."

"Bad luck," sympathised John. "Ivan's fond of them."

Timo shook his head and winced again. "Ours. When I lit one, some of the petrol got on me." Then he smiled, the open guileless smile of a child. "We burned 'em up proper, though." When he got no response, he frowned and went on. "The Reds were in a house.

Marius, my mate, Marius and me got on the roof, got inside." His spoke quickly, insistent, a boy eager to impress, waving his bandaged hands, words gushing over each other. "Pulled up the slates." He winced, stopped the flow of words and stared at his hands for a moment, then laid his forearms carefully across his thighs. "Marius and me, we dropped 'em down the stairs and ran. *Whoosh!* Went right up!" He grinned again and repeated, "*Whoosh!* Whole house caught fire. That's when I splashed myself," he added ruefully, looking at Greger and Kaarle who had stopped playing by now and were watching him.

Sabaev nodded. "Anyone get out?"

"No," said Timo with great satisfaction, turning back to him. "Well, one ran out on fire but one o' me mates shot him."

"Well done," said Sabaev quietly.

"Thanks. You should have heard 'em yelling." Timo's eyes sparkled.

He's really proud of that, John realised. Burning men alive. How old is he? Timo saw John's expression and his pleased grin faded.

Frowning at John, Kaarle held out his canteen and smiled at the boy. "You do good."

Timo sniffed and shook his head. "I'm not old enough to drink."

"Sure," urged Kaarle. "Finn boy drink all time." He swallowed deeply from the canteen and again held it out but was refused.

Timo looked at John and seemed embarrassed. He levered himself awkwardly onto his knees and then lurched upright unsteadily. "I have to get back to the others. Moving out shortly."

Sabaev stood with him. "Where are you going?"

Timo looked at him earnestly. "Gotta report back to our barracks. Get fresh orders."

Sabaev nodded and placed a hand on Timo's shoulder. "Good luck, Comrade," he said gently.

Timo straightened. "Heil Hitler." He stood briefly to attention in front of them, raised a bandaged hand and then turned and strode away, arms held out from his sides.

Like a penguin, noted John. The image did not amuse him; instead he felt sad.

"A fine example of young Aryan manhood," Greger observed sardonically as Sabaev sat down once more. "The Führer's pride and joy."

Kaarle looked at him, puzzled. Then he took another swig from his canteen and stared after Timo who was manoeuvring himself awkwardly to sit by his comrades. "Boy not drink," he said wonderingly as if the concept was beyond him. He leaned his head against the barricade and sighed and shook his head.

Although it was a bright afternoon, the cellar was in deep gloom for it was lit only by a single Hindenburg lamp: they'd decided to ration them. Axel was invisible in the corner where he sat with Klara, but Tanya could tell from his tone that he was exasperated.

"I don't know why you're bothering."

Mrs Boldt turned briefly from the radio and then went back to spinning the dial.

Why does she bother? Tanya wondered. Mrs Boldt had been scanning the frequencies all morning but had found nothing except broken snatches of Russian: commands mostly, or questions, all sounding military. Once she'd caught a burst of martial music, but whose? Palanevich thought it might be German but it was too indistinct: all they could make out through the hiss, crackles and whines was the regular *thump, thump, thump* of heavy drums.

There seemed to be no civilians on the air at all.

"It's getting on my nerves." Axel sounded petulant, but Tanya had to agree with him. Not only were there discordant sounds emanating from the speaker but the dynamo emitted a low hum.

"And mine. Why not try again later?" She tried to sound solicitous. "You must be getting tired."

But Mrs Boldt was having none of it. "You'll see," she rasped, her gaze fixed on the radio's luminous front panel which lit up her face eerily, a ghostly gargoyle like something out of a magic lantern show.

Palanevich waded in. "What exactly *is* it you're hoping to hear?" Tanya turned her head in surprise. He'd been sleeping on top of the few crates they'd moved from the cellar; he'd been sipping champagne all morning, a solitary tippler, and had dozed off just after midday, but clearly the noise of the radio had awoken him: his voice was a little slurred.

Mrs Boldt stopped cranking the handle for a moment and turned her head towards him. "The counterattack. You'll see. It'll be starting soon and then you'll all see."

Axel groaned. "Good God, woman! You don't believe that rubbish?"

"Axel!" Klara admonished him in a low whisper but it carried across the now quiet cellar.

"Rubbish? How dare you! The Führer himself promised it!" Mrs Boldt was not whispering.

"Like he promised Stalin would never get to Berlin?" Palanevich sounded amused.

Mrs Boldt turned back to the radio. "You'll see. You'll all see. The Führer's planned it all." She seemed to be speaking to the radio. "It's a trap to lure the Reds into the city and then destroy them. And the new weapons. Yes, you'll see!"

"We'll see all right." Axel sounded weary.

Mrs Körtig was sitting in the alcove with Monika. Tanya could just make out a shrug and knew what Mrs Körtig was thinking: the Nazis had been promising wonder weapons for some time; new offensives to drive the enemy back and save Germany; the unholy alliance of western capitalists and eastern communists grinding Germany into dust would fall apart. Well, wonder weapons *had* appeared, but the Nazi rockets hadn't even slowed the Americans and British, nor halted the bombing of German cities unprotected by an emasculated Luftwaffe, and the unholy alliance seemed to hate Germany more than they hated each other. The war went on.

But not for too much longer, Tanya pleaded. Please God. Germany was beaten; she knew it, they all knew it, except, it seemed, for Mrs Boldt. Am I glad? Tanya asked herself, watching the block warden's obsessive tuning. Anyone sane would want the war to end, but what lay in store for them then? She thought of the sour joke she'd heard whispered many times in private: 'enjoy the war while you can; the peace will be terrible.' But no one, surely, really wanted the war to go on. Did Mrs Boldt believe what she'd said? She must know that, even if the Russians were driven out of Berlin, there were still the Americans and British. And even if they were all driven back, what sort of Germany would that leave? A heap of rubble inhabited by the maimed and blind and hopeless? Better that we lose now, she mused. Then she shivered: it would not finish there. She feared that more horrors were to come. If half of what Goebbels and his propagandists predicted was true…well, best not to follow one's thoughts down *that* road before one had to.

Klara crossed the cellar and joined her at the table where she'd been trying to read by the light of the lamp: a forlorn attempt, but better than just sitting, and the feel of the book in her hands was a tiny comfort.

"Is she right, do you think?" Klara whispered when she'd sat down. She sounded desperate for reassurance.

Tanya couldn't give it. "No. She just doesn't want to face the truth."

Klara bit her lips. "She's not the only one." Her voice trembled slightly.

Tanya laid down the book and took Klara's hand. "My mother was like that, clinging to the hope that things would get back to what they were. She lost her world to the Revolution. When we left Russia without Father, we had nothing except each other. In Paris she'd visit the émigrés' office every week." Tanya paused; the recollection was surprisingly painful. "She must have known there was little hope, but she persisted. It wasn't until *he* came to see Mother that she stopped looking back." Tanya nodded towards the recumbent form of Palanevich who seemed to have gone back to sleep. It was he who'd come to see them with awful news. She remembered the flowers, the long talks, her mother's tears, and smiled sadly at Klara. "Before then we had a photograph of Father on the wall. She'd talk to it, tell him of things that had happened, of our plans as if he was there." Tanya stopped, surprised at the emotion she felt and at her need to tell. She was supposed to be comforting Klara and here she was pouring out her woes.

Klara squeezed her hand. "Go on." The tremble was gone from her voice now.

"I hardly knew Father, really. I last saw him when I was four years old. I can't remember his voice, and without that photo probably wouldn't know what he'd looked like. It wasn't so bad for me really, but it must have been so hard for Mother."

Klara said nothing, but she placed her second hand on top of her first and nodded.

Tanya bit her lip. "The day after Victor Mikhailovich came we went to Sainte Geneviève des Bois. There's a Russian cemetery there. We took Father's picture from the wall and buried it. Mother and I laid flowers."

"Go on," Klara repeated gently.

"After my stepfather died, she stayed in Breslau where they'd retired. He had family there, you see. She's still there."

Klara said nothing. Breslau had been besieged by the Red Army for over two months.

Tanya took a deep breath. "Goodness. Just listen to me, laying all my troubles on you. I'm sorry."

Klara shook her head. "It's all right."

But Tanya slid her hand free; she didn't want to think about her mother. She said with a brightness she didn't feel, "Shall we have tea?"

Klara nodded. Tanya went to the stove, tipped tea and boiling water into Mrs Körtig's old silver English teapot. It was a cherished heirloom, left to her by a favourite aunt. The tea in fact was dried blackberry, strawberry and mint leaves mixed with finely chopped tree bark, but it would do. Waiting for it to brew, Tanya went to the window in the alcove, smiling at Mrs Körtig and Monika. Only the old woman smiled back. Tanya stood on her box and drew back the blackout curtains to peer through the small greasy panes, and froze.

In the courtyard were four soldiers in brown uniforms carrying rifles, their legs wrapped in bandages from ankle to knee: *puttees*. Their long narrow cloth caps reminded her of the one Walter had worn when he was in the Deutsche Jungvolk, before he'd moved up to the Hitler Youth. Schirmmütze, they were called, but these were not schirmmütze. They were pilotki and the soldiers were in the Red Army. Shabby with round Asiatic faces, they clustered by the door to the coal cellar.

"God," she said too loudly and feared the soldiers would hear her. She turned her head and saw that everyone, except for the sleeping Palanevich, was now looking at her.

Mrs Boldt stopped tuning the radio. "What's going on?" she rasped.

"Soldiers," Tanya said and Klara put her hand to her mouth.

Axel walked to the window and she stepped down. After a long look, he went to take Klara's hand.

"Ivans," he said in a deadpan voice.

Tanya looked again. The soldiers were hammering on the coal cellar door with the butts of their rifles, shouting, the noise echoing around the courtyard.

"What's going on?" Mrs Boldt called out again. She went to the table, resting her hand on it as if for support. Palanevich got to his feet and stood by her side, an incongruous pairing.

"Shush!" Tanya waved her to silence. Then she turned her attention back to the window as the hammering and shouting stopped. Mrs Körtig held onto Monika's hand, murmuring soothing words.

Diederich had emerged from his apartment carrying a white cloth above his head. His wife stood in the doorway behind him. The soldiers stared at them, their rifles half raised. Then one of them, shorter than the rest, said something and the rifles were slung onto shoulders. Cautiously Diederich approached. He held out his other hand, offering a cigarette packet. One soldier took it, handed it around. Two of the soldiers pushed past Diederich and his wife into the apartment. The short soldier pointed to the coal cellar.

"What's happening?" Mrs Boldt hissed.

Tanya shushed her again without turning her head; her attention was wholly on the courtyard. Diederich went back into his apartment, pushing his wife inside. Then he reappeared with a crowbar. The short soldier levered the padlock off the coal cellar's door and kicked it open. He disappeared inside, and moments later re-emerged laughing and beckoning to his comrades.

Tanya turned and briefly explained what was going on. Mrs Boldt was waspish.

"Damn thieving Slavs!"

Tanya didn't respond but turned to watch as the two soldiers reappeared, bottles tucked into tunics and pockets. They grinned at Diederich; one slapped him on the shoulder. The two who had gone into Diederich's apartment now reappeared clutching a few items, but when they saw their comrades they dropped them and rushed into the coal cellar to re-emerge with their arms full of bottles. One fell to the floor and smashed but they ignored it. Then they all left, grinning broadly. Diederich watched them go with a fixed smile on his face. His wife picked up the dropped items and then they turned and went back inside.

"Thank goodness!" Tanya tugged the curtains fully closed and stepped down. Monika's pale face stared up at her anxiously.

"Gone?" asked Mrs Körtig and Tanya nodded. She explained what had happened.

"Well," said Mrs Körtig, "let's hope they're all so easily pleased."

Mrs Boldt looked at her, started to speak, and then someone knocked hard on the door.

Everyone tensed.

The knocking came again. "It's me. It's all right."

Tanya smiled. "It's Diederich." The tension in the cellar eased palpably and Axel trotted up the steps and opened the door. Diederich came in and stood at the top of the steps. He looked shaken and began to explain.

"I saw it all." Tanya walked to the steps.

He nodded. "Ivans like to drink. I found that out from the in-laws. Give them a bottle and they're happy."

Tanya smiled thinly at the comment. Then he remembered and smiled apologetically at her, and she felt her resentment to be absurd and smiled back. Palanevich just shrugged and took out his cigarette case; Tanya noticed that his hands shook slightly.

"I thought," Diederich continued, "better they take the wine than...well, best not to annoy them."

Axel nodded. "Look, it can't be safe for you out there on your own. The two of you, I mean. Especially..." He paused and Diederich flushed. They all knew he meant 'especially for your wife.'

"Join us," Mrs Körtig said. "Safer together."

Diederich shook his head. "Thank you, but we'd rather stay in our own home. And the wife, well, being Polish should help."

He stopped and looked anxiously at Mrs Boldt. She snorted, but they all ignored her. Axel looked doubtful and Tanya wondered how much Diederich could rely on Russo-Polish friendship. The two nations hardly had a history of it; they'd fought one war barely twenty years before, and when Germany conquered half of Poland in '39, Russia took the other half.

"Anyway," Diederich looked around, "I'm not sure that being here...no, we'll stay home, thank you."

Tanya knew what Diederich was thinking: a cellar containing two men of military age, a boy and four women was not necessarily the safest location in Berlin. She kept the realisation to herself but her stomach twisted.

"Are you sure?" Axel asked.

"No," Diederich smiled doubtfully, "but we'll make do." Axel nodded and Diederich turned and walked out.

"Good luck," Tanya called after him. Diederich waved his hand without turning his head.

"Survive," said Axel softly, the now popular Berlin farewell. Then he locked the door.

Ridderstolpe came with orders to move. Berg, he told them, was to join up with forces concentrating deeper in the city. Charlemagne's detachment was to come with them, leaving the barricade to the Volkssturm.

It was starting to get dark when their column turned a corner in a sprawling nondescript residential district and ahead saw yet another barricade. Half a dozen Volkssturm were busy passing rubble from hand to hand in a line. Leaving it a bit late to set it up, John noted. Then he realised that they weren't building it, they were dismantling it.

Ridderstolpe, just in front of him at the head of the weary column, must have realised the same thing for he raised his hand for them to halt and shouted, "What the hell are you doing?" The Volkssturm looked at him startled and stopped. When Ridderstolpe motioned with his hand they dropped their stones. They looked like a group of schoolboys caught out in a piece of mischief.

One of the Volkssturm stepped forward. His long, dark overcoat was open and underneath he wore a black shirt, a band of white showing at his throat. He walked purposely towards Ridderstolpe and didn't salute when he halted a few paces away. "Pelzer. I'm in charge." Ridderstolpe ignored the proffered hand. "Father Pelzer."

"Ah. Catholic?"

Pelzer nodded.

Ridderstolpe smiled in a way that John had seen before: seemingly relaxed, but if John had been Pelzer he'd have been very wary indeed. "Building a barricade, Father?" Behind Pelzer some of the Volkssturm shuffled. He met Ridderstolpe's gaze steadily without answering. "Don't let us delay you, Father. Do get on with it." Ridderstolpe's tone was still amiable and he was smiling, but his eyes were flinty and his face hard. Pelzer hesitated visibly, and when he opened his mouth to say something Ridderstolpe dropped the smile and spoke coldly. "I'll leave a couple of my men here to help supervise." Pelzer closed his mouth. Then he nodded, turned to his waiting men and began giving commands in a weary voice. They set to work once more, passing the stones back the other way.

Ridderstolpe pointed to John and then to Sabaev behind him. "You and you." He pulled out his by now very crumpled street guide and consulted it, then he glanced up. "We'll be about five hundred metres up that road. There's a bus station on a main junction. We'll bed down there for the night and push on in the morning. I'll send Corporal Børgesen back to relieve you when we've set up. Make sure," he lowered his voice, "that *he* does what he's told." Ridderstolpe jerked his head towards Pelzer. Then he shook it; there was exasperation on his face. "It's a bad idea to bring God into this sort of thing, eh, Marlow? Confuses people." Then he walked on, waving the column to follow him. Kaarle and Greger grinned at John and Sabaev as they passed.

When they'd turned out of sight, John and Sabaev went to sit on the side of the road. They eased their feet and smoked, watching the Volkssturm as they slowly and sullenly built up the barricade using the rubble they'd piled to one side. Pelzer looked at them now and then but said nothing. They moved quickly, and it did not take many cigarettes before the rubble was back in place and the Volkssturm slumped down behind it, looking exhausted and resigned.

Pelzer however walked over to them and they stood to meet him. "We've finished."

"I can see that." Pelzer stared at John angrily. "Look, uh, Father," John tried to sound conciliatory, "it's always best to obey orders." He felt embarrassed. He was not Catholic, not even a believer, but respect for men in dog-collars had been inculcated into him by his father who'd often mentioned the fine padre he served with in Flanders.

"Tell me, just what is the point now?"

John frowned at Pelzer's question, glanced at Sabaev who stood behind him impassively. "Point? We have to defend ourselves."

"Is that what we're doing?" Pelzer shook his head. "These men" he waved at the huddle of elderly and late middle-aged sitting watching them "are going to die here. And for what?"

"We have to fight." John shrugged, suddenly angry. What was the man's problem? It was obvious, wasn't it?

"Don't talk to *me* about fighting." There was sudden venom in Pelzer's voice. "I was at Verdun. Got the Iron Cross, First Class."

Not another one, John despaired, glancing at Sabaev again. The Frenchman smiled wryly.

"And I fought the Reds in '18, in the Ukraine." Pelzer let out a slow, tired breath and calmed his voice. He pointed along the undamaged street. "This will be destroyed. For nothing."

John shook his head. "Not for nothing."

"Look." Pelzer grabbed John's sleeve as if desperate to make him understand, but John jerked his arm away. "You get to a point where you're not fighting for your country, not for the Kaiser, Fatherland or folk. You're not even fighting for your family or your friends. You're fighting because that's all you do. It becomes pointless."

Out of the corner of his eye, John caught Sabaev nodding. It annoyed him, but it was Pelzer he glared at.

You're like a dog in a pit fight. John observed Pelzer sounded like a man in a pulpit. You can't let go, and all you want to do is tear the enemy's throat out. And that's all we're doing here now.

"We'll make them bleed," John heard himself say, "make them pay for it." Sabaev's smile was now directed at John. He felt himself flush and resented it.

Pelzer looked disdainful. "They're not the only ones bleeding. 'Blood and soil', is it? Too much blood. Look…" He reached under his coat and pulled out a small triangular piece of stone. "I found it in the rubble."

John took it. It was the size of his hand. One edge was jagged, the broken-off corner of a rectangular slab. Etched deeply into the stone were a few characters John recognised immediately: 'Jewish.'

"Hebrew," said Pelzer quietly. "Part of a gravestone."

"What?" Sabaev stepped forward and took the fragment out of John's hand as Pelzer went on.

"There's a Jewish cemetery over there." He pointed over the roofs of the adjacent buildings, waving vaguely. "*Was* a Jewish cemetery," he corrected himself. "Used to be a Synagogue, too. Now it's a warehouse. But you can still see where the cemetery was. They dug it up."

"So?"

Pelzer reacted angrily to John's question. "*So?*"

Sabaev looked studiously neutral and handed the stone back to Pelzer.

"People's *graves!*" Pelzer held the stone up, ran his fingers gently along the Hebrew characters, caressed them. "Do you know what this says?" He shook his head at them, didn't wait for an answer. "*Po nikbar*: here lies. That's all. 'Here lies'. Someone's name was on this stone. A person's name, gone now."

"A Yid." John said it in English to Sabaev and shrugged.

"A child of God." Pelzer looked at John with pain in his eyes. "We're all children of God." He looked at the stone again and suddenly turned away. In a low sad voice, he said, "Even the SS."

John stared after him, angry. Sabaev touched his arm. "Leave it," he said quietly as Pelzer walked away.

John stiffened, a rebuke in his mouth, but when Sabaev took his hand away and shook his head gently, John said nothing.

Sabaev stared at the barricade and the weary Volkssturm sitting silently waiting for Pelzer. "How does that poem go again?"

John looked at him, puzzled. Then he understood. "'I have a rendezvous with Death, at some disputed barricade,'" he said slowly and his anger faded.

Sabaev nodded, looked down the road and smiled. "Here's Børgesen," he said brightly.

The sound of shelling had gone on sporadically for most of the afternoon, usually not close, but when several loud explosions vibrated the floor and ceiling, everyone in the cellar crouched back against the walls. It didn't last long, however, and when it finished Tanya and Axel went outside to take a look. The street was even more cratered, strewn with rubble, the air thick with brick dust. That was not what shocked them, though: white tablecloths and sheets now hung from most of the windows or balconies. A week before they'd been draped in red, white and black; some German national tricolour flags, but mostly Nazi swastika banners and all in honour of Hitler's birthday. Now the banners were the white of surrender.

They didn't mention it to the others when they returned to the cellar, but they did discuss quietly what needed to be done. Diederich's close encounter with the Red Army soldiers had shaken them all, and even Mrs Boldt acceded that anything that might antagonise the Bolsheviks needed to be got rid of. They all trooped upstairs to search their apartments, save for Klara who stayed with Monika. Palanevich went with Mrs Körtig to replace his uniform with an old suit of Eugen's. It fitted well, and of course looked elegant on him; much more elegant than it had on its original owner.

They took anything with a Nazi connotation downstairs, save for Walter who announced that he would remain in Mathias' apartment. Axel considered it to be a bad idea, but Walter found an unexpected ally in Mrs Körtig.

"Let the boy be," she urged. "He's sensible; he'll come down if it gets dangerous, and he's too cooped up."

Like the rest of us, Tanya thought.

No one argued and Walter was left to his own devices.

Back in the cellar, they spent a long time slowly feeding the stove, stirring the ashes to make sure no trace of Hitler's regime remained. When her turn came, however, Mrs Boldt couldn't bring herself to do it and Axel volunteered, Klara favouring him with an exasperated look when his satisfaction showed as he pushed Mrs Boldt's Nazi paraphernalia into the low flames.

Evening came on slowly as they burned and stirred, Palanevich watching them, sipping at champagne. He made no comment as they burned his uniform and Walter's too.

Mrs Boldt finally stopped tuning the radio and went back to knitting in the gathering gloom. Tanya and Mrs Körtig played cards with Axel and Klara around the table. Monika slept, curled up in the little alcove wrapped in Mrs Körtig's overcoat. It was a nice coat but was getting shabby, as most clothes were these days. Mrs Körtig had sighed wistfully when she'd brought it down from her apartment and wrapped it around Monika.

"He got it in Gerson's for my birthday," she'd said sadly. Gerson's hadn't been Gerson's for some time. Tanya had looked at the old coat and wondered what had happened to the store's Jewish owners. Then she dismissed them form her mind: they were only Jews, after all.

Monika had stared listlessly into space.

Tanya finished the round of whist, declined the offer to play yet another and went to sit on the edge of the champagne crates with Palanevich.

"Have some," he offered in Russian, holding up a half-empty bottle. There was another empty at his feet.

How does he do it? Tanya wondered. She shook her head, but when Palanevich insisted, Well, why not? she told herself and went to fetch a mug.

She stopped him when he'd half-filled it.

"*S'daroveeyah.*" Palanevich saluted, draining his own mug and refilling it while Tanya sipped. It was warm; Palanevich smiled mirthlessly when she grimaced. "Champagne," he explained in Russian, taking another swallow, "should be drunk cold on a hot day."

Out of the corner of her eye Tanya caught Mrs Boldt staring at them. Palanevich followed the direction of her glance and raised a mock salute.

"Block wardens," he muttered, "the Führer's loyal watchdogs, or watch bitch in her case." He stared into his mug. "We ought to have some cucumber."

"Or blinis and caviar," Tanya said wryly.

Palanevich smiled. "You're a cultured lady." He raised his mug again. "Here's to culture. To art." He glanced again at Mrs Boldt.

Her head was bowed and the knitting needles *clack-clacked*. "The bitch should appreciate that," he murmured.

Tanya shushed him, although his voice was very low and still he spoke in Russian. "Why?"

"Why what?"

"Why should she appreciate art?"

"The little corporal's an artist. So he says." Palanevich grimaced. "He once told me that he preferred art to politics."

Tanya was startled. "*Hitler* told you?"

"I met him once. In Munich, in '39." Palanevich paused, belched slightly. "I do beg your pardon. At the arts festival. Huge affair. Hitler loved it. He told me that after the war he'd retire, paint pictures and design buildings. He loves architecture. Really passionate about it."

Tanya was exasperated. "There's not many fine buildings left in Berlin. Or in Germany, for that matter."

Palanevich sighed. "Now Göring, there's a real art lover for you. Carinhall's stuffed full of it."

Tanya nodded. Carinhall was Göring's pride and joy: his residence outside Berlin.

"Quite a baroque monstrosity of a house," Palanevich observed. "I was there a lot."

Yes, thought Tanya ruefully, I'm sure that you were. Palanevich, she knew, held some sort of post in Göring's household, and everyone in Berlin knew of the Reich Marshal's passion for fine living and elegance. Carinhall would have suited Palanevich well.

"He liked to talk about Tsarist art and how it compared with Bolshevik. He knew quite a bit. He's quite a fan of Musatov." He paused, and added, as if Tanya would know, "That's Borisov-Musatov, of course." Tanya looked at him blankly, but he didn't seem to notice. "Also liked some of the post-revolutionary work. Deyneka, Galakhov, artists like that. Surprising really. That man has good taste."

"Hitler?"

"God, no! Not him, *Göring*."

*

Mathias' apartment had never really felt like home, but Walter had lived there for over two years and he was glad he'd stayed when the others returned to the cellar. Closing the door behind Mrs Körtig, he went first into the living room and threw back the blackout curtains. Outside, despite the dust it was a bright late afternoon. He went to his mother's bedroom to get what she'd always called her memory box. It was small, the size of a shoebox, and precious, given to her by her own mother. She had died before Walter had been born, but his mother had spoken of her often, venerated her, and he felt that he knew her. Faded paintings of flowers covered the memory box under cracked varnish; its brass hinges and clasp were tarnished. Walter had never seen inside it, but it had no lock. Carefully he tipped the contents onto the bed, hoping to find something, anything, to bring his mother back.

He sorted through the jumble on the coverlet: an elegant pearl necklace reminiscent of a bygone age; a chipped champagne glass wrapped in faded and brittle pink tissue paper; a lacework handkerchief yellowed with age. His achievements book, the official record of his time at volksschule, lay face down. Next to it was a bundle tied with an old ribbon. On top was a postcard, a faded sepia photograph of a ruined castle set on a steep hill with steeply gabled half-timbered houses clustered below it on narrow cobbled streets: a typical German scene. The word 'Hanstein' was printed in the top left-hand corner of the card. Underneath were several photographs. Carefully he untied the ribbon and turned the postcard over. The other side was stamped, franked and addressed to his mother using her maiden name. It had only one line of message: *My darling Ida, how I miss you* and was signed *F xx*. For a while he sat and looked at it, felt the card's fibrous texture, sniffed its stale mustiness. Then he set it aside and went through the photographs one by one. Some showed his father and mother in youthful days; some showed other members of the family. There was an improbably young Uncle Mathias standing awkwardly in a railway uniform, posing stiffly in a studio against curtains and standing by a large potted fern. There were pictures of Walter himself: christening, first day at kindergarten, confirmation and first communion. One showed him on his first day in the Pimpf, the most junior branch of the Hitler Youth. He was grinning into the camera, an awkward little boy in black uniform shorts and brown shirt, grey socks pulled up above his knees. There was another taken on the day he was promoted from the Pimpf at age ten into the Deutsche Jungvolk; now in dark shorts, he had a dark-blue jacket over the brown shirt and he looked serious, as befitted his greater years. The last photograph showed a group of young teenagers standing in two groups in front of low tents: short-haired boys in dark blousons and long trousers; plait-haired girls in dark skirts and white blouses. Most were grinning, but he was standing between Friedrich and Rolf and looking at the camera with an earnest expression.

The scene was like something on a poster and he could imagine the caption: 'The nation's youth at summer camp enjoy the healthy pursuits which the Führer has made possible in the New Germany.' The photograph had been taken at the start of harvest duty in 1942, the last time he'd gone. After that he'd been drafted into the SHD.

He smiled at the photograph sadly. It had been good, despite the hard work interspersed with route marches and parades; he felt only unutterable sadness looking at it. When he'd come home from that last camp his father was gone; he'd been called up, one of many older reservists summoned back into uniform to help fill the ranks depleted by the terrible fighting in Russia. They'd had no opportunity to bid farewell to each other and Walter had never seen his father again.

He sat on the bed and stared at the picture until his eyes ached.

"Thinking about that boy with the machine gun, Comrade Lieutenant?"

Leonid grimaced at Agranenko across the low table which sat between them in the foyer of the small family hotel they'd taken over a few hours before. The proprietor, a cadaverous man with an equally mortal-looking wife, had greeted their arrival with intense anxiety and excessive obsequiousness, but still he had tried to allocate the rooms. Agranenko had soon disabused him and the couple had retreated to the attic.

It was early evening and they were waiting for Gushenko to confirm where he wanted them to go next. Leonid hoped that they might rest for the night; they were all exhausted, but Gushenko was under pressure from Zeldin to get on.

Polyanski had come to see them that afternoon to emphasise the need to advance, or, as he'd put it, to "…push your bayonets deep into the belly of the fascist beast."

"Remind you of your brother?"

Leonid didn't answer but rested his head against the wall behind him and closed his eyes.

"He's not though, is he?"

Leonid kept his eyes closed, silent.

"A lot of blood's been spilled." Agranenko sounded weary. "And he *wasn't* your brother. All right, so maybe he was *someone's* brother, someone's son: they all are. Are you going to let them all get to you like this? There's too many of them. Just get on with it and wait for it to be over."

Leonid opened his eyes and shook his head, feeling the wallpaper rub against his gritty hair. "It was the tears. The blood, I mean."

Agranenko reached for his canteen. "In Leningrad, there was a lot of blood, and a lot of tears." He paused and then spoke slowly in a low voice. "'For what they say of Leningrad is true: the tears have frozen in the people's eyes. We cry no longer, for no tears could quench our burning hate.'" He smiled grimly. "Poetry goes with Russians." He sipped from the canteen and smiled briefly. "And suffering." He passed the canteen across the table. "Suffering is very Russian too."

Leonid took a mouthful of the brandy. "You know a lot of poetry."

"So do you." Agranenko accepted the canteen back and drank,

deeply this time. "But I learned most of it at the University. We studied it."

Leonid thought of Mr Gerstein and smiled sadly. "I had a good teacher." He paused, recalling the hours he and Cheslav had spent in Gerstein's little library, their teacher selecting passages for them to read aloud. There'd been a lot of poetry. He whispered under his breath the words Gerstein loved to quote. "'Poetry comes nearer to vital truth than history.'" Seeing Agranenko frown, he repeated them more loudly. "Plato," he explained. "What was that poem you quoted earlier?" He remembered only the first few words of the German Agranenko had spoken so well. "'Your sons...'"

Agranenko held out the canteen. "'Your sons will no longer play as children.' Ernst Toller, *Deutschland*."

Leonid took another drink. "Why that one?" Agranenko didn't answer, and Leonid knew from his expression that he shouldn't press him but something drove him on. He gave the canteen back. "Did that boy remind you of someone?" Agranenko stiffened silently. His own son, perhaps? Does he have a son? wondered Leonid.

"It's just a poem. It seemed," Agranenko hesitated as if searching for a word, found it, "apt."

"You quoted it beautifully."

Agranenko smiled wryly. "I learned it at university." He shook the canteen and frowned. Then he laid it on the floor next to him and settled back against the wall. "German literature. It's not something I talk about these days." His smile vanished. "Not wise to advertise it." He held Leonid's gaze. "I studied with Germans, you see. They were our, well, not friends, but it was acceptable to be around them then, subject to supervision of course. But Hitler attacked and contact with everything German was suspect. You know that, Comrade Lieutenant." He waited as if expecting an answer, but when none came Agranenko pursed his lips. "No flies in a closed mouth. That's what they say, isn't it?"

Leonid hesitated; Agranenko was inviting him to share something. For the first time he seemed to be really confiding in Leonid. It was the opportunity to get closer to him that Leonid had been hoping for, but he was wary: it was a lifetime habit. Then he made a decision. Perhaps it was his exhaustion, perhaps it was the brandy, perhaps it was Agranenko's grief at the boy weeping blood; perhaps it was Agranenko's own candidness and Leonid being tired of hiding things.

"I learned German at home. We spoke it when I was a boy."

Agranenko seemed unsurprised. "Go on."

"Papa, he was Volga German. Our name was Gartner."

"But not now."

Leonid shifted uncomfortably. "No. We grew up in a village near Bradander. Germans settled there a long time ago. Papa was born there, and his father, and his. Our home is Russia."

"You don't live there now?"

Leonid shook his head. "Papa…Papa went away."

Agranenko had the grace to look awkward: such things were not usually spoken about openly.

"When he…went away, Mama remarried. A good Party man. Russian, like her." Leonid was surprised at the undertone of bitterness in his voice. "Then we moved."

"I see." Agranenko shifted his shoulders, stretched. "As awkward for you as for me." He smiled ruefully. "We speak the language, we knew Germans. And you had a German father…"

"He was Russian."

Agranenko shook his head. "Not to Comrade Stalin."

"We're Russian. We've been in Russia for two hundred years. We're loyal."

"Think that makes a difference?" Agranenko shook his head again; he seemed irritated by Leonid's simple claim. "They're not big on things like loyalty to the Motherland, except when it suits them, like now. Class consciousness, that's what counts. Loyalty to the Party."

"I'm a Barakovski now. I'm Russian." Leonid knew it sounded like a child's stubborn claim. "My brother and me."

Agranenko picked up the canteen and stood up. "We need some more refreshment, Comrade."

*

Cheslav lay near a wrecked car, the smell of burned rubber in his nostrils. He'd tried to sleep, but despite his numbing, bone-aching weariness, could not. The background noise didn't help: explosions, shooting, sometimes the squeal and clatter of tracks or the rumble of engines. Once, distant shouting in a language he couldn't discern. The tumult had not died out after dark; something was going on ahead, but he didn't care: he was too tired, but still he could not sleep.

Those around him seemed to have no such problem. His side of the street looked as if passing refugees had dropped their bundles as they fled, but the dull brown mounds were not empty clothes. Sleeping forms cluttered the pavements.

The company had halted at dusk, the last of many halts that day. They'd seen little fighting: a few skirmishes with isolated pockets of last-ditch defenders bypassed by the units marching ahead of them. The defenders were Hitler Youth mostly, with some SS. The Volkssturm and regular army tended now to surrender or flee after firing a few shots; often after firing no shots at all. It was the fanatical teenage boys and the grim veterans of Himmler's elite who did most of the fighting, the killing and the dying. Cheslav wondered at it and had concluded that the boys fought because they were confident in the arrogant way of adolescence, uncomprehending of their mortality. The SS fought because they were all too comprehending: they knew that surrender was not an option, not after what had been done in the Soviet Motherland. Invariably SS prisoners were shot if they were fortunate, bayoneted or knifed if they were not. Sometimes they were interrogated first, but usually not. It depended on whether an NCO or officer was around to take an interest in a tongue.

Giving up on sleep, Cheslav pulled out Leonid's book and tried to read it by the light of the full moon overhead, but that was no good either. Charles Dickens made no sense to him on the dusty cold road. He tossed and turned and fidgeted, and it was while he was trying out another position he hoped might be comfortable that something moving caught his attention. Across the road at the entrance to an alley was an old standpipe. He'd had a look at it when the company had halted. All of iron, it had a levered handle set at the top of a thick vertical tube curving over like a shepherd's crook. Lopakin had explained that the water pumping system in Berlin had failed thanks to bombing and shelling, so now they used standpipes. Cheslav found this ironic: Germany, the birthplace of a man he'd been taught was the most advanced thinker of his time, Karl Marx; Germany, with its industry and science, famous for its chemists and engineers; Germany with its great musicians and writers; Germany, whose people now were reduced to drawing water from the ground like the peasants in his home village.

A woman had emerged into the moonlight and was walking down the alley towards the standpipe. She wore a dark dress and a shawl which covered her head, and from her bent back and slow shuffle she was clearly old. She carried a bucket in each hand. Close to the standpipe stood two soldiers detailed to keep watch while the rest slept. They were from another platoon and Cheslav didn't recognise them. He watched them as they watched the woman. As she got close, one of them, a gnarled and elderly man with the thick grey beard of his generation, crossed himself and walked rapidly away to stand near Cheslav. The other soldier didn't move and the elderly man beckoned urgently.

"Misha. Get over here, boy!"

Bodies stirred about them. Cheslav sat up and shushed the old man, who looked at him in annoyance.

"What's up, Gregorii?" The second soldier walked across, looking anxious.

"Never you mind, boy," Gregorii answered testily, "just stay over here with me."

Misha shrugged, then grinned at Cheslav and raised his eyes to the sky as if to say, 'old men!'

Gregorii looked sour. "It's not good," he said.

Cheslav smiled and nodded. "No."

Gregorii crossed himself again. Misha stared at him, shook his head and sighed.

Cheslav levered himself to his feet and stretched. "A woman carrying empty water buckets is bad luck until the buckets are filled."

Misha stared at him for a moment, glanced at the old woman who had set her buckets down by the standpipe and then grinned in derision at Gregorii. The old woman bent over the standpipe and started to pump water into the buckets. She was slow about it, each laborious lift of the handle followed by a long pause, then down it went. One, two, three…Cheslav found himself fascinated by it. *Creak*, pause, *creak*. On it went. Gregorii watched calmly, but Misha fidgeted, shuffled his feet, blew out. After a while he turned to Gregorii.

"How long is this going to take?"

The old man shrugged. "Who cares? You thirsty, boy? Need to get some water?" He shook his head at Cheslav as if saying, 'what's his hurry?'

"The sergeants said we should stay by the pump."

"Never mind the sergeants, until she's done, we stay here."

Misha pursed his lips, fidgeted some more. Finally, he'd had enough. "Oh, fuck this," he muttered and stomped across the road. "Hey, you!"

The old woman stopped pumping and looked at him.

"Go. Now. Piss off." He stopped in front of her and waved his rifle. She ignored him and went back to pumping. "I said, piss off." He reached out to grab her arm.

She swore at him and he stopped, hand hovering inches from her arm.

"What did she say?" Misha turned towards them. Gregorii shrugged and Cheslav, who knew what she'd called him, just grinned. It wasn't complimentary and he wasn't about to translate.

The old woman picked up her buckets and shuffled back down the alley. Misha stared after her. "I wonder what she said," he called across to them.

Gregorii turned to Cheslav. "Nothing nice, I'd guess."

"No, I guess not," Cheslav agreed.

Gregorii shook his head. "A dog is wiser than a woman," he said. "That's what they say, don't they? Wiser than a woman: it doesn't bark at its masters." He sauntered back across the road.

Masters? wondered Cheslav. He looked at the company sleeping around him: masters of Berlin; of Germany. I suppose we are now.

FOURTEEN

No one came to fetch Walter and he didn't go down. It wasn't a conscious decision, it just turned out that way. He spent the evening curled up in this chair or that, or moving about the apartment touching familiar things. Before the light faded he opened the blackout curtains and looked at Mathias' old railway magazines while listening to some of Mathias' classical records. Then he got his homework out and sat with it at the dining table as he always used to do. By then it was too gloomy to read, but still he turned the pages of his text books.

When the moon rose and the room glowed pale blue-white he went into his mother's room. In the ghostly light he went through the clothes in her little wardrobe, burying his face in the cloth, drawing in the aromas of mothballs, lavender scent and wool. He ran his fingers over her jewellery, stroked her hair brush, dabbed his wrists with the rosewater she kept on her tiny dressing table. Then he sat on the bed and looked at the silver-framed wedding photograph on the side table. Ida and Fabian stared at him through the glass, standing on the steps of a chapel, awkward in Sunday best, faces formal but glowing with joy in the bright moonlight.

He didn't notice he was falling asleep. When he awoke, sprawled cold and stiff across the bedspread, dim dawn light stroked his face through the window. Then he retrieved his school satchel from the dining room, emptied it and crammed in some clothing, his Hitler Youth knife and the wedding picture.

He walked through the city, following his familiar Sunday route, not so familiar now. He was used to changes; anyone living in Berlin during the previous few years had to be. It was something people joked about. Hitler, loving building projects, had once boasted: "Give me ten years and Berliners will not recognise their city." The promise had become reality thanks to years of bombing. The authorities had always been quick to clear up the mess: buildings were shorn-up, rubble pushed to the side, roads reopened. Order was re-established, Berliners were reassured. 'Berlin will always be Berlin', the old saying went. But now the bombs had been replaced by shells and the mess lay untended; chaos supplanted order.

It wasn't just physical; the social orderliness for which Germans were famous was also breaking down. Not long after leaving the apartment, in a relatively undamaged street, Walter came across four carts piled high with loaves of bread, hundreds of them. He would have helped himself for he felt very hungry, but a mob of women surrounded the carts, jostling and pushing. Brief scuffles broke out as more women hurried to join the fray. He stood and watched as an old woman, respectably dressed in black with a shawl and highly polished town shoes, rushed past him holding three round loaves close to her chest. Her expression was one of feral satisfaction; it was almost sexual. No one shouted or swore; they made no sound and somehow that made it worse.

Discomforted, he walked away quickly. Rubble forced him to follow unknown secondary roads and he lost his bearings for a while, but eventually he came to a road bridge across a canal he recognised. On the other side was a small crowd, this time with a few young boys and old men amongst the women. They held bags and bundles; a few pulled dog carts. More people were constantly appearing, swelling the crowd. They couldn't cross for the centre of the bridge was a mass of barbed wire. Two field police stood behind it, highly polished silver gorgets winking at their throats, machine-pistols slung over their shoulders. An officer in a peaked cap stood with them, remonstrating with the crowd. Someone called back angrily.

On the near side was a large sandbagged sangar protecting a machine gun and several Hitler Youth. The sight of them made Walter stop suddenly: he might be asked why he wasn't in uniform and where he was going. He feared being re-enlisted; there was no way he wanted that, but he needed to go forward. He ducked into a doorway and scanned the canal: which way was best? Should he backtrack? As he hesitated, the mass of people moved forward slowly. There were perhaps a hundred or more by now and the growl of low voices was menacing.

Suddenly the officer shouted, drew his pistol and fired three shots into the air; distinct, precise: *crack, crack, crack!*. The crowd stilled, and in the silence Walter heard the officer order them to go another way; shouting that the bridge was closed. And then Walter heard another sound; it seemed familiar, but he couldn't place it.

A voice in the crowd called out, "Ivans," and then Walter knew that it was the sound of tank tracks.

The crowd rippled with movement and after a moment burst apart. People streamed away to the left and right down the footpath edging the canal. There was chaos for the path was narrow; people pushed and shoved, trippied over carts or struck their neighbours with bundles as they turned to flee. The officer and the two field police ran back across the bridge and ducked into the sangar, crouched low out of sight.

The sound of tracks was louder now, echoing off the buildings. Walter saw tanks lurch into view down the road which led to the canal. Each carried several infantrymen. At the sight, panic broke out in the crowd: people struck each other more violently, voices called out and one hapless woman lost her footing at the canal edge and tumbled in, arms flailing. Some of the crowd ran across the bridge and pulled unsuccessfully at the barbed wire with their bare hands, their bare, bleeding hands.

Walter stood transfixed, fascinated and horrified as the lead tank approached. He saw the officer in the sangar take off his peaked cap, reach down and do something with a box at his feet.

The bridge blew up.

Walter cringed. There was no flash such as one saw in the cinema, no great roar of an explosion, although later he supposed that there must have been one. The middle of the bridge seemed to lift in slow motion, taking with it the barbed wire and the people on it, and then it erupted, shattering into pieces which spiralled outwards and upwards. The tanks halted, the soldiers scrambled off and threw themselves flat or dashed behind them. The two ends of the bridge which were left sticking out from the banks of the canal, fell away and dropped into the water; the surface stippled with debris. To Walter, it all seemed to happen in complete silence.

He stared, and then he noticed something bright by his feet. He peered down and saw a tiny arm lying by his boot. It was clad in pink satin and looked like part of a doll, but it wasn't; and with a cry of disgust he kicked it from him. It was then that his hearing returned and he heard the sudden chatter of machine guns. Feeling sick, he bolted from the doorway and ran, and ran; and ran.

Leonid stood at the front door of an apartment building transfixed by the spectacle: the sun, a riot of colour, was rising through the smoke and dust above the rooflines. It was a beautiful sight and he felt at peace; even the distant sounds of battle seemed almost like some bizarre musical orchestration: a symphony of destruction. He let himself drift, not thinking, not feeling, just *being*, and then he was abruptly jerked back to reality.

"Tea," Tajidaev said.

Leonid turned and was offered a chipped enamel mug. He smiled: it was hot tea and very sweet. He nodded his thanks and watched Tajidaev head down the hall behind him and through a side door into the room where some of the platoon had bedded down for the night. Moments later he emerged with a small white cloth bundle and went further down the hall and out the back door. His curiosity aroused, Leonid walked after him.

He found himself in a storeroom. Markov, Ivanova and Rybczak were sitting on the floor smoking makhorka, watching their breakfast stew in a cooking pot set on a fire made up of the shelves which they'd obviously stripped from the walls above their heads. There was no sign of Tajidaev, but he could only have gone out through the door Leonid saw in the far wall. Ivanova nodded to him as he passed, picking his way carefully over outstretched legs.

He passed through another storeroom, empty shelves on the walls, out into an enclosed garden. It was no more than ten metres across, just a patch of brown soil with a gnarled old tree-stump at its centre. Several new branches sprouted from the stump bearing tiny buds of lilac.

Tajidaev stood facing the tree, his head bowed, holding the white cloth bundle and chanting. It was an unearthly sound, a low moan rising slowly in pitch then falling away immediately, only to rise again. It seemed to start in Tajidaev's boots, struggled up through him like a diver climbing back up through water and into the air above, where it vanished. Leonid paused; he was suddenly back in his childhood, standing amongst a crowd in his village church, darkness dispelled only by a small flame on the altar. It was Easter and midnight. His mother had roused him and Cheslav from bed, taken them through a cold spring night to stand by her in the press of warm bodies. He remembered the scent of incense amongst the odour of unwashed clothes and human sweat. He remembered listening to the sonorous chanting of the priest, watching a candle being lit from the altar flame and then brought forward, people lighting their own candles from it, and how the flame was then passed from one to another until light spread throughout the church. He'd been spellbound then and was now.

Unmindful of Leonid's presence, Tajidaev unwrapped his bundle and took out a piece of black bread. He bowed and placed it on the broken stump. Then he tied the white cloth to the largest of the branches and stepped back, still chanting. The stump was half in shadow, but the rising sun was dispelling the gloom, and in the growing light it seemed to glow as if the offering of bread had revived it. Leonid's scalp tingled. He waited quietly as Tajidaev brought his chant to an end and turned from the tree.

He beamed at Leonid. "Spirit here." Tajidaev glanced behind him. "Tree live."

Leonid nodded as if he understood, but he didn't.

Tajidaev pulled out his canteen and dribbled amber liquid onto the ground between them. He muttered something Leonid couldn't make out and then offered him the canteen.

"Life," Tajidaev said.

"To life," Leonid saluted silently, taking it and swallowing a mouthful of something sweet and powerful. He coughed and handed it back.

Tajidaev grinned and took a sip. "I pray. Give bread, feed spirit of tree."

"Your people are Tatars, aren't they?"

Tajidaev frowned. "No Tatar. Father Tatar. Mother Shalgan. I Shalgan. Not—" he spat the word out like something bitter "—father."

"I see..." said Leonid, again nodding as if he understood.

"Father bad." Tajidaev took another swallow from the canteen. "Mother good. Her father shaman. Close to spirits." He offered another drink and Leonid took it; it was too good to turn down. "Father—" Tajidaev's voice developed an edge, "—leave when I baby. Bad man. Not believe spirits." He tucked the canteen away. "Father give me name but mother name me *Kögudei*, big hero. Warrior."

Leonid looked at Tajidaev's crinkled baby face and skinny frame and suppressed a grin, but he knew the name was appropriate. He'd seen Tajidaev fight, and despite the little man's appearance, he was indeed a warrior.

"After war, I shaman."

Leonid's eyebrows rose. "Like your grandfather?"

Tajidaev nodded, again looking at the tree. "White shaman." He rolled up the sleeve on his left arm. "See." There was a vivid strawberry-coloured birthmark running from his elbow halfway to his wrist. "Sacred mark. I talk spirits, talk animal. I be shaman."

"That's why you were praying?"

Tajidaev looked at him sombrely. "I pray. But no…" He stopped and frowned. Then he made a movement with his hands as if holding something in his right and beating it with something held in his left.

"Drum?" guessed Leonid. Tajidaev shook his head, made the gesture again. Leonid was about to ask Tajidaev what he meant when he heard a voice behind him.

"Comrade Lieutenant." He turned to see Rybczak hovering in the inner door. "The Comrade Political Officer wants you."

Leonid nodded. "I'll be right there." As Rybczak disappeared inside he turned to Tajidaev. "I'd like to know more." Tajidaev nodded. "Later," Leonid said and hurried after Rybczak; it would not do to keep Polyanski waiting and perhaps provoke his curiosity as to what Leonid had been doing. The Party disapproved of religion and of those who showed too much interest in it. They disapproved too of anyone who showed too keen an interest in culture other than proletarian and the Party's approved way of life. To make things worse, Tajidaev's appearance was Asiatic, with swarthy skin and almond-shaped eyes. Never mind that racism officially was counter-revolutionary, any hint of empathy with him would not go down well. I'll talk to him later, Leonid told himself as he hurried through the building, when we're alone. He hoped Rybczak hadn't heard too much.

Later that morning Walter stood at an empty booth by a quiet suburban crossroads leafing through the stack of magazines and newspapers he'd found inside. He couldn't resist them. He'd always been an inveterate reader of weeklies and dailies and he'd been starved of any real news for some time, so he stopped and, looking around the empty streets to make sure no one was watching him, helped himself.

There were plenty to look through, although all were several days old: *Der Angriff, Der Stürmer, Das Reich, Der Völkischer Beobachter*; all the usual, pushing the Party line. There were a few copies of *Deutsche Allgemeine Zeitung*, not much better, and the previous day's edition of *Der Panzerbär*. It was the most recent newspaper on the stand. He picked it up, hoping that it might tell him something useful. The picture on the front showed a steely-eyed SS trooper lying on a grass bank, a *panzerfaust* beside him. The headline was simple and to the point: 'Bulwark Against Bolshevism.' Below it, in smaller type, was another line: 'Berlin: Mass grave of Soviet tanks.' Walter thought of the SS trooper in the hospital and of what he'd said to him and Friedrich, his sour disillusion, and he thought of Mathias lying dead and Friedrich falling at the bridge. He threw the newspaper from him, then in a sudden fit of rage, he seized more of the stack and hurled them away, the noise of the fluttering pages sounding like the beating wings of some awful carrion bird. He shivered and looked up at the surrounding apartments; the windows stared down at him and he felt suddenly very alone.

"Why did you do that?"

At the sound of the soft voice behind him he turned, dismay displacing anger: throwing official newspapers to the ground could get you into trouble.

"Don't worry." A young woman was standing a few metres away, dressed in a mid-length slightly shabby grey coat, smoking a ready-rolled cigarette. He wondered where she'd found it, for such were now luxuries reserved for the military and Party hacks. Her shoulder-length hair was black, shiny-clean; vivid green eyes looked at him from a pale, fresh, elegant face, pure and without any makeup save for glossy red lipstick which jarred badly. She smiled at him as if she was playing a part in a film, but not doing it very well: it was an invitation.

"Hello," he croaked and, embarrassed by the sound of his voice, he flushed and cleared his throat.

"Hello." Her voice was light, but now there was tension in it. The smile wavered and disappeared and her gaze dropped momentarily. The cigarette trembled slightly and ash fell to the cobbles.

"I'm Heike," she said. When he told her his name, her smile returned and she nodded brightly. He held out his hand for her to shake, but she stared at it. She didn't take it, instead drawing a deep draught from the cigarette, blowing it out and looking over the smoke towards him with hooded eyes: another movie image, like Marlene Dietrich. He almost giggled at the absurdity.

"Where are you going?"

He shrugged.

She looked down again, licked her lips. "You're nice." Then she looked up and seemed determined. "Do you want to come with me?"

The question startled him. "I don't under—" he began, but she stepped forward and ran her forefinger down his cheek. The touch was soft, although her fingernails, unpainted and unbitten, scratched him a little. His skin tingled; he'd not touched himself for days, not since marching to the bridge, and his arousal was sudden, demanding. He flushed again, very hot, and felt sweat break out on his forehead.

"How old are you?" she asked, resting the finger on his cheek for a few seconds before taking it away.

"Fifteen." Then he added, he didn't know why, "Today."

"It's your birthday?"

He nodded.

Her eyes glittered. "Have you ever done it?"

"What?" But he knew what she was asking and his mouth went dry; he felt the swelling in his groin harden, but his stomach churned.

She grasped his right hand and placed it on her left breast. He felt the pliant softness beneath the thin coat before he pulled away, his face burning.

"Please," she entreated, suddenly sounding desperate. "Please, a birthday present. For you. Please. You're nice."

He shook his head. He didn't know what to say; he wanted to, and then again he didn't. He blurted out, "I don't have any money." He didn't know why he said that either for he doubted she was *that* sort.

She looked puzzled, then she herself flushed. "I don't want money!" She sounded angry, then hurt. "I'm not...I don't want *money!*" Her eyes moistened and he felt ashamed.

"Sorry. I thought…"

"I've never done it." She sounded wistful. "They say that when they, the Russians I mean, they say when they get here…" She looked away, anxiety tautening her voice. "I don't want them to. I mean, I want my first time to be…" She stopped. "You're nice. A nice boy." Her voice dropped, pleading like a child. "*Please.*"

He couldn't meet her gaze. He knew what she wanted, had heard other boys speaking of it, some shocked, some lascivious with hopeful yearning: women and girls losing their virginity with almost anyone they could before the enemy arrived, wanting their first experience to be with a decent German. Any German. Why not? he considered. Better me than some Red. But then he remembered something else he'd heard, a shameful, desperate saying: 'better a Russian on your belly than a bullet in your head.' Anyone would do: was *that* how he wanted it? He was totally inexperienced, aside from a few rushed furtive experiments with Friedrich: nothing more than excited, nervous fumbling and stroking. He knew that other boys in the section did that too, had heard them in the camp dormitories sometimes. No one spoke of it, but it happened. He'd never done anything with a girl.

Some of the boys boasted they'd gone *all the way* with girls. The BDM were supposed to be readily available at camp, if only one knew which ones to ask. He'd discounted such crude talk as mere bravado. Now he had the opportunity which he and Friedrich had fantasised about together, the chance they'd talked about: the *first time*. He looked at Heike, her pale face, her shockingly red lipstick; he looked around at the sullen grey streets and he knew that he wouldn't. Heike was nice, he could see that, but there was a sordidness about it. He'd be taking advantage and he wouldn't do that; or perhaps it was cowardice.

He drove that suspicion away, and more harshly than he'd intended, snapped, "No. Go home." Seeing her look of surprised disappointment, he added lamely, "I'm sorry."

"Please," he heard her say again as he walked away.

"I'm sorry," he repeated, but too quietly for her to hear.

*

Cheslav had hated doing it in training and he hated doing it now: scrambling across two ropes pulled taut, one foot on each rope, one hand grasping the third rope stretched above his head. In training he usually fell off and was made to do it again, soaking wet, but this was not training, and if he fell into the canal he might very well drown, laden as he was with kit and wrapped in a heavy woollen greatcoat. It was the only way across, however; the canal's swing-bridge lay on the far bank in pieces, pulled back and comprehensively wrecked.

Cheslav slid forward gingerly, the rifle slung across his left shoulder rhythmically bumping his head and buttocks. Behind him a crowd of soldiers waited their turn around a squat, angular monster.

'Beast killer,' Lopakin had named it: a tank with its turret replaced by a fixed steel box housing a massive gun.

"One five two mil," Bartashevich had commented admiringly when they'd arrived. "Great bit of kit."

Great or not, it was stuck. Until sappers arrived to bridge the gap, only infantry could move on, and the only kit crossing the canal was what a man could carry. Cheslav didn't envy the company's heavy weapon crews.

When he reached the other side, he fumbled for a cigarette. Beridze lit it for him. The boy didn't smoke, but he'd acquired a fancy lighter from a dead German officer and displayed it whenever he could: he was proud of it.

Cheslav looked on as the company eased its way across. This part of Berlin was full of little canals, each not much of an obstacle, but they imposed delay and the afternoon was wearing on. They'd not done any fighting that day and he was beginning to hope that perhaps they wouldn't before nightfall brought an end to the advance. The idea had no sooner occurred to him when he heard a shout of warning and the screech and rattle of approaching armour from *this* side of the canal.

"Take cover." Pankov's voice was almost drowned out from the other side, but it didn't matter: everyone was already running into nearby alleys or dodging behind whatever they could find. There wasn't a lot. The beast killer burst into life with a guttural cough of its engine and turned ponderously to point its gun directly down the road which approached the canal between apartment blocks. Sparks sprayed off the splintering cobbles.

Two squat grey shapes clattered down the road towards them.

"Ferdinands," said Kolchok, squatting next to Cheslav behind a shuttered booth bedecked with newspaper and magazine posters. It screened them from sight, but would provide no protection if anyone chose to fire at them.

"Sturmgeschütz III," Cheslav noted. STUGs: they'd seen a lot of them before. Self-propelled guns built on tank chassis, much like the Beast Killer but half its size.

"No infantry."

Cheslav nodded at Kolchok's casual observation: that at least was something. The STUGs would be easier to deal with on their own. He glanced back to the beast killer which was moving in small jerks to left and right now, no doubt laying a bearing on the lead STUG: at least he hoped so. The STUGs halted abruptly as if startled by what they saw, and their machine guns opened fire at once, tracer flickering redly down the road. Ricochets whined from walls and cobbles and screeched off the hull of the Beast Killer, but no one fired back. Small arms would be useless against the STUGs' armour so what was the point of drawing attention to one's positon by firing? The beast killer had no such inhibitions and its gun blasted out a massive jet of flame. Cheslav's ears rang painfully and he was sure that he felt the round pass him, warm air pushing against his face despite the trajectory being metres away.

A cloud of red points of light erupted from the front and rear of the lead STUG, and in line with it, another sparkling cloud burst out of the front of the second. Two loud *clangs*, fractions of a second apart, almost indistinguishable from each other; both vehicles rocked.

There was silence, and then Kolchok said in amazement, "Shit, straight through!"

Cheslav tried to take it in. Surely not, he doubted, but the crews of both STUGs were bailing out and it was then that everyone opened fire, the crew ducking low behind the STUGs and sprinting back up the road and out of sight. It was over as quickly as it had begun.

When they moved cautiously down the road, Cheslav examined the STUGs. He saw a small hole, not quite big enough to put his fist in, punched into the cone which formed the base of the gun on the lead vehicle. Kolchok, walking in front of him, pointed out another hole in the vehicle's rear, punched out like the petals of a half-open flower, and on the second STUG, on the front glacis plate below the gun, was yet another hole. Two *beasts* killed with a single shot.

"Marvellous," said Cheslav, but Janko, walking behind, disagreed.

"No."

"Why not?" Cheslav half-turned his head but kept walking.

"Better the shot had stayed inside, chop 'em up."

Kolchok nodded slowly and Cheslav felt slightly queasy as his imagination painted a picture: the slug of red-hot steel bouncing around inside the STUG, tearing up equipment and the soft bodies of the crew. He didn't say it, but he was glad the round had passed straight through.

Beyond the vehicles, where the road became a T-junction, Kolchok pointed out a hole smashed through the brickwork of the building facing them.

It's the round, Cheslav realised and on impulse he reached inside the hole. Something very hot touched his fingertips and he yanked his hand back with a yelp of pain. Behind him, Janko chuckled.

Walter had to make several detours, some to bypass blocked streets, others when he heard the sound of fighting coming too close, so it was mid-afternoon before he reached the woods. As he'd hoped, it seemed the same: the pine trees, the open glades, the scent of damp grass and pine resin, and the scent of lilacs. He stood on the path for a while, drinking it all in, relishing an atmosphere free of dust and smoke and fear. Then he wandered about, meeting no one, hearing birdsong and the wind and ignoring the sounds of the embattled city around the little enclave of peace.

It was what he'd needed: to get away, and instinctively here was where he'd come.

He sat with his back to a tree and fell asleep for a while. When he awoke, the light had changed: the day was beginning to draw in and he knew that he should go back. He couldn't stay here, and where else but back was there for him to go? After all, when his mother returned, he must be home to meet her.

He was making his way back through the fringe of trees when a German soldier stepped out onto the path in front of him.

"Hey, kid," the soldier asked, "do you know this place?"

Walter stared at him dumbly: he didn't recognise the soldier's accent, and the soldier carried a stubby Russian sub-machine gun, the sort with a drum magazine. There was something not quite right.

"Not really," Walter lied. He heard the dryness in his voice and felt a tight knot in his abdomen. "I'm trying to get home. I think I'm lost."

The soldier stared at him, scanning the trees and bushes before bringing his gaze back.

"I was at Grandpa's." Walter felt uneasy: more German soldiers with Russian guns were emerging from the trees, staring at him. He realised suddenly that there were no rank markings on their greatcoats, no eagle and swastika badges on their helmets, and two words stabbed him: 'Seydlitz troops.' He felt afraid; he'd been warned about them: German soldiers who had switched sides, fighting for Stalin under the command of turncoat General Seydlitz, infiltrating German lines and spreading mayhem. 'Traitors.'

He licked his lips. What might they do? What should *he* do?

The soldier facing him cocked his head disbelievingly. "You're lost?" Behind him, his comrades spread out, watching.

Walter shrugged. "I, uh, think my home is that way." He pointed in the wrong direction.

"Which way is the centre?" The soldier looked around him. "Tiergarten?"

Walter shrugged again. "Uh, I think that way." He pointed south, knowing that it lay to the west, the direction from which Walter had come. He didn't want them going *that* way.

The soldier smile wryly. "Yes, boy." Then Walter watched with dismay as he turned and pointed down the path to the west. "It's that way." The soldier grinned at him. "Get out of here, kid."

Suddenly he could no longer smell the lilac and the pines, only smoke and dust drifting over the trees; suddenly all he could hear were the sounds of battle, and he felt afraid. The woodland was no longer his, no longer a sanctuary: it was a trap. He nodded nervously, fearing a blow or bullet. He wondered if he would hear the shot, but all he heard was the diminishing crunch of boots as the soldiers headed down the path in the direction he wanted to go.

He decided to take the long way home.

John left the bus station at dawn with the others. They picked their way across rubble and walked down undamaged streets, seeing civilians here and there and the occasional group of defenders, but not many. At mid-morning, not far now from the city centre, Ridderstolpe halted them at a road junction blocked by half a dozen hedgehogs bound together by a long, thick coil of barbed wire. SS troopers sat on the pavements in camouflage smocks with more of the Storm Rifle 44s John had so admired in the hand of the officer with the medals. An SS colonel came out of one of the buildings accompanied by a sergeant. After a deal of saluting and conversation, Ridderstolpe pointed to where John stood with Greger and Kaarle and the sergeant walked up to them.

"There's a bunch of children in there," he said. John noticed his empty eyes, the dullness of his tone: it wasn't what you'd expect from an SS NCO. John exchanged glances with Greger: *children?* "You're their reinforcements." He grinned mirthlessly, jabbed his thumb at the restaurant sitting at the corner of the crossroads and walked rapidly away.

Greger took John and Kaarle inside while Ridderstolpe moved amongst the rest of the detachment, detailing groups to occupy adjacent buildings. Inside the restaurant they could see it once had been, as Greger observed laconically, "Quite a decent little establishment." Now it was filthy and decrepit.

Several boys sat apathetically amongst the tables, their bloodshot eyes staring dully from grimy faces; others sprawled on the floor asleep. They wore olive-drab uniforms and the tabs on their standard-issue army tunics had white piping. Piled up against the far wall was a stack of Mauser rifles and several boxes that looked like grey metal suitcases with wooden-gripped handles. John noticed the marking: *15 Stiellgr 24*. The metal suitcases held grenades.

A lieutenant in army field-grey sat apart at a short bar, a near-empty bottle of cognac in front of him and a full glass in his hand. The lieutenant didn't return Greger's casual military salute as they passed him but stared vacantly into his glass, then gulped down half and refilled it. Those boys awake also ignored them. As he passed the nearest, John noticed a black lozenge-shaped badge on the boy's upper arm bearing in gothic script the white legend: 'NPEA Berlin-Spandau.'

"What's wrong with them?" John whispered as they clambered up the stairs behind the bar. Greger said nothing, Kaarle shrugged.

They set themselves up as well as they could in the apartment above the restaurant, the living room of which overlooked the hedgehog barrier. They used furniture to build an inner refuge at the centre of the room: it would give them some protection from grenades or shell blasts. Then Greger went down to the restaurant and came back with several hand grenades and two bottles of French wine.

"Courtesy of the lieutenant," Greger explained as he poured out a mug-full for each of them. Kaarle grinned appreciatively and took one.

"He spoke to you?" John asked, taking another. "What's his problem?"

Greger sipped some wine. "Didn't say a word when I asked about the grenades. Just pointed to a pile of them in the corner and then handed over the wine. He's got Yelnya Face. Seen it before." Greger shrugged indifferently. "Guys get it when they've seen too much."

John nodded. "In the British Army they call it the 'thousand-yard stare.'" His father had told him about it, and later he'd seen it at Salla: the limp, unfocused gaze of the battle-weary.

Someone kicked the door and Kaarle opened it. Sabaev grinned at them, his arms full of grenades. Then his glance took in the small stack of them Greger had put on the floor under the window and his grin faded.

Greger smiled at him. "You can never have too much of a good thing." He held out a half-empty bottle of wine, but Sabaev shook his head. "I never thought I'd see a Frenchman refuse wine."

"And French wine at that."

Sabaev smiled wryly at John's observation, picked up the bottle and squinted at it. "It's Alsatian. Not the same these days."

John smiled. "Well I will," he said and held out his empty mug.

They were savouring the wine when a very young voice spoke through the open doorway. "Hello." A boy stood there. John guessed he was barely into his teens. He was bare-headed with a shock of yellow hair and blue eyes. "I'm Christhof, from downstairs. Can I come in?" His arms too were full, this time with tin cans.

Greger beckoned to him. "Food. Good."

Christhof placed his load on the floor next to the wine bottles. "The lieutenant said you might want something to eat."

Sabaev held one of the cans up to the light from the window and inspected the colourful label. "Peaches?"

Christhof nodded and watched Greger pull out a pocket opener and eat straight from the can. Syrup ran down his chin. He wiped it off with the back of his hand, licked it and smacked his lips appreciatively.

Seeing Christhof's eyes on the can, Greger picked up another, opened it and held it out. Christhof looked down, and then with a very shy smile he began spooning slices of fruit into his mouth with his fingers, one at a time.

John felt like asking him how old he was, but instead he said, "How long have you been here, kid?"

Christhof swallowed a peach before answering. "This morning. We marched all night."

"All night?"

The boy looked sheepish. "We were lost," he admitted.

The four men looked at each other.

"So." Sabaev smiled at him and introduced himself. "Charlemagne," he added.

Christhof straightened. "National Political Institution, Berlin-Spandau." John was amused that he actually clicked his heels, but tried not to show it. Greger frowned and looked puzzled.

"*Napola*," John said. "Party boarding schools, for the political elite. Set up to provide future Nazi leaders. You have to be special to get in." He smiled wryly at Christhof.

"Very special." Christhof beamed proudly. "Set up by the Führer for those destined to serve the Reich at the highest levels. Only pure Aryans of exceptional ability can attend. It's an honour." He stood a little straighter.

Greger pursed his lips, and Kaarle, not seeming to grasp fully what Christhof was saying, looked puzzled. John kept his face studiously neutral, but Sabaev smiled and nodded.

"Yes it is." He sipped at his wine and looked at Christhof intently. "Seen any action yet?"

"Not yet." Now Christhof seemed embarrassed, and then he added with a note of concern, "I hope we do our duty."

Kaarle beamed at him. "Not worry." Christhof beamed back.

John looked between the two of them and was struck by their youth; the realisation saddened him, but there was a toughness about Kaarle, a ruthlessness that in one so young frightened John for a moment. He held out his mug for Greger to fill and thrust it at Christhof.

"Go on."

The boy put down the now empty tin, took the mug and

swallowed appreciatively, then he emptied it and held it out for Greger to refill.

All of them chuckled, except John. Christhof reached inside the bread bag attached to his belt and pulled out a long cloth bundle. "Mother's always sending me these." He unwrapped it to reveal a dark smoked sausage. "From our farm. Please. I have more."

Greger took it and nodded his thanks. "We'll share later."

"Where is your farm?"

Christhof beamed again at John's quiet question. "Near Küstrin." He frowned. "She hasn't sent me any for a while." John cleared his throat. "Oh, I know the Reds are there. But she'll be all right. Our farm's outside the city." He looked anxiously around as if for reassurance. There was an awkward silence and Christhof's baby face fell.

Sabaev punched him lightly on the shoulder. "Sure she will." He took the sausage from Greger and made a show of sniffing it and grinning. "This is good."

Christhof smiled artlessly around the group. "Everything will be all right." They all nodded, save John who again glanced between Kaarle and Christhof and his sadness deepened.

Klara had stewed some of their potatoes with sauerkraut; it was nothing special, but the aroma was tantalising. Tanya watched with amusement as Klara laid out bowls and spoons on the table with care, checking that each was clean, wiping them, inspecting again. She was so German, so neat, such a *hausfrau*.

"Looks good." Axel, the first to collect his share, complimented her with a bright smile which Klara returned. Tanya felt a moment of pleasure. Then she wondered if she should wake Walter. He'd returned two hours previously, filthy with dust and soot, stumbling down the steps past Mrs Boldt, answering no questions. He'd fallen asleep in Ida's chair under a blanket; he was still there, buried under the grey woollen cloth, motionless and silent. He should eat, she disapproved. As Klara slopped stew into the bowl Tanya held out, she imagined her mother: solid, matronly, standing at the stove in the Paris apartment. And she saw herself as a girl, watching dutifully, encouraged to cook, but it hadn't been her forte. Food didn't interest her much, which was one reason, she'd always believed, that she kept her figure while her mother lost her willowy slenderness. Most Russian women seemed to; most German women too, for that matter.

She pushed thoughts of her mother away and went to Walter. Gently she tugged back the blanket. Walter was deep asleep and she touched his shoulder with her free hand.

"Here."

He blinked, sat up and stared at her. After a moment he took the bowl. "I wanted to find her." His voice was dry; he coughed.

"Your mother?" It was a stupid question; she knew it and flushed slightly.

Walter nodded. "It's my birthday, you see." He whispered it and no one else seemed to hear him. Startled, she touched his arm again, not knowing what to say. He pulled back from her and some of the stew slopped on the blanket.

Louder, he said, "I'm fifteen today." Heads turned across the cellar.

"Happy birthday, Walter," Mrs Körtig called out after a moment's silence. He looked at her shyly and then he smiled. Tanya resisted the urge to touch him again.

"She always sang to me, you see." He sounded bewildered, lost.

Mrs Körtig, sitting with Monika on her sofa, smiled. "What did she sing, Walter?"

"'The Cuckoo is Calling from the Wood.'" He looked down, embarrassed. "She used to sing it to me every birthday."

He took the spoon Tanya proffered and began to eat. Then a cork popped. Palanevich stood by the table, pouring champagne into mugs. He took two and brought them to Walter, giving him one. and clinking his own against it.

"Happy birthday, boy."

"May you have many more," Tanya said softly in Russian.

365

"Yes." Palanevich nodded. "Everyone, please take some." He gestured at the table and went back to sit on his crates.

Tanya took her share, Axel and Klara too, but Mrs Boldt, she noticed, didn't stir from her place at the bottom of the steps, and Monika, although Mrs Körtig gave her a mug, put it on the floor after staring at it.

Tanya pulled a chair from the table and sat by Walter. He put the now empty bowl by his feet and sipped gingerly from his mug.

"I used to get a plum cake. She'd write my name on it with icing." He sounded almost cheerful and Tanya felt unutterably sad.

"Here." Palanevich got up to top up Walter's mug. Then he waved the bottle; his jollity seemed artificial to Tanya. "Come on, it's the lad's birthday." He went around the cellar, sloshed more champagne into mugs, then he opened another bottle. "How does that song go?"

"'Cuckoo, cuckoo is calling from the wood'," Mrs Körtig said. Then she sang a few bars in a reedy voice. "'Let us sing and dance and jump. Now, how does the rest of it go?'" She frowned. "Oh yes. 'Spring, spring is coming soon.'" She stopped then and smiled, and Walter smiled back.

Tanya didn't smile. Yes, she acknowledged sadly, spring has come, but what's come with it? She shivered slightly.

Palanevich raised his mug. "Bravo." His hand, she noticed, shook slightly, spilling champagne onto his sleeve. "Bravo. Encore!"

Axel and Klara echoed his demand and Mrs Körtig looked embarrassed.

Walter took a big gulp of champagne. "May I please have some more?" He held out mug. "It *is* my birthday."

Palanevich laughed and poured some for him.

Cheslav supposed that each street they cleared that day must have been different, but all he would later recall was a featureless collage of sights, sounds, smells: a composite experience. He lost track of how many roads they advanced down, cautiously picking their way, watching the windows, the alleys, checking buildings. Cobbles, pavements, rows of apartments, small shops, crossroads, rubble, wrecked vehicles, dead animals, dead people. White flags hung everywhere by now: sheets, shirts, towels draped from windowsills, from balconies and gutters, and even from an occasional flag pole. Every street seemed keen to surrender, but every street still had to be checked; a few had to be cleared because some hadn't got the message: it's over, it's done with. Give up. Stop killing. Stop dying. But there were fewer and fewer like that, and mostly it was women and children and old men they encountered. Some of the platoon eyed the women speculatively and grinned, but that was all. The old men they ignored; the children were given food and patted on the head. Babies were cooed over and laughed at. The children watched them wide-eyed and the babies cooed and laughed back; the women and old men did not.

Once they came across two men and a young boy in civilian clothes, cowed and frightened. They'd lost their papers, they said. They were of course vouched for by the anxious women, searched and relieved of their watches. Cheslav took a rather nice Helma from one of the men, a thin figure in a smart suit which contrasted oddly with his unshaven face and filthy hair. Cheslav already had a Raketa, and unlike most was content to have just the one watch, but the Helma would make a nice gift for Leonid so he pocketed it.

Bartashevich told the boy to stay with the women and sent the two men back to battalion under the watchful eye of a fat company cook. He wrote two notes saying that the bearer was a prisoner of the state, signed and dated it and gave one to each of the men. They seemed to find this reassuring. How they love paperwork, Cheslav wondered. Order. How cooperative they are.

But some were not cooperative. They were moving down yet another anonymous street adorned with white flags when three bullets fired from the upper storey of a nondescript red brick building hissed past in quick succession; there was no warning. The first passed over Cheslav's head and everyone ducked. The second struck the wall next to Cheslav, ripping out a shard of brick which punched through the sleeve of his greatcoat, through his tunic and then through his undershirt. It hurt like the devil and he dropped his rifle.

As he fell to his knees in pain and surprise, the third bullet passed through the space he'd occupied a moment before and struck Janko who was walking behind him. Janko twisted, fell against the wall and then slid face down onto the ground, jerking and coughing, his hands around his neck. Janko's legs thrashed and blood ran between his fingers. There was shouting and the sound of firing and running feet. Janko twisted onto his back, and Cheslav scrambled over and cradled his head as he twitched and gasped. Cheslav didn't dare pull Janko's fingers away to see what lay beneath. Instead he watched as Lopakin led men into the red brick building at a run. Cheslav heard a door crash open, the characteristic deep growl of a papashay sub-machine gun. He thought that he heard a woman shriek and a baby cry, but later he couldn't be sure. Then he stopped listening as Beridze dropped to his knees next to him and glanced at Janko. Cheslav looked down and saw the man's staring eyes, felt the lack of movement and gently laid his head on the bloody pavement.

"Stay still," Beridze urged softly and eased Cheslav's coat off his arm and rolled back the bloody sleeve beneath, clucking like a fussy mother. He was careful in his ministrations but still it hurt like the devil. As Beridze bandaged the gash, Cheslav gritted his teeth and tried not to wriggle. To distract himself he focused on the panduri strapped across the boy's back and thought, he's got a musician's touch all right. Gentle, like a lover's.

"Thank you, Comrade," he said and picked up his rifle with his good right arm. Beridze smiled shyly, glanced again at Janko staring up into the dusty darkening sky and his face fell. They both looked away.

Lopakin came out of the building and walked over to them. "Lost the fucker," he said. "Bastard got out through a hole in the attic."

Cheslav nodded; it was standard procedure to knock holes in walls between adjoining buildings: escape routes and means to move about safe from observation and fire. Lopakin looked at Janko and shook his head. He seemed annoyed more than anything else.

"All right?" he asked Cheslav. "Fit enough?"

Cheslav nodded again. Lopakin picked up Janko's rifle. They followed him down the street. At the end of it, Cheslav looked back. This street he *would* remember, for really this one wasn't any street: it was the street where Janko died. Later he couldn't remember what it looked like; he could only remember Janko's white face and staring sightless eyes.

They all drank more of Palanevich's champagne, but not very much for Walter soon went back to sleep on Ida's chair. Monika still sat on Mrs Körtig's sofa, eyes closed. She was not asleep, but Mrs Körtig nevertheless drew the blanket curtain across the alcove before joining Axel, Klara and Tanya at the table in a game of doppelkopf. Mrs Boldt maintained her solitary vigil at the radio; it still had nothing hopeful to offer her, but she cranked the handle anyway and leaned in close to listen.

Palanevich announced that he would seek fresh air and left, nodding to Tanya as he walked, somewhat unsteadily, up the stairs. Tanya watched him go and wondered if she should join him, but she didn't want to break up the game. She and Mrs Körtig were doing well paired against Axel and Klara.

They'd played half a dozen games before she changed her mind. It was relatively peaceful outside and she wanted to take advantage of that before dark fell, so she murmured when they'd finished the latest hand, "I'm just going upstairs."

Mrs Boldt glanced at her but said nothing.

Mrs Körtig smiled. "Very well, m'dear." She gathered up the cards and shuffled them. "Skat?" Axel and Klara nodded and she began to deal.

The cellar door clicked shut behind her and Tanya paused for a moment to let her eyes adjust to the musty gloom. It was almost silent in the hall; the outside noises were muted through the heavy front door, and she heard a low murmuring voice clearly. For a moment she froze; anxiety welled up, and then was pushed back down as she recognised a familiar sound from her childhood. The dark space, the closeness, the rising and falling cadence struck a chord, and for a moment she was back in Kazintsev's church in Paris. Softly she moved forward down the hall.

Palanevich didn't notice her: he was kneeling in front of Mrs Boldt's alcove. On the chair from which Mrs Boldt had once kept watch were a small icon and a Hindenburg lamp.

"O God, our help and our aid in distress," Palanevich prayed in Russian, "who art just and merciful and who inclines to the supplications of His people, look down upon me, a miserable sinner, have mercy on me and deliver me from this trouble that besets me, for which, I know, I am deservedly suffering."

He sounded tired.

Tanya knew the prayer: her mother had used it often in Paris.

Palanevich paused, reached out, lifted the icon and kissed it. Then, replacing it, he crossed himself. Tanya did so too.

"I acknowledge and believe, O Lord," Palanevich whispered, "that all trials of this life are disposed by Thee for our chastisement, when we drift away from Thee and disobey Thy commandments. Deal not with me after my sins but according to Thy bountiful mercy, for I am...I am." He paused, took a deep breath and repeated, "Deal not with me after my sins but according to Thy bountiful mercy, for I am..." Once more he stopped and, after a few moments, reached out gently to stroke the icon with his fingertips.

Moved, Tanya finished for him in a whisper, "For I am the work of Thy hands and Thou knowest my weakness."

Palanevich turned his head in surprise, then he smiled briefly and returned his gaze to the icon. Tanya knelt behind him.

"Grant me, I beseech Thee," he continued, and together they went on, "Thy divine strength to endure my tribulations with complete submission to Thy will." The words rolled on and Tanya pictured another small icon lit by a simple light. She must have been about four years old, the year that her mother had taken her to Paris. Before they left, they'd knelt with her father in the house in Petrograd; she remembered his broad back and his light voice, melodious like a flute.

She stared at Palanevich's icon. It was like the one in her Petrograd home: two flat panels of wood joined by a hinge like an open book, covered in dulled gold and silver leaf laid onto faded paint. Unlike the icon back home, however, this was scratched and parts of the paintwork were missing. One panel of Palanevich's icon held an image of the Holy Mother and Child, the other the head and shoulders of Our Lord. As the images stared back at her over Palanevich's shoulder, the eyes seemed alive in the flickering light.

Tanya felt a sense of great age, of timelessness. Here and now shrank into the background. "Look," the sacred images seemed to say to her, "what do your troubles matter? We've seen it all before. Lay them down here and let go."

As she spoke the final words of supplication with Palanevich, it seemed that all the suffering and loss around her was as insubstantial and transitory as the flickers of the Hindenburg lamp.

"...in due time, when Thou knowest best," she and Palanevich whispered, "thou wilt deliver me from this trouble and turn my distress into comfort, when I shall rejoice in Thy mercy and exalt and praise Thy Holy Name, O Father, Son and Holy Spirit..." they crossed themselves, first two fingers of their right hands touching tips with their thumbs, held to forehead, then heart, right shoulder, left shoulder, "...now and always and unto ages of ages. Amen."

They knelt in silence for a while and then stood. Palanevich turned and smiled wryly. "Tomorrow is Palm Sunday," he said.

She started; she'd forgotten that.

Palanevich seemed about to say more but he didn't. Instead he bent down, blew out the light, picked up the icon, closed it and put it in his jacket pocket. Then he walked down the hall and out into the street. The door banged open and the sounds of destruction flowed into the hall and out again as he closed it behind him. Tanya remained where she was, silent and still.

*

Leonid sat with his back to a tree in a small orchard, holding Cheslav's book but not reading it. The orchard belonged to a house which once must have been rather fine, but which had been converted into apartments at some point in its life and was now rather dilapidated. The inhabitants were rather dilapidated too, poor and old. They'd had little worth appropriating. The building was damp and smelled of paraffin, and it was more comfortable to camp amongst the neglected fruit trees; the blossom smelled better than the stink of boiled cabbage which permeated the place.

He had his eyes closed, remembering. Despite the murmurs of war, the lightning-like flickers above the rooftops, it might have been a spring evening outside his boyhood village. There had been an old house there too, a ruined dacha. It had been a gentleman's summer residence in the days when Russia had gentlemen. The Revolution had appropriated it as a village infirmary, then as offices for the local Party, then as storerooms. Hard use and lack of proper maintenance ruined it and it rotted away, but its orchards remained, a place of peace and beauty where Leonid and Cheslav sometimes went to be alone together.

The company had lit fires in the orchard using wood pulled from the adjacent fences and fallen branches. Leonid could smell meat cooking. There was a low murmur of conversation, the occasional clink of metal mugs and glass bottles. He looked at his platoon, laughing and joking together, but he felt no urge to join them; he doubted they'd welcome him. It didn't do for officers to be too familiar in case it undermined their authority. He winced at the thought: *authority*. They would obey him, habit and training ensured that, and he'd noticed that the platoon's obedience *had* become more accepting, less grudging over the months. Shared dangers and discomforts had seen to that. He had obedience, yes, but not full respect and not full acceptance. Perhaps he'd never have it. It was not something given to everyone, he'd been told by a captain in the academy: a frontoviki. It had taken him, the instructor had told Leonid one evening during a drinking session, a year to become accepted fully by his own men.

A shadow fell across him. "I brought you something to eat," Agranenko said and sat down in front of him. He held out a steaming bowl. "It's not bad."

Leonid laid down the book and took the bowl gratefully. He tasted it: it was better than not bad.

Agranenko lit a cigarette and they sat watching the fire together as Leonid ate. When he'd finished, Agranenko cast away the stub and spoke softly:

> In Vyazma is an ancient house
> Which once one night was home to us.
> That night we ate whatever came,
> The source of drink was much the same.

Agranenko lit another cigarette and held it out to Leonid, who shook his head; he'd been smoking too many of the damned things lately. Leonid knew the poet: Simonov, a favourite of Agranenko. The authorities liked him too, printing his works in the army newspapers and leaflets.

Leonid laid his head back against the bole of the tree and quoted:

> Again I'm in the country, once again!
> I hunt, write verses and am free from care;
> Yesterday, tired with tramping through the swamps,
> I strayed into the barn and slumbered there.

Leonid explained. "Nekrasov." Agranenko looked quizzical. "You don't know him?"

Agranenko nodded. "Yes. But not that one. What's it called?"

"'Peasant children'."

That seemed to amuse him briefly. "You a hunter, Comrade Lieutenant?"

Leonid smiled. "I'm from the country, but no, we didn't hunt. Well not really. Mushroom picking was the most we did."

Agranenko smiled sadly. "We did that in Leningrad too. Well, not *in* Leningrad. We'd go out of the city every autumn to pick mushrooms at Toksovo. The University had a dacha for students there in the woods. Good they were too. Nice fried with butter." He looked wistful, cast away his cigarette stub and murmured:

> I try to find that joy
> In softly dappled woods
> Amidst the call of birds
> Where once I was a boy.
> When we would stroll and talk
> And laugh our days away
> Together just we two
> Amidst those trees we'd walk.

His face darkened and he went on:

> And as the shadows fell
> We'd sit beside a fire.
> No words were spoken then
> For silence served us well…

"Go on," said Leonid gently when Agranenko's voice trailed away, but he didn't speak. Instead he lit another cigarette and puffed at it. Then he smiled sadly up at the darkening sky and murmured:

> I would that you were here
> To walk with me once more
> To sit and watch the flames
> A moment we would share.
> But I shall never see
> Your cherished face again
> Nor walk nor speak with you
> By fire never be.

Silence fell between them. Leonid didn't know how to respond: there had been such repressed pain in Agranenko's voice. Suddenly he remembered Agranenko quoting another poem; and remembered the dead blond boy; Agranenko anguished as he was anguished now. Who did he remind you of, he wondered, that boy? Are you thinking of him now? Was he a friend? Your brother?

Laughter drifted over from the platoon, then Babich began to sing. The illiterate morose Chechen radio operator was very inarticulate when he spoke, but his voice was golden. He was the best singer in the company, perhaps the best in the battalion, and all through the orchard conversation stilled, voices were lowered.

"All is still once more, still until dawn," Babich sang in a lilting melody, "no door will squeak, no light will flash…"

Someone spoke too loudly and was shushed.

It was another poem, set to music; a popular folk song with a sentimental tune. Just the sort soldiers loved, were always moved by, especially when drinking. Leonid looked at Agranenko.

"Who wrote it?" he asked.

"Mikhail Isakovsky." Agranenko sounded irritated. "You should know that, Comrade Lieutenant." Isakovsky was author of the very well-known *Katyusha*, another poem which had become a popular song.

Leonid shook his head. "No, not Babich. I know that. The one you were just quoting."

Agranenko listened to Babich for a few moments more. Then in a sudden fluid movement he scooped up the empty bowl, stood and turned away. "You wouldn't know his work."

"Is he Russian?"

Agranenko stared into the distance. "Oh yes, Russian. He's Russian all right. From Leningrad." And with that he strode towards the fire and Babich's golden voice.

That evening, Cheslav saw a vision of home.

They had entered a small square, quite undamaged save for a house on one corner, the façade of which had collapsed in a heap in front of it. Opposite the ruin was a brick church, squat, simple, its onion-shaped cupolas and three-armed cross reminding Cheslav of the one which had stood on the edge of his village. That is, until it had been broken for building materials to be used on the new collective farm.

The platoon deployed cautiously across the square, spreading out into a line, while behind them Gushenko and the rest of the company waited. Lopakin went up the steps and pushed at the church door.

It didn't open and he raised his rifle and struck it, but still nothing happened. He struck it again and this time the door was slowly pulled half open. Lopakin spoke for a while to someone they couldn't see, then he turned and waved to Bartashevich to join the discussion.

After a while Bartashevich hurried back and then on to Gushenko. Lopakin came to join them.

"Plenty of room and good walls," he advised, lighting a cigarette. "Good place to bed down."

Cheslav felt slightly shocked at the suggestion, and then felt slightly surprised that he did so. A church, after all, was just a building. It *would* offer good accommodation and they all needed a safe rest; exhaustion was etched on their faces and the light was fading fast.

Gushenko, it seemed, shared that view. When Bartashevich returned it was with orders to occupy the church. "But keep your hands off things," he told them. "This church is now the property of the Soviet State."

As the platoon shuffled past him up the steps, Lopakin was terse. "That mean no fires inside. No smoking either. And clear up your mess. If you need to take a shit, do it outside." He glared them. "And no fucking souvenirs. Not one."

Inside it was as Cheslav remembered from the wooden church of his childhood: a vestibule with seats lining its walls and an icon on a stand. Through two beautifully carved doors was a long high-ceilinged space, at the far end of which was a tall screen covered in rich paintings dimly discernible by candlelight. Automatically he took the pilotka off his head; to his surprise, so did Lopakin. It was then that Cheslav noticed a priest standing in the gloom beyond the double doors. A small man in a long black robe, he was slightly built with black beard and black hair; in stark contrast his face and hands were pallid. There was no welcome in his dark eyes as they flickered over them, and Cheslav avoided his chill look as he went in.

Cheslav bedded down in one of the two smaller areas facing across the long space just before the low platform on which sat the screen. His eyes adjusting to the gloom, Cheslav could see better how beautiful the screen was, but the eyes of the images held as little welcome as the priest's and he sat with his back to them. So, he noticed, did everyone else.

Kolchok joined him. "Lopakin says we're on first watch." He looked around him. "This place gives me the shivers." Cheslav noticed that Kolchok too had removed his hat. Scratch a New Soviet Man and find an Old Russian, he thought with some amusement.

Kolchok scratched his head, seemed to find something, examined it closely and flicked it away. "Let's grab a smoke."

Cheslav nodded and followed him out. He lit a cigarette while Kolchok filled his pipe. Then they sat at the bottom of the steps leading to the church, carefully shielding the glow behind their hands as night closed in. In the square all was quiet, and beyond it the sound level was falling slowly. The fighting wouldn't stop altogether, but it would dwindle until dawn, when no doubt another day of slaughter would begin.

Cheslav picked out a low guttural hum and raised his head. Kolchok too looked up.

"Night witch?" he ventured, but Cheslav didn't think it was. The sound was deeper than the clatter of the biplanes. A dark shape flashed suddenly over the square and then was gone, leaving behind a brief, dull echo of noise.

"Fritz?" Bartashevich opened the church door and stood above them, staring over the surrounding buildings in the direction of the vanished aircraft.

They stood to meet him as he descended the steps. Cheslav nodded. "I think so, Comrade Lieutenant. But it was difficult to tell."

Bartashevich lit himself a cigarette from Kolchok's pipe.

"An Arado, maybe."

"A what?" Bartashevich turned to look at Cheslav.

"An Arado, Comrade Lieutenant. A light training aircraft. I, uh, remember it from the lesson."

Cheslav saw Kolchok look at him with amusement and flushed slightly.

Bartashevich blew out smoke. "Arado. Good. Well, keep an eye out. I want to know if it comes back." He looked up into the sky for a moment: it was dark with a thin line of orange-red above the rooftops like a dusty summer sunset. "We've been told to look out for any light aircraft flying out of the city. Seems Hitler's got an airstrip somewhere. He might make a run for it." They looked at him in surprise and he drew on his cigarette deeply, deftly flicking his wrist to detach the ash at the tip. "I doubt it myself. Where'd the bastard go?" He looked over the rooftops again and went back up the steps.

"'An Arado, Comrade Lieutenant,'" Kolchok mimicked when Bartashevich had gone back inside and they'd sat down again on the bottom step. "Blessed Mother," Kolchok snorted, "the boy fucking memorised it all."

Cheslav grinned sheepishly at him. Kolchok had slept through the training session on aircraft recognition; many did, but Cheslav lacked the status that gave Kolchok and the other frontoviki the confidence to sleep through lessons.

"Well," Kolchok looked closely at his pipe, tapping it against the step beside him, "if it was Adolf we missed the fucker. No Hero of the Soviet Union for us, eh?" He snorted again and began refilling his pipe.

FIFTEEN

When it came to it, the inner refuge they'd constructed in the apartment proved no use at all.

Kaarle spotted the approaching soldiers in the eerie grey predawn light, made eerier by the orange glow reflected down from low cloud: the glow of the burning city. It was his watch, but they were all awake and responded to his urgent summons immediately.

They squatted beneath the window, Sabaev and Greger to Kaarle's left. John took up positon to Kaarle's right after he'd called down a warning to the boys in the restaurant. For several minutes they watched brown figures move cautiously along the street towards them. Adding a strange solemnity to the scene was the faint tolling of a bell, just audible above the dull report of explosions, the clatter of rifle and machine gun fire and occasional indistinct shouting. As he watched the figures advance, John thought of the words of one of his father's favourite poems: 'What passing bells for these who die as cattle?' He smiled grimly and answered softly under his breath: "'Only the monstrous anger of the guns. Only the stuttering rifles' rapid rattle.'"

Sabaev glanced at him and muttered, "No tanks."

"Yet." John squinted along the barrel of his rifle, laying the blade of the foresight onto the leading figure. Tanks were the things they worried most about, or self-propelled guns, or artillery dragged by hand down the roads where lorries could make no headway. The Reds were using everything they had to blast away defenders with no concern for collateral damage. In order to own Berlin, they seemed more than willing to destroy it.

"Hold your fire," Greger whispered.

John grinned. "Ready for confession?"

Greger cocked his head and grinned back. Kaarle peered at them with a puzzled frown, and Sabaev, glancing at him, whispered, "Sunday."

The bells tolled twice more and then fell silent. Kaarle nodded. Sabaev looked solemn, and to John's surprise he crossed himself.

"Catholic?" John was annoyed with the tone of his voice; he didn't wish to offend Sabaev for he'd come to like him well.

"*Was* a Catholic."

The leading figure raised a hand and the soldiers all halted; they didn't take cover. Sloppy, John thought and shifted his aim to the man who'd raised his hand. He thought of Father Pelzer.

"Was?"

"I saw things. In Russia."

"Things?"

Sabaev shook his head. The man raised his hand again and the brown figures resumed their advance.

"We had a visit from our priest before we left for Russia." Sabaev adjusted his own aim.

John considered this for a moment. "*Your* priest? You mean he was the unit chaplain?" Sabaev nodded, his gaze unwavering along the barrel of his rifle. "In the SS?"

Sabaev grinned. "Yes…" He squinted at something, tensed and then relaxed. "He, well…" John glanced at him, saw his eyes glitter bright in a grimy black face. Sabaev went on, his voice firmer. "I believe in what we're doing, all right? Stop the Bolsheviks, keep that bastard Stalin out. But this priest! What he went on about, like it was a religious war or something."

"You mean a crusade? You know, like in the Middle Ages." The figures were close now, bunching in the middle of the street, driven there by high mounds of rubble stacked along the pavements. Nicely does it, John told himself. His rifle remained unwavering on the leading figure; he could see him more clearly now. He was slightly built, no more than a boy, yet he wore shoulder boards: an officer or NCO.

"Middle Ages. Yes…" Sabaev gently worked the bolt on his rifle, "…fucking medieval all right, what we did."

"'Gentle Jesus, meek and mild.'"

"What?" Sabaev's gaze flicked briefly towards John.

"Words on the wall at Sunday School when I was a kid." He thought of the plaque: a lurid picture of Christ, brown hair and beard, long white robe, seated, surrounded by children. Some were niggers, he reminded himself. He remembered how that had annoyed his mother when she'd first seen it.

"Any second," Greger warned them calmly and four fingers tensed on four triggers.

Closer now, John's target seemed even younger. "'Suffer the little children to come unto me,'" he murmured, centring his aim on the boy's chest.

"Let them get closer," Greger said softly, but suddenly a storm of fire broke out from below them. "Fuck, damn kids!"

Brown figures scattered down the street. John could only see a couple lying still in the roadway. Too soon, he cursed mentally and picked a figure to fire at; but before he could pull the trigger all had vanished from sight.

Greger turned to say something else but it was Kaarle who spoke, once more drawing their attention. John followed the direction of his pointing hand and his stomach turned over. A huge shape had lurched into view down the road: squat, angular, with a massive gun. They didn't need Greger's shouted order before making a bolt for the door, ignoring the inner refuge: the thing down the street wasn't about to throw grenades at them.

John was out first, taking one last look at the self-propelled gun now pointing at the restaurant. Dashing into the bedroom which lay behind the lounge, he made for the small hole they'd cut through the wall into the adjacent building the night before. He was yanking Sabaev through the hole when the building bounced, knocking John to his knees. Sabaev shot through the opening like the cork from a bottle, sending John sprawling on his back. He saw the floor behind Sabaev erupt upwards in a cloud of fragments; Kaarle and Greger vanished from sight. The sound of the explosion stunned him for a few moments and Sabaev rolled off him limply. He struggled to his knees just as the wall in front of him began a leisurely collapse outwards. Grabbing Sabaev by his webbing, John dragged him towards a door in the wall behind him. Outside he could hear a storm of gun fire and another massive explosion.

"Out," was all he could think of to say, "out."

Cheslav dreamed of a tolling bell and woke, rubbing sticky eyelids with the back of his hands. He glanced around from the wooden seat on which he'd spent a stiff, cold night and saw dark shapes in the gloom. A single candle in front of the painted screen at the far end of the church cast muted shadows on dulled colours.

"Awake then," Kolchok whispered; he was sitting on the floor with his back propped against the seat, close enough for Cheslav to smell his sweat.

Cheslav levered himself to his feet, stretched aching shoulders and grimaced. "I wasn't sleeping. Not much, anyway."

Kolchok stood up and scratched his head vigorously; a few specks of dust puffed up, showing against the dim candlelight. "Never had any trouble sleeping in church."

"You?"

"When I were a little 'un." He twisted his head from side to side, squeezed the nape of his neck.

"Me too." Cheslav looked at the screen, felt the sad memories crowd in.

"I need a piss," said Kolchok and headed for the door. Cheslav followed; behind him the platoon began to stir slowly. Someone coughed, the sound echoing loudly around the dark space.

The vestibule was a mess: dirt tracked across the floor, weapons and kit piled against the wall. The paintwork was marred here and there and Cheslav wondered what Bartashevich and Lopakin would say. A candle still flickered in front of the icon; Cheslav wondered who had kept it alight: the priest? Outside the church several of the company stood clutching steaming mugs and mess tins near a pot with a sealable lid and two shoulder straps. It looked like a steel rucksack.

"Tea, Comrades," said a fat soldier with Asiatic features standing by the container with a ladle. Cheslav recognised him: one of the company cooking detail. After relieving himself against the low wall fronting the church, his back turned to the others for modesty's sake, he collected his tea and went to stand with Kolchok further along the pavement.

Lopakin walked past. "Sleep all right, Comrades?" But he didn't wait for an answer and strode up the steps.

He won't be happy, Cheslav realised, watching him pass into the vestibule.

"That one was up half the night."

Cheslav looked at Kolchok in surprise.

"Praying." Kolchok grinned briefly at the look on Cheslav's face. "A few of the guys took turns."

"Vigil?" Cheslav dragged the word from the depths of childhood memory. "They kept vigil?"

Kolchok nodded, put his fingers to his lips. "But not so loud, all right?

Cheslav looked around; no one seemed to have heard. He winced at the sudden pain his movement caused, eased his left arm.

"Here, let me look at that." Kolchok set his mug down on the wall and helped Cheslav shrug off his coat. Unwinding the bloodied bandage, Cheslav saw that the wound was still partially open and seeping. Kolchok pulled out a bottle. "This will sting," he said and upended it along the wound. Cheslav yelped. "Vodka. Good for anything." Kolchok took a swig, handed him the bottle and pulled out a needle and thread.

Cheslav gritted his teeth as Kolchok, with the deftness of a seamstress, closed the wound. The pain was intense, the sewing seemed to take an age and he emptied the bottle.

When he'd finished, Kolchok inspected his handiwork critically. "Good enough for the army."

"Mother used to put honey on wounds." Cheslav heard his voice shake and felt embarrassed by his weakness.

Kolchok didn't seem to notice. "Mine too." He glanced up. "Here we go," he muttered.

Cheslav turned to see Lopakin clumping back down the steps, his face set. "Cleaning detail," he bellowed. He stopped, stabbed the air with a forefinger. "You, you and," he pointed at Kolchok, "*you!*"

Softly, Kolchok said something inappropriate for a Sunday and Cheslav grinned, his pain forgotten.

"What's the matter, m'dear?" Mrs Körtig tilted her head towards Palanevich who was sitting on his crates, staring at the wall and fiddling with his briefcase.

Tanya smiled wanly at her and accepted the proffered mug of tea. "He went up to have a look."

"Bad?"

"Very bad," Tanya confirmed. "It's a complete mess. Red Army here, Germans there. He says that he met Frenchmen at the end of the street."

Mrs Körtig nodded; she didn't seem surprised. But then, thought Tanya, Berlin is awash with foreigners: half of Europe it seems. She thought of the Red Army men in the courtyard. And half of Asia. She glanced around at her companions and smiled to herself.

Tanya sipped the bitter tea and lowered her voice so that only Mrs Körtig could hear it. "He wants us to join a breakout."

"Breakout?" Mrs Körtig's whisper was a shade too loud for Tanya's comfort but luckily no one seemed to notice.

"The French told him that there's to be a breakout west. Some general called Wenck is supposed to be relieving Berlin."

"But if he's coming to save Berlin…"

"Victor said there's no chance," Tanya cut her off. "He says it's better to try to get out now by ourselves."

Mrs Körtig considered for a moment. "What do you think?"

"I'm not sure. We *might* be better staying here. Safer."

"It's not safe anywhere."

Tanya nodded and sipped more tea. "You think we should go, then?" She glanced at Palanevich. "He's planning to go when it's dark."

"Perhaps you should consider going with him." Mrs Körtig laid her hand upon Tanya's arm.

"What about you?"

Mrs Körtig shook her head. "Where would I go, m'dear? Without Eugen…"

Tanya took her hand gently. "Well," she said, "think about it."

Ivanova told Leonid it was one of those things; it wasn't his fault. It was war, she told him, but her words didn't help and he felt sick every time he thought about it later, which was often.

He'd been leading the handful of men that was now the platoon cautiously down a half-ruined street towards an official-looking two storey building. Bullets zipped past him and everyone had scattered. He had taken refuge in a doorway, craning his neck to look back the way they'd come and silently urging, come on. As if in response to his mental summons, the two tanks had swung clumsily into view around the corner he'd turned minutes before. They'd accelerated, jerked to a halt in clouds of dry dust and elevated their guns, rocking on their chassis. Two rounds howled like express trains past him; two huge clouds of dust and brick fragments flew outwards from windows on the ground and upper floor. Then there was stillness, broken only by the clatter of debris bouncing on the roadway. A pause, the tanks' machine guns fired and, without orders, the platoon rose from cover, dashed forward and inside, all before the dust had settled. All routine and not a man lost.

Not then.

Leonid and Agranenko had followed the men in. There were a few dead Fritzes on the ground floor, badly mangled from the shell burst. Leonid felt like a cigarette and gave one to Agranenko. They stood together, smoking, weapons laid against the wall as the platoon clattered from room to room. Leonid knew that the building was not yet officially cleared, but what the hell?

Later he told himself he should have been more careful.

He had watched in frozen horror as one impossibly mangled body raised a bloody hand clutching a pistol. Agranenko saw Leonid's stare across his shoulder, turned and he too froze. Leonid knew he should move, pull the revolver from his holster, push Agranenko to one side, rush forward, do *something*. Instead he stood rooted to the spot as Agranenko was shot through the chest, and he remained so as the pistol rose slowly to point at his head. They stared at each other for an eternal instant, the German and he. Leonid felt oddly detached as if watching a scene from a film: a close up of the German's face, eyes squinting with effort; shift the camera to show the German's hand trembling, the barrel of the pistol making little circles.

Then pull the view back to show Tajidaev rushing in behind the German, raising a rifle and smashing in his head, clubbing it until Ivanova screamed at him to stop. Still Leonid just watched.

They stood, the three of them, staring at each other over the body of the German; over Agranenko's body. Tajidaev's tunic was speckled with gore, Leonid remembered later. At the time, he didn't notice.

Then Leonid stirred and knelt by Agranenko. He lifted his head, listened to the breath wheeze from ruined lungs, watched red bubbles on greying lips and knew there was nothing to be done. He held Agranenko in his arms as he would hold a baby, head in the crook of one arm, the other under the man's back, and felt sticky wetness. He held Agranenko until the light left his eyes, and then something left Leonid. He knelt that way for a while until Ivanova gently shook his shoulder and told him it was one of those things.

Then he laid Agranenko on the ground and stood, not knowing what to do next.

Ivanova gently touched his sleeve and he started. What should he say? Something must be said, but he couldn't find the words. Tajidaev knelt, gently opened Agranenko's bloody coat and removed a small bundle of cloth, the personal *something* which each and every soldier carried as a legacy, just in case: letters; mementoes; something real to accompany the terse official communication of their death.

Tajidaev gave Leonid the bundle. Leonid felt helpless. They were looking at him; he couldn't meet their eyes.

He cleared his throat and took a deep breath, looking at Agranenko, the lover of poetry. Then at last words came to him.

"'It's not for us to calmly rot in graves,'" he said. He was surprised: his voice was steady. "'We'll lie stretched out...'" Then his voice caught in his throat and he had to stop. Tajidaev nodded at him and he drew another breath and went on:

… We'll lie stretched out in our half-open coffins
And hear before the dawn the cannon coughing,
The regimental bugle calling gruffly
From highways which we trod, our land to save.

Tajidaev nodded again; Ivanova turned her head away. "A poem by Nicolai Mayorov," Leonid said simply. Then, "Sergeant Agranenko was a good man. A good comrade." Too simple perhaps but they both nodded. He looked at Agranenko's white face and could say no more. Ivanova gestured to Tajidaev and they left Leonid standing alone.

When they were gone Leonid felt the strength leave his legs and he sat suddenly by Agranenko. The bundle fell to the floor. It contained a postcard of a painting, a tattered notebook and a round pendant of pitted brass with an engraving showing a man in archaic armour. He was seated on a horse trampling a dragon underfoot; the man was stabbing the dragon with a lance. The reverse side was plain with an inscription in the formal Russian now only used by the very elderly, and that seldom: officially it was frowned upon as the language of deference, of hierarchy, of religion. The inscription read: 'Holy Martyr George, the victorious, defend me.' It was a sacred medal meant to keep the wearer safe. Leonid wondered who'd given it to Agranenko, and why Agranenko hadn't worn it, as many others wore good luck charms, medals and icons under their uniforms.

The postcard was normal, the sort issued by official Soviet shops. It was worn, edges curled, colours faded and stained. It showed a group of raggedly dressed men; Leonid counted eleven. They had straps around their chests attached to a long rope, and with it they were pulling a barge along the bank of a silver-grey river, the sky above livid blue. All the men looked weary except for a fair-haired youngster in the centre of the group. He alone had his head raised. On the back was writing: 'Bargemen on the Volga by I Repin.' Leonid had never heard of him.

He turned to the notebook. It was the sort issued to schoolchildren; he'd used them when he was young. It was full of writing, some in pencil, some in ink in different colours: poems, crossed out in places, corrected, added to. They were not poems Leonid knew.

Carefully, he rewrapped the three items in the cloth and tucked the bundle into his satchel. Then he searched for, but couldn't find, the small Bakelite tube issued to every soldier into which they were supposed to put their personal details to identify them if dead or too wounded to speak. Many soldiers believed that doing so marked them for death and disobeyed the regulations, but Leonid was surprised that Agranenko seemed to have been one of them.

"What's going on?" Moiseyevich walked in.

Leonid stared up at him and anger flared. He stood abruptly.

Moiseyevich blinked, saw Leonid's face and stood very still. He turned his head away. "What do you want, Private?" Leonid closed the satchel, fumbling with anger. Moiseyevich looked sullen. "Well?" Leonid insisted. He wanted to hit the boy; felt the urge to smash *his* head in, shoot *him* in the chest.

"The captain wants to know what's happening."

Leonid glanced down at Agranenko and said in a voice like ice,

"Tell him we're moving. Building cleared." He felt his throat tighten and then added, "One casualty."

Moiseyevich too glanced at Agranenko, opened his mouth, then closed it and sloped away. He didn't salute.

"We'll rest a bit." John helped Sabaev down a short lane into a tiny square surrounded by linden trees and settled him onto the steps of a small post office. There were also cafés and a couple of shops; all the display windows were bare of goods. He tried to imagine what it must have looked like once, busy with people sitting at tables savouring coffee and cakes, talking, reading newspapers, watching their children play. Couples wandering arm in arm, others bustling in and out of the shops, perhaps to buy, perhaps just to browse. There would have been laughter, the hum of traffic from the street beyond the alley, birdsong from the trees. Now the square was silent, the tables gone. He bit his lip and suddenly felt very, very tired.

He lowered himself next to Sabaev, laid his head back against the brickwork behind him and closed his eyes.

"Papers!" John woke with a start; he must have dozed off. Standing above him were three young soldiers, clean and tidy. John saw polished boots, polished helmets; even the machine-pistols slung over their shoulders gleamed. Their faces were smooth shaven and John thought that he caught a whiff of Eau de Cologne. He knew he must stink but really couldn't smell it.

Not now, he thought and stood slowly, his legs not wanting to cooperate. Sabaev just stared up at them. One, a corporal, held out his hand. On his cuff in silver letters on a black band was the legend: 'Leibstandarte Adolf Hitler.' The Führer's personal bodyguards were out looking for deserters.

"I'm sorry, I don't have my soldbuch. It got lost." He fumbled inside his coat for the letter-headed paper he'd been given in the barracks and handed it over.

"You are not German," the corporal said, glancing at John's collar tabs.

John shook his head. "*Svenska*. Swedish."

The corporal jerked his head at Sabaev who had pulled out his soldbuch and held it up.

"Vichy."

The corporal beckoned Sabaev to stand. "He's hurt," John explained and took Sabaev's soldbuch and handed it over. "Look," he explained as the corporal flicked through the pages, "we were Detachment Berg." The corporal's face remained impassive. "We're all that's left." John thought of the chaos of that last engagement: Greger and Kaarle disappearing with the room; dragging Sabaev down the stairs of the adjacent building and out into the street; the Red infantry; the gut-churning screams of *urrah*; the clatter of tracks; the explosions. He recalled the mad scramble, no time to think, somehow pulling Sabaev away. Now he had the time to think and it was hard to keep control of his voice.

"You are not German," the corporal repeated. He did not return the papers.

"Look," John repeated testily, "I told you. I'm Swedish. This man is Vichy. We were in Detachment Berg. There was a fight. Ivan. The rest…" and his voice failed him. He shook his head.

The corporal seemed unimpressed. "You're deserters."

"Deserters? Listen to me: we've been fighting for fucking days." John's nostrils flared; he felt Sabaev tug on his trouser leg in warning.

The corporal shook his head and glanced back at his companions.

Then Sabaev spoke for the first time. "Here." They looked down; he was holding up his two medals. "I got these killing Ivans in Russia." He stared up into the corporal's face. "How many have you killed, *boy*?" Sabaev's voice was tired, but it dripped disdain: he was the adult dismissing an impertinent child. The corporal's face flushed.

John remembered something his father had said to him the first time they'd visited Königsberg: "'Never back down in front of a Hun official. They're pompous little Kaisers, every one. Stand your ground.'"

"And me." John leaned forward, thrusting out his jaw pugnaciously. "I've killed dozens since I got here. How many Bolsheviks have *you* killed?" John watched the corporal hesitate; for the first time the man seemed unsure of himself. He glanced at his companions, then down at Sabaev's pinched, angry white face.

John pressed the point. "Everyone else was killed. Now I need to find my comrade some medical attention. And I need to join another unit. To *fight*."

The corporal glanced again at the other two troopers.

"Satisfied?" Sabaev held up his hand and the corporal stared at the medals. After a moment he returned them.

"There's a group of foreigners like you up the road. We'll make sure that you get there."

Tanya sat in the alcove trying to read, but couldn't. The singing pained her; she had too much of an ear to ignore it. When she was six years old, despite their poverty her mother had paid for music lessons from an elderly Russian aristocrat. To Tanya's distress, they were discontinued because, really, they couldn't afford them, but she'd kept an appreciation of good music well performed. This wasn't it. Palanevich had a decent baritone voice and Axel was a passable tenor, but they'd had too much of the champagne. They were sitting together on the crates, working their way through a repertoire which included Mahler and Mendelssohn. She suspected they'd chosen the two Jewish composers to annoy Mrs Boldt, but Tanya doubted that she noticed. Hearty German folk songs and rousing marches were more Mrs Boldt's style and the block warden just sat and knitted and ignored the two men.

Mrs Körtig, however, approved. "Bravo," she said, clapping when they finished Franz Lehár's 'You'll Find Me at Maxim's'. Mrs Boldt actually smiled. But then, noted Tanya, she would. The favourite composer of the Führer would most certainly be Mrs Boldt's favourite too.

Axel bowed at Mrs Körtig and began another song. "'Hail to thee in victor's crown, ruler of the Fatherland, hail to thee, Emperor,'" he began, but stopped abruptly. "Can't remember the rest." He grimaced, looking hopefully at Palanevich who shook his head.

"Oh well. Never mind. A fine tune though." Axel's voice was slurred and Klara, sitting at the table with Mrs Körtig and Monika playing German whist, looked at him with a slightly disapproving frown. "From Schleswig. I'm from Schleswig. Fine place. Fine songs. Do you know the tune?"

Tanya shook her head. "But I'm sure I've heard it somewhere."

Axel seemed amused. "Oh, I'm sure that you *have*. But not recently. No, it's the tune the English use for their national anthem." Mrs Boldt glared at him. "Funny that, eh?"

"Actually," interjected Palanevich, "it's Danish." He looked at the near-empty bottle in his hand, frowned at it.

"Danish?"

"Yes." Palanevich put the bottle down with a sigh. "Schleswig was part of Denmark then. But the composer's German. Harries, I think. Became the National Anthem of Prussia." He smiled wryly at Tanya and slapped Axel gently on the shoulder. "Enough for now." He picked up the briefcase at his feet and came to the alcove, leaving Axel to lie back on the crates, his eyes closed. "May I?"

Tanya nodded.

He sat opposite her, placed the briefcase across his knees and mused quietly in Russian, "Odd, isn't it? The National Anthem of Prussia, National Anthem of England." He hummed a few words. "'Hail to thee in victor's crown, ruler of the Fatherland...'" Then he shook his head. "And here we are in Berlin, capital of Prussia, capital of the New Europe." He leaned forward slightly, earnest. "Don't you wish you weren't here, that we were back in Paris again?"

Paris? she wondered. What made him say that? Yes, despite the hand to mouth existence of her childhood, she *did* wish it in a way. She'd loved the city, felt safe there, but she also loved Berlin: it had become her home and, despite everything, still was.

"I do," he said, suddenly sounding very tired. He closed his eyes, his hands clutching slightly at the case. She touched his arm gently and he looked at her.

"Why are you still here?" she asked softly. "All the others left."

He didn't answer immediately. Then, "Well, I did try to leave. You know that."

"You left it very late."

He smiled ruefully. "I had something to do first. You know I was Göring's advisor?" She nodded. "My job was to identify the art he'd collected, help him decide which to keep, which to sell off, which to give to museums. He had lots of it. Fantastic stuff. Warehouses full of it." He snorted. "Collected? Looted. Such lovely pieces."

He glanced across the cellar. "Close the curtain," he said quietly.

She looked at him for a moment and then did as he asked. As the blanket slid across she saw Mrs Boldt watching her with narrowed eyes, but she no longer cared what Mrs Boldt thought.

With strange deliberation Palanevich unlocked the briefcase, undid the two restraining straps, extracted a thick flannelette bundle and laid the case at his feet. He placed the bundle on his lap and gently unwrapped it to reveal a book about thirty centimetres long and six thick. Its brown cover was faded and slightly crinkled; she smelled musty leather and old fabric.

She reached out but Palanevich abruptly held up his hand. "Please," he admonished gently, "don't touch it with your bare hand. You might damage it. It's very old, you see." He smiled down at the book with the tenderness one might bestow on a baby. Then, using a corner of the flannelette cloth, he very gently opened the cover to reveal a page almost entirely taken up with an illustration. "Lovely," he murmured. The page was darkened by age and slightly stained, the colours faded, the images worn in places, but yes, it *was* lovely.

"Here." He held his forefinger over the image. "See the proportions? The figures look almost solid in places. You can almost see them move and speak." He shook his head in wonder. "Amazing. Such talent the illuminator had."

She too wondered; she'd never seen Palanevich like this. "Who was he?"

He shook his head. "We don't know. It was made at Noyon but that doesn't mean he was French."

"Noyon?" She'd heard of it. "Near Paris?"

He nodded. "There are very similar German Psalters, so he might have been German. But really he might have come from anywhere. Medieval craftsmen were in demand all over Europe." Carefully he turned a few more pages, found another illustration. "They're all pictures inspired by the Psalms. This is King David." He pointed. "Marvellous work." He sat back, closed the book and rewrapped it, careful not to touch it.

"How old is it?"

Palanevich shrugged slightly. "Who knows for sure? But I'd estimate seven hundred years at least."

She was startled. Such an ancient thing, she wondered, precious. Why has he got it with him here?

As if reading her thoughts, Palanevich whispered, "It's my passage."

"I'm sorry?"

"My ticket out. It's very valuable, and it gives me credibility. As far as anyone's concerned, I'm a French art expert sent to Germany to work for the authorities." He replaced the bundle in the briefcase. "Unwillingly, of course." Again he leaned forward. "I'm going to join Wenck's breakout to the west. Give myself up to the Americans and British." He sat back and looked at her intently. "Come with me."

She stared at him.

"Yes," he insisted. "You can't stay here."

She shook her head. "I'm not sure."

"It's too dangerous to stay."

She licked her lips. The idea appealed: Paris had so many positive memories for her and beckoned like a protective mother, but she shook her head. "It's too dangerous to go. Anyway, what makes you think the Amees won't send you back?"

He reached down and tapped the briefcase. "I have papers. There'll be lots of people like me. People going home. Too many for them to check on one little art dealer. I'll tell them the Psalter was looted from France, that I was working on it for the Germans. Now I'm taking it home with me. They'll believe me."

Perhaps he's right, she conceded. There would be millions of people on the move when the war finally ended. Palanevich could be very plausible when he wanted to be; his story *might* get him through.

"And me?" she asked.

"You're my assistant."

"My papers…"

"Were lost in the chaos. I'll vouch for you."

For a moment, she felt the urge to agree. But then the moment passed. She didn't really believe he would succeed, and anyway, whether he was likely to get to Paris or not, she must stay in Berlin. Her mother might come looking, or she might be able to go looking for her mother; assuming, that is, her mother was still…

She suppressed the thought, but she knew that she couldn't leave without finding out. She shook her head again. "I have to stay."

He gazed at her and smiled. "Just like you mother," he said gently. Then he picked up the briefcase, closed it, stood and drew back the blanket. "Stubborn."

John and Sabaev were taken by the Leibstandarte patrol to a street studded with nightclubs and seedy bars. Windows were boarded up or gaped open and glass crunched under their feet; some walls were pitted and cracked, but all the buildings still stood. One even had an awning, striped and gaudy, above steps leading to a below-ground entrance; on it were words in red curly script: 'Café Falstaff.' John couldn't help smiling.

Two heavily armed men in SS camouflage smocks stood under the awning. One wore the collar tabs of the Charlemagne division, the other those of Nordland. John knew neither of them. After a brief explanation, the corporal and his men strode off; sour looks followed them. The Charlemagne trooper muttered something in

French under his breath and it didn't sound complimentary. John eased Sabaev down the steps into the nightclub with his help.

As they passed through the glass door, John stopped in surprise. In the dim light of assorted candles, Hindenburg lamps and a single ancient oil lamp, half a dozen men lolled about a table filled room like exhausted survivors of a fancy dress party. One slumped on a stool, face down on the bar which ran the length of the left-hand wall. He was wearing a long-tailed frock coat over his grubby camouflage smock. Another sat at a table in an old-fashioned British Army red coat, drinking straight from a bottle. A third wore a woman's dress, like a saloon bar whore in a cowboy film: low cut bosom, frills and flounces, worn with muddy combat boots and several days' growth of beard. Others sat against the walls: those that seemed awake ignored them.

They eased Sabaev across the room to join the only man John recognised: Børgesen, sitting against the padded bench running along the right-hand wall. His smock was draped loosely over a naked torso swathed heavily in bandages; an ominous dark stain covered his chest. He smiled wanly as they eased Sabaev onto the floor near him.

"Thank you," John murmured to his helper and gently turned Sabaev onto his front and began stripping off his tunic. The trooper peered at Sabaev who was wincing and grunting under John's ministrations.

"I'll get something for the pain," he said and headed for the bar.

When he pulled off Sabaev's filthy undershirt, John swore softly. Sabaev's lower back was a distended purple mass.

Sabaev twisted his head towards him. "What?"

John tried to smile reassuringly but only succeeded in grimacing. "Bad bruises, that's all." He heard the insincerity in his voice. He eased Sabaev onto his side, pulled two plush cushions off the bench and placed them under the injured man's shoulder. Sabaev sighed and closed his eyes. John watched Sabaev's breathing slow, realised that he was asleep and went to sit with Børgesen.

"Bad?"

"Internal bleeding." John kept his voice very low. "I think."

"Medicine!" The trooper returned with an opened bottle of cheap cognac and squatted in front of them. Then he shook John's hand. "Bertrand Gosselin."

"Marlow. John Marlow."

"John Marlow? That's an English name." Gosselin spoke fluent German; it was better than John's but the accent was unmistakably French. "You're English?"

John nodded, then archly he muttered, "And Swedish."

Gosselin's eyebrows rose a fraction. Then he took a swig before offering the bottle to Børgesen, but the corporal too had closed his eyes, so instead Gosselin offered it to John.

He took a mouthful and nodded towards Sabaev. "He needs a hospital."

Gosselin shrugged.

"Do you have a medic?" Another shrug. John took a second bigger gulp of the rough brandy and slowly looked around the room.

Gosselin grinned. "We had a party."

John smiled ruefully. "Why not."

Gosselin grinned again, went to a nearby wicker basket, flipped it open and extracted a horned metal helmet: the sort Vikings wore in movies.

"Here," he offered.

John put the bottle down and placed the helmet on his head.

"*Voos et urn gerriar norse.*" Gosselin nodded and added, "A brave warrior."

John suddenly felt ridiculous and placed the helmet on the bench.

"Sabaev too."

"You know him?" John settled back against the bench; he felt drained and listless and the brandy burned in his empty gut.

"Sabaev? May dacor." He took the bottle and settled beside John. "We joined together. The *Legion Volontaires*. Colonel Paud.

Then, Charlemagne." He reached up and touched the helmet. "Wasted." He drank deeply.

"Wasted?"

Gosselin shook his head very slowly. "We win the first war. Then the Reds, the Unions, the Jews, they pull us down." His face hardened. "I'm no Nazi, but Hitler's right. No Reds, no Jews, no English." He grinned apologetically and offered the bottle. "Present company excepted, of course."

"That's all right." John accepted the offer; now the brandy didn't taste too bad. He raised the bottle. "No Reds, no Jews."

"No Yanks either."

John drank again, handed the bottle back and nodded once more towards Sabaev. "He likes Americans."

Gosselin took the bottle. "There's no accounting for taste," he observed with a grin.

Cheslav sat in the church and wrote. He'd started a letter to Leonid, but then to his surprise he found himself composing poetry. Verse, Leonid would probably call it, but Cheslav was pleased with it. They'd both loved poetry since they were children. He looked at the papers on his lap and recalled one special moment: Leonid sitting on the bottom step of their family hut in pale sunlight. Cheslav had been drawn outside by his brother's voice reciting a poem by Tyutchev: There comes with autumn's first appearance, a brief spell full of wonder and delight. When Leonid saw him watching he'd not stopped reading, nor had he shooed Cheslav away as he often did. The words had rolled on in soft cadences, praising the beauty of changing seasons, and Cheslav had sat on the top step and listened, enraptured, to his older brother. A magical moment; intimate: it had been the first of many times Cheslav had sat listening to Leonid read. When he was older and his reading good enough, Cheslav had returned the favour. Then they'd started writing poetry, sitting together reading their own faltering attempts to each other, praising, making suggestions.

Cheslav wondered if his brother was reading poetry now. He looked at what he'd written:

> Stilled by painted ancient faces,
> Silenced by gilded awful eyes,
> Instruments of death,
> Harbingers of freedom
> Resting from their labours,
> In peace they lie.

He frowned at his words: not one of his best, but not bad under the circumstances. He looked up as the door through the painted screen opened and the priest appeared. Nobody stirred; they'd become used to his occasional forays into the church. Cheslav noticed that he wore the same vivid green robe he'd worn all day. Does the colour mean anything? he wondered. It must do, he reasoned, for he knew that priests wore different colours at different times, but he couldn't remember why.

The priest took up a position at one end of the dais and announced in a loud voice that it was the day of the Lord's entry into Jerusalem. A few bodies stirred; a few heads turned. They should pray, he adjured them, and give thanks. Then softly he began to intone and Cheslav listened in fascination to the beautiful, lilting Russian words gently rising and falling.

"'Blessed is He who comes in the name of the Lord. We bless you from the house of the Lord...'"

Really it was a poem of a sort.

Several of the company sat up. One knelt in front of the dais, his lips moving from time to time. Another began rolling a cigarette, but a soldier sitting next to him reached out and touched his arm. The man hesitated then rose and went outside.

"'And Babylon, the glory of kingdoms, the beauty of the Chaldees' excellence,'" the priest chanted, "'shall be as when God overthrew Sodom and Gomorrah.'" He crossed himself three times, looked down the church and returned behind the screen.

That was really quite good, Cheslav thought as he wrote the words down, but who or what is a Chaldee? Sodom and Gomorrah he remembered as cities destroyed for wickedness. What point was the priest making? Did he mean Berlin? Or Moscow? Both? He thought of more of Tyutchev's words:

> Who would grasp Russia with the mind?
> For her no yardstick was created:
> Her soul is of a special kind,
> By faith alone appreciated.

He stared at the priest's words on his notepaper and then at the faces on the painted images. They stared back and he looked away.

SIXTEEN

John dozed through most of the dark hours in Falstaff's Café, rising from time to time to check on Sabaev. As the night wore on, Sabaev's back became darker and more suffused. His skin felt hot and his brow was feverish. John found it progressively more difficult to wake him; he felt he ought to do so, as if bringing Sabaev back to consciousness would hold death at bay. Finally, not long before dawn, John couldn't rouse him anymore. He knew Sabaev wouldn't waken again; reason told him he should go now, but he could not.

"This place is as good a place to be as any other," Gosselin reassured him.

And perhaps he's right, John admitted to himself. After all, he had no destination in mind, no plan, but he felt uncomfortable waiting nevertheless.

Outside the battle still raged, mostly distant, but an hour or so after sunrise they crouched under tables and against walls as a short, sharp bombardment fell on the street. Dust cascaded from the ceiling, glasses and bottles rattled, the floor vibrated, but still Sabaev didn't waken.

A little later they listened tensely to the rattle of tracks and the rumble of engines as a column passed by. The lookouts dashed in to tell them they were Red Army tanks with infantry sitting on them, but no one moved to fight and the column was soon out of earshot.

Shortly before midday Sabaev began a low intermittent moaning and John went to sit with him, holding the wounded man's hand the way his mother used to hold his when he was sick. He didn't know what else to do. Like his mother, he murmured soft words of consolation, but Sabaev didn't respond.

Børgesen was phlegmatic. "Not long to go." He'd hardly stirred from his place against the bench, spending most of his time dozing, getting up only once during the night to relieve himself in the little courtyard out back which they all used since the lavatory had ceased to work. Now he was wide awake, playing endless games of patience using one of several packs of cards found behind the bar.

John felt a flare of annoyance but suppressed it and gave him a cigarette. "What happened?"

Børgesen seemed puzzled by the question.

"At the barricade, I mean," John explained.

Børgesen shook his head. "Gone." He drew in a deep draught of smoke, nodded appreciatively.

"All of them?"

Børgesen shrugged. "Most."

"The priest?"

Børgesen shrugged again.

John thought of Pelzer; he'd quite liked him. "Pity."

"Russian bombers." Børgesen made a swooping motion with his hand, smoke trailing from his cigarette as if from a burning aircraft. "I was lucky, really. One of the old guys got me away."

"Volkssturm?"

Børgesen nodded. "He carried me. We met a patrol."

John smiled wryly. "Leibstandarte? A corporal and two men?"

Børgesen nodded. "Brought us here. The old guy left." He sighed wistfully. "I wish I could go home that easily."

John held out the packet of cigarettes: there was only one more left. When Børgesen hesitated, John pushed the packet at him. "Go on." The stain on Børgesen's bandages seemed to be darker, his sweaty skin paler and his eyes glittered intensely. John felt it might not be long for Børgesen either, but he didn't say so.

Børgesen nodded. "All right. Share."

So they took turns with the cigarette and waited, Børgesen playing cards and John holding Sabaev's hand.

Leonid had always believed that he'd be completely lost without Agranenko, to whom he'd been so used to deferring. And who would follow him? Yet they did, and he found that leading wasn't so hard. Faced with the necessity to move forward, he and they just got on with it. What else could they do? There was a job to be completed, but first they needed to say goodbye.

Markov and Ivanova gently laid Agranenko's body on the street where it would be found and retrieved by the burial detail. Then the platoon filed past slowly. Some stopped to whisper a few words, some crossed themselves, some simply paused and then moved. A few placed a branch by his body: it was an old Russian tradition and there was a shattered lilac tree nearby to help matters.

After that, the same routine: advance down the streets, check the buildings, advance again. There was no resistance.

In the afternoon, shortly after they'd paused in a narrow street to eat, Ivanova came to Leonid. She was trying to look calm but anxiety showed through her eyes, and he followed her without question to a three storey apartment building. Babich stood by the front door, eyeing two young prisoners in shabby German Army uniforms who sat together against the wall. Eyes cast down, shoulders bowed, they looked like delinquent schoolboys waiting for the headmaster. Babich was smoking a cigarette; his rifle was slung over his shoulder, but he didn't take his eyes off the two boys as Leonid followed Ivanova past him. As he passed the prisoners, they looked up at him and Leonid glared at them. They both flinched and looked away. He realised with a tinge of surprise that he hated them, yet they had done nothing to him: it was the sort of hate one felt towards rats. He stopped being surprised and accepted it. They were Fritzes, after all: they were hateful in themselves, like rats.

Ivanova led him past the inevitable concierge's room, past the main stairs and through another door. Beyond was a short passage and she stood to one side to let him step through. She was hidden in the gloom, but he could sense her tension as he passed her.

He found himself in some sort of storage room. By the pale light streaming through a tiny window set high in the back wall he saw shelves with boxes. On the floor were mops and buckets, but it was not these his eyes rested on.

Sitting with her back to the shelves was a half-naked girl, a torn-open blouse hardly covering her torso. Below the waist she wore nothing. She was very young, her breasts hardly more than bumps, her body slim and pale. Honey-coloured hair hung in unkempt locks around her shoulders. The eyes in her bruised face were a vivid, lovely green, but they didn't move as he entered and were utterly devoid of feeling.

She sat in a pool of blood. His eyes were drawn downwards to the mess between her legs and suddenly he tasted bile. He felt ashamed at the naked intimacy of his stare, but he couldn't look away at first. Then the shame grew and he did, and saw a bottle smeared with dark blood lying on the cold stone floor nearby. It had broken in half and he couldn't see the missing piece. The smell struck him, warm, coppery and bitter, and his unwilling gaze was drawn back between the girl's legs. He had never known a woman, never touched a girl *there*; just thinking about girls in that way when he pleasured himself was something he would feel guilty about afterwards. Girls were to be treated gently and with respect, his father had always told him. Now to see a girl like this was intolerable; his mind reeled away from what it imagined.

He turned from the girl, blundered into Ivanova as he lurched through the door and retreated back down the hall. He didn't make it to the door before he heaved and vomited onto the polished wooden floor; he tried to avoid his boots but failed, and another smell was added to that of the girl's blood. He pressed his head against the wall to quell his dizziness and to try and blank out the terrible thing he'd seen, but it didn't work. Then he realised that Ivanova was speaking to him, her hand laid gently between his shoulder-blades.

"Tajidaev found her." Her voice wavered ever so slightly. From the off-white canvas shoulder bag with its Red Cross stitching she pulled out a plain metal canteen. "Here."

Gratefully he swallowed rough brandy. She copied him, then replaced the canteen in the bag. "I saw something like this before. In Poland." He stared at her. "A few guys got drunk and had a go at a woman where we were billeted. One of them had too much vodka in him. Couldn't get it up, so he used the bottle instead."

Leonid swore softly under his breath, foully, several times.

"She was lucky."

The words startled him.

"The woman in Poland, I mean. *That* bottle didn't break." She looked back towards the storeroom. "I guess *he* didn't like not being able to do his stuff in front of his mates."

Leonid realised that, at that moment, for her the word 'he' tasted bad. She was angry, and momentarily he felt shame simply for being a man. He reached out for her shoulder, but then snatched his hand back; touching a woman at this moment seemed a vile thing to do.

Ivanova lost her anger and said coldly, "We'll get her fixed up." Then it was she who touched him, laying a hand briefly on his arm.

He nodded. "I'll organise something." He hesitated. "Who did it?"

Ivanova shook her head. Then she shrugged. "The fucking war."

Outside the passage the stink of the city was a welcome relief with its peculiar combination of bitter dust, acrid smoke and sweet decay. He drew in deep draughts of it, trying to steady himself, and looked at the two prisoners. His hate welled up again, this time cold and implacable. He thought of the girl; of Agranenko; of the others. Men like these two, *boys* like these two, had slaughtered and burned and violated. Fresh faced boys with dull eyes and dusty uniforms; he'd seen what they'd done, all of them. They were all guilty, the whole stinking fucking German lot of them.

"Have you made arrangements to get these back to HQ yet?"

"No." Babich looked at him warily.

"Don't bother," he said casually, and then, just as casually, he pulled out his revolver, cocked it, stepped forward and fired two shots into the wide-eyed faces of the boys. The sounds echoed down the street, and blood and grey matter splashed on the wall as two heads cracked back, leaving smears. Babich stiffened and stared, first at the bodies and then at Leonid. Ivanova appeared through the door in a rush, clutching her medical bag. She stopped abruptly and she too stared at Leonid. He turned away and saw others looking at him. He ignored them, put away his revolver and went to report to Gushenko: building cleared, no casualties, no prisoners.

Cheslav had never seen so many books in one place before: more than in his village school; more than in the Factory Apprentice School; perhaps more even than in the small municipal library in Bradander. He was in a large detached house, one of a row of such houses set back from the road, each at the end of a wide brick drive, each surrounded by hedges and fronted by neat lawns. Inside the house the platoon found elegant carpets, old wooden furniture, oil paintings on the wall. There was even food in the cupboards in the spacious kitchen, and in the large larder a bonanza they were quick to appropriate. There were no people.

While the others busied themselves wandering through the house taking whatever would fit easily into pocket or backpack, Cheslav stayed with the books.

From floor to high ceiling each wall was covered in heavy wooden bookcases, dark with age and polish. The only breaks were for casement windows, a wide chequerboard of small square panes admitting some light, but not enough to illuminate fully the large, long room. Cheslav liked it that way. He walked along the shelves, running his fingers down the spines of the books, breathing in the smell of old paper, waxed wood and oiled leather. Now and again he'd pull out a volume, rub the pages between his fingertips, feel the embossing, savour the dry aroma of words. The books were beautiful, elegant: works of art in themselves whatever lay inside. He thought of those back home, poor worn things with dirtied and crumpled pages and stained covers, and he felt awe that one house, one family, should possess such a treasure trove. He and Leonid had fantasised that one day they would share a house of their own and it would have a library, but they had never dreamed of one like this. He felt sad that Leonid was not here to see it; Cheslav must show him a tiny glimpse of what neither of them would ever have for themselves.

He scanned the shelves slowly, trying to decide where to start. He heard the thump of boots through the ceiling, the sound of muffled voices through the door, the faint rumble of destruction outside, but his mind was on the books. Which to choose? At random he pulled one out, a mottled brown volume with faded gold printing on leather: Gottfried Keller, *Der Grüne Heinrich 1–2*. He put it back. Further along the shelf another caught his eye. It bore an ornate leaf pattern in faded gold and red, bordered by scarlet and gold: Jausef Lauff, *Die Overstolzin*. That one didn't appeal either and was slipped back into place. He sighed and looked about him. Then across the room his eye lit upon a bright strip of colour. He went to it and pulled out a cloth-bound book about twenty centimetres high. On iridescent pink and green brocade the cover showed a woman in a blue gown reclining on an orange bed. Around her stood female attendants; near the foot of the bed a woman knelt holding a baby which had a halo. He guessed at once it was a religious book, but he had difficulty in reading the title, even though it seemed to be written in Cyrillic. This writing was strange, a form of Russian he couldn't read easily. The words said something about rebirth and happiness. He puzzled over it for a while, trying to recall the old script which Mr Gerstein had explained to him and Leonid. Then it struck him: *Joyous Resurrection*.

He smiled and opened the book. Inside were page after page of more brightly coloured pictures, images of what must be Christ, the Virgin Mary, angels and the magi bearing gifts. It reminded him in some ways of the images on his mother's icons and in the old churches, yet these images didn't look old. The colours were bright and lacked the patina of years, and the style was modern.

Inside the front cover he found modern text which he had no trouble reading. It told him that the book had been printed in Prague only seventeen years before. A new book, but he felt sure that Leonid would love it so he carefully wrapped it in his spare shirt.

As he was doing so, Lopakin walked in. "We're going." He glanced at the cloth bundle Cheslav was tucking into his backpack and then looked around the room. "I might have guessed I'd find you here, Comrade. Come on." He smiled but sounded impatient, and he left without waiting for a reply.

Cheslav heard the sound of others leaving the house and voices outside, but before he went he took one last long look at the room, savouring it, trying to fix it in his mind's eye. How Leonid would have loved it.

Tanya sat at the table trying to read by the inadequate light of a Hindenburg lamp, while next to her Mrs Körtig and Monika played cards. Walter sat with Axel and Klara playing 'Bombs on England.' Mrs Boldt stood on Tanya's box in the alcove and peered through the small window.

"They're up to no good, you mark my words. They're showing a light." Mrs Boldt sounded smug, as if she was seeing no more than she'd always expected to, one day. "Why show a light unless they're up to no good, eh?" She tugged the blackout curtain closed and stepped down to resume her knitting; no one answered her. Only Palanevich looked at her.

Monika and Mrs Körtig, having finished one round, went back to sit in the alcove. Monika couldn't concentrate for long on anything. Tanya watched Walter moving counters with glee across the game board. It'll have to go, she realised. It was too dangerous to have a Nazi war-game in the cellar. Walter would be outraged but it would definitely have to go. She smiled as she recalled Mrs Boldt's reaction when Axel had insisted on burning her copy of *Mein Kampf*. It was the nearest thing the Nazis had to Holy Writ, written by Hitler, a record of his ideas. Tanya had bought a copy shortly after the Nazis came to power; most people did for it was politic to have one visible at home, evidence of loyalty. Most people did no more than buy one, but Tanya had actually read it. At least, she'd dipped into it chapter by chapter; a slow process for it was turgid and rambling and in places almost indecipherable. After some months she'd finished with a sigh of relief and even less respect for Hitler than when she'd started.

"Thinking again?" Palanevich commented, pulling a chair out from under the table and sitting next to her.

She turned from watching Walter and shook her head with a rueful smile.

"Inadvisable at the moment," he said in Russian: it was how they mostly spoke to one another now. He looked drained.

"I was just..." she began, but Palanevich held up his hand.

"...wondering," he finished for her. He pulled out his silver cigarette case, and she as usual declined his offer.

"Yes. Mrs Boldt's *Mein Kampf*."

He smiled briefly at her. "Yes. Quite a scene, wasn't it?"

She shook her head, explained that she'd read it but couldn't make sense of it. She still didn't understand the Nazis, what drove them.

"Ideas," he said in a way which made the word sound like an obscenity. "Ideology. Belief." Slowly he blew out a cloud of smoke; he was taking more time over his cigarettes, she'd noticed, making them last. "I stopped trying to make sense of things after the Revolution; after I left Russia. When I left your father..." He stopped. "Anyway, it's not worth thinking, not now." He blew out another cloud of smoke. "Look at this." He gestured around the cellar with the cigarette, the glowing tip waving in the gloom like a circling firefly. "This is what *ideas* get you. Master Race. Germany. Europe." He snorted and smoke flowed out of his flared nostrils. "Nazism, Communism, damned democracy. Religion." He reached out and placed his free hand on her arm. "Marx was right. Religion is just the herd making itself feel comfortable. Don't think, don't question. Do what the priests tell you. Where he got it wrong is that it's true of all big movements, big ideas. Marxism is a religion just like any other, and Nazism."

She looked at his face and saw sincerity, then she saw him kneeling by the icon in Mrs Boldt's alcove, praying, and was puzzled.

"Isn't there anything you really believe in?"

"Friendship," he said, simply. "You must trust the man, not the idea." He paused. "Your father was my friend; we were like brothers. He saved me from drowning in my own shit when I was about to go down for the last time. I owe him everything for that." Tanya was startled; she didn't know what to say. Palanevich had never, in all the years she'd known him, said so much about his friendship with her father. The subject had been taboo. All she knew, and that from her mother, was that Palanevich and her father had been cadet officers in the Semonovsky Guards before the Revolution. They'd been close, and after Father had disappeared in the Revolution, Palanevich had helped her and her mother from a sense of honour, of obligation, but the rest he kept to himself, and her mother had told her little.

Now she wanted to know much more for that way she could learn about her father, but as she opened her mouth to speak he headed her off with another wave of his cigarette.

"No," he said quietly, "that's it. No more. Your father looked out for me. I made him a promise about you and your mother. That's it." He stood. "I keep my promises, when I can."

Sabaev died near midday. John knew it immediately. He was sitting against the bench, half-asleep and not paying attention to much at all, when suddenly he'd felt a stillness next to him, an absence. Something was different, like picking up a flicker of movement out of the corner of an eye. He looked at Sabaev: *something* had left the room. Wearily he levered himself up onto the bench and then onto his feet. His movement woke Børgesen, who blinked sleep out of his eyes and peered up at John, and then looked at Sabaev. He nodded with a strange air of satisfaction as if seeing the expected, closed his eyes once more and went back to sleep.

John retrieved Sabaev's dog tags and his soldbuch. Inside his jacket he found a faded photograph of a middle-aged woman standing by a small farmhouse with a boy, ten or eleven years of age. They stared at the camera in grim sepia tones, their faces markedly similar to Sabaev's. Gently he tucked the picture inside the soldbuch and made his way outside, nodding to the two lookouts sitting under the awning. One, he realised, was the trooper he'd seen dressed like a woman the previous day. Now he looked every inch a toughened SS veteran, and John wondered what had happened to the dress. He refused their offer to drink from the wine bottle they were sharing and instead stood a little way away on the pavement. He fumbled in his pockets for a cigarette but then remembered he'd shared his last with Børgesen. As he searched, his fingers brushed against a small book and he pulled out *Poets of the Great War*. It fell open to a poem by Alan Seeger and he smiled at the appropriateness. He glanced at it, didn't need to read the opening lines for he knew them well enough to quote softly, peering up into the dusty sky:

> I have a rendezvous with Death
> At some disputed barricade,
> When Spring comes back with rustling shade
> And apple blossoms fill the air...
> I have a rendezvous with Death
> When Spring brings back blue days and fair.

He stopped when he thought of all those who'd kept that rendezvous: Olé, Mimmi, Kurschat, Sundberg, Greger, Kaarle, and now Sabaev. And me? he wondered and quoted the rest of the poem:

> It may be he shall take my hand
> And lead me into his dark land
> And close my eyes and quench my breath...

He paused, glancing behind him. The two troopers were watching him; he ignored them and went on:

> God knows 'twere better to be deep
> Pillowed in silk and scented down,
> Where love throbs out in blissful sleep,
> Pulse night to pulse, and breath to breath,
> Where hushed awakenings are dear...
> But I've a rendezvous with Death
> At midnight in some flaming town,
> When Spring trips north again this year,
> And I to my pledged word am true,
> I shall not fail that rendezvous.

Carefully he tucked the book away and went back inside.

There was little conversation amongst the platoon. Some sat eating, some smoking, some gazing into space, but most slept. Cheslav looked through the pages of *Joyous Resurrection*; Beridze sat next to him restringing his panduri. In the red glow above the nearby roofs the colours of the book were garish. Cheslav looked at the woman on the cover: Mary, he'd realised, mother of Jesus, of God. He thought of his own mother and how much God had once meant to her; perhaps He still did. Although she'd put away the icons and never spoken of her faith again, she'd hear no blasphemies, tolerate no disrespect towards God or the church, and her sons and new husband quickly learned not to speak of God at all. When his father had been taken away, Cheslav had first had thought that she'd lost her faith, but looking back now he wondered whether perhaps it was simply that she'd locked it within her, cherishing it silently.

I wish I believed in something like that, he told himself suddenly and, closing the book, ran his hand across the cover.

"Beautiful." Beridze smiled at him shyly.

Cheslav nodded. The panduri too was beautiful and he said so.

Beridze beamed. He stroked the strings and cocked his head, nodding in approval. Then he put the panduri away in its leather bag and gestured at *Joyous Resurrection*. "Holy Book?"

"In a way." Cheslav held it up to show Beridze the cover. Then he opened it to show him a few of the pictures inside and explained simply and carefully what each was. As he went through each page in turn, Beridze nodded with pleasure. Like Cheslav, Beridze had been born into an Orthodox household; unlike Cheslav, he'd remained in one all through his boyhood, and it showed. He knew the subjects, he knew the stories, and he approved. In places, it was Beridze who told Cheslav what they were looking at, and when they reached the end of the book, he opened his tunic and pulled back his discoloured undershirt to reveal a tarnished brass chain around his neck. With an eager smile he pulled at it and a medal tumbled out. Beridze rested it on the palm of his hand for Cheslav to see.

It was beautifully made, brass like the chain, and small, quarter the size of a playing card. It showed a man in ancient armour, a halo about his head, stabbing down at a dragon which his horse was trampling underfoot.

"Did your father give you this?"

Beridze shook his head. "Grandmother. Very old."

Cheslav could see that: the medal was much worn. "A family heirloom?" Beridze frowned, puzzled. "It is very special to your family?"

Beridze nodded once more. "Very holy. Blessed by the Holy Father."

Now Cheslav was puzzled: he'd thought the Holy Father was the Pope, a Catholic, but he didn't say so.

"Very holy," Beridze said again and kissed the medal before tucking it away. "You have holy medal? Keep you safe?"

Cheslav smiled sadly. To his surprise he wished that he did. He closed the book. "No," he said.

With Gosselin's help, John moved Sabaev's body into the room at the far end of the bar: a large room with a stage. They covered him with a red cloak taken from the basket of costumes. After that John did nothing, stretching out on the bench at the far end where he'd not be disturbed, drifting in and out of slumber as darkness drew in once more. He felt drained, physically and emotionally, and it would have been so easy just to wait passively for the inevitable, but then Gosselin came to him with a proposition.

"La rezignaseeon eh la more de lespoor."

"What?"

Gosselin grinned. "Resignation is the death of hope."

John frowned. He didn't understand, and then a moment later he did. He sat up wearily, swinging his feet onto the cold floor.

"You're leaving?"

Gosselin shrugged.

John hesitated. "I can't."

"Why not, my friend?"

John didn't know. Why not indeed? But it felt wrong, an abandonment. He might no longer be fighting, but to run away was a step too far: a betrayal.

"It's all over. You know that."

John did, but he didn't want to acknowledge it. Casting about, he saw Børgesen sitting against the bench, watching them. "Duty, perhaps."

"'My honour is loyalty?'" Gosselin quoted the SS motto wryly, and when John didn't answer he asked, "Loyalty to what?" Still John didn't answer. "Look, my friend. It's finished. Here, anyway. Hitler's done for. The Reds have Berlin. Who knows, maybe they'll have all of Europe."

John shook his head. "The Yanks. The deal…"

Gosselin interrupted him. "Maybe." He sounded exasperated as if with a child's foolish hopes. "But whatever happens, we should get out of Berlin. What's the point of staying just to die?" John looked at Børgesen again and saw he'd closed his eyes; his face was yellow-white under the grime. Following his gaze, Gosselin laid his hand on John's arm and said softly, "He's not got long, I think. You can do nothing for him now. He's going the way of Sabaev. Come with me."

John looked at Gosselin's earnest face and felt a lift in his spirits: there was something about Gosselin that seemed irrepressibly positive, even now.

"Anyway," Gosselin squeezed his arm, "two of us stand a better chance."

John nodded. What is there to lose? he asked himself. He stood up slowly, every muscle aching. "Yes."

They helped themselves to overalls from a store under the cabaret stage, for Gosselin had a plan. They'd go west, hoping to slip through the ring of encircling Soviet forces by passing themselves off as forced labourers. Footwear was a problem. They couldn't wear their military ankle boots: they would give them away too easily. The baskets only contained dancing pumps, but after rooting about for a while, Gosselin found a bag of tennis shoes in another cupboard. Hardly ideal for a long hike, but they'd have to do.

Weapons and identity papers they left behind, even their dog tags, but John took the folio case. There was nothing in it that would look suspicious, he was sure. It was the sort of keepsake a man sent abroad might have, a memento of home; in any case John was determined not to leave it behind. *Poets of the Great War* went too, tucked into the case with the rest.

In the fading light they slipped out of the building. John didn't say goodbye to Børgesen for he was fast asleep. Instead, John wrote a brief note of farewell wishing him *bonne chance* and tucked it into his top pocket.

In the street there was no one: the lookouts were gone. They moved alone through the eerie shadows cast by the red light flickering across the skyline.

The platoon lay asleep in a little cul-de-sac, clustered together around the fire they'd built out of the rubble of the street beyond. Only Leonid was awake, brooding, staring into the glow of burning furniture at his feet. By him Babich was curled up like a child, hands clasped at his mouth; Ivanova hugged her medical bag as if it were a lover; Tajidaev sprawled on his back, legs twitching, no doubt dreaming of horses. Someone in the cul-de-sac snored, the sound louder than the occasional *thud* of an explosion and *tack-tack-tack* of machine gun fire; the clatter and squeal of caterpillar tracks; the shouts which drifted in from outside. Leonid took no notice of any of it. Only once did he stir: when a building collapsed somewhere nearby with a noise like the roar of water tipping over a weir and the ground vibrated. At this he looked up, and then he returned to the flames. From time to time he sipped from the vodka bottle Ivanova had given him.

"Drink, Comrade Lieutenant. Sleep," she'd urged. Well, he could manage the first but not the second. He couldn't rid his mind of images: Agranenko shot; Agranenko falling; Agranenko talking about Leningrad; Agranenko with the POWs in the brewery yard the night before the assault. How long ago was that? An age, it seemed. Leonid pulled out the postcard: *Barge Haulers on the Volga*. He remembered that he *had* seen it before, in an article in *Pravda*. It was, *Pravda* had trumpeted, one of Stalin's favourite paintings. The implication was clear: the Great Leader appreciated art. Leonid smiled grimly; who'd have imagined that the old bastard would like a painting that Agranenko could like? He stared at the postcard, contemplated consigning it to the fire and then put it away.

Other images came: the girl in the storeroom; the broken bottle; the pool of blood. He drank more vodka. He recalled Kolchok's words: 'Vodka isn't tea; you can't have too much of it.' He smiled and drank again, and then he remembered Ivanova's words and the smile dropped from his face. 'One of them had had too much vodka. Couldn't get it up, so he used the bottle instead.' Bile rose in his throat and he washed it back down.

He thought of Cheslav. Where is he now? he wondered. What had he seen? He felt suddenly tired that Cheslav should witness what he had witnessed, experience what he had experienced. Leonid wanted to shield him from vileness, as he always had when they were growing up, but he couldn't, not now, not ever.

He brooded. How would he cope without Agranenko? But then thinking of Cheslav he knew that somehow he *must*. He must see it through, make it to the end. Cheslav needed him. He held the bottle up against the flames: it was almost empty. He drank the last, upended it to make sure and laid it gently on the ground by his feet.

"Sleep," Ivanova had urged him and he nodded, pulled his greatcoat tightly around him and lay down, watching the flames dance until finally darkness took him.

It was night, but the full moon lit the hallway like a lantern. Tanya stood with Palanevich just inside the street door.

"Ancient beauty." He sounded lyrical. He was holding the icon they'd prayed before, having taken it from the briefcase resting on the floor by the alcove and laid it on the palms of his hands as if making an offering in church. In a more practical tone of voice, he observed, "But paint on wood, nothing more. He took it with him to the war, said it might keep him safe." He smiled sadly.

"Your father?"

He gave her a long contemplative look and then shook his head. "No. Yours."

"My father?" She looked at the icon and emotion welled up in her.

He held up the icon. "Your great grandfather had it with him during the war against the Turks and the English. Your grandfather had it when he fought against the Japanese. He gave it to your father to protect him when the last war broke out. Please. It's yours."

She hesitated and then held out her hands. Gently he laid it on her palms: an offering. Palanevich drew out his silver case; the Semonovsky badge caught Tanya's eye as he lit a cigarette. He didn't offer her one.

"I was stationed in Petrograd. When your father came home on invalid's leave in '17, he left the icon with me, told me that I should keep it safe and give it to your mother if…"

He shrugged.

"I remember him coming home that time." The icon felt rough on her skin and the colours looked jaded, but the silver glowed in the moonlight and the nape of her neck tingled for a moment as she looked at it.

Palanevich drew smoke deeply into his lungs with evident relish, paused and then blew out an aromatic cloud.

Like incense, she thought and savoured it. She sounded sad as she said, "It was a short visit."

"Well, it was a light wound and they needed everyone at the front."

"*You* weren't sent at all, I recall."

His eyes narrowed briefly and then he nodded. "I was lucky, privileged perhaps. Prince Golitsyn liked to talk about art with me." He grinned briefly at her expression. "That's right. His Imperial Majesty's last prime minister. Russia was bleeding to death, the Reds were on the streets and Golitsyn wanted to talk to me about *paintings*." He drew in more smoke. "I did get to see action eventually, though. On the streets of Petrograd. Damned near killed by my own men during the February uprising. Even the Guard was in revolt by then."

"That's when you left?"

He shook his head. "Oh no. I have more sense of duty than *that*." There was slight mockery in his voice and she looked away momentarily in embarrassment, taking the opportunity to place the icon face up in the small alcove: she was afraid of dropping it. When she turned back, Palanevich had moved into the doorway.

He cast away his cigarette stub. "I met your father again at General Yudenich's headquarters," he said without turning around. "He was in charge of the White forces outside the city." He stepped back and looked down at the icon. "I did try to give it back to him, you know, but he insisted that I should hold on to it. Shortly after that we were separated, and then later he was killed." Palanevich lit another cigarette slowly. "I suppose you're wondering why I still have it." He contemplated his cigarette case and then put it back unopened. "Your mother didn't want it. She said that it was *his* family's, that he'd given it to me for safekeeping. She didn't want *it*, she wanted *him*. So I kept it."

"It seems to have protected you all right," Tanya murmured.

He cocked his head. "You should have it."

"No."

He didn't seem surprised and carefully picked it up, wrapped it in its cloth cover and put it back in his briefcase. "Well, I suppose I could hold onto it for a little while longer."

"Keep it," she said.

Palanevich stared at her and then nodded. He buckled the straps on the briefcase and tucked it under his arm. They stood by the door and peered out into the street, turning when the door to the cellar creaked open behind them.

Axel led Klara down the hall carrying a shiny crocodile skin valise. It looked incongruous against their dusty, crumpled clothes and grimy faces. "We're going," Axel said as if announcing the start of a holiday trip. Palanevich seemed unsurprised.

"To Wenck?"

Axel and Klara nodded. Then Axel placed the bag on the floor and held out his hand. Palanevich shook it firmly.

"Bonn shawnz."

"Is it safe? They must be all around the city by now."

Axel smiled at Tanya's question and shook her hand too. "There's bound to be gaps. There always are. Anyway, why would they bother with civilians? They'll have enough on their hands as it is."

"It's safer than staying here," added Klara, but her voice trembled slightly.

Tanya looked at her, then at Axel and nodded, although she didn't agree.

"You'd have been better leaving sooner," observed Palanevich.

"So would you," replied Axel and the two men smiled wryly at each other.

"Ah, but at least I did try." Palanevich turned to Klara, bowed over her hand, kissed the back of it gently. "Go with God," he said in Russian.

"Thank you," Klara whispered, "and with you." Then Axel picked up the case and took Klara by the elbow. She looked around her. "I've always been a Berlin girl, you know. Never really been anywhere else, just to Neuruppin every summer."

"The Ruppiner Lake?"

Klara smiled sadly at Tanya. "Yes. Why, did you go too?"

"No. But the Schleys went there in '41; they told me about it. It was the last holiday they had together. I remember Ida talking about it all the time."

"Now you're going for a longer holiday." Axel spoke reassuringly. "We must go."

Klara nodded. "You can tell me all about it when we come…" Her voice trailed off and she blinked back tears.

"Good luck," said Tanya.

Axel nodded thanks and guided Klara out through the door. At the threshold he stopped and turned, and in the gloom Tanya caught a glimpse of a broad smile. Then he said something which made her start. It seemed like an expression of goodwill, but she didn't understand the words for they were English, and so, suddenly, was his accent. She recognised it; she'd heard it before on the radio and at the cinema: cultured, precise and clipped.

"But you're…" she began in amazement, and she and Palanevich stared at Axel.

He shook his head abruptly. Reverting to his usual voice, he said, "I spent some time in England, in the theatre." He said no more but took Klara's arm and together they walked out into the street.

Palanevich looked at Tanya in surprise, and then in atrociously accented English he called after them, "Good luck, old chap."

Neither looked back.

SEVENTEEN

Tanya was crammed in next to Walter at the tiny alcove window, peering into the dimly-lit yard watching six soldiers standing outside the door to Diederich's apartment. The soldiers wore Russian Army uniforms and carried the sub-machine guns with round magazines the Russians always carried, but they weren't Russian.

"Polacks." Walter's voice was hoarse with tension.

Tanya nodded: the soldiers were wearing rogativka, the square-topped soft caps of the Polish Army. She'd last seen them in the papers and on the cinema screens nearly six years before as Germany invaded Poland. Now, it seemed, it was their turn to do the invading. One banged on Diederich's door with the butt of his sub-machine gun and shouted something indistinct.

Mrs Boldt called across the cellar, "What's going on?"

Tanya admonished her without turning her head. "Keep your voice down." Then, realising she herself had shouted, added in a stage whisper, "They might hear." Looking at the anxious faces around her, she added, "Polish soldiers."

The door to Diederich's apartment opened and he came out. She watched, her stomach tight with anxiety as he said something, shrugged and then shook his head. One of the Poles shoved him hard with the muzzle of his sub-machine gun and he staggered back inside, out of sight. The Poles followed him. A minute or so later two of them came out again, crossed the yard and disappeared down the passage to the street, and her stomach twisted more.

"They're coming here," she announced, surprised at the calmness with which she said it. She yanked the blackout curtains closed and stepped down from the window, pulling Walter with her. Palanevich ran up the steps and checked that the door was firmly locked. He looked around.

"Can we barricade it with anything?"

Then someone hammered on the door. A voice demanded insistently, "*Tvush teh drrzhvee!*" No one moved. Tanya bit her lower lip and hoped that the door was sufficient barrier in itself. It was old but stout, sturdily made of wood in the way doors used to be: heavy, with solid metal hinges and a lock twice the size of her hand. It looked as if it belonged in a medieval castle; she hoped it would take a battering ram to break it open.

The door was struck again and a voice demanded, "K'to tam yest?" The question was repeated after a long pause. Then suddenly a large splinter of wood erupted from the back of the door with a loud *bang* and Palanevich ducked away, pressing himself to one side. There was a *ping* as if a coin had been dropped onto the stone floor, a buzzing like a demented bluebottle, and more pings, decreasing in pitch. Then silence, which seemed to Tanya to be the loudest noise of all. She heard voices raised in argument beyond the door:

"Otvush teh drrzhvee!"

"Nyeh man ne cogo."

"Mooshee bytch."

"Khodjimeh."

"Yestem gwodnyeh!"

"Vyem, soy yestesh gwodnyeh!"

For a moment she wished Diederich was there to translate, then she pictured the soldiers who had gone into his apartment and she felt sick for him and his dumpy wife.

The voices beyond the door faded away.

After a long pause, Mrs Körtig asked softly, "Are they gone?"

"Yes. I think so. Perhaps they are searching upstairs." Palanevich, his ear pressed to the door, sounded surprisingly calm.

Light flickered and Tanya turned. Walter had drawn back a corner of the blackout curtain and was peering out. "They're going," he whispered back across his shoulder. Motioning Walter to step down, Tanya looked for herself. The courtyard was empty and Diederich's door was still open. She felt someone tap her arm and looked down.

"This landed by my foot." Mrs Körtig held out her hand. Tanya took something the size of an almond from her, held it up to the light from the window: it was a twisted cone of metal.

"A bullet!" Walter seemed fascinated.

"Yes," she agreed. That's what it was: the bullet that had passed through the door and bounced around the cellar, buzzing and pinging. They were lucky it hadn't hit anyone.

Mrs Boldt interrupted her musing. "What did you see?" She came to stand by Tanya and craned her neck up at the window.

"They've gone." Tanya stepped down and let Mrs Boldt take her place.

"Diederich?"

Tanya shrugged. "I don't know. We should see if they are all right."

Mrs Boldt dismissed Tanya with a sneer. "He'll be all right with his Red friends."

"How can you say that?" Tanya shook her head. "He's not a Red."

Mrs Boldt snorted. "He's a Red, all right." She flicked her wrist dismissively. "And he married a Polack." She glanced at Tanya with a sneer. "A *Slav*."

"But she was German." Walter looked at Mrs Boldt. "Uncle Mathias told me."

Mrs Boldt pursed her lips. "Boy, she grew up with Slavs, didn't she?"

Tanya looked at her with contempt, then with disgust at Walter when he nodded agreement. Seeing Tanya's expression, he looked away and went to sit at the table.

"I don't understand it. We beat the Poles. How is it that they're here? We crushed them."

Palanevich came down the steps and smiled grimly at him. "Face it." He looked at Mrs Boldt and ran his hand across his head, adding, "It's Germany that's crushed. Again." Then he looked at Tanya sadly and in Russian said, "They that live by the sword…"

Tanya finished for him in German, "…shall perish by the sword."

They all stared at her, then at Palanevich as he sat back on his crates and reached for a half-empty bottle lying by his feet.

Walter shook his head with a jerk. "No!" His voice cracked and Tanya saw tears in his eyes. "Shut up! Germany's *not* finished!" He pressed his hands together on the table, eyes cast down. "Shut up. We're not."

Tanya took a step towards him, entreating, "Walter…" She stopped when Mrs Körtig shook her head.

"Here," Palanevich spoke gently, holding up a bottle, "have a drink, boy." But Walter laid his head on his arms and closed his eyes.

"You know, we ought to check on Diederich," said Palanevich, taking a swig of champagne.

Leonid woke, cold and stiff with the April chill, and cold with hate. The chill faded with dawn, but the hate remained, numbing his pity like the deep Russian winter. It stayed with him through the day as they worked their way down the ruined Berlin streets. He was relentless, as the Russian winter is relentless. Gone were his doubts, his uncertainties, his fears: hate had frozen them out.

The ammunition boxes brought forward from time to time bore the legend 'Don't economise'. Polyanski, making the rounds, told Leonid it was a sign that the end to the fighting was in sight; saving resources was now unnecessary. Ammunition was to be expended instead of men and Leonid made the most of it.

Still, they lost men.

They'd been following an elevated railway line that ran high above the street, and came to a station sitting at the top of a very long flight of steps. Its defenders were stubborn, that is until Leonid called forward the tanks. A few rounds of high-explosive and the defenders fled along the railway tracks. Rybczak led Babich up the steps at a trot, reckless as ever, and he made it unharmed, as ever. He waved down to Leonid, and as the rest of the platoon approached, Rybczak came down the steps again. One moment he was trotting down, the next he tripped and fell against a safety rail buckled by the tank fire. It tore free, and Rybczak fell with it. He seemed suspended in mid-air for a moment, and then he thudded to the ground a couple of metres in front of them.

Leonid couldn't take his eyes off Rybczak's head as Babich clattered down to join them. It was twisted at an awkward angle, eyes staring upwards; he looked as if he was smiling at something.

"Shit, that's bad luck."

Leonid lifted his gaze to Babich, who shrugged and turned away.

Tajidaev held out his canteen. "Here, boss."

Leonid rinsed out his mouth and spat; it was water, the first he'd tasted that day, and it was good, washing away the bitterness in his mouth. He took another mouthful and this time he swallowed it.

"Thank you, Comrade." He looked at Gushenko and Polyanski, who were standing further down the street, watching. They would expect a report, but what was he to say? 'Beg to report, Comrade Captain. Objective cleared. The enemy ran away. They didn't kill anybody and nor did we. Oh, and by the way, Private Rybczak tripped and broke his neck.' Suddenly he felt desolate: Rybczak, the man who survived a punishment battalion; Rybczak, the man who ran unscathed through minefields; Rybczak, the man who dodged bullets and shells; Rybczak, the man who almost made it home.

Tajidaev held out a different canteen.

"Thank you, Comrade," Leonid said again, and then, "I've had enough." He swallowed a mouthful of vodka, looked at Rybczak, then at Babich, nodded at Tajidaev and offered back the canteen.

"You keep, boss."

Leonid nodded again slowly, drinking as the two men picked up Rybczak and carried him under the steps and laid him down.

It was only later that he realised Tajidaev had called him 'boss'.

*

Cheslav watched a short column of dirty, exhausted men and boys pass by, guarded by an equally dirty guard. Unlike the prisoners, the guard looked cheerful.

No one jeered as they might have done days before. These pathetic figures were not the army of the Master Race; not the cruel soldiers who'd carved a bloody track across Mother Russia's body: they were a pathetic rabble not worthy of abuse.

Beridze, sitting next to Cheslav, observed, "They've had it."

Cheslav nodded and looked around at the wrecked street: mounds of rubble, cracked or missing walls, gaping windows, open roofs. Opposite him was a bar, next to it a small grocery store. The bar was intact, the grocery store was not. Its window was smashed, its door broken open. Boxes, jars, tin cans, paper bags and hessian sacks were scattered across the threshold, along the pavement and onto the road. They were broken, their contents trampled and smeared; the passing prisoners left a trail of floury footprints. The mess sickened Cheslav. The comrades who'd done this would have suffered great shortages during the war, as he had. Some must have grown up in homes where little was plentiful and much absent, as he had. The habit of thrift would have been seared into the men who'd gutted this store by persistent want, so how could they do such a thing?

Are we going to be like the Nazis? he wondered. Despoilers? He remembered something his Marxist teacher Sarafanov had kept quoting in the schoolroom: 'Private property must be abolished and in its place must come the common distribution of all goods.' He'd been fond of quoting it during the times of shortage, as if somehow good communist theory made up for empty bellies and naked feet. Well, they were abolishing German property all right. He looked at the food on the ground and sighed.

Beridze looked at him quizzically.

"It's such a waste," Cheslav explained. "Mindless looting. It's wrong."

Beridze looked at the scattered containers and sticky remnants for a few moments and then nodded. They sauntered across the street and Beridze kicked at the litter for a while before bending down suddenly to retrieve something.

"Here, Comrade Corporal," he said and held out a jar of preserved fruit. Cheslav leaned forward to see better: peaches, by the look of it. He hadn't seen a peach in years, but he hesitated.

"Take it," Beridze urged. "It's ours. It's all ours. They owe us." His normally placid youthful face was hard, his eyes glittered. "*Siskhlis vali.*" He held out the jar once more, this time quite forcefully.

Cheslav took it and smiled ruefully: 'the common distribution of all goods.'

"*Siskhlis vali.*" Beridze said again and smiled, the gentle boy once more. "They owe us."

Cheslav held the jar up to the light. "Yes," he murmured and popped off the top with his thumbs, cramming the jar's sweet contents into his mouth. "Yes," he repeated out of a full mouth. Peach juice ran down his chin and he wiped it off with a grin.

What struck John most as he and Gosselin turned the corner into a narrow street was the disregard the women showed towards the corpses. Two dark crumpled shapes sprawled in the gutter a few metres away from them, and yet everyone in the queue for the standpipe seemed unconcerned, as if they were piles of empty clothing and not young men twisted with the awkward stiffness only the dead convey. John and Gosselin stopped for a moment to take in the scene: a short line of housewives holding pots and pans, buckets and pails. One, John noted with amusement, clutched a brown pottery rumtopf: the pot German housewives used to mature fruit. Two were walking away carrying a tin wash tub, water slopping over its edges.

The women had been gossiping, but when the two men appeared they stopped and turned their heads. A stout woman stood by the standpipe; next to her a young brunette was pumping water slowly into an enamel bucket, and suddenly John felt dreadfully thirsty. He stepped forward.

"Please. We need a drink." His voice rasped. The brunette stared at him and then glanced down at his tennis shoes. The stout woman eyed them suspiciously. John noticed that her hair was a peculiar shade of russet brown.

"Guest workers," she said, placing her hands on her hips. It wasn't a question and it wasn't friendly.

He'd met the type before, usually in the uniform of some minor Nazi functionary. This one wore a flowered wraparound pinafore and looked like a cleaner. He suppressed a smile at her pompous self-assurance. Where's your mop? he asked himself.

"This water is for Germans only. Go." She spoke as if to a dog and he bristled.

The brunette frowned and turned her head briefly. "Oh, for heaven's sake." She held up her half-full bucket. "Here."

He took it, spilling some down his front as he drank. The stout woman tsk'ed.

"It is forbidden to help foreigners!"

John met the brunette's gaze over the rim of the bucket and they smiled briefly at each other before he took several more gulps and passed it to Gosselin.

The stout woman reddened and someone in the queue giggled. She glanced along it without response and said again, "It is forbidden." She wagged her forefinger at the brunette. "You could be reported!"

John took the bucket from Gosselin and passed it back to the brunette. How pretty you are, he wondered. I should like to touch your face. He didn't.

Gosselin was more courageous: he took her hand in both of his, bent low and kissed the air above it. "Zher voo remersee, bell dam."

She coloured. "Mersee, missyer."

Once more the stout woman snorted. Gosselin straightened, turned to her and was about to say something when the shell struck. Only one. Later John wondered if it was a ranging shot, but then who was there to observe its fall? Probably it was just a stray. That's how these things happen, he reasoned. In war they just do.

Everyone scattered with practised speed as the noise of the explosion engulfed them and dust billowed down the street, the brunette tripping over the bucket. John and Gosselin remained completely still and then blinked at each other. After a moment, with the dust settling, John looked around. The women had all disappeared, save for the stout woman who, like them, hadn't moved. She was staring at the brunette now lying face down, covered in dust.

John suddenly felt very tired. Oh God, he despaired, looking at her, but then she raised her head, smiled at him and stood up, brushing herself down in a peculiarly prim way.

"I'm all right," she told him, and then turned to the stout woman who stared at her for a moment longer before sinking slowly, reaching down with her hand to support herself and sitting heavily. Then, just as slowly, she lay back and closed her eyes, a dark red pool spreading out around her hips.

John knelt by the fallen woman and pressed his finger into her throat to feel for a pulse, but he didn't need to: he knew she was dead.

"Help me."

John and the brunette turned to Gosselin. He too had sunk down and John's stomach twisted, but Gosselin was sitting upright, clutching his lower leg and grimacing. "It's my fucking ankle." He glanced up. "Sorry, "

The brunette shook her head and knelt by him. John knelt too as she carefully removed Gosselin's shoe and peeled back his blood-soaked sock to reveal a ragged gash. It was bleeding, but John was relieved to see that the flow was slight.

"Splinter?"

The brunette nodded at John across Gosselin's bowed head. She sat back and sighed. "Can you walk?"

Gosselin smiled grimly. "Help me up."

John took one arm and she the other as Gosselin clumsily levered himself to his feet. Gingerly he took a step forward, put weight upon the injured leg and almost fell.

"Fuck!" He looked at her and apologised again, and again she shook her head. She smiled gently at him and John saw sudden tenderness. For some reason that annoyed him.

"Leave me." Gosselin grasped John's wrist. "I'm not going far on this."

"It needs dressing." The brunette looked down at Gosselin's bare foot; it was swelling and turning an angry red colour. Behind her the women had reformed the queue and, ignoring the sprawled body at their feet, were busy pumping water once more.

John opened his mouth to protest, to make some speech to Gosselin about how he would not leave him, could not leave a comrade. Then he closed it again: he knew he should and could and would, so instead he spoke to the woman.

"I'll help you carry him."

Gosselin shook his head. Not far away more shells were bursting. "No, I can manage with her help."

"It's not far." She tucked an arm around his chest and draped his arm over her shoulder.

John nodded. "All right." He thought he should say something more, but before he could do so Gosselin grinned at him.

"You damned English are always running out on us."

The woman looked puzzled; John grinned. "Bloody Frogs," he said in English. Then, "Bon shawnz."

Gosselin winced. "You English speak French so badly."

They looked at each other for a moment and their grins faded. "Thank you," John said to the woman. As he walked away, he heard Gosselin say to her, "Zher voo remersee, bell dam. Je swee Bernard."

He didn't hear her reply, if there was one.

Leonid shouted at the window, "*Herawss kommen. Handee hock.*" It was yet another street, yet another surrender ostensibly no different to all the others. As soon as the tanks rumbled forward, Leonid's men packed close behind, a white flag was thrust out of the second floor window of the building on the junction they faced. Moments later a Volkssturm stepped out of the front door with hands raised, licking his lips nervously.

"*Kommen. Heer.*"

The man raised his hands and shuffled towards them. A moment later a second appeared, then a third and fourth, none of them under fifty. Leonid gestured at the wall and they lined up compliantly, eyes to the ground, hands raised. They always were compliant, now.

Another easy one, Leonid had believed, but this time he was wrong. Suddenly there were shots inside the building. He pressed against one of the tanks, swinging his sub-machine gun to cover the doorway; around him his men scattered, lay down, raised weapons. The Volkssturm froze in place.

For a long moment nothing more happened. Then another Volkssturm appeared in the doorway, but this one got no further, for more shots rang out, louder, closer. The Volkssturm jerked forward, eyes widening in surprise, mouth opening in a silent cry. Then he fell forward, hitting the ground with a dull thud.

The Volkssturm against the wall threw themselves to the ground as the platoon opened fire on the windows and the door; ricochets howled about them. Babich shouted, ran forward and tossed something through the open doorway; moments later a grenade detonated. Everyone stopped shooting as Markov ran up to lob in a second. Then the two ran inside.

Silence fell.

Leonid looked around. Everyone was getting up save for the four Volkssturm who continued to press themselves into the cobbles along the base of the wall. "*Unten bleiben*," he shouted. One of them raised a face taut with fear for a moment, then pressed it down once more. Leonid saw that he was shivering violently. With a snort he walked up to him, prodded him with the toe of his boot none too gently and repeated his command. This time the Volkssturm scrambled nervously to their feet. He could see them staring at the machine gun in his hand and half raised it, enjoying the fear that appeared on their faces.

"Comrade Lieutenant." He turned to see Moiseyevich staring at him. "I'm to bring the prisoners back."

"What?" Leonid's eyes narrowed.

Moiseyevich glanced behind him along the street. He licked his lips and then looked at Leonid in the same manner as the Volkssturm: uncertain, afraid. The realisation that Moiseyevich might fear him brought a frisson of pleasure and Leonid smiled. Then he shook his head and lowered his gun.

"Take them, then."

Moiseyevich hesitated, glanced backwards again, and then, avoiding Leonid's amused stare, stepped over to the nearest Volkssturm.

"*Komm*." He tugged at the man's sleeve and, still holding it, led them all away. Leonid watched them go for a moment, then he turned back to the building as Markov came out. He was sombre.

Leonid stiffened. "Babich?"

Markov wouldn't meet his gaze. "An SS pig shot him. I killed him." The statement didn't seem to bring Markov any satisfaction. "The other one was dead already." Leonid tilted his head quizzically. "One of those," Markov explained, pointing at the dead Volkssturm lying by the doorway. "Shot in the back."

Leonid nodded. He understood: the Volkssturm had been killed by their own. Some stupid die-hard SS bastard, he reasoned He looked at the Volkssturm shuffling along under the watchful gaze of Moiseyevich. Vicious dogs, all of them. Moiseyevich looked back at him and Leonid turned away to give his orders.

Ironically it was Mrs Boldt who discovered that Hitler was dead. It was after Palanevich returned blank-faced from Diederich's apartment with the news that he and his wife were dead. He'd given no details and no one asked for any. No one said anything at all, for a while but sat in grim silence, doing nothing much.

Mrs Boldt was the first to stir, moving to the radio where she sat, cranking the handle, determinedly. The rest did what they always did and played cards or dozed. Palanevich, Tanya was not surprised to see, opened a bottle; but he only sipped at his glass and did not pour a second. He caught her glance just once and held it, expressionless, until she turned back to the book she was trying to read by the flickering lamp-light.

On the radio was nothing but static, snatches of Russian voices and once a brief burst of music. Something classically modern, Tanya mused, but couldn't identify it. Then she heard a German voice. Difficult to pick out over the crackle and hiss, it was nevertheless clear what it was saying: Hitler had fallen at his post, the new Führer was Grand Admiral Karl Dönitz, the head of the Navy, such as it was.

Tanya looked up when she heard the announcement, and then, after a shocked disbelieving moment, she looked around the cellar. Everyone was frozen into immobility as she was, disbelief on their faces too. She felt the stirring of relief and the others too stirred, but once again they froze as the announcer went on to say that Germany would not surrender. Dönitz had ordered continued resistance to save them from the advancing Bolsheviks. The announcer was saying more, but Mrs Boldt bent her head and stopped cranking and silence fell, broken only by her subdued, breathy sobs. Mrs Boldt was weeping.

Walter too wept, silent tears running down his miserable face. Mrs Körtig and Monika held hands, their faces expressionless. Palanevich inclined his head slightly, lifted the corner of his mouth in a half smile and stood up. No one paid any attention as he made his way to the steps. For a moment she thought he was going to say something to Mrs Boldt as he passed her, but, to Tanya's relief, he didn't. He didn't even spare Mrs Boldt a glance as he made his way out of the cellar.

Gathering herself together, after a few minutes Tanya followed and found Palanevich standing by the open front door, smoking. There was something about the cast of his shoulders and the way he held his head which signalled determination.

"Are you leaving?"

He reached out and touched her arm without looking at her.

"Not yet. When it's properly dark." He sounded remarkably

sober all of a sudden. He turned a wan smile on her. "You're better off staying here."

She shook her head.

"It'll be dangerous out there now."

"What do you mean by *now*?"

He chuckled. "Now that *he's* gone, God knows what will happen to order and discipline."

She pictured the chaos on the streets during the previous days and shook her head. "It can't get any worse, surely?"

He didn't answer her directly, but said softly, "There's an opportunity, of course, a chance of slipping through in the confusion."

"They said Dönitz is in charge now."

"No doubt," he said wryly. "And they'll fight on for a while to buy time to do a deal. It won't work. We're past deals now." He cast the stub of the cigarette into the street, watched the firefly-glow skitter across the ground and go out. "I shall try to get out."

She thought of the tales she'd heard, of the propaganda words: slavic hordes, bolshevik beasts, torture, murder, rape. She thought of the newsreels and of poor, terrible Nemmersdorf, and she shivered. Perhaps I should get out too.

Palanevich seemed to guess what was in her mind for he looked at her with pity. "I have some papers. Forged, of course. Quite a work of art in themselves."

Yes, she told herself, they would be.

"But I don't have any for you. So it would be too dangerous."

She sighed, supposed that he was right, but the prospect of what might befall her in the city was frightening. Perhaps it might be better to go; she couldn't decide. She ran her fingers through her hair and grimaced at the greasiness.

"God, I need a wash." It sounded so banal.

Palanevich chuckled. "Oh yes, a bath, a nice hot bath. Real scented soap."

"A hairdresser," she sighed. "And a manicurist."

"You're just like your mother," he snorted.

"What do you mean?"

He lit another cigarette before he answered. "She was a real lady. Elegant. Feminine. She always looked the part."

To her surprise Tanya felt tears well up. Annoyed with herself she wiped them away.

Palanevich looked out through the door and sounded wistful. "Do you remember that time I took you both to the Café de Flore? On the Boulevard Saint Germain?"

She did: the Art Deco interior, the red-plush seating, the mirrors! They all drank champagne. "Yes," she said. "You took us to see the artists."

"Visit the exhibition of exotic specimens." He turned and touched her again, more briefly this time. "Your mother was so elegant, and you were so small." He chuckled again, but it was a sad, lonely sound. "I poured you a glass even though your mother thought you too young."

"Yes." Tanya stepped forward and stared out into the street. It was dim with dust and smoke and the approaching dusk; her throat was dry with the acridness. "She asked you to look after me if anything ever happened to her. You promised her that I should have champagne every day." She looked at him wistfully, remembering. "Well, Victor Mikhailovich, you brought me champagne."

"Yes," he murmured, "but you didn't drink it." He hesitated a moment, then he reached into his jacket pocket and withdrew a revolver. He held it on the flat of his hand.

"What is this?"

"For you," he explained. "It won't do *me* any good. If they find it on me…" He shrugged. "But you might find it…useful."

She stared at his hand. "What good would it do me? I can't shoot every soldier that might…" Then she stopped, realising that it wasn't enemy soldiers the pistol was meant for. "Oh," she said and shook her head.

"Hide it," he urged. "Keep it." His voice shook slightly and he went on in a near-desperate tone she'd never heard from him before.

"Just in case. It may save you a lot of…for your father. For your mother." His voice choked, and he paused and cleared his throat: once more he was self-assured Victor Mikhailovich Palanevich.

He held the revolver out to her by its barrel. "I'll be going soon. I'll try to get back to Paris. Then, I'll send for you."

She stared at the pistol and shook her head, and he lowered it to his side. "Yes," she accepted, "you go. I'll stay. But don't promise things now, Victor Mikhailovich. None of us can make promises now."

"I must," he said.

"For my mother?"

He smiled sadly. "And for your father. A pledge. I told him too that I would protect you. In whatever way I could." He held up the revolver one last time. "Please."

One last time she shook her head. "I'll manage," she said, and he put the pistol away. They stood together in the doorway, watching the darkness deepen.

After leaving Gosselin, John meandered in a vaguely westerly direction. He picked his way carefully across rubble, walked through undefended barricades, passed smoking shell holes and burning buildings, all the time trying to avoid direct contact with anyone. It hadn't been difficult: there were few civilians to be seen and even fewer military. Artillery roared and barked in the distance, but he heard little small-arms fire and came close to no actual fighting. No one challenged him, although a few glanced at him, but he was not the only one on the streets dressed as a foreign labourer and he was ignored.

As the light faded, he tried to decide what to do: should he press on in the dark and risk getting lost or suffering an injury that would immobilise him like Gosselin? Or should he take shelter and wait for the dawn, even though that would mean losing several hours' travel time? He was still pondering when a heavy artillery barrage began ahead of him. At first he ignored it, but when shells began to explode in large numbers in nearby streets, he took shelter under one of the brick arches of the elevated railway that ran through this part of the city.

His only company was a suspicious feral cat which joined him halfway through the barrage and stayed when it ceased shortly after sunset. By then his decision seemed to have been made for him: it was too dark to press on. The arch was comfortable and offered a degree of protection, and he was disinclined to leave it; the halt had drained him of energy. All he wanted now was to hibernate, so he remained where he was. Despite the damp chill and the continuing, if diminished, sounds of the city's destruction, he dozed off almost immediately. He awoke when the light of the rising full moon filled the arch, the glare pulling him out of oblivion. The cat had moved to lie across him, seeking warmth. Bomber's moon, he observed. Once such clear moonlit skies would have brought the RAF, but now it was the time for shells.

EIGHTEEN

Dawn painted the sky dismal grey. John bid the cat good luck and left it sitting in the arch. He could hear some very distant artillery but there was not much, and there was no tank or small-arms fire at all. Was this a ceasefire? Was the fighting over? He shook his head, unwilling to countenance the prospect, and walked on.

Everywhere was the detritus of war: wrecked cars and carts, dead people and animals, and an armoury of weapons. John could easily have equipped a whole platoon, a company perhaps, maybe even a battalion from what lay in the streets. He resisted the temptation to pick up a gun: it was safer not to. A foreign worker caught armed by the authorities would be shot out of hand, and the Reds had made it very clear through leaflets and broadcasts that gun-toting civilians would be shown little mercy.

The further west he went, the more people he saw. They were mostly small groups who, he guessed, were also making their way out of the city. He was glad for the cover they provided. Everyone looked grim and exhausted. He saw fewer and fewer uniforms, and their wearers were now mostly unarmed and looked uninterested in anything, but still he feared running into another roaming patrol. That might prove fatal. Once he saw a group of Hitler Youth manning a light anti-aircraft gun behind a sandbag sangar. They stared at him as he passed, and when he looked back they were still staring at him. One was fingering a rifle nervously, and John hastened around a corner out of sight. There he paused, feeling vulnerable, and debated hiding again until dark, but he knew that he had to get out while he could. He had little choice but to take risks, so he suppressed his fear and walked on.

Midway through the morning he turned another corner and stopped dead in his tracks.

Ahead of him was a group of Soviet tanks. He didn't need to see the red stars under the dust and soot to tell him that: they were unmistakable. His stomach clenched and instinctively he stepped back out of sight. Then something struck him about the scene. Cautiously he peered around the corner. The tanks were stationary, their hatches open, and the crews were standing around, relaxed and unconcerned, smoking, chatting, eating and laughing, calling out occasional comments or whistling at the few civilians who passed them.

The implication struck John immediately: the fighting was done. It was all over for the city. And elsewhere? He stood up, uncertain as to what to do. The idea of handing himself over to the Reds was still unconscionable: even if they handed him safely over to his fellow countrymen, he would still be in peril; and he wasn't ready for surrender quite yet. Better to slip away and hide amongst the masses of refugees there undoubtedly would be on the roads out of Berlin. He might get back to Sweden somehow; it was worth a try, at least, but how to get past the tanks? He'd come down a long arterial road with no side turnings and he was loath to backtrack. In any case he'd become increasingly conscious of how he stood out: a lone man in overalls, younger and fitter than most on the streets. He needed to find a group to attach himself to, but who was likely to accept him?

As he pondered this, an opportunity presented itself. Two middle-aged women approached from behind pulling an overladen cart by canvas straps. They looked tired and were struggling with their load. As they passed him, one nodded and a sudden thought struck him.

He smiled, stepped forward and said quietly, "One moment please, ladies. If I may?" They stopped immediately and looked at him suspiciously. Perhaps it was the incongruity of being addressed with such formality by an unshaven man in grubby overalls and tennis shoes, but the woman who'd nodded smiled a little. Her companion just stared at him.

"I hope that you don't mind." He kept his voice low, his tone unthreatening and placatory: a harmless man, well-mannered and sorry to be disturbing the ladies. He used what he hoped was an accent that fitted with the story he'd being making up for himself as he'd walked: "I'm trying to get back to my family. I, uh, was working in a factory. It was bombed. I wondered if I might walk with you? Just a little way."

The women looked at each other. He noticed that they had exactly the same nose. Sisters? he guessed. The smile slipped from the first woman's face and she shook her head.

"Please." He cast a glance meaningfully at the cluster of Russian soldiers, none of whom seemed to be taking any notice of them, yet. "It would be safer for all of us, and I can pull the cart."

They followed the direction of his gaze and then looked at each other again. The second woman put her hand on the other's arm. "Perhaps, Katrina? I don't feel safe with *them* around. It might help. And I'm so tired."

The first woman looked at John for a moment as if weighing him up. "Very well, Elsa. But only a little way."

John nodded. "Thank you." He took the straps from their hands and draped them over his shoulders.

"Who are you?" Katrina asked as he settled them in place and took up the slack.

"Ulrich. Hans Jost. From *der Neyderlandt*." He hoped he sounded Dutch. A man called Jost had served with John at Salla and John was familiar with the accent, had acquired a few Dutch phrases; hours spent with Jost in a cramped stinking dugout had seen to that. They should be enough for his story to pass muster, providing neither of the women knew the language.

He seemed to be in luck. Elsa looked reserved, but nodded;

Katrina relaxed. The Netherlands had been conquered by Hitler five years before, but many Dutch supported his anti-communist crusade nevertheless. Dutch volunteers fought for Hitler against Stalin in Russia; many more volunteered to work in German factories. Being Dutch was a good enough cover story for now.

Neither of the women said anything more as John led them towards the tanks. They all tensed as they walked by and the crewmen watched them curiously, but none approached them or said anything, and as they passed the last tank John relaxed. Easy, he told himself, but it was then that a Russian voice called out. He ignored it and kept going, but Liesel glanced behind her.

Elsa snapped, "Don't look!"

Then the Russian called out again and John heard running. His mouth went dry and he knew that he'd have to stop. Releasing the straps, he turned reluctantly. A very short crewman trotted up and grinned at them with gold teeth. For a moment they all stared at each other. Then the Russian hugged him and John winced. He smelled raw garlic and vodka on the man's breath and sweat and dirt on the man's body. The Russian slapped John on the back.

"*Tavarsich rabotnik.*" He bowed slightly in turn to Elsa and Katrina. "Frau, Frau." They stiffened and he grinned at them with undisguised interest. John stiffened too and clenched his fists, but the Russian just nodded at the sisters and then walked away.

John drew in a long ragged breath, picked up the straps and started off again down the street with Katrina and Elsa walking either side of him. Their faces were white and they held hands.

They were not bothered after that. Although they plodded through the morning in silence past increasing numbers of Soviet soldiers, tanks, horse-drawn carts, lorries and jeeps, they were left alone. The enemy seemed intent on doing nothing more than standing about. There was an expectant air as if they were waiting for the party to begin, and John wished he knew what was going on. The two women only shook their heads when he asked them, and he didn't dare approach anyone else, least of all the soldiers.

Then they left him. They directed him off an avenue lined with linden trees into a side street where Elsa told him to stop. She gestured up at a tall apartment block.

"Our brother's place." Then she went inside, leaving Katrina to thank him and press on him a jar of which she extracted from the bundles on the cart.

"Go with God," she said as Elsa came back out followed by an older man who had the same nose as the two women. He nodded at John, a dismissal.

"West is that way." Elsa pointed. It was all she said before she turned to help her brother and sister unload the cart. John felt a flare of anger at her curtness, but then supposed that he should expect no more, so he smiled fulsomely at Liesel before walking back to the avenue and resuming his journey.

He'd not gone far before the avenue joined a wrecked plaza full of Soviet soldiers and parked vehicles. Without letting himself pause he entered it, but he made sure that he kept close to the edge, not wanting to risk drawing attention to himself by crossing the open space too blatantly. Then he heard something behind him and stopped. Down the avenue he'd just left came the whine of an engine driven in very low gear and a voice, tinny and crackling, from a loudspeaker. All across the plaza soldiers turned towards it. He stared behind him, but could see nothing over the heads of the soldiers who clustered around the end of the avenue. Something was going on. He looked about him anxiously and spotted the entrance of a U-Bahn station on the opposite side of the plaza. The station sign had disappeared, but the concrete base on which it had sat remained and he saw steps leading down into darkness, which seemed warmly inviting.

He strode across the plaza and scrambled onto the base to get a better look across the heads of the soldiers. A faint aroma of smoke wafted gently up the steps from the U-Bahn entrance and he fancied he could hear music, but other sounds had his attention at that moment. The engine noise had stopped, but the tinny voice was louder and he heard rifles being fired across the plaza, more and more. Then he began to distinguish words:

"...reached an agreement with the Russians for a ceasefire..." For a moment the voice was drowned by shouting and whistling, cries of *urrah*! Then, in a lull, he heard, clearly and terribly, "...battle for Berlin is lost." Again the voice was smothered by *urrahs* and an accordion began to play the communist *'Internationale'*.

It sank in: it was over, all right. Slowly John stepped down from the plinth, feeling numb. He'd expected it and half of him was relieved, yet the other half couldn't believe that the city really had fallen, the enemy had won. He felt the disbelief of one hearing of the death of a loved one.

He was brought back to reality by a sharp slap on the shoulder. He spun and a grinning Asian soldier waved a bottle under his nose. "*Ee, Tavarisch! Moi pieta! Yevo bulyeh!*" The soldier laughed and said something else, but John didn't hear him; all he had ears for were the words pouring out from the loudspeaker, still audible even above the noise of celebration.

"I order the immediate cessation of resistance. Weidling, General of Artillery, former District Commandant in the defence of Berlin."

The soldier gulped from the bottle and waved it. "*Gitler kapoot!*"

John stared at him. Hitler's dead? Really dead?

The soldier held the bottle under John's nose. "*Izdyeess, vodka. Gitler kapoot!*"

John looked across the plaza, so full of celebration and devastation. He looked at the grinning face of the soldier in front of him, looked away, looked back again, and that was when his nerve broke. Pushing in blind panic past the exuberant man, he fled down the steps into the darkness of the U-Bahn.

A cry of "*Yevo bulyeh. Gitler kapoot!*" followed him.

Tanya couldn't put her finger on it, but it was there: a feeling like the tension before a storm, or the stillness of a summer morning before sunrise and the dawn chorus. Expectancy. She sat upright in her chair and looked around the cellar; the others too seemed to have sensed it. Mrs Boldt was staring at the little window above Tanya's head, her knitting on her lap, her lips pursed, her eyes narrowed. Walter sat at the bottom of the steps with his head tilted slightly to one side, his eyes closed.

Mrs Körtig sat in the alcove opposite Tanya, holding Monika's hand. She shook her head, and in a slow, wondering voice said, "They've stopped."

"Yes," Tanya replied, "yes."

"What's happening?" Walter stood up; he sounded bewildered.

"The guns have stopped." Tanya climbed up on her box to press her ear to the window. There was nothing: no sound, no vibration. The silence was oppressive, ominous. She thought she'd welcome it, but now it had come, she didn't.

"It's over, then."

Tanya smiled down at Mrs Körtig and Monika, and then across the cellar at the others. No one smiled back as she stepped away from the window.

"It might just be a pause."

Mrs Körtig glanced at Mrs Boldt in annoyance. "Well, perhaps they're discussing surrender."

"Nonsense!"

Mrs Körtig shook her head in exasperation.

"Oh God," said Monika listlessly, "God," and she closed her eyes.

Mrs Körtig put her arm around Monika, pulled her into her shoulder and murmured, "There, there, it'll be all right. It's all over."

"Nonsense," Mrs Boldt said again, but now there was fear in her voice.

Walter looked at her and went to the radio. It crackled softly as he cranked the handle and slowly turned the dial. Whines and screeches leapt out of the speaker grill and a background hiss filled the cellar. Indistinct voices faded in and out as Walter worked his way across the frequencies: some German, some Russian. One might have been French but the words were indistinct. Only the tones were discernible, sombre and portentous. With frustration on his face, Walter reached the end of the dial and began turning it back once more, listening intently.

Suddenly one voice spoke out, sharp and clear above the background static: Russian. Walter jumped, his hand twisted the dial involuntarily and the voice vanished.

Tanya had heard enough of it, however, to know that she wanted to hear more. "Get it back. Quickly!" She walked to the radio as Walter did as she instructed. The voice returned, stern and solemn. Everyone looked at Tanya.

"What…?"

She cut off Mrs Boldt's question with a peremptory flick of her hand, her attention fixed on the radio. As the voice ran on through an announcement she felt detached, as if she was sitting on one side of a glass screen staring into the cellar. She saw everyone, but she didn't really notice them; she was struggling to make sense of the words which came at her. She knew that she understood them and followed what the mellow, authoritative male voice was saying without any problem, but for some reason she couldn't hold the words in her head. It was as if they slipped tantalisingly into her consciousness and then wriggled away before she could pin them down.

Everyone stared at her.

Then, suddenly, the words firmed up in her head. While we all sat here, she wondered.

"What…?" Mrs Boldt began again, this time with a note of pleading: a note Tanya had not heard Mrs Boldt use before, but again she waved her to silence. A new voice came on the radio, and in a Russian accent announced in excellent German, "General Weidling, German commander of Berlin."

A pause, more crackle and hiss and then a third voice, commanding and dignified. "On April the thirtieth, 1945," it said, "the Führer committed suicide, thereby leaving everyone who followed him to their own fate."

"Nonsense," whispered Mrs Boldt with intense anguish, and as the voice rolled on, calm and terrible, she put her hands over her ears and turned her face to the wall and sobbed softly.

Cheslav had only just sent Beridze to Battalion Headquarters with a message. It wasn't urgent, so he was astounded when he saw Beridze dashing back towards him so soon. Beridze was shouting, rifle in one hand, panduri in the other. Heads followed him in curiosity as he pushed his way excitedly through knots of soldiers.

"*Es aris ze meti!*" Beridze gasped, grinning broadly as he came to a halt in front of Cheslav. "*Es aris ze meti!* Dead! Given up! Given up!"

Cheslav stared at him. For a moment he didn't take it in. Then it struck him: it was as simple as that. He looked at Beridze's flushed face, his undisguised joy, the laughter in his dancing dark eyes and smiled.

"Tell the boss," he said softly, and as Beridze rushed away grinning, Cheslav went to sit on a nearby broken wall. He propped his rifle carefully against the brickwork and opened his backpack as all those around him took in Beridze's shouted news, digested it, spread it further. Some rushed about slapping their comrades' backs and hugging them; some shouted "For the Motherland!" or "Thank God!" He heard none shout "For Stalin!" Some stood mute, looking uncertain, drinking from the bottles which everyone now seemed to be pulling out of their pockets and packs. One woman, a medic in Third Platoon, extracted a red cloth which she waved above her head. A short man, a grandfather with a white beard from Company Headquarters, stood with legs apart and fired a pistol into the air: *bang, bang, bang,* until it was emptied. Then with great deliberation he reloaded it and did it again; and again; and again until finally he ran out of bullets, at which point he too pulled out a bottle.

Cheslav looked at Beridze gabbling at Bartashevich. The lieutenant clutched his peaked cap in both hands as Beridze rushed away again, dashing to others with the news. He's crying, Cheslav realised with surprise, peering at his officer, and then his own tears came, rolling slowly down his face. He didn't wipe them away.

In the distance were more shots, more shouts; the hubbub grew. Cheslav thought that he could make out a tinny voice, a loudhailer, but the words were indistinct, lost amongst the rubble and smoke, drowned by the sounds of growing celebration. Then he did wipe his eyes using his field cap, and he took out the bundle containing the book he'd kept for Leonid and placed it on the wall next to him. He didn't unwrap it; he just ran the back of his fingers gently across it, to and fro as if stroking a face. A shadow fell across him and he looked up. Kolchok looked at him unsmilingly, but his eyes sparkled. They remained that way for a few moments, young man and old, seated and standing, gazes locked. Then Kolchok reached into his pocket, pulled out a cardboard key and looked at it intently. The red letters printed on the side facing Cheslav were worn and discoloured but still legible: 'To Berlin.' Kolchok turned the key over and Cheslav read the words on the other side: 'Red Army Soldier. The hour of revenge has come.'

Cheslav nodded. Yes, he agreed.

Then Kolchok dropped the key onto the ground. "Done." He was matter-of-fact.

Cheslav bent down and retrieved it.

"Don't need it no more, Comrade." Kolchok now smiled. "Door's open. We kicked it open." Then he turned and walked to Beridze, who by now was sitting by himself on the nearby kerb strumming the panduri. He sang, his light boy's voice rising and falling, the words unfamiliar but the meaning clear: joy. A small crowd gathered to listen and, as the rhythm picked up, they began to clap in time to the jaunty tune. Someone began to play an accordion, not very well.

Cheslav sat quietly, listening and watching for a while. Then, tucking Kolchok's key inside his tunic, he unwrapped the book. He looked at the pink and green binding, the blue gowned woman on the orange bed, the woman attendant holding the haloed baby. He suddenly thought of his own mother, and then he thought of the small church in the square not so far away where the platoon had stayed. He felt that at this moment he should go there, so he rewrapped the book and went to find it.

Leonid stood watching a man. He was a civilian, wore worker's overalls and was unarmed. He was like so many others Leonid had seen, yet there was something different about him. Leonid could see that he was nervous, but surely that was unremarkable, and he chided himself for his suspiciousness. Maybe it's the drink. But he wasn't drunk, unlike most of his platoon and despite Ivanova having pressed German brandy on him. "For medicinal purposes," she'd said, smiling as celebrations broke out all around them across the plaza they'd ended up in. It'd been good brandy, but he'd not drunk much of it.

What *was* the man doing? Why don't you just go down the steps if you're frightened? Leonid wondered, watching him standing on the concrete base of a vanished U-Bahn sign. He was torn between ignoring the man and challenging him. He knew that it was his duty to do so; regulations were firm about potential saboteurs and counter-revolutionary elements, which meant anyone acting oddly, but he was tired and worried about his own feelings. Shooting the two prisoners the previous day had brought him a sense of satisfaction, but his anger at Agranenko's death still flared up whenever he saw a German, especially one in uniform. He'd had to turn his head when they'd passed prisoners sitting under guard that morning; the rage he'd felt at the sight of the dishevelled, pathetic men had worried him then, and it worried him now.

What have I become? Moiseyevich was standing a little way off and Leonid looked at him. Like you?

"Boss." Tajidaev's voice prodded him out of his musings. He was walking up to Leonid carrying two identical small green bottles. Both had been opened; one was half empty, and he held up the full one.

Leonid shook his head. Where are they getting all these bottles from? he asked himself. Perhaps he should stop them: they seemed pretty drunk already, but the whole company was drinking, even

Polyanski, who stood some way off, was sharing a bottle of something with Gushenko.

"Drink, boss. Finish."

Leonid shook his head again, but Tajidaev grinned and pressed the bottle on him such that he had to take it, lest it fall. Leonid looked at it: the label bore a picture of a man wearing a jaunty feathered hat above a round red face, beaming like Tajidaev's. "Come," the picture seemed to be saying, "it's all over. Why not have a drink?" 'Jägermeister', the label said.

Across Tajidaev's shoulder he saw Moiseyevich watching him. Moiseyevich was not drinking. That decided him.

The hell with you, Leonid thought and upended the bottle. He tasted something thick, like nothing he'd had before, cloying with some sweetness. He didn't like it and coughed, made to hand it back, but Tajidaev shook his head, grinned and placed his hand on Leonid's shoulder. Then he raised his own bottle, toasted Leonid and walked back to where the rest of the platoon stood laughing and chatting.

Leonid turned and saw that the man had vanished.

Music, Tanya knew. It's time for music.

She and Mrs Körtig were in Tanya's apartment: the cellar had seemed all too inappropriate. When she'd let Mrs Körtig in, Tanya had joyously pulled back the blackout curtains and opened her window wide. Through it they could hear shouts, gunshots, a distant accordion playing jolly tunes. Men laughed, a bottle broke. Someone sang in Russian, a mellow, beautiful baritone. Tanya knew the song, a soldiers' song she'd learned from the teenage son of an émigré general who was working at the Renault factory near their apartment in Paris; a popular song amongst the workers: 'Kamarinskaya'. She smiled at the word but didn't translate when Mrs Körtig asked what they meant. Words like that were not for her genteel ears. Instead, Tanya went to the cupboard standing in the corner of the room by the gramophone. Opening it, she looked through her stack of records.

"What are you looking for?"

"Something appropriate," Tanya said. She held up a recording of the Berlin Philharmonic Orchestra's performance of Beethoven's Ninth Symphony.

"Furtwängler?"

Tanya nodded. She'd attended the live performance conducted by the famous conductor and composer three years previously. She smiled at Mrs Körtig, pulled the record out from the sleeve and let her see it: a Victor Records recording of 'Sweet Jazz O' Mine' by Duke Ellington and his Cotton Club Orchestra.

Mrs Körtig smiled back. "Are they all jazz?"

"No," Tanya inserted the record back into the sleeve, "but I thought it wise to keep these ones out of sight." Mrs Körtig nodded. Then Tanya went through the stack of Mahler, Bach, Wagner and, of course, Franz Lehar's 'The Merry Widow', announcing the actual contents of each to Mrs Körtig as she did so: Theo Mackeben and Peter Kreuder; Count Basie; Earl Hines. All banned by the Party, but who cared now? She pulled out one that had been safe to keep in its original cover: Hans Bund and his Dance Orchestra. Properly German.

She came across another in its original sleeve. "Oh yes," she murmured. This one was most appropriate: The Jarosekas Quartet. Mrs Körtig took the sleeve to read while Tanya placed the record gently on the gramophone. She wound the handle, and as the opening bars of a jolly dance tune began to play, she and Mrs Körtig looked at each other with great satisfaction.

"We'll have to go down soon," Mrs Körtig murmured.

"Not yet." Tanya took Mrs Körtig's hand and they danced around the room as through the open window came sounds of others celebrating too.

As he reached the bottom of the short run of steps into the U-Bahn, John saw a glimmer of light coming up a second set of steps beyond the ticket barrier. He paused, wondering, but the jubilant sound of gunfire and cheering behind him urged him on. Better to risk going forward than go back, and waiting wasn't an option. He took an unsteady breath and walked through the open barrier and down the steps into another world. Like something from Jules Verne, he wondered, pausing to let his eyes adjust and to take his bearing. Lit partly by the faint sunlight spilling from the street and partly by the light of lamps and makeshift braziers, he saw many people. They were of all ages and types, huddled together in small groups along the platforms. All heads turned towards him, and then most turned away.

Here and there blankets and sheets had been strung between pillars as partitions; along part of the wall boxes and barrels had been arranged to make crude tables and stalls on which were stacked various goods: food, drink, clothing, bric-a-brac. It reminded John of the flea markets in London's East End. The whole scene was surreal. The atmosphere was heavy, but not unpleasant: wood smoke masked the ranker odours. A low babble of conversations, stilled when he clattered down the steps, started up again, and ahead in the gloom someone was playing a mouth organ: a jolly tune written for dancing.

"Mamma." He turned his head when he heard that word and saw a little girl, no more than six or seven years of age, dressed in an outsized coat and trousers, standing next to a woman who looked old beyond her years. The woman wore the same sort of workers' overalls that he did. She stared at him and shushed the little girl. John tried to summon up a reassuring smile, but all he managed was a grimace. In return, the woman nodded sombrely, a movement that somehow reassured him, and so he walked forward towards the mouth of the tunnel at the platform's far end. He had some vague idea of losing himself. As he walked along the platform, he caught snatches of conversation around him: a woman whispering in French; another in Russian, or perhaps it was Polish. A teenage boy spoke to a child with guttural words that made John turn his head for he thought they must be Swedish, yet after a moment he knew that they were not.

He passed people lying or sitting on blankets and bedrolls, their meagre possessions laid around them. Two young couples sat by a fire burning inside a bucket on which stood a steaming kettle. One of the women actually smiled at him and he smiled back. It reminded John of the scenes in the London Underground stations he'd read about and seen pictures of in the British newspapers his mother sent him, but this was less tidy and more settled. This was somewhere to live, not just a temporary bomb shelter. It felt safe and he began to relax.

He was almost at the tunnel when he heard the clatter of feet on the steps and all conversation stopped abruptly once more. Then the feet were stilled and a voice called out, *"Ros tam. Puh die chee!"* He turned but could see nothing. The words came again, louder and clearer in the sudden silence.

The little girl by the woman began to cry and the clatter of boots resumed. For a moment John froze, but only for a moment and then he spun around and ran. The tunnel was a Stygian blackness, and when he came to the end of the platform he hesitated, but then he saw the flicker of handheld electric torches coming down the steps from the ticket hall and heard more shouts.

"Sig die yest! Roo cheg vyach!" Brown figures clutching guns followed the beams of light and John fell to his knees at the platform edge, swung his legs over and dropped onto the tracks. He stumbled into the tunnel, crouching down to avoid any shots that might come, but none did.

He reached out and felt rough brick under his fingers. Somehow reassured by this, he stumbled on into the dark. Ankle-deep in water, he splashed on, careful not to trip, running his hands along the slimy wall to steady and guide him. Behind him voices commanded and the little girl cried. He fumbled his way in the dark, and around him heard the rustle of rats above the splashing of his feet. He hated rats, had come to loathe them at Salla where they infested the warm dugouts, but thankfully none came near him here.

After a while he felt the wall curve away and he stopped. He fumbled and found he was by an alcove, not large. Then his hand found the rungs of a metal ladder. He could see nothing, but he pulled himself upwards until he bumped his head with a soft curse and found himself beneath what felt like a metal hatch: a manhole cover. For a long time he hesitated; he pressed one ear awkwardly against the cold metal, but could not discern any sound and felt no vibration. All he could hear were the very faint noises coming from the platform. Taking a deep breath, he pushed hard against the metal, and to his surprise it yielded with no resistance and flipped easily onto its back with a clatter. He froze then. Sunlight blinded him and he heard the sounds of distant shooting and voices; a vehicle drove past nearby. He waited, ready to drop back into the darkness if he must, but nothing happened and so he pulled himself out and found he was between a mound of rubble and a street wall. He could see no one else and so he replaced the cover and pulled some of the rubble across it.

That'll slow them, he told himself and walked quickly away down a mercifully empty street, but at the next corner he stopped. Here soldiers danced and sang, stood in groups chatting and smoking, or staggered about waving bottles. He saw a cluster of pale-faced boys in the grey overalls of Flak Helpers, unarmed, helmetless, ignored by all around them. Near them two old men in dirty overcoats tried to smile but failed as a very drunk soldier capered in front of them, grinning and waving a sausage from which he cut chunks with a vicious looking knife. These he offered to them, and each time he did so the old men shook their heads and the soldier ate them instead.

John looked behind him carefully to make sure no one was paying much attention to him. He looked at the sun, faint through the low cloud, dust and smoke, and realised that west lay down the street past the dancing soldiers. Staring resolutely ahead, avoiding anyone's gaze, he walked on. He passed the old men; he passed the boys. Then, as he came to the end of the street, a very young, very blond Russian soldier ran up to him. The boy had half a dozen watches on each arm, a sub-machine gun draped over his chest and a bottle of vodka in one hand. With the other he grabbed John by the shoulder and then kissed him full on the mouth like a lover. The boy tasted of alcohol and cheap tobacco. John recoiled, astonished.

"*Gitler Kapoot*," the boy shouted and ran off.

John watched him go for a moment and then carried on into a square with a church and a ruined building on the corner. Steadily he made his way down one edge of it towards a street leading out the other side. He was halfway there when a big American lorry with a red star painted on its bonnet roared down the street and took a turn about the square, the driver grinning at John as he passed, sounding the horn. John stopped and watched the lorry disappear the way he had come. It was then that he saw three soldiers walk down the street he'd just left, pause, look about and then stare at him. Trying not to seem in a hurry, John resumed his journey, resisting the urge to look back. He was about to leave the square when he heard a voice calling.

The three soldiers were walking after him. The leader, an officer he could see now, was waving to him. He paused. Their guns were still slung over their shoulders: should he make a run for it? Should he wait? It was as he agonised over what to do that the lorry came back down the street ahead of him and roared past. The driver, still grinning, still sounding his horn, turned into the square once more in front of the soldiers and then stopped with a squeal of brakes. John was now screened from the three soldiers, and on a sudden impulse he took to his heels.

Behind him someone shouted angry imprecations.

Cheslav savoured the peace. He'd found the church much as he'd left it that morning: the door unlocked, a candle burning in front of the icon in the vestibule, another in front of the painted screen, but instead of fellow soldiers inside there were civilians. Clustered around their belongings, they all stared at him as he entered. They stared even more when he removed his field cap, crossed himself and went to sit in one of the chairs along the nave. The looks on the faces of the people saddened him: misery, anxiety, uncertainty. One little boy's face twisted in hate, the sort of intense feeling only a child can display: vivid, sudden, but short-lived. The boy then turned his head; his mother did not. She stared at Cheslav, her hand on the child's head, until Cheslav looked away.

The mood changed when he walked in: it seemed tangibly to thicken, but then, when he went to sit in his usual chair along the nave wall, it lightened. The low babble of conversation started up once more. Cheslav opened his pack, took out *Joyous Resurrection* and sat in silence. In the gloom he couldn't make out the printing in detail, but shapes and colours were evident as he slowly flicked through the pages. He felt the textures under his fingers.

He sat that way for some time, glancing up now and again to look at the figures on the. The priest made an entrance and stopped at the lectern. Those of the congregation not already on their feet stood up and Cheslav did the same, laying the book down gently on the adjacent seat. The priest glanced at him, stared for a moment and then nodded briefly. He crossed himself.

"In the name of the Father and of the Son and of the Holy Spirit, Amen," the priest began in a sing-song lilt. "O God be merciful to me, a sinner…" It was Russian but the inflections were odd, archaic.

Cheslav couldn't remember how these things went, but he copied the congregation. When they crossed themselves, he did; when they bowed, he did it, albeit awkwardly. The responses he found more difficult, but mumbled something under his breath. Somehow it felt right, and once again he felt himself to be in the little village church with his mother.

Then it was done. "Lord have Mercy, Lord have Mercy, Lord have Mercy." The priest closed the book and crossed himself three times. "Oh Lord Jesus Christ, Son of God, through the intercessions of your most pure Mother and of all the Saints…" Cheslav glanced at the screen: the images seemed to be watching him as the priest finished, "…have mercy on us, Amen."

The priest paused, stepped back from the lectern and cast his gaze over everyone impassively. "Today," he said in the rich, sonorous formal language which had vanished everywhere in Russia with the

Revolution, except in the churches, "is Great and Holy Wednesday. Today is the time when we receive healing for our bodily ills and for our spiritual weaknesses. On this day perhaps we shall need it more than most. I shall be celebrating the Sacrament of the Holy Unction this afternoon as always, come what may." The priest looked directly at Cheslav, who dropped his gaze. "All are welcome who come in the true Orthodox faith in humility, repenting of their sins."

Watching the priest return behind the screen, Cheslav was discomforted. Several of the congregation looked at him again. He couldn't precisely recall what was meant by unction but he was determined to find out: he would come to this celebration. Right now, however, he felt that he should get away from everybody and seek some fresh air. He collected his things and went out into the vestibule. As he passed the icon he hesitated, and then he faced it, crossed himself three times as he'd seen the priest do and left. It felt right.

As he opened the front door he heard the scream of brakes and shouting: something in Russian, shockingly foul mouthed to be coming into the church. He glanced at the icon on its stand as if fearing the saint might hear. He crossed himself again and strode outside.

A lorry, big and angular, olive-drab and dusty, had halted on the far side of the square at the end of a street. The driver was leaning out of the window being roundly abused by one of three soldiers standing on the pavement. Cheslav watched the driver grin, gun the engine and drive across the square and out the other side, still sounding his horn. The three soldiers turned to watch it depart before heading down the street. One clearly was an officer; Cheslav could see that, but then he started, for as the officer turned away he got a very brief glimpse of his face. It was enough to identify him; that and his gait. He knew it well.

Leonid? Cheslav wondered. Leonid! He'd expected to meet his brother again and knew Leonid couldn't be that far away, but like this? It seemed absurd, unlikely, but he'd seen the man's face and knew that he must make sure. That Leonid might have been so close and he'd not gone to him was an insufferable idea. So Cheslav ran down the steps and after the three men as they disappeared at a rapid walk out of the square.

Markov and Tajidaev followed Leonid into the street into which they'd seen the man run. It was a dead end and empty save for a boy standing by an entranceway next to a passage leading into a run of apartment buildings. The boy froze as they approached him.

Leonid took in the thin body, the face pale beneath straw-coloured hair, vivid blue eyes avoiding his own. He noted the small rucksack on the boy's back. "Where?" He asked in German, his voice harsh.

The boy licked his lips and Leonid could smell the fear on him. Suddenly he felt ashamed. More gently, he repeated, "Where?"

The boy swallowed and then slowly, as if forcing it, turned his head to look behind him.

Leonid strolled briskly forward. "In here?"

The boy nodded, again very slowly and ignoring him Leonid clattered up the steps into the building followed by Tajidaev and Markov. As he did so he balanced back briefly to see the boy walking away, his gaze fixed rigidly ahead.

They walked down a gloomy hallway to a stairway down which drifted faint sounds of music. But Leonid's attention was on the door at the far end. Behind him Tajidaev cleared his throat, a sound shockingly loud. "Stay here." Leonid indicated the bottom of the main stairway to Markov and tried the handle on the door. It turned but the door didn't open, so he knocked. There was no reply and he knocked again: nothing. Losing patience, he drew his revolver and hammered with the butt.

"Open up," He bellowed in German.

This time he got a reply. "Who's there?" It was a woman: she sounded nervous.

He repeated his demand, and then, becoming angry, shouted,

"Open this damn door or we'll break it down!" His voice echoed along the hall; Markov stiffened, and Tajidaev swung the rifle off his shoulder.

After a moment of intense silence, Leonid heard the lock click and the door swung slowly open to reveal a fat women standing at the top of a run of steps down into a musty cellar. Her face was puffy, botched with tears. She glanced at the revolver in his hand and he lowered it. Gesturing for Tajidaev to follow him, Leonid walked forward, and the woman gave way and stumbled slowly down, never turning her back. Leonid paused at the top to peer carefully into the dimness. By the light of two narrow windows high in the wall and a couple of flickering lamps he noted a table, chairs, boxes. He saw a tiled stove in the corner, so much like the one he'd grown up with and smiled briefly. At the back a drawn-back curtain revealed what must be a makeshift lavatory.

The fat woman stopped at the bottom of the steps, licking her puffy lips and peering at him nervously. A younger woman sat wide-eyed with fright on a sofa in an alcove: it was a look he'd gotten used to. Leonid walked down the steps, gesturing Tajidaev to remain at the top. "Names," he demanded, again in German. It was the fat woman who told him that they were Mrs Boldt and Miss Eberhardt. The younger woman jerked at the sound of her name and trembled under Leonid's gaze.

"Have you seen a man?" Immediately he regretted the question. He felt its absurdity. There was no one else here: the cellar was too small to hide anyone. Both women stared at Leonid and, irritated, he spun on his heel and walked back up the steps.

Music still drifted down to the hall and gesturing to Markov to remain where he was, he followed it up Tajidaev trailing in his wake.

He passed the doors on the first floor landing, the music drawing him on and up. As he reached the second floor, it stopped abruptly. No matter: he had noted its direction and pushing at door, he found it unlocked. His pistol pointed ahead of him, cautiously he pushed it open and stepped into a short corridor. Pale light streamed down it from a room at the end and he sensed there was someone there. He smelled cigarette smoke.

He walked down the corridor and stopped.

Two women faced him. The younger was defiant; the old woman next to him was impassive. Behind them stood the man he had followed. They stood quietly, hands empty.

Stepping aside to allow Tajidaev to enter the room next him, rifle in his hands, he holstered his pistol.

"Who are you?" he asked, again in German. None of the three facing him moved at first and then the two women glanced at each other. "Papers," he demanded and again the women glanced at each other. Then the younger went to a cabinet, opened a drawer and pulled out a small booklet.

He glanced through the pages, noted the details with surprise and looked at the young woman. "Comrade Klarkova," he said, this time in Russian. Behind him Tajidaev stirred briefly.

A flicker of anxiety showed in the woman's eyes and she answered him in German. "I left Russia when I was a child. I have German nationality."

He stared at her for a moment, then nodded and smiled wryly, and switched back to the language she'd chosen. "Well, Russia has followed you, Comrade." Out of the corner of his eye he saw the old woman wince; for some reason, that pleased him. He turned to her.

"This is Mrs Körtig," the young woman said.

Leonid peered at the old woman for a moment and then turned his attention to the man. No one spoke and he turned back to the young woman and tilted his head questioningly.

She hesitated, looked helpless and looked away.

You don't know him, do you? he thought and again looked directly at the man. "What's your name?"

"My name is John Marlow." The answer was in German, but Leonid thought the accent strange. He'd heard a lot of German accents during the previous months, men and women from all over the Reich and some Volksdeutche from outside it, but none had sounded like this.

"Where are you from?"

"Jersey."

Leonid stared at him.

"England," John explained.

Leonid shook his head. "What are you doing here? You're dressed as a civilian. Prisoner of War?"

John shook his head.

Irritated, Leonid held out his hand. "Papers."

John shrugged. "I don't have any. They were lost."

Leonid looked at him in disbelief. Everyone had papers.

"I'm forced labour."

Leonid looked him over. He'd encountered such before in factory barracks; in makeshift refugee camps; on the roads trying to make their way home. The man was wearing a labourer's overalls but there was no letter sewn onto them. Something was wrong.

"From England? Hitler didn't get to England. What are you doing here?"

"Jersey is a small island near France. The Germans got that far."

Leonid tried to recall his school geography lessons, what he'd learned about England, but it wouldn't come.

He shook his head. "You lost your papers?" He knew there were severe penalties for not carrying them, and it was inconceivable that anyone genuine would be wandering around without them. Is he a spy? Leonid wondered, but what would a spy be doing wandering around Berlin in this mess dressed as a labourer? And surely a spy would have a better cover story, and papers.

John fumbled at his overalls. "There was a fire. At the factory I worked in. The barracks." It sounded like he was making it up as he went along and Leonid stared at him.

Instinctively Leonid stepped back as John's hand disappeared from view like a gangster in a movie reaching for a pistol. Tajidaev raised his rife and the women stiffened.

John's hand paused. "Look, it's just something I brought from England, from Jersey. To remind me of home."

Leonid held John's gaze, then glanced at Tajidaev: the rifle was pointed firmly at John's midriff. "Slowly," he warned.

Very carefully John unbuttoned his overall and withdrew a small folio case.

Leonid relaxed, replaced his pistol in its holster and reached out. The contents were definitely English, he saw as he leafed through them. He was intrigued by the newspaper clippings, the poetry, the postcards. Then Leonid looked up.

"I carry it everywhere," John explained. "My mother gave it to me when I left England. Jersey."

Leonid considered this for a moment; he was still not convinced. He wondered what John was hiding. "Roll up your sleeves."

John looked surprised and then complied.

Looking at the unmarked flesh, Leonid felt a little more reassured, but only a little. He tucked the collection of memorabilia back into the case and put it into his satchel.

"You must come with me." He turned to the two women. "If I were you, I'd be more careful what strays you take in." Then he turned abruptly on his heel leaving Tajidaev to fall in behind John.

At the bottom of the steps there was no sign of Markov. Waving for Tajidaev and John to remain where they were, Leonid looked in the cellar once more. There was still only the two women, Eberhardt sitting on the sofa in the alcove, head in hands; Boldt sat in a chair at the bottom of the steps looking lost. Annoyed, he went back up the stairs.

Standing beyond Tajidaev and John was a new figure; and Leonid's annoyance vanished.

"Cheslav," he whispered.

After he saw the Russians go into his apartment building, Walter knew he must stay out of the way. He would have to wait, perhaps hole up somewhere for a while. It wasn't safe to walk the streets but, he told himself, it would be even less safe inside the apartment building. He thought of the woodland, *his* woodland; his sanctuary. Yes, he would go there.

It was impossible to keep a steady course in the city: obstacles to detour around, people to avoid, and soon he was tired and depressed and shuffling along. Thoughts came which made him more listless: the little bridge by the grubby canal; Friedrich and Mathias; Vogel; Rolf. He thought of the old men of the Volkssturm, of Fenstermacher. He thought of the cellar: Tanya and Mrs Körtig; Palanevich and Mrs Boldt; all the others; and he thought of his mother. His father he couldn't picture clearly for some reason, and that failure distressed him.

Images intruded from outside his mind too: wreckage, frightened Berliners, campfires, horses and guns. It was like some grim movie epic with a soundtrack of laughter, singing, the rumble of a passing loudspeaker van replaying Weidling's message of betrayal and surrender. He saw a soldier playing an accordion as others danced around him, none too elegantly. He heard flurries of shots fired into the air, other sounds too. Once he passed a building, all its windows missing. Inside a woman screamed incessantly, calling out, "God, oh God, no, oh no. Stop, please stop."

He hurried on.

This movie had smells too: the acrid stink of smoke and gritty dust; the chemical tang of explosives and burned rubber; the taste on his tongue of charred wood and overcooked meat. And sometimes, here and there, the sweet aroma of lilac which Berliners loved to plant in their gardens; in their courtyards; along their streets. He saw none, but the bushes were there all right, the scent wafting up from the rubble. He felt dirty, exhausted, and his feet hurt where his shoes rubbed. He wanted desperately to sit down, but instead he kept going, back to his woodland and reassurance.

It was an easy decision. Leonid assumed Markov had gone back for some reason; and that angered him. He wanted to find the man; and he knew that he should take the Englishman back to headquarters, but then he thought, the hell with it. That can all wait. Cheslav comes first. He trusted Tajidaev to see John safely delivered. So he sent the two away and stayed with his brother.

It was a quiet reunion: Cheslav and Leonid had never been ones for demonstrative affection. Their feelings for each other ran too deep to need exuberance. They stood on the pavement while Tajidaev led John away.

"You're looking thinner." And Leonid *was* thinner. Cheslav saw that his brother's face was no longer round and fresh like a boy's but narrow and weathered. Leonid smiled but his look held a tinge of reserve; there was something about his expression that disturbed Cheslav slightly. There was a distance between them, not great but definitely there, which there hadn't been before Leonid left for the academy.

Well, of course, Cheslav told himself. He's been through a lot; it's bound to have affected him. I suppose that I'm a bit different too. To Cheslav, Leonid now seemed the epitome of a frontovik: his gaze held a touch of the veteran's thousand-yard stare. There was something else too and Cheslav felt a tremor of ill-ease, but he suppressed it. Time could heal all ills, he knew. He squeezed Leonid's shoulder. Whatever it was didn't matter: they were together once more.

There was nothing reserved about Leonid's answering grin. "You too. You've lost that puppy fat." He pushed Cheslav playfully in the belly.

"I have something for you." Cheslav grinned back and swung his pack from his shoulder. "Here." He pulled out the book.

Leonid took it with an impassive face, but his eyes gleamed with pleasure, and Cheslav too was pleased, watching Leonid turn the pages, savouring the images, the feel of the paper, its smell, as Cheslav himself had done. We're still close. On impulse he briefly put his hand over Leonid's.

Leonid smiled, but the smile faded too quickly.

"I don't have a gift for you."

"But you've already given me one!" Cheslav fumbled again in his pack, pulled out and unwrapped *A Tale of Two Cities*. "See. A fine gift."

Leonid tucked *Joyous Resurrection* under his arm, took the Dickens. He considered the cover, stroked it, then handed it back. He didn't open it. "I'd forgotten."

"Well." Cheslav rewrapped the book and put it away. Then he repeated softly, "It's a fine gift."

They looked at each other for a moment. The sounds of celebration seemed distant; here it was quieter. Then a bell tolled, startling them both.

Cheslav glanced towards the end of the street. "Sacrament of the Holy Unction," he murmured.

"What?"

"The priest in the church around the corner mentioned it."

"What is it?"

"I don't know exactly. Shall we go and see?"

Leonid frowned at him. "In the church?"

Cheslav nodded and stood up. "Come on."

Leonid shook his head slowly. "You go." He tucked *Joyous Resurrection* into his satchel. "I should check on the platoon. See what they're up too. I need to see to that Englishman, too."

Cheslav touched Leonid's arm. "Please. It won't take long."

Leonid shook his head again, this time forcefully, a jerk of dismissal. "No." Then his expression softened. "I'll come later. We can celebrate. Talk some more then."

Cheslav nodded reluctantly. "All right." The bell stopped ringing and on a sudden powerful impulse he reached out and took Leonid's hand. "Go with God."

Leonid looked startled and pulled his hand away, but then smiled ruefully. "You too, brother." He turned and together they walked around the corner. "I'll meet you outside the church. I'll bring vodka."

Cheslav grinned.

When Leonid arrived back at the platoon, Polyanski was speaking earnestly to Moiseyevich and Markov. The Englishman was nowhere to be seen. Leonid knew immediately there was something wrong.

The three men turned to look at him, but then Polyanski guided Moiseyevich further away by the shoulder and Markov followed with a brief, taut glance backwards. Leonid's stomach flipped over and he took a step to follow them, but stopped abruptly when he heard Tajidaev's voice behind him.

"Boss." He turned. Tajidaev seemed agitated.

"What is it?"

"Trouble, boss." Tajidaev threw a hostile glance towards Markov who now stood beyond Polyanski and Moiseyevich facing them.

Leonid took a deep breath. "Well?"

Tajidaev jerked his thumb at Polyanski's group; the political officer was nodding as Moiseyevich talked. "Him big mouth."

Leonid. "Moiseyevich?"

Tajidaev shook his head.

"Tell me."

Tajidaev unfolded a dangerous tale.

When he and John had walked into the platoon area they were immediately accosted by Moiseyevich, Markov in tow. "He knew about the Englishman, boss."

Leonid glanced at the discussion and his stomach flipped as Tajidaev explained that Moiseyevich had followed them to the apartment; and been inside.

"Big mouth," Tajidaev jerked his head at Markov. "Told him where you were. Went upstairs."

Leonid was puzzled. So Markov had directed Moiseyevich up to find him but he'd not seen Moiseyevich. Then it struck him. The boy would stand where he could hear. Thoughts came in a rush, making his blood run cold. Leonid had spoken to the two women and to the Englishman in fluent German, a skill had always striven to hide lest it provoked questions. And questions might lead to enquires, about a past best kept buried. And Klarkova had said she was Russian. More curiosity. On the surface, little enough, but little could get a man into trouble, especially a man with a father like Leonid's. It only took a little digging; and Moiseyevich was the sort to dig, or to encourage others like Polyanski to do so. The right words, the right innuendo. His chill deepened when he realised that Moiseyevich might have seen Cheslav with him.

"He come back with him," Tajidaev was glaring towards at Markov. "They talk much."

At that moment Polyanski and Moiseyevich turned started towards him, Markov following miserably behind.

"Go!" he hissed but Tajidaev stayed where he was.

"Go," Leonid repeated forcefully, but still Tajidaev hesitated. He met Leonid's gaze for a few moments, and then it was too late.

"Comrade Lieutenant." Polyanski sounded amiable as he strode up, Moiseyevich loping behind him.

"Comrade Political Officer." Leonid saluted, making his acknowledgement deliberately formal. Moiseyevich watched as if sizing up possible prey. Yes, Leonid thought, the wolf.

Polyanski didn't return the salute. "Tell me," he commanded. "About your conversation."

"I saw someone behaving suspiciously. I followed him to an apartment building. I found an Englishman. Sent him back for processing."

Polyanski nodded, still amiable. "Yes, comrade."

Polyanski glanced at Tajidaev, then at Moiseyevich.

"An interesting catch." Polyanski turned his attention back to Leonid. "Well done."

For a moment Leonid relaxed; but then he stiffened as Polyanski observed, still amiable. "Useful skill, German. Why have you never offered your services? Battalion could have done with a good German speaker."

Leonid could think of nothing to say.

Now Polyanski's tone hardened. "How did you come by this remarkable skill, comrade? It's not on your file. I wonder why not."

Moiseyevich, Leonid noticed, had a faint smile on his face.

What have you been saying? wondered Leonid. What have you hinted at? Suggested, even?

"I'm told you speak it like a German."

At Polyanski's words, Leonid truly wanted to kill Moiseyevich.

"I'm a loyal Soviet citizen, Comrade Political Officer."

Polyanski nodded slowly.

Then Moiseyevich asked, "Who was the corporal?"

Leonid tried to keep his face neutral. So Moiseyevich had seen Cheslav, but he couldn't know who he was. He directed his answer to Polyanski. "I don't know. He just came in." Neither Polyanski nor Moiseyevich said anything but just looked at him without expression.

Then Polyanski nodded curtly. "Who else did you find in the building?"

"Just the Englishman. And women, Comrade. That's all."

Polyanski smiled at him. "That's all?" He still sounded amiable.

Leonid nodded.

"Private Moiseyevich says one is a Soviet citizen."

Leonid shook his head. "German, Comrade. I checked her papers. Born in the Motherland but a German citizen."

"An émigré then." Polyanski said the word as if it was something dirty. "Whites. Or her parents were."

Leonid realised where this might go. More thoughts came in a frightening rush. Speaking with a German who undoubtedly was once Russian. Whites, counter revolutionaries, class traitors. Speaking with an Englishman, theoretically an ally but England was a class enemy. Concealing that he spoke German, how had Moiseyevich described it to Polyanski? 'Like a German'. And meeting some unknown corporal he'd just happened to meet. Thin stuff to reasonable people; but the Party wasn't reasonable.

Then a terrible realisation struck him. Cheslav would come looking for him if he didn't turn up. And if he saw Cheslav, Moiseyevich would recognise him as the unknown corporal. Polyanski would know for certain then that Leonid knew him, had lied. And as Cheslav had been there, that would be enough to cast suspicion on him too, that and the fact that he was Leonid's brother. Leonid pushed down the panic he felt beginning to bubble up.

Polyanski turned to Markov. "You can go, comrade. I will want to talk with you later." He smiled at Leonid as Markov walked away quickly, seeming anxious to depart. Polyanski's tone was again amiable but his expression was cold. He nodded at Tajidaev. "You can go too. But don't go far."

He turned back to Leonid. "Let's have a chat, comrade. He turned on his heel, Moiseyevich turning with him.

In that moment when their attention was no longer on him, Leonid seized his chance. He met Tajidaev's gaze, held it for a fraction of time, his look pleading wordlessly: 'Warn him.'

Tajidaev's expression didn't alter. "Yes, Comrade Political Officer," he said to Polyanski's back. Then he looked at Leonid and made a tiny nod, a gesture that said: 'Yes, boss, I will.' Leonid followed Polyanski and Moiseyevich.

Walter had walked all afternoon, bolting like a fleeing animal. His instincts had led him to his wood, of course they had, but it wasn't what he'd expected. He emerged from the trees onto the heath and stopped: he felt sickened by the devastation before him. The area had been worked over good and proper by the look of it. The far side of the heath had a battered look: craters littered the open space and spills of tossed earth lay across the charred sward. There were two new ponds where bombs had scored a direct hit on the little stream. Beyond, the next stand of wood was splintered, torn apart. Tears welled up; he wiped his eyes.

Stop it! he chided himself, shrugging. What did it matter now? What did anything matter? He must not be the child; he had decided what to do and he must do it firmly. He had realised that he couldn't go back to the apartment: there was nothing there for him except the Russians. Oma was in Breslau. His mother would have gone seeking her as he sought his own mother. He'd thought about it on his way through the city here and the more he'd done so, the more likely it had seemed. So he would go to Breslau. He felt relief that he now had a purpose.

He adjusted the rucksack on his back and as he did so his gaze caught a splash of colour. Curious, he approached it. At the edge of some scrub was a young lilac bush. He knelt, reached out and gently touched a spray of blossom. He lifted his fingers to savour the scent, then he fumbled inside his jacket and pulled out his knife. For a moment he looked at the inscription on the blade: *blut und ehre*; blood and honour. Then he carefully cut off a slender branch bearing tiny buds. Wrapping it in his handkerchief, he tucked it inside a pocket. His mother loved the scent of lilacs.

He put the knife away and set off to find her.

AUTHOR'S NOTE

Dictator Adolf Hitler led Germany to war in the autumn of 1939. By the spring of 1945, he had lost the war catastrophically. In the West, the combined forces of the United States of America, the British Empire and their allies were advancing rapidly into the heart of Germany. In the East the Red Army, the land force of the Soviet Union, was close to Berlin, Hitler's capital city and the heart of the regime. Everyone knew that the Red Army would attack Berlin; and everyone knew the outcome. Hitler's forces did not stand a chance. *The Scent of Lilacs* is the story of that battle seen through the eyes of the soldiers and civilians who suffered it.

The Scent of Lilacs is a work of fiction based heavily on fact. The story of the fall of Berlin to the Red Army is a vast one. Many books were read, DVDs were watched and radio documentaries were listened to in order to provide an accurate picture of time and place. There are far too many to list here. For those readers who wish to learn more about the momentous and terrible events of April and May 1945, however, the following three books are a good starting point:

- *Fallen Eagle – The Last Days of the Third Reich*, Robin Cross, Michael O'Mara Books, 1995.
- *The Fall of Berlin*, Anthony Read and David Fisher, W.W. Norton and Company, 1992.
- *The Fall of Berlin 1945*, Anthony Beevor, Penguin Books, 2003.

- Three movies are also recommended:
- *Downfall*, Directed by Oliver Hirschbeigel, Screenplay by Bernd Eichinger, Constantin Film, 2004.
- *The Downfall of Berlin*, Directed by Max Färberböck, Screenplay by Max Färberböck, Constantin Film, 2008.
- *I Was Nineteen*, Directed by Konrad Wolf, Screenplay by Konrad Wolf and Konrad Kohlhaase, DEFA, 1968.

A full bibliography and source list can be found on the author's website: www.haydncorper.com.

The intention was to tell the story of the people, not the place. The setting is important only insofar as it conveys a sense of what it may have been like to be there. The Berlin area portrayed in *The Scent of Lilacs* is accurate in the detail of the general topography and street scenes, but few actual locations are named or identifiable.

The timetable of events is as accurate as it could be given the need to tell a coherent story without going into tedious detail.

Poems and song lyrics quoted are taken from the public domain. In each case, where they exist, the author and source are identified within the text. They can all be found in the *Sources* page on the author's website. The writer Konstantin Simonov was exceptionally popular within the Red Army and Soviet society and is quoted more than others. Several quotations were taken from www.simonov.co.uk, which is a recommended source for readers who wish to know more. Heine's poem quoted on pages 43 and 44 is taken with permission from www.poetryintranslation.com/PITBR/German/Heine.htm.

The list of those who were helpful during the preparation for, and writing and production of, this book is too long to include here. The author is grateful to them all and hopes to be able to buy each one a drink at the next opportunity. Particular thanks, however, are due to Alison Jack for her meticulous copy-editing; Helen Hart of Silverwood Books and her production team who rendered a very professional service – thank you all. Carol and Russell Clarke of Xhost/D7 Enterprises maintained and improved the website to a high standard; and provided much moral support during a long, long gestation period.

Finally, thanks are more than due to the author's partner for considerable patience, and financial and emotional support over the years. Without his love and forbearance, this book would never have seen the light of day.